Dedalus Original

MEMOIRS OF A B\

Christopher Harris was born i. _____ in 1931. After studying art he had a vast array of different jobs before returning to
university to take a degree in biology and teach science. He
now lives in Birmingham with his wife, a university lecturer,
and writes full-time.

Christopher Harris is the author of two acclaimed novels
Theodore (2000) and *False Ambassador* (2001), and is currently
currently writing a novel on science, art and reptiles called
Brute Art.

For further information about Christopher Harris please visit
his website www.christopher-harris.co.uk.

Christopher Harris

*Memoirs of a
Byzantine Eunuch*

Dedalus

Published in the UK by Dedalus Ltd, Langford Lodge, St Judith's Lane, Sawtry,
Cambs, PE28 5XE
email: DedalusLimited@compuserve.com
www.dedalusbooks.com

ISBN 1 903517 03 6

Dedalus is distributed in the United States by SCB Distributors,
15608 South New Century Drive, Gardena, California 90248
email: info@scbdistributors.com   web site: www.scbdistributors.com

Dedalus is distributed in Australia & New Zealand by Peribo Pty Ltd,
58 Beaumont Road, Mount Kuring-gai, N.S.W. 2080
email: peribo@bigpond.com

Dedalus is distributed in Canada by Marginal Distribution,
Unit 102, 277 George Street North, Peterborough, Ontario, KJ9 3G9
email: marginal@marginalbook.com   web site: www.marginalbook.com

Dedalus is distributed in Italy by Apeiron Editoria & Distribuzione,
Localita Pantano, 00060 Sant'Oreste (Roma)
email: grt@apeironbookservice.com   web site: apeironbookservice.com

First published by Dedalus in 2002
Copyright © Christopher Harris 2002

Typeset by RefineCatch Limited, Bungay, Suffolk
Printed in Finland by WS Bookwell

Contents

And blessed is the eunuch, which with his hands hath
wrought no iniquity, nor imagined wicked things against
God: for unto him shall be given the special gift of faith.
Wisdom of Solomon

A eunuch is a debased creature, weak, devious, beardless,
soft-skinned, ungainly, credulous, untrustworthy, jealous,
cowardly, prone to anger, gluttony, obesity and incontinence.
Agapios of Alexandria,
Infirmities and Defects of the Nether Regions

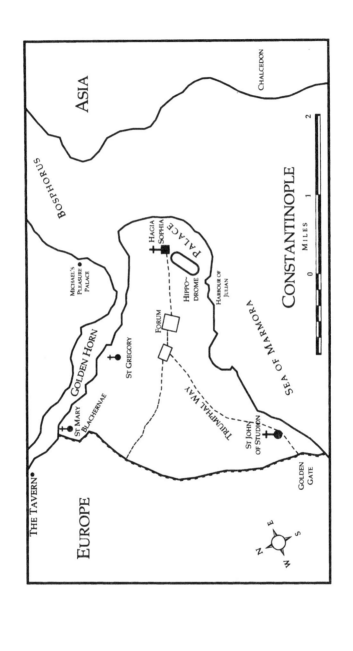

CONSTANTINOPLE

ASIA

CHALCEDON

BOSPHORUS

THE TAVERN

EUROPE

GOLDEN HORN

St Mary
Blachernae

St Gregory

Michael's
Pleasure
Palace

Hagia
Sophia

PALACE

Hippo-
drome

Forum

Harbour of
Julian

Sea of Marmora

Triumphal Way

St John
of Studion

Golden
Gate

N
E
W
S

MILES

0   1   2

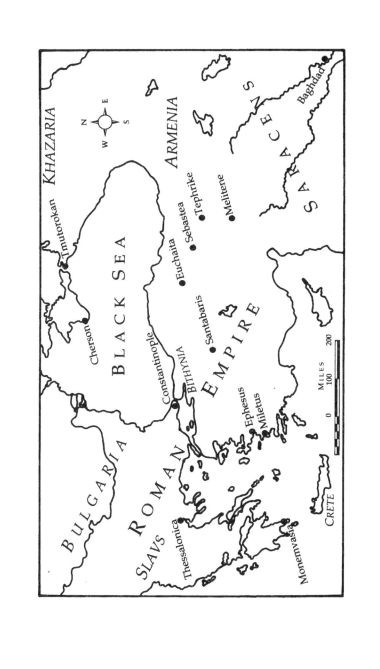

A ceremony
[AD 865]

"If you still had your balls," the charioteer muttered, "I'd cut them off."

How often I have heard that said! Whole men think it witty and original, and the fact that it is so often repeated tells us what low esteem eunuchs are held in. But the man who stood before me was not joking. He was quivering with fear, and so was I. My knife trembled like a leaf, its blade flickering in the dim light. The chalice I held in my other hand, an elaborate jewelled vessel obviously taken from some church or other, also shook, and I feared that I would never be able to carry out the task I had been entrusted with.

I stood as still and straight as I could, hoping my borrowed chasuble would make me look more dignified than I felt. Michael and his cronies, who could not hear what the charioteer had muttered, looked impatient. The emperor was dressed in more elaborate vestments than usual. The others, following his example, were dressed as bishops or as various sorts of priests, though their manner was far from reverent. They lounged in their finery, not caring that their snowy tunics and gold-hemmed capes were dragging in the dirt. Lamps and candles had been set up all over the room. Without providing much light, they risked setting fire to heaps of straw and fodder that lay all over the uneven floor. However, the lighting, faintly revealing the vaulted ceiling, as well as picking out odd details of our assorted costumes, did its job. It made the stable look like a church, albeit a church of filth and disorder.

A groom dressed as an acolyte held a silver dish bearing a mound of horse dung. It had been selected for its neat shape and resemblance to a small loaf, and the groom who carried it smirked at his burden, lifting the silk cloth that covered the dung, sniffing it with apparent pleasure, as though it really was freshly baked bread. No one else shared his joke, though a few courtiers, dressed in their own clothes, hanging back and

11

glancing at each other nervously, tried to give the impression they were enjoying themselves.

I wished, as I stood there with the knife, that I had not pursued the emperor's scholarly enquiry quite so vigorously. How was I to know that half-remembered superstitions about the potency of gladiator's blood could have any relevance to me? There are no gladiators in Constantinople, and it is centuries since there were any at Rome. When Michael asked about those ancient beliefs, I could have admitted that I knew nothing, and left it at that. But I suppose I must have absorbed something of my master's habits. Photius seldom admitted ignorance, except of things he thought beneath contempt, such as racing, or court gossip. When asked something he did not know, he prevaricated, then went and found out, usually consulting Leo or Theodore, or some other scholar with more time to investigate than he had. I followed his example, consulting Theodore, who produced an ancient book which, when interpreted by him, confirmed what Michael hoped, that the blood of a gladiator, if drunk fresh, imparts strength, vigour and dexterity. It was the emperor's idea to use a charioteer instead of a gladiator, and to offer the blood in a mockery of the Eucharist.

"Get on with it," Michael said. "How can we have the ceremony without blood?"

A horse pissed noisily, filling the air with foul steam. Hoping that the horse would not give Michael ideas, I pressed the blade against the charioteer's skin, then cut very gently, just below the ear. I would much rather have cut somewhere else, a finger for instance, but that was not deemed dignified. For the rite to be solemn, the cut must be dangerous. My victim held himself rigid, giving me a sideways glare, and I knew that if he ever caught me alone, my life would be over. I allowed his blood to flow into the jewelled chalice. Each drop gleamed as it trickled down the bright silver, joining the dark pool at the bottom of the bowl. When the chalice was almost full I drew it back, allowing the charioteer, pale and trembling, to raise a hand and staunch the flow.

"You may go," Michael said to him. "And it's no good looking at me like that! It serves you right for losing."

The charioteer slunk away, holding tightly onto his neck with bloodstained fingers. Michael waved a hand and a couple of thurifers leapt forward, brushing the straw from their silk cassocks. They were guttersnipes, recruited for the occasion, and not at all sure who we were or what was expected of them. On Michael's command they threw grains of asafoetida into their thuribles and began to swing them enthusiastically, filling the air with acrid vapour. It might have been worse. The emperor's first idea was to use brimstone, but he had abandoned it when Basiliscianus, who had been a sailor and claimed to know about such things, pointed out that in the confined space of the stable the fumes would have killed us. I disliked Basiliscianus, who was a pretty, simpering sort of youth, who always demanded more attention than anyone else. It was hard to imagine him lasting long as an oarsman, though it was easy enough to picture him drawing attention to himself, flaunting his oiled body and being plucked from the rowers' ranks by an indulgent emperor. Whatever his past, we all had cause to be grateful to him then, as no one else could have contradicted the emperor and been listened to.

When the charioteer was out of sight and the air was full enough of fumes, Michael began to intone. He, of course, had the emperor's privilege of entering the sanctuary at Hagia Sophia and witnessing the Mystery. He knew the appropriate words, and could repeat them accurately, but on that occasion Michael did not repeat the formulas used by his patriarch. He uttered words of his own, improvising and elaborating as he went on.

When he had gone on for long enough Michael held out his little finger, reached beneath the silk cloth and scooped up a small lump of the horse dung. He held it beneath his nose, sniffing it for a moment before popping it into his mouth. The others held back, watching their emperor rolling dung round his mouth like sturgeon's roe, knowing that they would be required to do the same. He swallowed the dung with a loud gulp, smacking his lips for effect. "Delicious," Michael said. "It reminds me of tripe. However well they clean tripe, it always retains an odour of the farmyard. That is one of its charms, don't you agree?"

A few of the courtiers agreed nervously, recalling banquets of offal they had been obliged to eat, while others continued their efforts to shuffle backwards unobtrusively.

"Come forward my flock," Michael said, "and receive the Sacrament."

No one moved.

"Who will be first?" For a moment Michael looked vulnerable. His eyes filled with fear and his lip trembled until he looked like small boy who had been denied something he longed for.

"It was a good idea, wasn't it?" Michael said, his voice almost inaudible.

There was a chorus of inarticulate sounds that might have been interpreted as agreement. Michael looked a little happier. "Who will join me in the Paulician mass?" he asked.

The courtiers and grooms looked at each other apprehensively. What would happen if no one obeyed him? Would they all be horribly punished? Or was the whole business so embarrassing that Michael would not dare to do or say anything?

"Who will partake in this unholy meal?" Michael asked. "Who will join the community of sinners?"

Worshipping the devil did not, in itself, seem such a bad idea. What repelled me was the silly ritual, devised by an emperor who knew nothing of Paulicianism, and was known to dislike ceremony. As for the devil, he was as good as any other god. Perhaps I should have prayed to him, rather than to God, when they sliced off my balls. The Evil One might have kept me whole. The genital organs are the devil's favourites, being the source of all temptation and most pleasure.

Basiliscianus stepped forward, smiling and looking back at the others. "I will be first," he said, kneeling at Michael's feet, a posture he was rumoured to adopt often. He looked up expectantly, parting his lips slightly. Michael broke off a little of the dung and placed it on his friend's lips. Basiliscianus turned to the others and swallowed it ostentatiously. Then Michael held out the jewelled chalice and allowed Basiliscianus to sip the charioteer's blood, muttering a few words as he did so.

One by one, the others all came forward and knelt to receive the flesh and blood of the devil. I held back, hoping that my role as an assistant celebrant might somehow make my participation unnecessary. But it did not. Like the others, I was obliged to ingest a little of the dung and drink some of the charioteer's blood, joining, not the community of sinners, but a company of dissemblers and sycophants.

How did I, Zeno of Tmutorokan, a eunuch, come to be serving the Emperor Michael III at a heretical mass held in the Hippodrome stables of Constantinople, while dressed in the cast-off vestments of a Metropolitan of Thessalonica? It is a question I have often asked myself. I suppose that my life, that any life, could be represented as a series of accidents. But that is not entirely true. We make plans, and so do others. The gods watch over us, and use us for purposes of their own. Demons lie in wait for us, eager to lead us astray. And the result, which no one will deny, is that things seldom turn out as expected.

Perhaps you doubt that the gods take any interest in creatures like me? Well, here is a fact that will make you think again: the most significant event in my life happened in the year of Our Lord 837. And that was the year the Great Comet blazed in the sky, lighting the darkness with its portentous tail. If that is not enough for you, there were omens on the Earth, as well as above it. I became a eunuch, and thus began my adventures, because my attention was distracted by a talking bird. And birds, as the Paulician heretics assert, are creatures of the devil.

The Rus
[AD 837]

The magpie spoke harshly, but its words were clear. "Mary was no virgin," it croaked. "God fucked her."

The sailors sniggered. "God's a spirit," one of them said. "How'd he do that?"

I barely understood the words I heard. I was only seven years old. I had defied my father's orders and crept away from school to mingle with the marketplace crowds. They were all around me, foreigners, sailors, barbarians, nomads from the steppes.

"God's prick," the magpie croaked. "God's prick."

I had pushed through the crowd, breathing strange smells, looking at the gaudy clothes of the foreigners, hearing the babble of their speech. Who, in mud-bound Tmutorokan, could understand all those languages? There were Armenian merchants, Persians and Arabs, Jews from Itil, as well as humble peasants squatting on the ground by heaps of vegetables or stinking cheeses. Trappers came from the Far North with bundles of furs and skins, sailors from South, with ships full of wine, grain and oil, and fishermen with glistening hauls of herrings and anchovies. Sometimes there were grave-robbers selling antique trinkets and Scythian gold.

A tethered peacock shrieked. In the pale spring sunlight the caged birds gleamed like jewels, their feathers fluttering against bars of green willow. They were all for sale: pheasants, white doves, quails, linnets and nightingales, brightly coloured bullfinches, and rare parrots from the distant East. And there was the magpie, hopping and strutting, twitching its long tail, spouting blasphemy while Greek sailors laughed.

I did not really notice the shouting at first. I thought it was the traders crying their wares, or buyers arguing over a price. Then I heard the thunder of heavy-booted feet, followed by a terrible scream. It rose somewhere behind me, shrill and harsh, ending with a sudden thud.

The magpie fell silent.

The sailors looked up.

"God's prick!" one of them muttered. There was a look of horror on his weather-beaten face. The marketplace had filled with armed men. I stared at them, amazed. They were huge, built like oxen, with broad chests and powerful arms. Their bodies were clad in gleaming chain mail, their heads topped by steel helmets. They had hair the colour of straw, faces reddened by the sun, and long beards hanging halfway down their chests. The earth shook beneath their feet, and their wolfskin cloaks flapped as though driven by a storm.

They were giants.

The sailors leapt to their feet, knocking me roughly aside. I fell backwards among the cages, bursting them open, sending up a covey of mixed birds. Snapped willow dug sharply in my back, but I dared not move. Through a cloud of fluttering feathers I saw a red-faced giant launch a huge axe at an old man. The long shaft whistled through the air. The blade buried itself the old man's head. He toppled like tree, falling his full length, coming down beside me. His head cracked open like a ripe pomegranate, splashing me with blood, dappling the doves' white feathers with crimson.

I screamed and ran blindly away from the dead man. But the giants were everywhere, swinging long swords and heavy axes, knocking men to the ground, kicking at pots and baskets, trampling fruit and vegetables. They took pleasure in their own strength, shouting gleefully with voices like thunder.

People ran wildly in every direction. Even the nomads ran, heading for their horses and escape. I saw hands raised in fear and hacked off, blood gush from sword-slit throats, severed heads rolling in the dust. I covered my eyes and tried to flee, but ran straight into one of the giants. I bounced off the skirts of his mailcoat and fell to the ground. He looked down at me. His eyes were clearest blue, and his hair was like shining gold. There was a faint smile on his red lips. He hefted his sword. Its tip hung above me, glinting in the sun. That bright point of light was all I saw. Everything else, the lumbering giants, their victims, the chaos in the market, disappeared.

But the sword did not fall. Instead, the giant reached down and grabbed me. His huge hand gripped my ankle, then he swung me up into the air and over his shoulder. He did it so easily I might have been a rabbit. I jerked and swung on his back. I hammered at him with my fists and kicked with my free leg, but it made no difference. He was so strong that he carried me dangling over his shoulder while he swaggered through the market.

Men and women lay on the ground, dead or afraid to move, and I feared that I would soon be lying among them, that I would be dashed to the ground and trampled by the giants. They were all around me, their faces streaming with sweat, their blades dripping blood. I saw the world turned upside-down and spinning around me. I was tumbled off the giant's shoulder. I felt rough cloth against my skin. Then I saw nothing. I had been thrust into a sack like a pig. The giants were going to eat me. Was that my punishment for listening to a blaspheming bird?

The first thing I saw when the sack opened was a twisted leg. It was bound up with thick cloth and webbing, but I could see that it was weak and malformed, not the limb of a gigantic warrior. Hands tugged at the sack, raising its mouth. A face appeared. The owner of the crooked leg was staring at me, looking at me curiously.

"You hurt?" he said. I was surprised to hear him speak Greek. It sounded odd, like the talking birds in the market. He poked me in the ribs. "Get out," he said, pulling at the sack.

I struggled out, and fell onto rough timbers. I was on a ship, a long narrow one manned by two dozen giants. Most of them rowed, while the rest slept. Beyond the oarsmen was a post topped with a carved bear's head, its wooden fangs bared in a snarl. A red sail hung slackly from the mast, flapping occasionally in the feeble breeze. The giants were rowing, slowly and steadily, as though they had been at it for hours. Their mailcoats and weapons lay at their feet. Some of them had taken their shirts off, letting shaggy beards fall over bare chests. Though their arms and faces were red, their bodies were as white as fresh cheese, and stank almost as bad. The deck was strewn with sacks and bundles, with barrels of wine and trussed pigs and chickens. They had emptied the market-place into their ship.

The man with the crooked leg was not a giant like the others. He had the same fair hair and pale skin, but he lacked their strength and calm. His face scared me. Perhaps it was his eyes, which were bluer than any I had seen. They were like gaps in his face, holes through which the sky shone, as though his face was an empty mask.

"Stand up," the cripple said.

I stood, steadying myself on the rail, looking out to sea. All I could see was a few sleek ships, their oars rising and falling in unison. There was no land in sight. Before I could panic the cripple poked me again, touching the bloodstains on my tunic. "You hurt?" he repeated.

I did not know what to say. I ached, and was bruised and bewildered. There were too many things to be scared of: the cripple, the giants, being eaten, the open sea. I longed for home, and my mother and father.

"Undo," he said, tugging at my belt. "Let me look."

"Don't feed me to the giants!" I cried.

"Giants?" The cripple laughed. "We are the Rus."

"Don't let them eat me!"

He laughed again. Some of the giants looked to see what amused him. The cripple grabbed my belt and pulled me towards him. I struggled and screamed, but he slapped my face. "Keep still," he hissed. I stopped struggling and let him unfasten my belt. He reached up and felt beneath my clothes, running his hands over my chest, back and belly. Then he raised the hem of my tunic high, and leaned forward, staring at my private parts. Gently, with a finger and thumb, he lifted my penis. Then he tugged at my balls. His smile told me he was pleased by what he had seen. He let my tunic drop, then sat back against the side of the boat, pulling his red cloak around him.

"What is your name?"

19

"Zeno."

"There's no meat on you, Zeno," he said. "We not eat you."

I did not believe him. He was a trickster: I could see it in his face. I watched him carefully, fearing his cold stare, his narrow lips and sharp teeth, waiting while his eyes slid shut, hiding those patches of cruel sky.

The world jolted and lurched. I fell against hard timber. The ship had run aground. I stood up and rubbed my eyes. Some of the giants vaulted over the side. Nearby, other ships had already beached. The giants were jumping into the shallow water, scrambling ashore, securing ropes, shouting instructions and throwing sacks and bundles. For a moment I forgot my fear. Then I saw the giants driving captives ashore from the other boats. There were cowed nomads, sobbing peasant women, a few children like me. I did not recognise any of them. The cripple gave me a sack to carry and shoved me forward. He stumbled along beside me, gripping my shoulder, as much for support as to stop me getting away. The sharp smell of wormwood scented the air. The place looked like an island, but it was hard to tell. I trudged forward, up the shore and into the ruins of a town, its walls and pillars reddened by the setting sun.

The cripple was watching me when I awoke. He was sitting on a rock, rubbing grease into a long, curved oxhorn, polishing it to bring out the colour. The giants were asleep. The Rus, the cripple had called them. Were they really men? They sprawled on the ground as though felled by a wizard's magic. I had heard of such things, while lurking in the market at Tmutorokan. It was not a very Christian place. All gods, and a good many demons, were worshipped there. It was common knowledge that a wise man could defeat a strong one, if he knew the right spells. But it was not magic that had laid the Rus low.

They had drunk all night, feasting among the ruins, gorging on roasted pork, tearing at the meat with the same knives they used for fighting. And while they feasted, the night sky was lit by the comet. It hung above us, still, yet seeming to rush, its long tail, stretching to the East. It had brought the Rus to Tmutorokan, and they had carried me away across the sea. What further evil might it bring? What would happen when they had eaten all the pigs and chickens they had stolen? Would they eat me, and the other captives? Would I end up killed and spitted, cut to pieces with daggers?

The Rus giants lay for hours in the shade, sometimes waking to scratch themselves or pick lice from their beards. Then, late in the afternoon, the cripple summoned them. He hopped onto the stump of a pillar, raised the oxhorn to his lips and blew, filling the island's air with a discordant, bellowing blast. He took breath and blew again, varying the sound, making it high or low, but always harsh. Then he lowered the horn and called out, his voice not loud and commanding, but soft and insinuating. Only a few of the Rus noticed him at first. They nudged their fellows, and pointed at the cripple, and scrambled up to hear him clearly. The rest roused themselves and gathered round. There must have been over a hundred of them, all watching and waiting, tugging at their stained and crumpled clothes, running rough hands through tousled hair.

The cripple began his speech, softly at first, so that the Rus shuffled forward to hear him better, then raising his voice to a shout. Though his limbs were weak, his voice was strong. The rise and fall of his words was like the sea, and he carried the Rus along, just as the sea carries ships. He gestured, reaching his arms upwards, pointing suddenly at one or other of the men, putting his hands on his hips and leaning forward, then rocking back and puffing out his skinny chest.

The Rus listened, nodding at some of the things the cripple said, frowning at others. Then, when he had finished, they sent up a great cheer and stamped their feet. While the sun dropped behind the abandoned town the Rus went to their tasks. They gathered wood and lit a circle of fires. They rolled barrels from the ships and broached them. They slaughtered squealing beasts, then set the carcasses to roast. Or were they beasts? In the half-light I could not tell. They might have been children like me.

A gang of giants dragged a large log into the encampment. They followed with another, then with a collection of poles and curved branches, all of which they dumped in the middle of the ring of fires. Under the cripple's direction, they cut and shaped the timbers with knives and axes, lashing them together into a structure that rose high into the darkening sky.

I backed away into the shadows. There were plenty of places to hide. The town was full of roofless buildings, collapsed cellars and patches of dense undergrowth. The camp only occupied a small part of it, and beyond the town was a wilderness of low trees and scrub. But it was city of the dead, inhabited only by ghosts and bones. With night falling, and the comet hanging overhead, the place terrified me. I slipped into the shelter of a ruined house, stepping carefully over toppled stones and broken tiles, hoping no one would see or hear me.

Sacrifice
[AD 837]

There was another blast of the cripple's oxhorn. The Rus advanced with drawn swords, goading a captive before them. He looked like a nomad, small, wiry, and bow-legged. They drove him towards the fires, feinting at him with sharp blades and flaming torches. Would they slaughter and roast him? Would we all die that night?

The Rus stopped before they reached the fires. One of them filled a drinking horn from a wineskin and offered it to the captive. The nomad looked scared, but he took the horn and drained it, holding it out again hopefully. The Rus looked at the cripple. The cripple nodded. The drinking horn was refilled and emptied, then the nomad was led to centre of the fire ring. He stood by the wooden framework, swaying slightly, blinking in the firelight, while the cripple addressed the crowd. His voice was soft and musical, but the Rus answered him with a clamour, their voices deep and rumbling, echoing from the ruins. When the cripple finished, nine of the Rus stepped forward, carrying with them a length of ship's rope. They circled the nomad, chanting savagely, ringing him with rope, closing in on him until I could see nothing but their broad backs.

The nine men bent over the nomad. There was a cry. They flung the rope over the wooden framework, caught its end, then yanked it down. Strong arms heaved on the rope until the nomad rose high into the air, his twitching body lit by the flickering fires. The nine men stepped back, then one of them thrust a spear at the victim, piercing his side. The others raised their hands in salutation, then turned away, leaving the dying man to swing.

The Rus sat and feasted. Lit by flaring fires, their faces glistening with grease and spittle, their clothes stained with wine and blood, they shoved the meat into their huge mouths, gulping it greedily, throwing it down their throats like starving dogs. Despite what I had just witnessed, my guts rumbled as I smelled roasted meat. I wanted to eat, and I wanted to get away. I was afraid of the Rus, and of the dark, and of the empty city and the wilderness that stretched out all around it. The whole island was filled with things that scared me. Even the star-flecked darkness above was troubled by a glowing portent. I pressed myself against a wall, comforted at least by the rough solidity of its stones. No one could creep up behind me.

When they had filled their bellies, the Rus sang. Their voices were loud enough to drive away any lingering beasts or ghosts. I was hungry enough to risk leaving the wall to search for something to eat or drink. I scanned the fires, looking for a discarded loaf, an untended wineskin, a carcass that had not been picked clean. But the only carcass I could see was the one that swung at the centre of the fires. I gazed at it, watching it gently rotate in the firelight. The nomad's face, contorted by pain, pulled awry by the rope, frozen by death, glared at me like a Gorgon.

Faced by that horror, I dared not move.

The song of the Rus was faltering. As the last ragged verses died into silence I heard a footstep nearby, and the sound of a pebble skittering over dry ground. A voice came out of the night, soft and wheedling. How did the cripple know where I was? Could he see in the dark?

"Zeno?" he called. "Zeno? You are there?"

Without really meaning to, I answered him.

I heard footsteps again, pressed myself harder against the wall. I wished I could slip through the stones like a spirit, that I could fly through the sky like a comet, that I was not made of flesh that could be roasted and eaten. Something bobbed and twisted in the dark. I raised an arm to shield my eyes against the fire-glare.

A moment later a hand lunged out of the darkness and grabbed my wrist.

"Got you!" the cripple said, jerking me away from the wall. Ignoring my cries, he dragged me over the rubble-strewn floor, out of the ruined house, towards the drunken, gluttonous giants.

When we were near the fires the cripple called out to one of the Rus, who brought a horn of wine. The cripple smiled at me in his cold, cruel way, then handed me the drinking horn. It was a heavy burden for a young boy. I felt the slick horn slide between my hands. It almost fell, nearly plunged its point into the ground, or into me. I steadied my grip, hugging the horn against my body, feeling its contents trickle down my tunic.

"Drink," the cripple said

I hesitated. I was very thirsty, and would have drunk gladly. But I had seen what they did to the nomad after giving him wine.

"Go on," he said. "It will make you brave."

Holding it firmly, I raised the horn to my mouth and drank a little of the wine. It tasted sour.

"Drink more," the cripple said. "You will need it."

I obeyed him, taking a deeper draught, then another, feeling the wine sear my dry throat. The cripple took the horn back, then pushed me down to ground, making me sit on the damp grass. The fire warmed me, and so did the wine. It fuddled me too, and made me malleable, as the cripple knew it would.

When he judged that enough time had passed, the cripple called out. Two Rus appeared, and stood on either side of him. They loomed over me, black shapes that blocked out the stars. When they reached out and pressed me down, there was nothing I could do. I struggled, but it made no difference. I cried out, but they ignored me. They pressed me flat against the ground and knelt beside me, gripping my wrists and ankles in their huge hands. The cripple also knelt, settling himself between my open legs. He felt under my tunic, found my penis and tweaked it. Then he held my balls in his warm fingers, rolling them like dice.

I was full of wine and fear. I pissed over the cripple's hands. He pulled them away and wiped them on his cloak, then reached into his pouch and pulled out a length of cord. The two Rus tightened their grip, pulling my legs wider. The cripple bent over me again. With a sudden pounce he looped the cord over my balls and pulled it tight. I cried out with pain, but he kept a grip on the cord. I feared he would pull so hard that my balls would drop off. But he did not. Instead, he spoke softly to one of the Rus, who reached to his belt and handed the cripple a dagger. It glinted as it passed from one hand to another, catching the firelight on its honed edge.

I made a last, desperate effort to break free, but the Rus pressed me against the earth so firmly that I might have been lying under a tree trunk. The cripple looped the cord a few more times and tugged on it, drawing my balls away from my body.

I prayed then for God to save me from that knife. But He did not save me. The Rus gods prevailed. The blade sliced below the cord and cut off my balls. I felt a sudden shock of pain. The cripple held the bits of my flesh in his hand for a moment, smiled grimly, then tossed them into the air. They streaked briefly through the night sky, rolling, tumbling, falling into the fire.

For days afterwards I could hardly move. The cripple inspected me regularly, poking at the swelling wound, dressing it with a stinging poultice of green herbs. He fed me too, bringing me bowls of broth and chunks of tender meat. His knife had made me valuable. He would not let me die.

I must have been on the island for months. I did not count the days, but knew the changing of the seasons. When I grew strong enough the cripple took me to Inger, the Rus who caught me in the market. He was my master and I had to serve him. I took him his food and drink, and his wine. I took him water, too, when he wanted it, but that was not often. I soon learned the Norse words for the things he wanted, and for the things he would do to me if I was not quick enough. But I also learned that he was kind, in his rough way, and would protect me if I served him well.

Once Inger went to the shore to wash, throwing his clothes off and wading into the water. He was huge and strong, his red face framed by fat plaits of blond hair and a bushy beard the colour of straw. His pale skin was matted with reddish hair. He was like a bear, like the shaggy beasts brought down from the mountains and made to dance in the marketplace of Tmutorokan. I had seen them goaded by their masters until they rose up on their hind legs and capered clumsily like men, poked and prodded with sticks to make their antics more comic. But Inger was like a bear that had not been caught and tamed, a man-beast who would submit to no one.

All that summer, ships came and went, discharging more loot and captives. The Rus feasted, drinking all they could, singing and arguing, dragging their female slaves into the bushes and doing things to them I did not understand. There was talk, as the days grew shorter, of what to do next, whether to go back up the great rivers to the North, or to go south to the famous city of Micklegard.

One night, the last I spent on the island, the question was decided.

The cripple wandered among the drunken warriors, sitting down here and there, whispering to one group, then moving on to another. He was like a beekeeper lifting hives, and wherever he went he left a buzz of anger. Men strode from one fire to another and confronted each other. Shouts filled the abandoned city, and hostile gestures, magnified by the flames, were shadowed on crumbling walls. One of the Rus, taller than the others, stood before Inger and challenged him. Inger rose, touched the small silver hammer that hung round his neck, then lunged. The two men did not use their weapons, but fought each other with fists and feet. They gouged, and boxed, and kicked, and rammed with knees and elbows. I was outside the ring, and could only catch glimpses of the fight. The tall man got Inger's thick neck in the crook of his arm and would not let him stand. The two grappled and swayed in the firelight. I feared that my master and only protector would be killed. But when the ring broke up it was Inger who was hailed as victor, and the other man who lay glaring on the ground.

Other fights broke out, and soon knives were drawn. As night deepened the island turned into a battlefield, with gangs of Rus stalking each other, lying in wait, rushing from the undergrowth and attacking their fellows. Terrified, I crept away and hid in the undergrowth, hearing shouts and screams all around me in the darkness. But I did not stay long, as men crashed into my hiding place. Driven by fear and confusion I crawled on all fours from one thicket to another until I found myself on the shore.

Behind me the sky grew red. The breeze carried the sounds and smells of burning. The brushwood was alight. The blood-coloured glow revealed the carved bear's head of Inger's ship. I climbed over the side, curled up among sacks and ropes, tried to make myself as small as possible. It was not long before I heard Rus voices, and felt the ship rock as men heaved it down the shore. I stayed where I was, pressing myself against the deck until I was sure we were out at sea. Then I crept out and looked back. The whole island was burning, a whirlwind of smoke, flames and sparks rising high into the night sky.

The tavern
[AD 838–845]

"You're a pretty young thing," she said, lifting my chin with a crooked finger. "You've got lovely eyes, and a smooth skin. Just like a girl." She put a hand under my tunic and felt my ribs. "But you're half starved. Sit there in the corner, and I'll make sure you get something to eat."

The tavern-keeper, a buxom widow with coarse straw-coloured hair, did as she promised. While the Rus wolfed watery stew and guzzled weak wine, I supped on good meat and soft bread. And while the Rus went on drinking, I curled up on the floor and slept. I had lost my freedom, my family, and my balls. But I was warm, dry and well fed, and in the care of a kind woman. After all that had happened to me, what more could I have hoped for?

The Rus were disappointed. The tavern, a big, low, wooden building with an overhanging roof, that stood in the shelter of a grove of towering planes, was no substitute for the fabled city of Micklegard. They had washed their pale bodies, combed their tangled hair and salt-crusted beards, put on their cleanest clothes and brightest jewels, yet they were still considered too barbarous to be allowed into Constantinople. Instead, the pilot-boat led their ship up the Golden Horn, an inlet that runs to the north of the city and beyond. And the prefect's men told them to wait. Or rather, they told me, and I did my best to explain things to Inger. They had left the cripple behind, and only I could translate for them.

Inger and his crew went to the tavern every day, passing the time by drinking and telling stories, gambling away their loot, wondering whether permission to enter the city would ever come. Because each day was the same, that time seemed to last forever. But in truth, the Rus were soon enough gone. All of them except for Inger. He had drunk so much the night before that he was unable to stand up. He lay on the tavern floor, wrapped in woollen blankets, his head propped up on a feather pillow. The other Rus jeered at him, saying that the mere sight of a great city had turned him soft. Inger groaned and rolled over, and muttered that he would see them in Hell.

They gathered up their possessions, and were about to set off for the city, then one of them tried to grab me. I knew why. I had heard them talk of the good price they would get for a gelded boy like me. I dashed to the widow and took shelter behind her skirts.

"You leave him alone!" she shouted. "I know what you've got in mind. You'll sell him in the slave market. Well I'm not having it. You can leave him here or I'll have the prefect's men on you!"

Meekly, knowing that they were in a strange land and under foreign laws, they went. The widow set me to watch over Inger, to mop his brow and bring him water. By the evening he was well enough to call for more wine. By the time he had finished it he was too drunk to notice that his comrades had not returned.

One by one, hearing that most of the Rus had gone, the widow's regular customers crept back. They came to drink, and to look at her two nieces, whose job it was to tease them, to lead them on, to get them to drink more than they might otherwise have done. The regulars were afraid of Inger, of his huge size and drunken ranting, but they gradually got used to him. His antics even became an attraction, something the regulars could remember and recount, laughing at what had scared them at the time. And Inger discovered that he had a talent. He was even better than the nieces at getting men to drink more than they meant to. He became very useful to the widow, and so did I. She showed me how to pour wine and serve it to the drinkers, how to get tips out them by smiling and chatting, and how to sweep the floors and wash the dishes when all the customers had gone home.

I tried to explain to the widow that there had been a mistake, that I should not be made to work, that I could read and write, that my parents were Roman citizens who had owned slaves in Tmutorokan.

"Never heard of the place," she said. "Whatever you were there, you're a slave here. But it's not so bad. There's people half-starved in the city, with nothing but the bread-dole to keep them alive. You'll do better than that here, if you're good."

Sometimes, when the tavern was empty, Inger would take me down to the waterside to look at the ship. There was not much left of it. The mast and tackle were stolen first, then the nails were prised out. The strakes fell to the ground or were carried away piecemeal, until only the ribs and keel were left lying on the shore like the bones of a beached whale. Inger would gaze sadly at the wreckage, blaming his comrades for leaving him stranded in a foreign land. On those melancholy afternoons, he talked of the far North, of endless night, of blinding ice-fields, and bears as white as snow. He told tales of Asgard and the gods, of Valhalla where the heroes dwell, of the World's beginning, and its end. In those days I knew more of the Rus and their ways than I did of the city that lay just a mile away.

Eventually, the widow took pity on Inger and let him marry her. I thought she loved him. Perhaps Inger did too. He was handsome when he was cleaned up, and could be kind and gentle when he was sober. But it turned out that the widow was being pressed by the guild of tavern-keepers, who wanted to put a man in her place, and were claiming that her house was disorderly. I can assure you that it was not. There are places like that in the city, as I will tell later, but they hide their low trade in back rooms and bribe the prefect's men to look the other way. Out in the suburbs, tavern-keepers must stick to the rules. A new husband was the widow's answer to the guild, and Inger was a man no one would risk provoking.

Inger became a Christian to be married, but I never knew him to go to church afterwards. He always wore Mjollnir, his silver hammer talisman, which looked enough like a cross not to be remarked upon. And he set up a little idol of Thor, carved from narwhal ivory. What an unlikely beast the narwhal is. Who could believe in a fish with a tusk like a unicorn's horn? I have never read of such a creature in the accounts of those who claim to have travelled beyond Thule. I have only Inger's word that the narwhal exists. Yet there are no elephants in the icy North, and the idol is undoubtedly made of ivory. I have it before me as I write. Inger prayed to the idol in his way, pouring it libations of best Monemvasian wine. It is still stained with the wine he poured.

After a year or so the widow gave birth to a girl. She was blonde, blue-eyed, and too beautiful for such a humble and squalid place as the tavern. She was like an infant goddess hiding among mortals. Inger wanted to call her Gerda, but the widow named her Eudocia. The nieces were jealous, and could not be trusted to look after her. When the widow was busy it fell to me to care for little Eudocia. I did everything but suckle her, and she came to love me as much as I loved her. She had no reason to despise me, did not even understand what I was.

Though he sometimes dandled her in his clumsy way, a daughter was no use to Inger. He salvaged a piece of oak from the wreck of his ship and carved another idol. I watched him work, saw huge-phallused Frey emerge from the weathered wood, and helped pour libations to the god. A god you can see was more real to me than a god you only hear about, and in those days I had not heard much about God. Frey mocked me, flaunting an organ that in my case remained small. He mocked Inger too, refusing to grant his wishes. He sacrificed a pig to it once, hoping the god of fertility would give him sons who would rebuild his ship and carry him back north. But no sons came.

Sometimes the widow took me into her bed. That was in the cold winter, when fog rose up from the Golden Horn as thick as blood soup, and wrapped the tavern in silence. Inger drank more in the winter. The short days and long nights reminded him of the icy North. Dragged down into drunken melancholy, he was seldom ready to do his duty.

"Why did I marry him?" she would say. "What's he good for, apart from drinking? That's all he does. He gets up, drinks, then falls asleep. I suppose he gets the others to drink, too. There is that. We sell more wine when he's drinking. But what's the use of him carving idols and pouring wine over them? If he wants sons he should be here in bed with me."

She used to hold me to her, ruffling my hair, pressing me against her soft flesh, enfolding me in her plump arms. She smelled of sweat, and onions, and stale wine. I had to lie with her all night, my head between her breasts, keeping her warm and comforting her. Even a eunuch can please a woman. He can do with his hand what he cannot do with his member. The widow showed me how, taking my hand in hers, guiding it downwards, pushing it between her fat thighs, pressing my fingers into a moist cleft that swallowed them eagerly. She writhed against me, moaning like the howling wind, quivering like the timbers of a beaching ship. The bed rocked, the floorboards creaked, the whole house shook as though battered by an earthquake. When the moment of pleasure came, her cry of triumph was loud enough to raise the roof. Dead drunk though he was, I do not know how Inger slept through it. But he did, and when he woke he never suspected that I had pleasured his wife, that I, a boy and a eunuch, had achieved what he could not.

I got no joy from that caressing. How could I? But it was my task at the tavern to please people.

When the widow did not want me I slept with the nieces. They dressed and undressed before me, and they washed in my presence, not concealing their most private parts, washing me too, provoking my little manhood, and taunting me with what I lacked. When they found that they could not arouse me they tried to convince me that I was like them. They dressed me in their old clothes, painted my face, plaited my hair like a girl's. But Inger soon put a stop to that. His rage showed what he thought of boys who dressed as girls. Loki could turn himself into a woman, but he was a god and a trickster, and not to be trusted.

33

When I grew bigger the nieces talked of places in the city where a creature like me could be sold for a handful of gold coins. They described the filthy old men who would pay to paw my body, and the indignities I would be forced to undergo. I do not suppose they would really have sold me. They would have had to do their own work then. But they made my life as miserable as they could, criticising my work, and stealing my tips.

I reached the age when uncut boys turn in to men. But I did not change. I knew the ways of women well, and might have become a sort of woman myself, mothering Eudocia, doing women's work, despising men's weakness, gossiping with the customers and bickering with the nieces.

Then, by chance, I was taken away, and began a new life among men.

Constantine
[AD 846]

"Cretan?" I asked. "Theban? Chian? Attic? Monemvasia?"

The young man looked puzzled. He was a gentleman, that was obvious, but not a type I had seen before. He was not like the young roisterers who sometimes ventured out from the city. They liked to do their drinking unobserved, among people who did not know them, and did not care if they drove away the regular customers with their shouting and horseplay.

The man who sat before me was younger, and less self-assured than those other gentlemen. He was, I thought, no more than twenty years old. His clothes were well-made and of fine material, but they were shabby and uncared-for. His hair and beard were unkempt. He was not proud or haughty, nor was he attended by any servants, unless he had left them outside.

"What?" he said, looking up at me vaguely.

"What wine would you like? Theban, Cyprian . . ."

"Wine?"

"Most of the customers drink something while they are here."

"Then I had better have some wine. Just the regular sort."

"Resinated, or not?"

"I don't mind."

"I'll bring you a cup of Monemvasia, sir. Or would you like a jug?"

"A cup will be enough."

While I went to get the wine, he looked around anxiously. It was obvious that he did not often visit taverns. Some of the other drinkers looked at him, no doubt wondering whether he was one of the prefect's men, or some other official sent out from the city to spy on us. One of the nieces was eyeing him up, and I could see he was not the man for that. If I was not careful, she would drive him away before I had got any money out of him.

I poured him a cup of Monemvasia. It was the most expensive wine we kept. He tasted it warily, then he looked around the room.

"What languages do these men speak?" he asked.

"They all speak Greek, of a sort."

"No other languages?"

"Maybe. They are all sailors and fishermen."

"Our Lord did not disdain fishermen." He spoke rather stiffly, as though trying to reassure himself. Then he raised the cup delicately to his lips, sipped, then set it down again, muttering something under his breath.

"Are you a priest?" I asked. The widow always feared that someone would find out about Inger's idols. The worship of icons had only just been restored, and there were many who still disapproved of Christian images. Pagan ones would have been unthinkable abominations.

"No. I am a scholar."

"What is your name, boy?"

"Zeno, sir."

"I am Constantine." He paused awkwardly, unsure how to proceed. I knew nothing of scholars. People of that sort never visited the tavern. But I could see that he was kind, and kindness was something that was lacking from my life in those days.

"Sir," I said. "What do you want here?"

"I've heard there's a Rus here . . . "

"Inger? He owns the place."

"I want to talk to him."

"You'll have a job. He's sleeping off last night's wine. You could wait, I suppose." Constantine looked uncomfortable. "You could come back in the evening," I said, "but the chances are he'd be far too drunk to talk, even if you could understand a word he said."

"When might I find him sober?"

"First thing in the morning, maybe, but he's always in a terrible temper then. The truth is there aren't many times when he's fit to talk. Not sense, anyway."

"I wanted to find out about his language."

"It's rough enough," I said. "But you'll find plenty here that speak just as roughly, if that's what you like."

"I don't mean sailor's talk. I mean his native language."

"It's like I said. When he's not asleep, he's too drunk."

Looking disappointed, Constantine drank some more of the wine.

"I know a few words," I said

The scholar's face brightened. "Tell me some."

"I'm busy," I said.

"It's all right," he said, scattering a handful of coins on the counter. "I'll buy another drink."

I scooped up the scholar's money, poured more wine, then sat down on the bench opposite him. I would not normally have done that with a gentleman, but I could see that he was ill at ease, and that the other drinkers were growing quieter, paying him more attention.

"What about these words," he said. "These words of Rus-speak."

"Norse, Inger calls it."

He leaned forward, his face full of interest. "Tell me as many words of Norse as you can."

I decided to make him feel sorry for me. He had overpaid for his drink, and might give me a good tip. "I only know bad words," I said. "Ones you wouldn't want to hear."

"Try me."

Looking around carefully to make sure Inger had not staggered in, I leaned across the table and whispered a phrase.

"What does it mean?"

"It means that Inger is going to hit me." That was not quite true. Inger never hit me. Hitting a boy, and a gelded one at that, would have been beneath his dignity. But he sometimes threatened it, and I had repeated his words accurately.

Constantine frowned. "He sounds a rough fellow. Perhaps it is just as well he can't speak to me. But don't you know any other words?"

"A few." I told him the words for bread, and meat, and

wine, and how to say "come here" and "get out" and "pour me a drink".

I realised that the scholar was keen to listen. Words and phrases came back to me, from Inger's stories, from my time on the island and at sea, and I went on, telling Constantine what I knew. Seeing his interest, I even exaggerated, telling him things I did not know, making myself seem more of an expert than I was.

The shy young scholar sipped his wine slowly and asked me endless questions. He wanted to know what the Rus meant by their words, what they believed, and about their way of life. He asked where I had come from, and how I came to be captured. I could see that Constantine was quite impressed. Though a few years older than me, he clearly knew less of life.

"This Inger," Constantine said when I had told him everything I could remember. "He is your master?"

"Yes. But he is a drunken ruffian. He would be no use to you."

"Would he sell you?"

"He'd sell anything if you showed him gold."

"I cannot show him gold, but I could promise it."

The scholars
[AD 846]

The first thing we saw as we passed through the gates was a gang of shaven-headed men shuffling grimly towards us. They were chained together at the wrists and ankles, their heads hung low with shame. Constantine leaped aside to let them pass, dragging me with him into an empty doorway. As they trudged to the gates, the guards lashed the prisoners with barbed scourges, making them skip over the cobbles and rattle their chains. Blood dribbled from the gashes on their bare backs, splashing onto the dusty cobbles.

"Criminals," Constantine said. "May God have mercy on them."

"What did they do?" I asked.

"I don't know, but it must have been something terrible to deserve that punishment."

We watched the criminals being driven out of the city. Constantine muttered a prayer, then led me on, towards the main street.

"Does your friend live near here?" I asked.

"He lives at the other end of the city, near the palace and the cathedral."

I had never been to that part of the city before, as tavern business had only taken me to the suburbs.

"This friend," I said. "Will he give Inger the money?"

"I am sure he will." Constantine looked worried. "I hope so, I have promised it."

"And he's a scholar like you?"

"A great and famous one. He will be delighted to hear your tales of the Rus."

I could hardly believe it: a great and famous man would be delighted to listen to me! For years I had had to listen to others and do their bidding. Now Constantine was taking me to a place where I would be welcome and respected. I skipped along beside him, delighted by everything I saw. Shops lined the avenue and the streets that led off it. They sold everything imaginable, and their goods spilled out onto the pavement in extravagant displays, guarded by stern and cruel-looking slaves. Some of the guards were so black that I could hardly make out their features, others were as pale as any Rus.

Above us, on columns and in niches, were statues of gigantic men, some of them half-naked, all carved from the whitest marble.

"Who are they?" I asked.

"Emperors," Constantine said, not looking up the statues. "Or old gods. It doesn't matter. Images are not important."

Despite the heat, the street was thronged with all kinds of people, many of them dressed from head to toe in the finest silks. Some were so rich that they did not have to walk, but were carried about in litters, from which they peeped out, parting gauzy curtains with jewelled hands, then sinking back on their soft cushions. Even the poorer people were clean and well dressed. A tavern in that place, I thought, would make a fortune for its owner. Those people would drink nothing but the finest wines, and would never expect change from a gold piece. But there were no taverns, just jewellers, tailors, money-lenders, furriers, ivory carvers, silk merchants, and purveyors of every kind of luxury. The taverns, I thought, must be somewhere else, perhaps down the streets and alleys I could see sloping away on either side of the avenue. In the distance, beyond the red tiled roofs of the narrow houses, I caught glimpses of the Sea of Marmora, the Bosphorus, the Golden Horn, glittering waterways that surrounded the city, guarded it and brought it wealth.

When we reached the quarter of the incense makers and perfumeries, Constantine, after a few words with a sullen gatekeeper, led me into a cool, shady courtyard. The calm and silence were almost a shock after the bustle outside. The courtyard was lined with marble columns, and had a pool with a gently tinkling fountain at its centre. Scattered artfully about were statues, and small trees and flowering bushes. Enough rooms led off the courtyard to house a shipful of Rus, yet the place was almost silent. Perhaps the inhabitants were all sleeping in the afternoon heat, and would soon rouse themselves and fill the house with noise and activity. Or perhaps Constantine's friend was rich enough to live there alone, with just a few fellow scholars for company.

I was looking at the mosaic floor, wondering why anyone would spend so much time and money on something destined only to be walked on, when I heard a mocking voice.

"What made you bring that *creature* here," it said. I looked up and, for the first time, saw Photius, whose fate was to be linked with mine for many years afterwards. I was struck at first by his smoothness, by the way his hair and beard were gently curled and scented with perfumed oils, and by the elegance of his dove-grey tunic. He was a young man then, not yet thirty, and handsome, with a confident manner that told me he was used to being listened to. I was used to listening to people. Clever or stupid, drunk or sober, it made no difference. But Constantine had told me that his friend would want to listen to me, so I was puzzled by his hostile tone.

"Creature?" Constantine said, looking crestfallen. "What do you mean?"

"That *eunuch*. You know I can't bear them. Nasty, hybrid, androgynous creatures, neither one thing nor the other. They violate logical categories, and break the laws of generation. A eunuch is an affront to nature, and to its Creator."

"Eunuch? He's just a boy."

"A boy? What an innocent you are!" Photius turned to me, glaring with almost gleeful anger. "You're a eunuch, aren't you?"

I stood there dismayed and confused. Only that morning, after taking a last look at Eudocia, I had left the tavern. She was five years old, and more beautiful than ever. Her blonde hair was neatly plaited, and her blue eyes blazed like the sky. It would not be long, I thought, before she was serving wine and charming the drinkers. No doubt the nieces would make her life miserable, and I would not be there to protect her. I was missing her already, and wondered whether I had been right

41

to encourage Constantine to buy me, to let him take me into a world I did not understand.

Photius looked at me with even greater contempt.

"A eunuch?" he repeated. I was not sure what he meant. The word was unfamiliar to me. It was not much used by fishermen and sailors. "It's stupid, too," Photius said, taking a step towards me. "Let's try a simpler question." He spoke very slowly. "Have you got any balls? Or have they been cut off?"

"No sir." I said. "Cut off."

Photius stepped back, a look of triumphant exasperation on his face. "I told you so! A eunuch."

"I thought he was just a boy when I bought him."

"You bought him! Why?"

"He is clever."

"He is clearly an imbecile."

"He speaks Norse."

"Another of your obscure tongues?"

"The language of the Rus. They are . . ."

"Barbarians," Photius said. "And best left in obscurity."

"I thought he could teach me. And then I could teach him. He might be very useful, a clever boy like him."

"A eunuch!" Photius said. "What on earth will people say?"

"Why should they say anything?"

"Buying a eunuch might be thought a little odd for one in your position."

"Odd?" Constantine said. "Why?"

"You are an innocent! People will think you bought this creature so that you can assuage your unnatural lusts!"

"Lusts?"

"Oh Constantine! I can believe that you are untroubled by lust, but others may not be so charitable." Photius paced slowly round me, looking at me with a slightly milder expression. "How did you pay for him?"

Constantine looked embarrassed. "I haven't, yet," he said. "I was hoping you would help."

"How much does his owner want for him?"

"Ten gold pieces."

"Ten! I could buy a book for that. Theodore has seen a fine edition of Ctesias that he could get me for not much more."

"You could borrow the book. This boy knows things that no one has written down."

Photius gave me a withering look. "But are they worth knowing?"

"He will be useful," Constantine said. "I promise you."

While they argued, I waited. That is what I had been taught: to wait on the orders of others. But I was bitterly disappointed. Constantine had told me that Photius would welcome me, and he obviously despised me.

That night, the first I spent in the scholars' house, I could not sleep. It was too quiet. There were no people about, no groans or sighs, no muttering, no sounds of snoring or pissing. I was alone, in a strange and silent house.

I rolled off my straw pallet, felt my way through a jumble of baskets, sacks and jars, then slipped out of the door. Faint moonlight bathed the far end of the passageway. My bare feet padding softly on the cool flagstones, I crept past the room where the other servants slept. None of them were eunuchs. They had not welcomed me, but had banished me to a storeroom.

I stepped out into the courtyard. The scent of roses and lilies was strong. The pool reflected a row of gleaming columns. At its centre a fountain tinkled gently, each drop of water a moonlit jewel. For a moment I thought I was being watched. Then I realised that the motionless figure was a statue. It stood proudly, draped in antique robes, its bearded face stern yet kind, its stony brow furrowed in ceaseless thought. It looked a bit like Photius, or how he might look in old age.

There were other statues, all of wise-looking bearded men. There were no images of saints in those days, so I guessed they must be philosophers. I wandered along the colonnade, touching the cool marble pillars, smelling the flowers, feeling the roughness of the mosaics beneath my feet, peering into alcoves and open doors. Most of the rooms looked empty, but in one a light showed. I crept towards it and peered through the door. Photius was there, lying on a carved bed of dark wood, his curled black beard sticking out over a thin blanket. His eyes were closed. He was alone. Surely he could not enjoy sleeping that way? Why did none of his servants keep him company?

I stepped into the bedroom. Its walls were painted with rustic scenes, but there was not much furniture, just the bed, a chest and a folding stool. Surely rich men had plenty of everything? Money, clothes, food, furniture, servants, friends. Yet Photius slept alone in a bare room. I tiptoed towards him. With his eyes closed and his mouth turned down, he looked sad. I wanted to comfort him, to make him happy. Then, perhaps, he would like me.

I had pleased the widow. How could I please him? Men were different from women. I knew that much. But their differences lay in the same place, and that place was the seat of pleasure.

As quietly as I could, I slipped into the bed beside him.

For a moment I felt the luxury of a soft mattress. It yielded beneath me, sagging, and tilting me to the bed's centre. Carefully, I reached out beneath the bedclothes, feeling for flesh. But I touched something rough and hairy. Surprised, I withdrew my hand. Photius was a smooth man, whose clothes were made of silk, and whose beard was oiled and scented, yet his nether regions were as shaggy as a goat. I reached out again, and encountered the same puzzling roughness. How could I please him if I could not find the right place? I felt a little higher, and touched hot skin.

Photius sat bolt upright and yelled.

The sound he made was wordless, but infinitely expressive of surprise, anger and outrage.

He leapt from his bed and ran to the doorway, calling for help at the top of his voice. Then he turned back and looked at me. He was wearing tightly laced drawers of the coarsest cloth imaginable. I wondered why a rich man would wear anything so uncomfortable, but only for a moment.

"You!" he shouted. "What are you doing in here?"

"I'm sorry sir. I wanted to please you."

"Please me?" Horror filled his face. "What do you think I am? An indulger in unnatural vice?"

If I had an answer to that question it was forestalled by the arrival of half-a-dozen servants carrying lanterns and sticks. They burst into the room, barely giving their master time to step aside, and took hold of my arms and legs, dragging me from the bed. I was too mortified to struggle, and allowed myself to be pulled into the courtyard, where I was pushed, pummelled, and hit with sticks.

"What shall we do with him?" one of the servants said.

"Shove him in the pool," another suggested.

"No!" Photius said.

"Shall we beat him? Lock him up? Throw him into the street?"

They held onto me firmly, almost tearing me in half. Photius's mouth opened and closed silently. He looked like a carp gulping air on a hot summer day. He did not know what to do, or what to tell his servants.

I longed to rub my bruised and aching legs. No doubt the servants longed to give me another beating. We stood there, frozen in the moonlight like a carved frieze of battling gladiators.

Then Constantine appeared. He looked sleepy, but quickly took charge, telling the servants to let me go, asking me what I had done, calming everyone down.

"It is not his fault," Constantine said, when he had heard my story. "He was trying to help. But he didn't know what was right. I will teach him."

Constantine was not like the teacher I had before I was captured. He was kind and considerate. He did not mind that I was a eunuch, or that I had made a fool of myself on that first night. He listened to me, took an interest in me, realised that what I knew was of value.

"Tell me about Tmutorokan?" he said.

"My father hated the place."

"Why? Was he an exile?"

"I don't know. He didn't say."

"Cherson is a notorious place of exile, but Tmutorokan is even more remote."

"That's what my father used to say. He said Tmutorokan was at the edge of the World. He said it was hardly a town at all, just a collection of shacks, tents and ruins, surrounded by shallow water that froze every winter. He used to complain about the dusty summers, and the winter winds that blew from the steppes, and the mud flats. He said they poked out into the sea like dead fingers, all covered in slimy seaweed."

"And what did you think?"

"I liked it, but I didn't know any better. I liked the market and the barbarians that came to it."

Constantine's face brightened. "What barbarians?"

"There were Khazars, Goths, and Magyars. And nomads I don't know the name of. They came from the steppes."

"From beyond the edge of the World?"

"Yes. From the North."

"Like the Rus. How often did they visit the place?"

"I never saw them before the day they captured me."

"So, they are on the move. You must tell me everything you know about them."

I told Constantine what I knew, and repeated all the Norse words I could remember. He wrote the words carefully, using invented characters to record unfamiliar sounds. When he had done that, thinking that I would make a useful assistant, he began the task of turning me into a scholar. I had not wanted to be such a thing before, but seeing how well scholars lived, I thought it worth making the effort. I certainly had no wish to be a house servant like the men who had beaten me. I could see that there would be opportunities in a house of scholars, but I had no idea what they might be. I would have to get to know them, and their way of life, before I could tell where life with them might lead.

We spent most of our time in the library, which looked out onto the colonnaded courtyard. It was an important room, and one of the best furnished, being lined with inlayed book cabinets, each equipped with a large lock. I had never imagined that so many books existed. My first teacher had been proud of his manual of grammar and anthology of verse, but owned no other books. Photius was rich as well as scholarly. Some of his books were bound with carved ivory and clasped with jewelled gold. Others, richly illuminated, looked like jewels on the inside. He had rare books brought from Egypt and Syria, and ancient ones that had been loved and studied for centuries. But most of his books were unprepossessing, much handled, meant for use rather than ornament, and full of knowledge and wisdom.

It was the books, as much as Photius's knowledge and ability, that attracted a circle of scholars to the house. They came to read, to discuss philosophy, to make useful contacts, and to attend the classes Photius and Constantine sometimes taught. When not teaching, Constantine worked in the library, cataloguing the books for Photius, making summaries, and compiling the information he would need for his great project of converting the barbarians.

"There are so many of them," he told me. "And all mired deeply in error. Take the Bulgars, for instance. Do you know what they believe?"

I assured him that I did not.

"They believe that the world was created by the devil." Constantine shuddered slightly on mentioning the Evil One. "According to the Bulgars, God sent the devil to the bottom of the sea to collect a handful of mud, which He used to shape the land."

It sounded plausible to me. My father used to say that the slimy mudbanks of Tmutorokan were the devil's creation.

"This means," Constantine said, "that they believe in two gods, the one remote and good, the other ever-present and evil. Well, perhaps not evil," he said, seeing, as always, good in everything. "Perhaps the lesser god of the Bulgars is more of a spirit or demon than a devil. Or a slave or workman employed by a fastidious master. Whichever it is they are utterly wrong, and I intend to lead them from error. But it will not be easy. Some of the peasants are receptive to the truth. But there

47

is the Khan to contend with, and his boyars. They are a bloodthirsty lot, by all accounts. They worship war, despise good Christians and fear all change. According to them, God or the devil laid down the law forever when the world was created. Imagine a law that comes from a handful of mud! They see no need to change their ways, to cease sacrificing to their gods and ancestors. I really need to find out more, to travel to deepest Bulgaria and investigate their beliefs. But whatever the Bulgars think, they are quite wrong to worship a lesser god. In that respect they are even worse than the Paulician heretics, and they are bad enough."

The more I heard about barbarians, pagans and heretics, the less I wanted to go and help Constantine convert them. A comfortable house in the city was a much pleasanter place than the forests, deserts and mountains described in the books Constantine liked. However, Constantine had brought me into the house because he thought me an expert on barbarian customs, and to keep him happy I had to sound like one.

"The Bulgars are just like the Rus," I said, with more confidence than I felt. "The Rus are fighters. But they have more than two gods. I don't know how many. But there are gods for everything. For war, thunder, fertility, poetry, justice, the sea. Everything. Inger told me all about them. And giants and monsters."

"How do they think the world was created?"

"From a giant's body."

I tried to tell Constantine a story Inger had told me. As well as the giant, it involved a cow, a block of salt, rivers of milk, and a mist-filled chasm. As I told it I realised that it made no sense at all. Constantine looked disappointed when I had finished.

"This giant," he said. "If the universe was created from his body, where was he living beforehand?"

"I don't know," I admitted.

"And the misty chasm. If it was not in the universe, where was it?"

"I don't know."

"And who could have caused any of these things to happen, if not Almighty God?"

"No one, I am sure."

Constantine was happy with my answer. But the truth is I could never quite believe in the Almighty God that Constantine proclaimed. Perhaps He exists, but only as one of many, an Olympian, an Aesir, a man-like god surrounded by rivals, beset by enemies, and far from certain to triumph. How else can we explain life's uncertainties and reverses?

A question
[AD 847]

I had been living at the house for about a year, and was well advanced in my studies, when Photius came to the library bringing with him a man I had not seen before. His guest, as Constantine explained afterwards, was Bardas: wealthy nobleman, successful soldier, uncle of the young emperor, brother of the regent Theodora, and, more important than any of his other qualities and achievements, a man excluded from power by his suspicious relatives because of his naked ambition and notorious womanising. That last point was the sort of thing Constantine, seeing, as always, the best in everyone, tended not to mention.

Not knowing any of that when Bardas first appeared, all I saw was a stiff, stocky, upright man, whose hair and beard were neatly trimmed, and who was dressed like any other gentleman, in a long, richly embroidered tunic that fell almost as far as his finely worked shoes.

"Scribble, scribble, scribble!" Bardas said, glancing at the table where Constantine and I worked. "Aren't there enough books already?"

"Constantine is trying to turn a eunuch into a scholar," Photius said.

Bardas looked at me more carefully, his mouth turning down with disgust. "I don't know how you can bear to have one in the house."

"A eunuch?" Photius said. "Perhaps you are right. I have never liked the creatures myself. But Constantine thought he might be useful."

I was hurt and disappointed. I had worked hard, tried to make myself useful, yet Photius, eager to please his friend, had echoed his contempt for my kind. Would he never forget the stupid mistake I had made on my first night? How could I make him like and trust me?

"Now that Ignatius is patriarch, they seem to be everywhere." Bardas said. "They are getting above themselves. Like that scoundrel Theoctistus."

"He is the Logothete. He controls the court. You can't get much higher than that."

"I'd cut him down to size. I'd gladly cut his balls off if it hadn't been done already."

"He must have had a hand in getting Ignatius made patriarch." Photius sounded rueful.

"It was Theodora as well," Bardas said. "My sister is under the thumb of those palace eunuchs. They made her put another of their kind in charge of the Church."

"Ignatius may be a eunuch," Photius said. "But he's hardly the same kind as those creatures that rule the palace. I can't imagine Ignatius mincing about the women's quarters doused with perfume and dressed in silks!"

"Perhaps not," Bardas said. "Have you heard the rubbish he talks? They should have cut off his tongue as well his balls. They couldn't have made him patriarch after that."

"What made them do it? I can see why they wanted another eunuch, but why Ignatius? He is far too stupid, ignorant and bigoted to be allowed any sort of high office. That is obvious to anyone of intelligence and good sense. So of course, Theoctistus chose him!"

"It's because of the icons," Bardas said. "Women and eunuchs love icons."

Photius looked at the image of Saint Jerome that Constantine had set up in an alcove. The flame of a small candle made its gilded frame glimmer. "There is nothing wrong with icons," Photius said. "Some of us have always defended them. As you know, my family was exiled for it. But where was Ignatius while the iconoclasts ruled? Hiding in his monastery, that's where! He didn't dare to come out in favour of icons until after Theophilus died. Then he claimed to have been leader of the iconodules all along."

Bardas looked disdainfully at the painted image, noting the saint's sombre habit. "The monks support Ignatius," he said. "They're just like eunuchs. They always support their own kind."

"The monks hate books as much as they love images," Photius said. "With Ignatius at their head they will do their best to spread ignorance and suppress learning." He looked around the room anxiously, as though a crowd of zealous monks might burst in at any moment and ransack his book cabinets. "Something must be done," he said. "Or Ignatius will take us back to those dark days when ignorance and barbarism almost triumphed."

"They are all in it together," Bardas said. I sensed that he was not particularly interested in books, and wondered why Photius liked him. "One eunuch runs the government," he said. "The other runs the Church. And their eunuch cronies control everything else. They do just as they like, whatever serves them best."

"I think removing their balls must remove their consciences."

"If I had my way, I'd clear them all out and bring the army in to run the palace,"

They talked for a while, naming court eunuchs and enumerating their many faults and few virtues. I kept my head down and pretended to work, running my stylus over the wax without marking it. But I listened carefully, learning what my kind were thought to be like. And I cannot say that experience has taught me to disagree with the views I heard then. Of course, I am reliable, honest and trustworthy, but most of the other eunuchs I have met, especially those who dominate the court, have been just the opposite.

After a while Bardas looked thoughtful, gazing around the library as though the books might reveal something without him actually having to read them. "What I want to know is this," he said. "Is a eunuch more like a man or a woman?"

"I have no idea," Photius said. "It is not a question I have thought worth considering. What do you think, Constantine?"

"I can't say I've thought about it either." Constantine turned to me and pretended to take an interest in the work I was pretending to do.

"It's hardly an important question," Photius said, though without his usual certainty.

"I think it's important," Bardas said. "It interests me, anyway. In war it's important to know your enemy. In peace, too. And just at the moment, the court eunuchs are our enemies. So I'd like to know whether they are more like men or women. I'd know how to deal with them then."

Photius looked embarrassed. He must have known his friend was a womaniser, though he always preferred to ignore what he did not understand. However, realising that his scholarly reputation was at stake, he began to extemporise. "Eunuchs are imperfect men," he suggested. "So perhaps they are more like women. After all, God created Man in his image, not Woman. Women are an afterthought, and are necessarily imperfect. Therefore . . . "

Bardas looked dissatisfied. "Imperfect?" he said. "Perhaps. But women have their charms. I've never seen much resemblance between a lovely woman and a eunuch. There are debased creatures who cannot tell the difference, but I am not one of them. I would still like to know the answer to my question."

"I'll try and find out," Photius said, looking hopefully at Constantine. "Perhaps there's something in Agapios."

Constantine, rubbing out a word I had misspelled, ignored him.

"I'd be glad if you would," Bardas said. "And while you're about it, here's another question for you. Does a man or a woman enjoy sex more?" He looked pleased with himself. "It's a good question, isn't it? If you two scholars can't answer it, who can?"

Photius and Constantine looked at each other questioningly, but said nothing.

When they left, Constantine directed my attention to our work. But I could not concentrate on transcribing theories from the *Christian Cosmography* of Cosmas Indicopleustes, even though it was a work Constantine particularly esteemed. I kept asking him questions, and was amazed to discover who the visitor had been. I knew that my master was rich, but to find that he knew the imperial family was startling. And to learn that his enemies were eunuchs was worrying. I was all the more determined to make myself useful, and to give Photius a reason for liking me.

"There are two things we must do," Constantine said. "In the first, I will guide you. But in the second, I will need your help."

It was only a short walk to the cathedral of Hagia Sophia, which rose above the other buildings on the eastern tip of the city like a mountain among foothills. Its great dome, the biggest ever built by Man, seemed to float as though suspended from Heaven by the hand of God. But the crowds in the cathedral square did not look up at the marvel that dominated their city. Gaily-dressed citizens hailed each other cheerfully, clutching at the sleeves of friends and acquaintances, talking expectantly about the sermon they were to hear, pronouncing the name of my master's enemy with awe.

Ignatius, Patriarch of Constantinople, spiritual ruler of all the Christians in the Empire, and a good many beyond it, defender of the Holy Images, was to preach!

Constantine, not caring about my humble status, took my arm as we neared the seven doors. He held on to me as we were borne by the jostling crowd through the porch and into the nave. And he led me to his preferred place beneath the southern gallery, allowing me to gaze with wonder at the gilded dome, the shimmering mosaics, the many-coloured marble columns, the gold and silver lamps, and the rich ornaments bathed in dappled light from the stained-glass windows.

When the service began, I followed Constantine's example, praying when he did, moving my lips in imitation of his singing, copying his movements and responses, trying to seem the pious believer I was not. It was easy to be carried along, to be overcome by the music, the brilliant colours, the precious ornaments, the intoxicating smell of incense. Beauty has an effect of its own, quite separate from that of truth, and in those days I knew little of either. I was happy to be in that wondrous cathedral, to be in the company of a good man and a scholar, to be among people so sophisticated that they could take such things for granted.

When Ignatius appeared I forgot everything else and concentrated on him.

Ignatius looked old, and yet not old. He must have been castrated young, as he had no beard, and the hair on his head was shaved in the monkish manner. He was small, frail-looking, dwarfed by the vestments he wore. Despite my master's inability to imagine such a thing, the austere monk was wrapped in the richest silks, and draped with every ecclesiastical accessory the patriarchal sacristy could provide. He flapped and rattled as he walked, and when the time came for him to climb into the pulpit, he could not manage it without a discreet shove from a couple of deacons. His chasuble was so heavy with jewels and gold thread that he could hardly raise his arms, and he struggled to perform the pious gestures required of him. His movements were jerky, spasmodic, and his hairless head, nodding slightly on a scrawny neck protruding from an inflexible collar, made him look like a tortoise. Ignatius glared at the congregation with eyes as black as dead coals. He was disgusted by what he saw. At first, when he began to speak, his voice had a reptilian hiss. His thin lips hardly moved, and after each wheezy breath he pressed them together so firmly that they turned white. The slit of his mouth was like a line ruled on parchment, a line drawn after every pronouncement, rendering it final and unanswerable.

Gazing wearily at his flock, Ignatius spoke slowly, stretching out every syllable, drawing out each pause. Like a torpid beast emerging from a cave into sunlight, he gradually warmed and stirred. His voice rose, changing from a hiss to a croak. Overcoming the stiffness of his sleeves, he raised his arms and waved them jerkily. His words speeded up until he began to gabble like a market trader. As he poured out blame, hatred, denunciation, loathing, threats of damnation, he hopped, jiggled, and almost danced. Bits of his costume came unfastened, bands and draperies dangled, and his pectoral cross swung loose. By the end of his sermon his lips were writhing and foaming like slugs that have been sprinkled with salt.

I would like to set down here some examples of Ignatius's rhetoric. Unfortunately I was so distracted by his manner that I hardly heard a word he said. Or rather, I heard, but did not listen, allowing the words to wash over me like the gushing of a waterfall or the howling of the wind. All I know is that he upheld blissful ignorance as a state to be longed for, and condemned sin in all its forms, but most especially lust. In truth, Ignatius hardly needed to speak. His appearance was enough. By the end of the service he looked like a dead sinner dragged from Hades, his flesh half-consumed by infernal fires, his limbs tormented by demons, his shroud-wrapped body set up before the faithful as a terrible reminder of what awaited them after Judgement.

The crowd was not quite so cheerful as it shuffled out through the seven doors and into the forecourt. Some worried citizens drew dull-coloured cloaks around their bright clothes and rushed off, frowning.

"Ignatius is a good man," Constantine said as we crossed the forecourt. "And sincere. What a pity he is so opposed to learning and scholarship. Can knowledge really be so dangerous? Surely not! If we are good by nature, we cannot be led into sin by what we know."

I kept silent. I had seen my master's enemy, the creature he and Bardas hated. And he was a eunuch, just like me. If an ignorant eunuch could become ruler of the Church, what might I, a would-be scholar, achieve?

Constantine was as ill at ease in the backstreets as he had been in the tavern. I went ahead of him crying out that everyone should make way for a gentleman and scholar. I cared nothing for my own dignity in those days. Indeed, I had none, being less than a man in every respect. However, our errand promised, if successful, to reveal something of my nature, and perhaps to advance my status.

Constantine flinched from the beggars, averted his eyes

from the unveiled women, trembled at the sight of street-corner ruffians, and pressed himself flat against the grimiest wall rather than get in the way of a hastening porter or well-laden donkey. The common people terrified him as if they had been wild beasts. But they did not scare me. In fact, they were much what I had been used to, and their increased number and activity were what made the great city of Constantinople so exciting. It was not the people we struggled through who puzzled me, but the scholars I had fallen among. Scholars valued knowledge, yet knew nothing. For every fact or opinion, they referred to books. It was only because there was no *Book of the Rus* that Constantine had sought out Inger and found me. Had there been such a book I would still have been serving in the tavern.

But Leo, I had been told, was different. He was not afraid to investigate, to find things out for himself. And his house was somewhere in the district of narrow streets that tumble down the slopes above the Sea of Marmora. But we were not sure where, and had been wandering for some time, unable to find anything except the miserable dwellings of the poor. They rose all around us, three or four stories high, their overhanging roofs almost blocking out the sun, their wooden facades as much patched as a beggar's cloak.

We had been jostled, importuned, jeered at, and almost soaked with slops. But I was enjoying myself. If Tmutorokan was at the world's distant edge, Constantinople was at its centre, and I was happy to be there. I had a riposte to every ribald wisecrack, and no work but to stroll the streets in search of the elusive Leo.

I felt a hand plucking at my elbow, and I was about to strike it away with a curse when I realised that it was Constantine's.

"We can't go on wandering like this," he said. "Can't you ask someone where Leo lives?"

I tried several of the more harmless-looking types, asking them about Leo, and found that they knew nothing, even when shown money. Some of them spat, or made superstitious gestures before sideling quickly away. Eventually an old beggar, more ragged and filthy than the rest, said, "Leo? I don't know about a philosopher, but there's a magician of that name. Would it be him?"

Constantine agreed that it might, and the beggar led us to a door that we already passed several times, differing from the others only in the many symbols that had been scratched or daubed around it. As well as roughly carved crosses, there were handprints, painted eyes, and marks so worn or faded that I could not tell what they were.

"How can they think Leo evil?" Constantine said, while we were waiting to be let in. "He used to be a bishop! That was in Thessalonica, when I was boy. He was good to me then, and I was sorry when they deposed him. Why did they have to punish him? He served under the iconoclasts, but he was never a zealot."

Leo's workroom was high up, at the top of several flights of rickety stairs. When we stepped inside it the first thing I saw was an inexplicable apparition. In the centre of the darkened room, lit by a shaft of light that came from nowhere, was a shimmering sphere of metal that hovered in mid air, spinning in a cloud of smoke. I leapt back in surprise, colliding with the doorframe and bruising my elbow. Constantine jumped too, and I stepped back to keep out of his way. I felt more comfortable in the doorway, through which I might easily escape if necessary.

I heard a deep laugh, but could see no one. Apart from the mysterious object at its centre, the room was dark. I peered round Constantine and looked again. The sphere was the size of a couple of soldier's helmets fixed together, and it was definitely revolving, without the action of any shaft or belt. I sniffed, expecting the sulphurous emanations of a magician's brew, but smelled nothing but dampness. The smoke was steam, and in the draught from the open door, it was dispersing. I saw that the sphere was supported by a pair of thin tubes rising from a brass cylinder.

As I stared, wondering whether the symbol-daubers in the streets were right, the apparatus was plunged into darkness.

An elderly man had emerged from the shadows and stood

in the shaft of light. He wore a long, dark tunic patched with many colours, and a peculiar fur hat of a kind I had never seen before. His beard was dirty white, and hung low over his chest. His appearance so unnerved me that I was prepared to dash down the stairs and out into the street.

"Leo!" Constantine said, his voice trembling with surprise. "What is it?"

The old man drew aside a curtain, allowing light from a latticed window to filter into the room. Stepping carefully forward, I saw a workbench scattered with brass rods and toothed wheels, bits of wood and ivory, and shelves stocked with flasks and caskets. There were wooden models of towers and other buildings, and spread out on a large table were charts covered with lines, circles and cryptic symbols.

"This?" Leo said, pointing at the sphere, which had slowed down and almost ceased to move. "It is, you might say, the opposite of a dark art. It works by light."

"But what is it?" Constantine repeated.

"Do you not recognise it? No? And you call yourself a scholar! If you had not wasted so much time trying to learn barbarian tongues you would know exactly what this is." The old philosopher stepped back, allowing the beam of light to fall again on the apparatus. I looked up to see where the light came from, but my eyes were dazzled by its brightness.

"This," Leo said, "is a machine invented by Hero of Alexandria, who lived many centuries ago. Can you see how it works?"

Constantine looked doubtfully at the sphere. Steam was emerging from two spouts on its sides, and it was starting to move again. "No," he said.

"I have given you a hint," Leo said, waving his hand in the beam of light. "I have combined Hero's design with another ancient idea. You will remember, no doubt, how Archimedes defended Syracuse against the Romans? He got a squad of soldiers to polish their shields and stand in formation on the harbour wall. The sun, reflected and concentrated by their shields, set fire to the Roman ships. Or so it is said. I do not have a squad of soldiers at my disposal. But up there," he pointed to an open hatch high above our heads, "is a highly polished concave metal disk, not unlike a shield. It concentrates the sun's rays, heating the water in this cylinder, turning it into steam that drives the sphere. Ingenious, isn't it?"

Constantine looked doubtful. He watched the steam spurting from the twin spouts as the sphere turned slowly in the sunlight. "What is it for?" he asked.

"For?" Leo said. "Why should it be for anything?"

"At least the languages I learn are for something. I will use them to convert the barbarians."

"Barbarians!" Leo said, his face creasing into a frown. "I saw enough barbarians in Thessalonica. They were no more interested in the truth than the beasts they drove to market. You'd be more use preaching to those savages in the streets . . ."

It was then, I think, that Leo noticed me. "Who or what is that?" he asked.

"Zeno," Constantine said. "A eunuch."

"Why have you brought him here?"

"Photius sent him."

"So he belongs to Photius?" Something like a smirk crossed the old philosopher's face.

"I suppose so. Photius has sent him with a question."

"Which is?"

"Is his nature primarily male or female?"

"Or," Leo said, "something in between."

"Photius did not mention that possibility."

"Proof then, that what I have always said is true. Photius is learned in his way, but he knows nothing of philosophy. It's all surface and style with him. So long as a book is rare, or elegantly written, he cares nothing for its true meaning. And when considering this eunuch, he ignored the most interesting possibility."

"Perhaps."

"Now, tell me this," Leo said. "Why does Photius want to know?"

"He was challenged to find out by Bardas."

Leo clutched at Constantine's coat. "Is Bardas back from exile?"

"He is here in the city. I saw him only a few days ago."

An anguished look crossed Leo's face. "I know what it is to be banished, to be deprived of everything one loves, to live without friends and influence. I daresay the emperor's uncle enjoyed a better sort of exile than I did. But if Bardas is back, then I will help him. On one condition."

"What is it?"

"That Photius gets me out of this place. I have been here long enough. Let him set me up somewhere safe and comfortable, his own house for instance, and I'll investigate any question he or Bardas cares to pose."

Sacks and baskets lay all over the floor, spilling out into the courtyard, where they were propped against chests and bundles of Leo's belongings. I had organised Leo's move myself. Though he was reputed to know everything, and could build ingenious machines and intricate models, he had no idea how to hire porters and donkeys or pack his books and apparatus into manageable loads. Constantine was just as bad, and I could not imagine him leading a mission to the barbarians. What would he do if he encountered a gang of pagan warriors on the lookout for loot and slaves? He might preach, but would they listen? He could pray, but their gods might be stronger than his.

Photius had only accepted Leo's arrival reluctantly, and was dismayed by the quantities of equipment he had brought with him.

"Once you are settled in I will order the servants to stay away from this room," Photius said. "You must be very discreet. There have already been stories. Quite unpleasant rumours, some of them."

Leo put down the glass flask he was holding, laying it back in its straw-filled basket. "You mean stories about selling your soul to the devil to gain all your knowledge?" he said.

"How did you know about that?" Photius looked startled.

"Because they told the same stories about me. That is why it was so difficult living where I did." Leo looked out at the

61

courtyard. "It's nice and peaceful here," he said. "Behind high walls, out of sight of the stupid and ignorant."

"But not beyond reach of the rumour-mongers. They exaggerate everything. The story about the devil started just because I bought some books from a Jewish merchant who brought them back from Alexandria. He asked far too much, and he came here several times before we agreed a price. Those who saw him coming and going claimed that the Jew was a magician, and that through his agency I signed a demonic pact. I suppose it is flattering in a way," Photius said, puffing himself up with pride, "that they find my knowledge inexplicable."

"Nonsense!" Leo said, twisting some stray locks of his white beard. "They tell the same stories about everyone who knows more than they do."

"Whatever the truth, the rumours are most inconvenient. People who ought to respect and admire me now regard me with suspicion."

An investigation
[AD 847]

I was not particularly keen to be studied by Leo. I knew what was in his baggage, and feared that he would dose me with noxious potions or probe me painfully with surgical instruments. But it would be wise to obey men like Photius and Bardas. If the emperor's uncle was amused by philosophical speculation, there might be rewards for those who helped him, even for a slave like me. And it might be interesting to learn something of my nature, to find out why my kind are so despised.

Even while we were unpacking, Leo asked me questions about my favourite colours, what foods I liked, and what pastimes I enjoyed. But the life I had led had not given me many opportunities to form tastes and preferences, and Leo was dissatisfied with my answers.

"Can you sing?" he asked.

I obliged him with a couple of choruses of *Another Jug of Wine*, a tavern favourite. But it was hard to sing well when surrounded by sober scholars.

"Evidently not," Leo said, giving Photius a sour look. "But the voice is distinctive. High, but not quite like a woman's, I would say."

"Do you have any stirrings of desire," Photius said. "For instance when you see a beautiful woman?"

That was the first time any of them had thought to ask my opinion. I suppose it was only natural. A slave's evidence is worth nothing in a court of law. Why should it be worth anything in a philosophical enquiry? "No sir," I said. "Not that I am aware of."

"What about boys?" Leo asked.

"No more than with women."

"And what about love? In the emotional sense, I mean. Are you capable of that?"

"I've not had much chance of that. Not so far. But I suppose I was fond of Eudocia."

"A woman?" Leo looked hopeful.

"A little girl. She was like a sister to me."

"Well, that is something. You are capable of affection. But it does not get us very far. Both men and women are capable of that. We will need to gather some evidence."

"It is pointless," Photius said. "Surely it is obvious that he can feel no desire."

"Suppose you lost your sense of taste," Leo said.

"I've never heard of such a thing," Constantine said.

"It can happen," Photius said. "As a result of a blow to the head, or something of that sort. Agapios of Alexandria, in his treatise *Maladies and Injuries of the Head*, claims to have examined such cases. I believe . . ."

"Exactly," Leo said. "Now, bearing that in mind, ask yourself: if you could not taste food, would you lose the desire to eat?"

"I've never much cared for fine food," Constantine said. "But I can taste it all right."

"I don't understand you," Photius said. "Scholars ought to be celibate. We who live by the mind must master the body. But there is nothing to stop us enjoying food or wine. God forbid that I should ever lose my sense of taste! However, if I did, my stomach would feel empty, my guts would rumble. I would still feel hungry."

"Precisely," Leo said. "Even if you knew you would not enjoy a single mouthful, you would still be compelled to eat. Now Zeno has been deprived of his balls, but that does not necessary mean that he feels no desire."

"But surely," Photius said, "in his case, it's more as though his throat's been cut."

"No it isn't! That is a very poor analogy." Leo turned to me. "Take down your drawers, Zeno, and show us what you've got."

I did as I was asked, standing in front of the three scholars with the hem of my tunic raised. My penis, already small, shrank under their combined gaze.

"There!" Leo said. "He still has his manhood. He is not one of those clean-cut eunuchs the Saracens favour."

"There is no reason why he should be," Photius said. "Christians have no need for such barbarities. The Saracens use eunuchs to guard their wives. Imagine having so many wives, or such wanton ones, that they need guarding!" Photius peered at me, inspecting what the Rus cripple's knife had spared. "It is a very small one," he said. "More of a boyhood than a manhood. And not likely to be of much use."

"A late-cut eunuch," Leo said, "one castrated after puberty, can satisfy a woman for some time before his potency fades. Eunuchs of that sort were once in great demand, according to the old poets, with women who wanted pleasure without the consequences. They must have experienced some sort of desire for that to be possible." Leo took another look at me. "But it appears that Zeno was not late-cut."

"So, it is as I say, he can feel no desire."

"There's only one way to find out," Leo said. "He must be exposed to temptation."

"How?"

"Now there is a good question. Just the sort of thing one must know in order to penetrate the Secrets of Love."

"The Secrets of Love?" Photius said. "What do you know or care about love?"

"More than you might think. I am compiling a book on the subject."

"You?"

"Why not me?"

"Anything you write about love is likely to be about as accurate as the works of Cosmas Indicopleustes."

"Why so?"

"Because I don't believe Cosmas ever went further than Palestine. Everything he says about India, perhaps even Persia, is cobbled together from hearsay, travellers' tales, and the imaginings of his own over-fertile mind."

"My work will naturally draw upon the opinions of the greatest ancient authorities," Leo said. "It will also incorporate the wisdom and learning of the Saracens. For some reason they are more advanced than we are in that particular subject. The beds must be softer in the East." Leo thought for a moment. "But perhaps you are right," he said. "There is always the risk that what ancient or foreign scholars tell us may be wrong. But my book will not just be a compilation. That is why it will be so useful to carry out some practical investigations. The Eunuch and his Nature might make an interesting chapter."

"Leo," Photius said. "I believe you have tricked me. You were brought here to answer a question for Bardas, and now it seems you intend to pursue your own work at my expense."

"Don't worry," Leo said. "I will settle the question for Bardas. And the expense will not be great. But I am sure Bardas would like the question settled thoroughly. First I will have to investigate Zeno's propensity to be aroused. If he is capable of arousal, then I can find out what arouses him. Then, after a little more investigation, we will know whether he is predominantly male or female. What could be simpler? And what more Aristotelian?"

Photius looked doubtful.

Leo took Photius's arm and led him out into the garden, picking a path through the jumble of baskets and packages, halting by a statue of a bearded man. It had a bundle of brass rods propped against its marble draperies. Leo reached out and laid a hand on the statue's shoulder. "Perhaps you prefer Plato's habit of metaphysical speculation?" he said.

Photius hesitated. To his friends, he was a man who knew everything. In the presence of the venerable Leo, he looked more like a nervous student, afraid of giving the wrong answer. But even I knew that Plato was out of fashion, thought unchristian by more pious scholars.

"No," Photius said. "You are right. We must be guided by Aristotle. What a pity he has not already answered the question for us. He hasn't, has he?"

"You would know," Leo said, a note of irony in his voice. "You are the scholar of great repute. I am just a humble philosophical investigator."

"It would have saved us some trouble if he had."

Leo smiled to himself. I suspected that he knew more about Aristotle's views on love than he was letting on. "There is something you must do before I start," he said.

"What?"

"Send to the marketplace and hire a whore," Leo said.

"Don't be absurd. How could a man of my reputation do something like that?"

Leo gave Photius a sceptical look. "Well, I suppose we could send Constantine. No one would suspect him of any wrongdoing."

"I would rather not go," Constantine said. "I have no idea how to do such things, and no intention of finding out. If you must do such a thing, and I think it very wrong, then you will have to send Zeno. He is incapable of that sort of wrongdoing."

"Constantine!" Leo said. "You are presupposing the very thing we are trying to find out."

"Do you think Zeno can be trusted?" Photius said.

"I can be trusted, sir." I was not at all keen on the venture Leo proposed, but it struck me that it would go better for me if I had some control over it.

"Very well," Photius said. "Hire a whore."

"You'd better pick up a boy too," Leo said.

Photius sighed. "Very well. Get one of each. And smuggle them into the house on some pretext. Pretend they're Leo's servants, or are bringing more of Leo's things. Something like that. Whatever you do, make sure no more rumours are started."

"There is one more thing," Leo said. "Make sure they know the time and date on which they were born. Be careful. So few of their sort do."

I sat on the damp marble steps of the marketplace fountain, wondering what to do. Photius had given me far too much money. It would have been easy to cheat him. His servants did it regularly, taking bribes from mongers and merchants, paying less than they pretended and pocketing the difference whenever they went to the market. I had already learned that scholars, however wise or worldly they think themselves, cannot do the simplest thing without help. I could have taken some of that money and spent it on myself. Yet what did I want?

A sweating porter grabbed one of the chained cups, filled it at the spout, then threw the cold water over his head, splashing much of it on me. He filled the cup again and gulped the contents down. He let the cup drop, hoisted his burden and trudged off. He did not look happy.

The women with painted faces who hung about the edges of the marketplace did not look happy either. In fact, they looked as miserable as Ignatius had when he condemned all fleshly sins in the cathedral of Hagia Sophia. Was the sexual act really such a miserable business? None of the scholars knew anything about it. They were as ignorant of sex as they were of any other worldly matter. Even Leo, who posed as an expert, only knew what was written in his Saracen books. And when they were asked a simple question by a rich and powerful man, they were unable to answer it without my help.

I found a boy and a girl, both a little younger than me, and bought things for them to carry, so that would seem like servants when entering the house. Photius looked at me strangely when I gave him change, as though he had never supposed such a thing possible. Then he retired with a book to the shade of the colonnade, unwilling to take part in Leo's work, or to leave him alone while he did it.

Leo began by asking the pair when and where they were born. He kept us waiting while he made some calculations, scratching numbers and symbols into a wax tablet, then smoothing them out again. He paced the mosaic floor, tugging at his beard and frowning, muttering under his breath. The girl looked at the old philosopher with disgust, no doubt wondering whether the money I had paid her was enough. The boy was bolder, and looked at Leo directly, waiting patiently until he finished his train of thought.

"You had better come inside," Leo said, "and see what I have rigged up."

In the centre of the room, hanging down from the ceiling, was a silken cord ending in a miniature noose. It swung slowly in the breeze, just above a small wooden stool. The cord was supported by a series of small hooks and pulleys which carried it across the ceiling until it disappeared behind a screen. I wondered how Leo had managed the work, considering that he was barely able to organise the packing and shifting of his books and belongings.

"What is it for?" I asked.

"Come and look." Leo led me behind the screen and pointed to the apparatus that sat on a small writing desk concealed from the rest of the room. The end of the cord was tied to a brass rod like the gnomon of a sundial, which lay against a polished disk engraved with lines and symbols. "A navigational device," he said. "But I have modified it so that it will serve our purpose." He reached out and twitched the rod with his finger, showing that it moved easily. "This will measure your arousal," he said. "If you are aroused."

"But how?"

"Is it not obvious?" Leo took my arm and led me back to the centre of the room. "There!" he said, pointing at the stool. "You are to sit on that. And the noose is to be tied to your penis. If there is the slightest movement it will be transmitted along the cord and I will be able to read off its degree on my brass scale."

"Is the noose really necessary? Couldn't you just watch?"

"Of course not! I would become part of the experiment, and that would affect the results. A philosopher must always be dispassionate. Surely you know that!"

Reluctantly, I removed my drawers and sat on the stool, allowing Leo to fix the noose round my penis. The boy-whore laughed while Leo adjusted the cord and balanced it with jewellers' weights. The girl looked bored. Though both young, they must have seen some odd things in the course of their work.

When Leo was satisfied with his apparatus he withdrew behind the screen and gave orders from there. I sat as still as possible, the hard wood pressing against my bare buttocks, while the two whores took off their clothes. The boy was muscular. His body, unlike mine, was tufted with dark hair. The girl was soft and rounded, her skin smooth and hairless. The female form was no mystery to me. It knew it well from my time at the tavern. I had warmed the widow in her bed, and comforted her. The two nieces had never troubled to cover themselves when washing or changing, and had often flaunted their nakedness to mock me. But unlike them, the girl-whore had depilated her entire body, pleasing those who like such things, revealing clearly the cleft that marks the female body like a defect, a reminder of what they lack. I could see why philosophers describe women as imperfect men. But who am I to talk of such things?

As Leo had instructed, the pair went to a couch and began to make love. There was little enthusiasm in their performance. He stroked her breasts a few times, causing her nipples to briefly harden, then switched his attention to her lower half. His hand slid between her thighs, plunging into soft flesh, probing her naked cleft. She moaned a little, and squirmed, then he climbed on top of her. I caught a brief glimpse of his erect member before it disappeared.

I willed myself to react. I thought as hard as I could about my penis, tried to imagine it swelling with pleasure. That was what Leo wanted, to see his gnomon jolted by a surge of desire. But there were others to consider. Photius disapproved of lust, especially the sort he called unnatural, and expected me to feel nothing. Bardas approved the desire for women, but despised eunuchs. He would expect me to be unmanly, to feel, if anything, unnatural desires.

Who should I try to satisfy?

I could not please them all.

I decided to be true to myself, to submit to nature.

I relaxed, settled back on the hard chair, watched the pair writhing on the couch.

But it was too late. I had thought too much. The pair, their perfunctory act coming to an end, did not excite me. Perhaps memory would do the trick? I remembered the widow and the caresses she had demanded. I thought of the softness of her flesh, the warmth of her bed, the way she groaned and shook when pleasure came. But I did not react. I felt nothing but the slight tickle of the silken noose. I experienced no pleasure, and my penis did not stir.

"I'm not getting a reaction," Leo said from behind his screen. "The gnomon hasn't moved."

"Perhaps the apparatus does not work," I said, hoping Leo would abandon it.

"Of course it works," Leo said, emerging from his corner. "I devised it myself." He tugged absent-mindedly at the cord, and the noose suddenly tightened. I leapt to my feet, yelping with pain. "I'm sorry," Leo said, releasing the cord. "But at least we know that your member has some feeling in it. If it can respond to pain, it may respond to pleasure. If only we can work out what moves you."

"I am sure the cord inhibits me," I said, untying it from my bruised penis.

"Perhaps we should test it on him," Leo said. The boy-whore, lounging naked on the couch, reached rapidly for his clothes. "Don't get dressed," Leo said. "We haven't finished with you yet. And don't look at me like that. You'll be paid well enough. And the girl. Now, come here and sit on the stool."

The boy-whore did as he was told, and, under Leo's direction I looped the noose round the boy's slippery member, noting that fear or uncertainty had caused it to shrink until it was not much bigger than mine. I stepped back, enjoying his discomfort, just as he had enjoyed mine.

Leo adjusted the cord and its weights, muttered something to the girl, then disappeared behind his screen. The girl raised her arms, crossing her wrists above her head, making her breasts stand proud. Then she closed her eyes and began to sway, gently rotating her hips. She moved her body like one of the great thuribles in the cathedral of Hagia Sophia, which swing on long chains, filling the nave with sweetness. Each orbit of her hips brought her pudenda nearer to the seated boy, but he did not react. Instead, his penis lay limply in its nest of dark hair, supported only by the finely balanced cord.

Perhaps the cord inhibited him, or he was tired from his previous efforts. Whatever the reason, the girl changed her tactics. She slowed down until her gyrations ceased and she faced the boy motionless. She lowered one hand, running it over her white breasts, then the other, licking a finger with her pink tongue. Sighing lasciviously, she ran the wet finger up and down her naked cleft, parting the rosy flesh.

There was a slight tremor in the boy's penis. The cord twitched, jingling the jewellers' weights that balanced it. Encouraged, the girl continued, swaying slightly while probing deeper with her finger. The boy's penis moved again, but only a little. The girl hesitated, staring at the still-limp member. The boy looked bored. She turned her back on him. I thought she was going to give up, perhaps to walk out. But she had her professional pride, and was determined to get a result. She wiggled her plump rear, making her soft flesh tremble, then she bent down so that her dark hair touched the floor and might have swept it had she been so minded. Her naked rump was only inches from the silken cord, but it was not her flesh that moved it. As though under orders from a fierce sergeant, the boy's penis jumped to attention, jerking the thread and causing the gnomon to crash loudly against its brass dial.

My heart sank as rapidly as the gnomon. I knew that the apparatus worked, that I would be tied to it again and subjected to an endless ordeal of quivering breasts and buttocks, rippling muscles, moist orifices and tumescent phalluses, displayed and deployed in as many ways as the pair could think of.

It was just as I feared. Leo subjected me to every temptation he and the whores could imagine. He paid them extra to simulate enthusiasm, modified the apparatus to make it more sensitive, tried his experiments at all hours of the day and night, but without provoking in me any measurable display of desire.

Perhaps in retrospect it does not seem such a torment.

Many slaves have endured worse. While I was being tempted, the other servants were working. They did not know what I was doing, but they knew it was not work, and they hated me all the more for it.

Eventually, after dismissing the exhausted whores, Leo dragged some old books out of a battered chest and began to consult them. Again, he scratched incomprehensible symbols on a wax tablet.

"What are you doing?" Photius asked, unable to stay away once the whores had gone.

"I am preparing for the next phase."

"Which is?"

"Aphrodisiacs!" Leo said, laying down his book. "Substances that inflame the passions and enhance fleshly pleasure. There are many of them. Rare foods, herbs, spices, fine wines, scents, ointments, the excretions of plants and creeping creatures, the inner and nether parts of animals, the vital fluids of men, women and beasts."

"I know what an aphrodisiac is. Or is reputed to be. But surely it is cheating to try to inflame Zeno's passions?"

"Not at all. It is like getting a man drunk. Nothing is so effective if you want to know his true character. Traits that have lain dormant are woken, and become visible, and can be examined easily, just as a tiny object is magnified by the concave face of a polished shield."

Photius looked puzzled, but he had not seen the way Leo had concentrated the sun's power with such a shield. "We all know there is truth in wine," he said. "But there are lies and boasts too."

"Lies and boasts are just as revealing as the truth."

Photius discovered that he had some business to attend to, and left Leo to try aphrodisiacs on me unsupervised. After sending me to various spice mongers and apothecaries to buy what he wanted, then grinding and blending the ingredients, Leo tried his concoctions on me. I chewed, sucked, drank, or anointed myself with whatever he gave me, and viewed again the naked contortions of the two whores, without feeling any twinge of

73

desire. One or two of the potions affected me, but only with a sort of drunken drowsiness followed by a dream-filled sleep. Leo asked me about my dreams, but was disappointed to find that they were not in the least lustful.

"What have you learned?" I asked, when we had exhausted all the possibilities.

"Nothing," Leo said. "I always knew the truth. I am sure you did too. Photius would have known it, if he had read as much of Aristotle as he claims to have done. The answer is to be found in the *History of Animals*. The Stagirite wrote that the soul is formed in embryo. The process takes forty days for a man, and ninety for a woman. But the time difference is immaterial. The man's embryo, being more thoroughly heated, is fuller of that energy which motivates us throughout life. We must never forget that women are defective, imperfect men."

"So I am like a woman?"

"Only in that you lack testicles, and in what follows from that. Women, because of the inferiority of their souls, lack other manly attributes, such as the power of reason, the capacity for true friendship, moral virtue, and so on. I suspect they are not capable of true faith, though some are susceptible to a sort of childish credulity. Of course, women lack bodily strength. And they cannot truly beget children, as their bodies are only fit to receive and nurture what is implanted in them by men. They are imperfect in many ways."

"If women are imperfect men," I asked, "does that mean that men are perfect women?"

"Of course not!" Leo said. "That would be absurd. It would lead, if taken to its logical conclusion, to the sin of sodomy." Seeing Leo in his patched and shabby robes, surrounded by alchemical apparatus and worldly books, it was easy to forget that he had been a bishop. But he had once shepherded all the souls of Thessalonica, and still sometimes remembered what was a sin and what was not. "In any case," he said, "you have missed my point, which is that, according to Aristotle, we are born with our souls fully formed, either male or female."

"Where is the soul?" I asked, wondering whether it might lie in that part of me that had been removed. I had already noticed that my ability to believe was no less impaired than my capacity to be aroused.

"That I cannot tell you, though I have searched for it." Leo glanced around, confirming that we were alone and that no servant lurked near the door, before speaking again. "This is between the two of us," he said. "But I have performed certain experiments, investigated the bodies of the dead. And the not so dead. Some of the work was very subtle, involving careful observation and precise measurement. Well, you have seen my methods, so you can imagine how thorough I was. But I found nothing that corresponded to the soul. Every part of the body seems to have some function, helping us to move, digest, procreate, and so on. I have concluded that the soul must be more of an essence than an organ. And though its nature is fixed, it can be affected by experience. You were born and brought up as a boy, so your soul developed as male. Then you were deprived of your testicles. That prevented the changes that turn a boy into a man. In that respect you are incomplete, incapable of doing what men do, feeling what they feel, or desiring what they desire. That makes you more like a woman. But your soul, your essence, remains male."

So I had a soul, and was male. That was something. And Leo trusted me enough to tell me his secrets. If I could win his confidence, I might yet succeed with Photius, perhaps even with Bardas.

"What will you tell Bardas?" I asked.

"That you are neither male nor female, but something in between. Bardas will be happy enough with that answer."

Was that true? Bardas wanted reasons for despising eunuchs, ways to exploit their inferiority. A non-committal answer was kinder to me, but would not satisfy Bardas.

"Did you know," I said, "that Bardas asked two questions?"

"No," Leo said. "What was the other?"

"He asked whether a man or a woman enjoyed sex the most."

"Really? Now that is an interesting question. Far more so

than the one we have just investigated. And Photius did not think to mention it. I wonder why not?"

"An oversight, sir, I expect."

"Perhaps. But Bardas will be pleased if I can answer both questions. And I have just the book that will help us. Give me a hand, will you, to shift these things."

I did as I was told, moving chests and baskets from one side of the room to the other and back again, disordering the heaps of apparatus I had stacked carefully earlier, getting covered with dust, until Leo found the book he wanted. It was an old Saracen text about the arts of love, which he seemed able to understand, even though it was written in an antique and oriental language. It may be that he was chiefly guided by the illustrations, of which there were many, all showing the various ways in which man and woman can achieve sexual congress. I might have been surprised to find that he owned such a book, had Leo not already exhausted my capacity for surprise.

When the two whores returned for their next session Leo instructed them, showing them the pictures that were to guide their coupling, then watching carefully to make sure they did everything right. He abandoned his habit of sitting behind the screen. My job was to record everything, timing each stage of every sexual act, at first with a sandglass, then with a water clock of Leo's own invention, or so he claimed. The cord and gnomon would have been of little use, even if there had been anywhere to tie it. But it was hardly necessary. The positions the two were obliged to adopt ruled out all pretence or concealment, and observations could easily be made directly. Leo, forgetting philosophical dispassion, studied the pair eagerly, and did not hesitate to point out their mistakes. Despite their profession they were sometimes clumsy, and could not always emulate the crane, elephant, tortoise, porcupine, or whatever creature the book's oriental author had fancifully named each act of congress after. I was amazed that there were so many ways of doing what can only have been intended as a means of increasing humankind. But I suppose I should not have been. There are even more ways of cooking, serving and eating food, which can keep us alive however monotonous it is. As Ignatius knew, there is logic in puritanism, however unattractive it may be to men who retain all their appetites.

"What have you learned this time?" I asked Leo when the pair had exhausted the book's menagerie of positions.

"I have confirmed what Tiresias revealed long ago. Women enjoy sex far more than men do. Though whether they enjoy it nine times as much, as Tiresias claimed, I cannot be sure. However, if I could devise an apparatus to gauge pleasure . . ."

"Will Bardas be pleased?"

"I cannot be sure. He is a great womaniser, and may take it amiss that his mistresses get more pleasure from their activities than he does." Leo paused, scrabbling at his beard with hooked fingers as though it harboured something of interest. "But, on the other hand, he may find justification in the thought that he gives more than he takes. I think it might be best to give him an account of my investigations. He is sure to enjoy that. Perhaps I will give him a copy of my book on the Secrets of Love, when I have finished it. He, unlike Photius, might appreciate it. And it is always wise to please great men when we have the chance."

Heresy
[AD 854]

I will pass over the years I spent turning myself into a scholar. They were not very eventful. Constantine helped and guided me, thinking that I would one day accompany him to darkest Bulgaria, where he hoped to convert the heathens. I had other ideas. Of course, I was a slave, and had to do what I was told. But I realised quite quickly that I might be told to do safer and more interesting things if I made myself indispensable to Photius. When Constantine went away and Photius insisted that I stayed behind, I knew that I had succeeded. And without Constantine's virtuous example, I was free to try and advance myself, which could only be done by advancing Photius.

My first opportunity came in the form of an unwelcome interruption.

"What are you doing?" Theodore asked. Gaunt and ill-kempt as usual, he seemed almost to be hiding the book-shaped bundle he held under his arm. His coarse woollen tunic was stained with food, wine, and worse. His beard turned up at the end like an old shoe, or a worn out brush. I had already decided he could be of no use to me, and was not inclined to pay him any attention. When not selling books, Theodore spent much time hanging around Leo, hoping to learn the art of astrology. Leo saw through him and refused to teach him anything. Constantine said that Theodore communed with demons, and perhaps was one himself. But if that was true, he would already have known what he sought to learn from Leo. And there were those who said that Leo too was a demon, perhaps the one to whom Photius had sold his soul in return for arcane knowledge.

Whatever the truth, Photius found Theodore useful, especially when he appeared at the house bearing long-lost antique texts. How he got them was a mystery, but Photius was always happy to pay.

"I am doing what my master has asked of me," I said, hoping Theodore would go away.

"Which is?" he asked, picking up one of the many books that littered the library table. They were drawn from the cabinets that stood around the walls, each devoted to a single subject. Several cabinets were filled with books on theology in all its aspects, others with volumes of history, philosophy, geography and medicine. The books I was using all had straws or ribbons stuck between the pages, marking the places referred to in Photius's extensive and ill-organised notes. If Theodore disarranged them my work would become more difficult.

Incidentally, I ought to record the curious fact that Photius could remember every word he had ever read. He could recite long passages from books he had studied years earlier, which was a useful skill in one who aspired to be the empire's greatest scholar. But it had its disadvantages. Though he liked to give the impression that he had read everything, Photius tended to explore the outer fringes of scholarship, leaving the well-trodden middle ground to others. Consequently, men like Leo, who began his scholarship in the middle and worked his way out, could easily guess the areas of my master's ignorance, and catch him out by his inability to recite from standard authors such as Plato or Aristotle.

However, I am interrupting the story.

Theodore was hovering over me, asking questions, putting me off my work.

"I am helping Photius compile a lexicon of rare words culled from ancient books," I said.

"I thought that was Constantine's work."

"It was," I said. "But Constantine has got himself ordained, and has gone off to visit his brother's monastery in Bithynia."

"So he's gone away?" Theodore said, picking up another book and letting the markers fall out. I could see that he was thinking about what I had said, fitting it in with what he knew already, trying to decide whether it would be any use to him. I immediately regretted having revealed anything. Theodore had a knack of turning any information, however innocent, to his own advantage. He was also, when discussing anyone's affairs but his own, thoroughly indiscreet. "I am surprised Photius trusts you to do this," he said, leaning over my shoulder to peer at the book I was using.

"Constantine taught me well," I said. "There is no reason why my master should not trust me with this task."

"I am sure you please him well," Theodore said. "Eunuchs have so many uses." He placed a hand on my shoulder and fondled the neck-band of my tunic. "Good stuff this," he said, rubbing the embroidery between a grubby finger and thumb. "Your master dresses you well."

There was a sneer in Theodore's voice. His breath smelled of garlic and sour wine. I wanted to end his insinuations.

"I bought this tunic myself," I said, jerking my shoulder away from his hand.

"Really? And how did you get the money for it?"

"Bardas gave it to me. For helping Leo with his philosophical investigations. He gave me a gold piece."

"Bardas? You were lucky. He's rather distracted now. But I expect you've heard the rumours?" Theodore leered at me, hinting that whatever was distracting Bardas would be worth hearing about.

I said nothing, but turned back to my task. I cannot honestly say that lexicography has ever been a passion of mine. It was dull work, finding the words my master had marked, and relating them to the notes he had sketched out.

Theodore reached out and picked up the book I was using. "Ctesias," he said, opening it and turning the pages. "I believe I supplied this volume. It has a fine description of India."

I gently took the book back and found my place again. Theodore unwrapped his bundle and took out another book. "A commentary on Dionysius the Areopagite," he said, holding up a slim manuscript, rather battered at the edges. "I daresay your master would be very glad to have this, and it wouldn't cost too much. It's full of rare words, I'm sure. He'd find it indispensable for this lexicon of his. Here, take a look."

Theodore's voice was wheedling and anxious. He obviously wanted money again. I wondered what he spent it on. It was clear from his appearance that he did not spend much at the barbers or tailors, and I doubted that he paid in advance for the books he hawked around to Photius and his friends.

"Take the book," he said, offering it to me. "Judge it for yourself."

"Only my master can decide what he wants to buy."

"You could make a recommendation. I can tell he trusts you."

I did not bother to point out that Theodore had earlier implied just the opposite. "I will tell him you called," I said, pushing back the book.

"By the way," he said, pausing in the doorway, looking ruefully at his book. "I have some news. I was going to tell Photius myself, but you can pass it on to him. Ignatius has written asking the pope to support him in his quarrel with the Archbishop of Syracuse."

Theodore's news meant little to me, but it infuriated Photius.

"How could Ignatius be so stupid?" he asked, turning his back to me so I could take off his coat. I removed it carefully and folded the stiff brocade so that it did not crease. Photius lowered himself onto the couch. "Why appeal to the pope?" he said. "He is only the bishop of Rome. How could Ignatius throw away the independence and authority of the Patriarch of Constantinople, just to win a petty argument with a bishop? No one can understand what the quarrel was about in the first place, so what is the point of submitting to the pope to win it?"

I had never seen Photius so angry. I poured him some wine, which he drank greedily.

"Ignatius is an imbecile. Just think! If they hadn't deposed his father, he might have been emperor. What a disaster that would have been. Ignatius as sole ruler of the Roman Empire! They did a good job when they castrated him. Unfortunately, losing his prospects as well as his manhood has made him bitter. I sometimes think all eunuchs are bitter at heart."

"I am not bitter, sir" I tugged off his boots and put a

cushion behind his head. "But I had no prospects when I was castrated."

"No? I daresay it improved your lot. But it was not like that with Ignatius. He turned against the world, rejecting what he could not have. He became a monk and a zealous puritan. Being ignorant, he turned against books and learning. That is why he likes icons so much. Any fool can understand a picture. So he posed as champion of the iconodules. He must have been bitter when they promoted Methodius instead of him. But Methodius didn't last long. What did he die of, I wonder? Perhaps the prayers of the iconodule monks killed him off. Or perhaps it was something else. There's a subject for one of Leo's philosophical investigations."

I had no views on the death of patriarch Methodius, but I was pleased by the way Photius confided in me, telling me openly what he thought, just as he would have spoken to Leo or Constantine. It showed that he had begun to trust me, and knew he could rely on me.

"Whatever Methodius died of," Photius said, "Ignatius was the least suitable person to succeed him. Why can't anyone see it? Why is he so popular."

Seeing Photius slumped on the couch, made miserable by the triumph and folly of the invincibly stupid Ignatius, I resolved to help him.

He was an intelligent man, there is no doubt about that. And he had read a lot, almost as much as he claimed. But he had a weakness. He did not know what to think about himself. Was he a pious Christian? Or a rationalist of the antique school? I cannot say his faith was false. Who can tell what a man truly believes? I am not sure what I believe myself. But I can say that my master's words were more pious than his deeds. If he was not as devout as he pretended, neither was he as rational. He believed in some quite odd things, especially towards the end. Sometimes he was bored by philosophy, weighed down by its complexity and contradictions. Perhaps he affected that boredom, just as rich men pretend to be bored by wealth. Some of his friends thought him too worldly, and wished he would devote more of his time to learning. Was he a scholar who mixed with gentlemen? Or a gentleman who dabbled in scholarship? Though I never could decide about the state or nature of his faith, I know that Photius was a real scholar, perhaps even, as many say, the greatest of the age. What he lacked was imagination. Like a lazy horse, he sometimes needed a kick to make him jump, a prod to make him see the potential in what he knew.

When Photius came to the library the next day, I was ready.

"Sir," I said. "If Ignatius is such an ignoramus, why not show him up as such?"

"It would be pointless. The trouble with fools is that they don't understand the extent of their own folly. If I accused him of ignorance he would take it as a compliment."

Photius had a point. The cadaverous figure I had seen preaching against lust at the cathedral might have skipped with delight at being called ignorant by his enemy. Ignatius was as freakish as any of the dwarfs or clowns who cavorted at the Hippodrome. Perhaps that was the secret of his success. He gave the public a performance as well as a sermon. It would be hard to devise a form of ridicule that would hurt him. There was no point in urging Photius to challenge Ignatius's view of lust. The two of them did not really disagree on that subject, though Photius preferred to ignore what Ignatius condemned.

"What is it that makes the people love Ignatius so much?" I asked.

Photius looked sour. He was not pleased to be reminded of the patriarch's popularity. "His rigid orthodoxy," he said.

"Then that is what you must undermine. You must make it look as though he does not understand what he professes."

"But he knows the orthodox creed thoroughly. It's the one thing he does understand. I can't catch him out there."

I remembered my master's taste for the recondite, his knowledge of the obscure.

"In that case, to expose his stupidity you must lead him into unfamiliar territory."

"How?"

"You are famed for your knowledge of theology."

Photius looked a little more cheerful. "I am," he said. "I think I may claim to know more about the history of Church Councils than anyone else."

He was almost certainly right. It was not a subject that inspired much interest even among the clergy, and it was an odd taste for a gentleman scholar.

"What is it about those Councils that is so fascinating?"

Photius thought for a while. "It is the doctrines the Councils condemned. They amount to a catalogue of error, a compendium of falsehood."

"You could be described," I said, "as a connoisseur of heresy."

"I'm not sure about that. You make me sound like a collector of silks or jewels."

"An apt analogy," I said. "I believe that those who love fine jewels appreciate their flaws and imperfections, as well as their beauty. It is clear that you have an interest in the defects of heretical doctrines."

Photius looked pleased but puzzled. "Perhaps," he said.

"You cannot deny that you know more about heresy than Ignatius."

"No," he said modestly. "I cannot deny it."

"Then heresy is the key to undermining Ignatius. The best way to make him look stupid is to come at him from an unexpected direction, to tax him with ideas that neither he nor his supporters have ever encountered before."

"I am impressed, Zeno, that you have given so much thought to the question. To think that you would still be serving in a tavern if I had not encouraged Constantine to buy you! Fate is odd, is it not? So tell me, exactly how can I show up Ignatius?"

"You must lure him into a debate."

"Impossible! He knows I am more intelligent than he is. And that I am more knowledgeable, and a better debater."

"You could try."

"No. Even if he was stupid enough to agree, his supporters would rally round. They would coach him and supply him with useful facts and arguments, which he would repeat like a talking magpie until I tired of refuting them. A debate would be useless."

"In that case," I said, "what we need is a way of making you seem a better Christian than he is."

Photius looked hurt. "I *am* a better Christian than he is. Ignatius knows nothing of tolerance or forgiveness."

"Of course, all I meant was that we must make that clear."

It was then that I had my great idea. I do not know where it came from. Perhaps it was at the back of my mind all along, waiting for the right moment to appear. It is possible that I remembered it from somewhere, heard someone speak of it, came across it in some old book, though I do not think so. Wherever it came from, I will not indulge in false modesty. These are my memoirs, and I am entitled to describe my successes, such as they are. It was a very good idea, and it led to all sorts of consequences, some predictable, others not. Above all, it was the moment I proved to Photius that I could be more than a slave, more than a secretary, that I could be a partner in his quest for power and influence. Not that he admitted to any such quest. Photius always insisted that he liked nothing better than his library, that the demands of public life were an unwelcome distraction. But it was obvious from listening to his conversations with Bardas that they both felt resentful and excluded from their rightful places in society.

"What we need," I said, "is a new heresy."

"A new heresy," Photius said. "Are there not enough heresies already? And how will a new one help? The task of a good Christian is to diminish error, not multiply it."

"In that case, make yourself seem a better Christian than Ignatius by alerting him to the existence of a new danger to orthodoxy. A new heresy will puzzle and surprise him. He must be given the impression that it is spreading wildly, that it is rife in the empire. As patriarch, he will feel obliged to preach against it."

"So he will condemn this imaginary heresy in his usual intemperate terms, lamenting its pernicious effects, condemning those who spread it, and the audience will see him for the fool he is."

"If they notice."

"You think they might be fooled too?"

"It is possible. The people, as you have often pointed out, are taken in by fervour. They may not realise that Ignatius is talking nonsense unless they are prepared. What we need is a few of your supporters scattered throughout the congregation. When Ignatius gets into full flow, they will start to nudge their neighbours and mutter, quietly pointing out the absurdity of the opinions he is condemning. As the congregation leaves, your supporters will laugh, and call out to each other, saying out loud what they muttered in the church. Soon afterwards, when the absurdity of the new doctrine has sunk in, we can reveal that the whole thing was a hoax."

"This sounds like an excellent idea. All we need is a suitable heresy." Photius thought for a while, and his furrowing brow told me that I had chosen the subject well, if not wisely. Unless I diverted him, I was in for a long lecture.

"Do you know what Origen thought?" he said. "To him, false doctrines were like lamps hung on a rocky shore by pirates hoping to lure unwary sailors to their deaths. He was right, and it is worse since his day, and partly through his fault. Heresies have multiplied, and are as many as the stars in the night sky. But how can we distinguish them? And what is the worst heresy?"

Heresies are all the same to me. One god, two gods, three in one, one proceeding through the other, many gods, gods that are not much more than men, gods in pictures or statues, invisible gods: all are equally plausible or implausible. I hazarded an answer which I though would flatter my master.

"Ignorance," I said.

"Yes. To turn wilfully away from knowledge, as Ignatius does, that is a sort of heresy. For him, the ancient philosophers are dangerous heresiarchs. He is afraid to know what they teach, in case he might come to believe it. There is no risk of that. He is too stupid. Even if Ignatius could be induced to read Plato and Aristotle he would not understand what they wrote. But ignorance is only a heresy for scholars. For priests it is a virtue. Have you ever slept out of doors, far away from the bright lights and choking smoke of the city?"

I thought of the nights I had spent with the Rus, sleeping on brushwood, looking up at the dark skies above the Black Sea. "I have," I said, wondering when Photius had done the same. He was not a countryman or outdoor type.

"Then you know that far more stars are visible from open country. Ignatius is like a man who has never left the city, who knows only the few stars that shine through the woodsmoke, and outdo the glare of the street lamps and linkmen's torches. He thinks that all heresies are listed in the Synodicon of Orthodoxy. As long as he avoids those obvious errors he imagines himself orthodox. But he is wrong. Whereas the truth is finite, error is infinite. There are so many things to be mistaken about, and man has an innate capacity to be wrong. Error may be gross or trivial, willed or accidental, persistent or fleeting. Where error is serious, it departs from mere heresy and becomes apostasy. Iconoclasm for example, is almost Islamic."

"You might catch Ignatius out in excessive idolatry."

"It would be easy enough to lead him into error, to show that he worships icons instead of venerating them, that he confuses the image with its prototype. But that would make him a hero among the zealots. And it might make me seem an iconoclast."

"No one could believe that. Your family were exiled by the iconoclasts."

"The zealots would believe anything. I must look further into the past. The Council of Chalcedon might be a fruitful starting point. There were some unresolved issues, some formulae that meant one thing to the Nestorians, another to the Cyrillians. Ignatius might be induced to condemn something that no one, in fact, believed in."

"Would anyone notice?"

"Perhaps not. Such subtleties might be beyond him. Perhaps I should go for something big, a false doctrine on the Trinity, or the Incarnation. Some variant of Monoenergism might be a possibility. Ignatius would not understand its Aristotelian logic."

"I am sure he would not."

"Perhaps I should delve into the Church's murky past, and dredge up something Origenist," Photius said. "Origen was wrong about almost everything. He was more of a neoplatonist than a Christian. Most of what he taught has been condemned as heresy. For example, the notion that Our Saviour is not the Son of God but an eternal sinless spirit."

"With respect, you need a new heresy, not an old one."

"Of course. So there is no point in trying to derive something from the Areopagite?"

"Probably not."

"What I need is something that sounds Cappadocian, but isn't."

"Perhaps."

"Or should I explore one of the less trodden paths of theology, pneumatology, for example?

"Would Ignatius or his supporters know about that?"

"I doubt it. If I could think of a suitable pneumatalogical heresy, it might well catch Ignatius out."

"I suggest you choose a heresy that is an echo of orthodoxy. It must be based on a doctrine that everyone agrees on, such as the two natures of Our Saviour."

"Yes. Human and divine. We won't get Ignatius to condemn that."

"But if we adapted the doctrine," I said. "If we applied it to men."

"Body and soul?" Photius said. "We won't get Ignatius to condemn that, either."

"It might be said that, just as Christ has two natures, man has two souls."

"Two souls? Of course, Epicurus proposed something similar, as part of his theory of atoms. And Aristotle considered the soul to be threefold: rational, sensitive and vegetal. Some savages believe that souls swarm in us like gnats, hardly to be distinguished from demons. But Ignatius wouldn't know any of that. He might be induced to condemn a twofold soul. Unless he agreed to it, of course."

"That might be no bad thing. If you could get him to support a heresy, you really would make him look foolish. But let us be sure of our tactics. Let us propose that of these twin souls, one is good and the other is evil."

"Too Paulician. Even Ignatius would detect the Manichaean taint in that idea. No. Two souls won't do."

Photius returned to his favourite topic of the Church Councils. He went on for some time, explaining the conclusions and compromises of each council, wondering how the resulting ambiguities might be used to trick Ignatius. But he was so used to demonstrating what he knew, and supporting his knowledge with scholarly authority, that he forgot that we were trying to invent a new heresy rather than dredge up an obsolete one. We had made little progress by the evening, when Theodore called by in the hope of being invited for a meal.

"Zeno has come up with a most amusing scheme," Photius said, while the food was brought. As they ate, he went on to tell Theodore what we had discussed. "The best idea we have thought of so far," he concluded, "is twin souls. One of which is good, the other evil. But I don't think it would fool Ignatius. There is something missing from it."

"Absurdity," Theodore said, brushing crumbs from his upturned beard. "That's what's missing. The idea of good and evil souls is quite plausible. Most men, however orthodox, have some notion of good and bad conscience, of being part angel and part demon. The heresy you dangle before Ignatius must be implausible, and nonsensical, but in a way he fails to notice."

"And I suppose you have a suggestion?"

"You must propose that one of the souls is fallible, the other infallible."

"It is too ridiculous."

"Not for Ignatius. It is just what you need."

Photius thought for a while. "It has possibilities," he said.

A sermon
[AD 854–5]

I knew our scheme was working when I heard two whores in the marketplace joking about the doctrine of the twin souls. One of them said that her infallible soul kept telling her to be good, but that her fallible soul always tempted her back into vice. The other said she hoped their customers felt the same way. Perhaps it was not the funniest of jokes, but the fact that it was made at all justified the weeks I had spent wandering the city, listening to idle talk, gauging the mood of the humbler citizens. Photius, with help from Theodore, had been spreading rumours of the new heresy among the educated and pious. For them it quickly displaced the Latin notion of the twin procession of the Holy Spirit as the topic most likely to rouse orthodox indignation. Some of the talk I heard in the streets and markets made me think we had been too successful, that we had devised a doctrine that the unwary actually believed in. There was much speculation on the fate of the souls after death, some supposing that the infallible soul was destined for Heaven, others wondering whether the fallible soul went to Hell or lingered to haunt the living. Gullible citizens rushed to their priests and begged to be exorcised of their fallible souls. After that, it was not long before Ignatius felt obliged to preach against the new doctrine.

We set off for the cathedral of Hagia Sophia in our finest clothes, joining throngs of others, as well dressed as we were, all converging on the cathedral. If only I could have stood atop the great dome and looked down on the eastern end of the city! The streets would have resembled intermingling rivers of shimmering, rustling silk. Even Theodore had tidied himself up, and walked beside us in a brocade coat he had borrowed from Photius, and which he later forgot to give back. Inside the cathedral the plan was for all my master's friends and supporters to be spread about the nave, ready to scoff loudly at whatever Ignatius said. Photius stood near the imperial enclosure, and I made my way to Constantine's favourite spot beneath the southern gallery, glad that he was not there to see the patriarch mocked.

Seven years in office had not changed Ignatius. He was still a thin, dried up creature, all bone and sinew, typical of what eunuchs turn into when they reject the world. His vestments hung on his gaunt body like the wrappings of a corpse, reminding all who saw him that life is vanity and death inevitable. Beneath a mantle the colour of dried blood he was burdened with an array of patriarchal accoutrements: belts, cuffs, stoles, ribbons, and medallions, each of them glimmering with gold, and symbolic of his intercessory role. Leaning unsteadily on a serpent-headed staff, he looked like an ecclesiastical old-clothes-monger who had elected to wear his entire stock.

Rather than processing gracefully into the nave, Ignatius hopped and skipped like a man desperate for the privy. And perhaps he was desperate. A weak bladder is one of the curses of the eunuch's condition. I have suffered from it myself in latter years. Ignatius, whether his anguish was bodily or spiritual, was agitated. He could hardly stand still during the solemn parts of the ceremony, and when he addressed the congregation he gesticulated, jabbing his bony forefinger at the sinners beneath him, then raising it high, pointing at the gilded dome above. He screeched at us, his high, harsh voice echoing round the vaults and galleries as though a bird had flown through one of the windows. His message was simple. Sin, unlike virtue, was a bad thing, and should be avoided. The consequence of not avoiding it was eternal damnation. The worst sin was heresy. The best way to avoid that sin was to believe only in what God had revealed. Anything else, elaboration of the faith, speculation, compromise, secular learning, and especially the purported wisdom of men who called themselves philosophers, was soul-rotting filth. Ignatius glared round the congregation, though whether at anyone in particular, I cannot say.

The patriarch's head lolled. He appeared to totter. His crosses and emblems rattled. I feared that he might foil our plan by dropping dead in the pulpit. He would have made a splendid corpse. But if he had died, what would that have said about God? That He despaired of having an ignorant fool as ruler of His Church? Or that He so loved Ignatius that He wished to preserve him from mockery? But it did not come to that. It was only a spasm, one the patriarch's habitual gestures, like the twitching of a basking lizard. Ignatius recovered his composure and went on, announcing the terrible news that a new heresy had afflicted the empire. It had spread from the East, the home of all lies, and was more dangerous than Paulicianism. It must be stamped out before it took root. Anyone who was taken in by it would be damned forever. When he had finished denouncing the doctrine of the twin souls, Ignatius concluded by condemning all who disagreed with him, or differed from him in any detail of belief or worship.

I played my part. As the congregation waited to leave, I smiled and chuckled to myself. While we streamed out through the seven doors, I laughed out loud. In the sunlit forecourt I accosted my neighbours and expressed amazement. Did Ignatius not know that the heresy of the twin souls was a joke? That it was so absurd that no one could possibly believe it? That Photius the great scholar had made it up? That he, the patriarch, was being teased? Elsewhere in the crowd others were saying much the same, and those who heard it passed it on, eager to be thought clever enough to have known all along.

As the worshippers headed for their various homes they took the story with them, and by nightfall it was all over the city. Ignatius, most holy and orthodox patriarch of the city, had been exposed as a fool by Photius.

I wonder how long it took before someone informed Ignatius that the doctrine he had condemned did not exist, and that the people of Constantinople were laughing at him? I have often not dared to tell Photius the truth, and he was much more reasonable than Ignatius. Perhaps it took days before Ignatius realised he had been tricked, and by that time my master's house was besieged by admirers and would-be followers.

"It's like a marketplace out there," Theodore said, as he shut the library door behind him. "There must be dozens of young men out there, all hoping for a word from you."

"I know," Photius said. "But they are not willing to buy. They expect me to give up my time freely, as though I had nothing better to do, not to mention borrowing my valuable books."

"Can you blame them? They despise the ignorance and zealotry of Ignatius. They want someone to lead them, someone to champion knowledge and learning. You made a fool of Ignatius. You are the most famous scholar in the city. And they know you are rich and generous." Theodore's tone was unctuous, as it often was when he had something to sell. I looked to see whether there was a book-shaped bulge under his cloak.

"It is all very well to give an occasional class, to discuss literature and philosophy with a few intelligent young men who are willing to learn. I have always done that. But have you seen how many of them there are? I don't have the time to teach a crowd like that."

"You could get someone else to do it."

"Why should I?"

"It would win you influence."

Photius thought for a while, gazing vaguely into the gloom of the closed and shuttered library. "It might," he said. "But it would be an expensive way to win it. I would have to appoint teachers and pay their salaries, and find a place for them to teach. This house isn't big enough. It would amount to founding a new school."

"That is something the city lacks," Theodore said. "All the schools are run by the Church, or by monasteries. And Ignatius makes sure they don't teach anything of value."

"There was a university," Photius said. "When was it closed? Under Justinian? Or was it later?"

"It was centuries ago, and the Church has controlled

learning ever since. No one has access to the wisdom of the ancients, except for rich men like you, who can afford to buy books and hire teachers." Theodore strode over to the library door and threw it open, revealing the eager throng outside. Some of the young men got up from their resting-places among the columns and statues and looked expectantly at Theodore. He stood in the doorway and raised his voice so that all could hear. "Where can eager young men like these go to learn about philosophy? Or mathematics? Where can they study astronomy, geometry, geography, literature or grammar? Nowhere! That's where! They must be given a school, a university!"

The men advanced towards the doors, shouting and cheering, ready to burst into the library.

"Yes," Photius said. "You've made your point. Now, please shut the door."

Theodore did as he was asked, then returned to sit by my master. "You must re-found the University of Constantinople," he said. "It is your destiny."

I could see the way Theodore's mind was working. A university would need teachers. Theodore and all his friends could all expect jobs. The students would need books. Theodore would supply them. One way or another, he would enrich himself. How had he managed to turns events to his advantage? Tricking Ignatius was my idea. Theodore only supplied a finishing touch to the scheme. Yet he was likely to benefit, and my master to bear the burden.

"It is a good idea," Photius said. "I can see that. Ignatius would be extremely annoyed. But I don't have the money."

"Bardas does."

"Bardas is no scholar."

"True, but he hates the zealots as much as any of us. He must have been pleased at the way you showed up Ignatius. I am sure he would like to be seen as a patron of learning. Why don't you ask him?"

"Did you know," Photius said, "that Constantine had the cheek to criticise me for the trick I played on Ignatius. He was in Bithynia at the time, but as soon as he got back he told me that I was guilty of spreading falsehood and confusing the faithful."

"Pious type, is he?" Bardas said. The two men had dined earlier. The doors were open and cool night air drifted in, giving welcome relief after the day's heat. Photius lounged on a couch, his head resting on soft cushions. Bardas never lounged. Even when reclining he was always tense, energetic, ready to spring to his feet and act.

"Pious?" Photius said. "He thinks of nothing but converting the barbarians." His tone was weary, almost dismissive. "The trouble with Constantine," he said, "is that he goes about things the wrong way. Even before he went to Bithynia, he was always fussing over his obsession with languages. Now he's back, he's worse. He keeps showing me some new alphabet he claims to have devised. I try to take an interest, but what can you say about a collection of baffling symbols supposed to represent the sounds made by savage tongues? He's convinced these alphabets will help him convert the Bulgars, or the Khazars, or the Moravians. He can't seem to make up his mind which it will be. I wouldn't go as far as the Trilingualists . . ."

"The what?"

"Those learned westerners who believe, and you must admit Bardas, this really is absurd, that the Word of God can only be expressed in Latin, Greek or Hebrew."

Bardas, perhaps fearing another theological hoax, kept silent.

"They are heretics," Photius said. "Utterly wrong. The truth is that no language can adequately express the Truth. I cannot believe that Latin is any better than the Slav tongue in that respect. Even so, Constantine would be better employed teaching those barbarians to speak a civilised language, such as Greek."

"Barbarians?" Bardas said. "Something's got to be done about them. They're everywhere. All around us, pressing on the frontier. Flooding into our cities and undermining our way of life. Have you been to Thessalonica? It's heaving with

Slavs. A few men like Constantine might be just what we need. Send them out into the field to teach the savages how to behave. Could be as good as an army."

"That's just what I've always thought," Photius said, though I could not remember him having expressed anything but mockery for Constantine's missionary enthusiasm. "But Ignatius won't send him. Or anyone else. He's afraid of annoying the pope. They are the best of friends, you know. The pope supports Ignatius, and Ignatius agrees to everything the pope says." Photius sighed and held out his wine cup. I got up from my place by the doors filled the two men's cups with darkest Cappadocian red. It was not my job to serve wine, but I was suspicious of the kitchen servants, and had already had a wine merchant dismissed for supplying inferior goods. I could not make myself indispensable if I let others serve my master.

Photius drank, and sighed again. "Constantine is a good man," he said. "That's why I resent being reproached by him."

I crept back to my place.

"You've nothing to complain of," Bardas said. "Everyone's done well out of your little joke. You'll get your university."

"It is for the city, not for me."

"You'll benefit. Everyone will. Except me! Theodora and Theoctistus are more suspicious of me than ever. They still won't let me into the palace. I'm not just thinking of myself, you understand. It's Michael's best interests I've got in mind. Is it right that a fifteen-year-old boy should be governed by a woman and a eunuch? What the boy needs is a man's influence. I'm his uncle, and I should be there by his side, guiding him."

"Of course," Photius said, but without much conviction. He was gazing out into the courtyard. A few lanterns made pools of light in the darkness, picking out a statue or a flowering bush. The fountain's spray, caught by the beginnings of a breeze, glimmered faintly.

"Michael is a weakling," Bardas said. "And he'll remain one, as long as Theoctistus has his way."

Photius turned towards Bardas. "What do you expect

from a eunuch?" he said. "They would unman everyone if they could."

"It's not just Theoctistus. Theodora's got the boy under her thumb. It won't be long before she finds a girl to marry him off to. Can you imagine it?"

"No," Photius said. "Marriage is a mystery to me."

Like most scholars, he never married. An appetite for books and ideas does not drive out all other desires. Scholars eat and drink, often with enthusiasm. My master ate well and enjoyed his wine, even if he was no epicurean. But he was never interested in women, or, I must make clear, in boys or eunuchs. If he was ever troubled by lustful thoughts, he kept them at bay with the coarse, itchy drawers he always wore in bed. There was an irony in that. Photius shared his celibacy with the monks and zealots he hated.

"I can tell you everything there is to know about marriage," Bardas said. "And I don't recommend it. Far better to make other arrangements."

Photius looked uncomfortable. By then everyone knew that Bardas was having an affair with his late son's wife. That was the real reason why his sister Theodora still kept him out of power and away from his nephew.

"What that boy needs," Bardas said, "is to get out of the palace and have a bit of fun. Wine, women, song, that sort of thing. A fight or two. No harm in him getting in a bit of a scrape. I know some lads who'd be only too happy to show him what's what. The question is, how to do it. I can get him out of the palace all right. Theoctistus doesn't control all the eunuchs. But where to take him? The city is teeming with the prefect's men, and the prefect is my sister's creature."

"I have no idea," Photius said. "I'm the last man to know about that sort of thing."

"There must be some way of getting Michael away from his mother and giving him a good time."

The two men lay on their couches, their wine untouched, their faces dark with thought. I sat in the doorway, remembering. And as the past came back to me I realised that I had another chance to help my master, one that might win him more than just the admiration of a gang of penniless students.

"Sir," I said, when Bardas had left. "I have an idea. As you know, I worked at a tavern before I came to live here. I was brought up there."

"You must be glad to have escaped."

"Yes, I am grateful. But I was thinking. Michael might enjoy visiting a place like that."

"Michael? Visit a tavern?"

"Yes, sir. It is up the Golden Horn, beyond Blachernae." Photius drank from his cup, but said nothing. "It is safely outside the city," I said. "We were seldom bothered by the prefect's men."

Photius leaned forward and held out his empty cup. I refilled it again, wondering how long he would sit up drinking. There were nights, even then, when things were going well for him, when he got so drunk that I had to put him to bed.

"Michael could get to the tavern by water," I said. "He could drink there safely. No one would know."

Photius drank again, and thought. Then his face filled with a broad smile. "Zeno," he said, "What a useful creature you are. Unlike the general run of eunuchs."

I was surprised by the smell of the place, which I had not noticed during the time I lived there. As soon as I stepped inside the tavern, my nostrils were filled with the reek of stale wine and piss, stewed onions, a maritime mixture of tar and fish, and the sweaty unwashed bodies of the poor. I realised that I had become fastidious while living with Photius.

The nieces did not recognise me in my fine new clothes, and were surprised to see someone of my nature visiting their rough tavern. I had no intention of dealing with them, and had chosen a time when Inger would be asleep. I ordered some wine, and sat in a corner and watched. The place was not busy. There were some carters, a couple of Bulgar merchants, and some men from the city who must have stopped there on the way to some outlying town. In the evening it would be livelier, fuller of sailors and fishermen, just right for a young man wanting a taste of low life. I sipped a little of my wine, winced at its sourness, waited for the widow to appear, so I could explain to her what I wanted.

A strange convulsion went through the room.

The drinkers fell silent, let their cups fall, sat upright with a jolt.

The most beautiful woman had just come through the door.

She was tall, and stood as straight as any man. The simple tunic and stained apron she wore could not disguise her figure. Her breasts were large and firm, her waist slim, and her hips wide. She had skin as pale as the finest parchment, hair the colour of honey, and eyes as blue as sapphires. The carters, the Bulgars, the travellers, all stared at her open-mouthed. The nieces glared.

There was no mistaking her. Eudocia would have been fifteen by then, and who else could have had eyes as blue as hers, or hair as golden? She was like Inger, transformed into a lovely woman.

I called her over, and, slipping a coin across the table, asked her to sit by me.

"Do you know who I am?" I asked.

She looked at me curiously. "I think I know you."

I could tell that she did not. "I am Zeno," I said.

"Zeno?" Her flawless brow furrowed. Her pink mouth turned down at the corners. She twisted a lock of her golden hair between a thumb and finger. "Of course," she said. "I knew it was you!"

Her voice was soft and seductive, with a charming hint of Inger's accent. She reached out and stroked my face with her hand. "Your skin is so smooth," she said. "And you are pretty, like a woman."

Eudocia clearly knew nothing of eunuchs. She had not learned that we are not susceptible to a woman's blandishments. Yet her touch had an effect on me. My heart beat faster, my face felt hot, my hands trembled. Unfamiliar emotions struggled within me. For the first time in my life, I felt the glimmering of desire.

How could that be? I had been tested by Leo. His instruments, and his theories, had proved me sexless. The two whores and their antics had not moved me. So why should Eudocia cause me such confusion? I had cared for her when she was a baby, watching over her while her mother attended the drunken Inger. She had been almost like a sister. If I felt anything for anyone, it should not be for her.

Eudocia was looking at me sadly. She must have seen agitation in my face, perhaps a hint of horror. I was filled with remorse. I felt as though the sun had gone in and a sudden chill had come over the day. I did not want Eudocia to be unhappy.

"You are very pretty yourself," I said. "Lovely, in fact. I might have guessed you would grow up to be beautiful." I reached out, took her hand and held it mine. "But your hands are red and rough," I said. "How did they get like that?"

"How d'you think? The nieces hate me. They're jealous. And they fear this." She raised a hand and pointed at her blue eyes. "The Evil Eye, they call it. They say the devil envies good people, and works his evil through me. One glance from me brings bad luck, according to them. Not that the customers care. They don't mind looking at me. Or being looked at by me. But the nieces keep me out of the way, and they cross themselves so often I sometimes feel that Christ is my enemy."

"Doesn't your mother protect you?" I asked.

"She's gone back to her village."

"With Inger?"

"No. He's still here. But the nieces are in charge now. And they make sure I do all the hard work. That's what I was doing just now. Washing up." She disengaged my hand from hers. "I can tell you don't do that sort of work."

"I used to, when I lived here."

"You're dressed like a gentleman."

"Not quite. I am still a slave."

I told her something of my life, but I wonder how much of it she understood. As I had already discovered, the life of a scholar is very different from that of a tavern servant.

"In two days time," I said. "In the evening, I will bring some people here. Some young men."

"That's good," Eudocia said. "We can always do with more customers."

"These will be special customers."

Eudocia's eyes widened. The sky shone out of them. How could anyone see evil there? She smoothed her apron, running her hands over her hips. "Gentlemen, are they?" she asked. "Like you've been telling me about?"

"You could say that. But they are not scholars."

"So who are they?"

"That's not for you to know. You must serve them, and be nice to them, and agree to everything they say."

"Everything?"

"You'll be well paid, I can promise that."

She simpered, as though to a generous customer. I felt misgivings.

"There's one other thing," I said. "You'll have to keep Inger out of the way. Get him drunk, send him to sleep, make sure no one sees him."

A contest
[AD 855]

The boat bumped against something hard. I put my hand out and felt stone steps, wet and covered with slime. A chink of light showed above us, there was a rattling of chains in the darkness, then a door was let down with a thunderous crash. Quickly, while servants held flaming torches out over the black water, six young men scrambled into the boat. An older man followed them, and sat down heavily beside me. I felt his curved scabbard jab against my leg, and knew he was a body-guard. A glance at his hook-nosed face, framed by dark plaits and topped by a fur-trimmed hat, told me that he was one of the Ferghanese guards. They were Turks from beyond Samar-kand, loyal to no one but the imperial family. I was glad to have such a man with me, but sorry he was alone. I tried to speak to him, but he growled a few words in his own tongue, then drew a finger across his throat. If he spoke Greek, he would not speak it with me.

The youths huddled in the bows, pulling their cloaks around themselves, whispering to each other. It was obvious which of them was Michael. The others sat apart from him, giving him more room to stretch his legs. I wondered how well they knew him, whether they even liked him. They had probably been chosen by Bardas rather than Michael. Even in swaying lantern-light I could see that there was something foolish about Michael's face. He constantly looked to his companions for reassurance, his expression innocent at one moment and sly the next.

When we were all settled, the oarsmen fended off and began to scull round the great curve of sea walls that protected the palace and its environs. I had not been out on the water at night since I sailed the Black Sea with the Rus. Inger and his companions had sung and chanted while they worked the oars, but the men I had hired rowed silently. The current in the Bosphorus was strong, and we hung for a while near the point, the glimmering lights of the city on our left, unable to make way. But the oarsmen were strong, and we rounded the point, and were soon scudding up the Golden Horn.

Out on the cold water I had a fit of misgiving. Why had I been so foolish? I had no idea what was permissible or advisable for young gentlemen out on the town in disguise, or how a eunuch slave might give advice to a boy destined to rule the empire. Was I in charge of them? Or could they do what they liked? What would happen to me if I reprimanded one of them, or if I failed to get them back to the palace? The penalty for displeasing the emperor's uncle might be terrible.

At the tavern, all was bright and warm. After our damp and chilly voyage even the frowstiness was welcoming. The nieces smiled winsomely, and led us to a glowing brazier. The tavern's customers looked particularly villainous that night, grizzled, dirty, ill-dressed, a few even lacked limbs or eyes. Some of them were dicing, gambling away tomorrow's catch or the proceeds of their next voyage. Others were just drinking, and telling tall tales of the sea. One group, their chins slick with pig-fat, picked over the remains of a stew of pigs' tails, noisily sucking small bones and spitting them back in the bowl. Michael watched them, his face filled with a strange yearning, as though he longed to join them and share their meal. Seeing him smile, I felt better. I realised that I had done the right thing, I had brought him to a place he would like, where he could have a safe adventure of the kind his uncle hoped for.

The Turkish bodyguard settled himself in a corner, unbuckled his sword belt, secured by gesture a cup of wine, and sat waiting. His heavy silk coat, shimmering with every shade of green, was so grand that it was obvious our charges were not the usual city roisterers. I knew he would be no help to me. He would only intervene if I did something wrong.

However, I had been instructed to show Michael and his friends a good time, and the only thing left to me was to get on and do it. I seated the six youths round the middle table, which the regulars, by reason of some seafarer's superstition, always avoided. Jingling my purse, I called for the best

Monemvasian wine, glad to be telling the nieces what to do. It was some small recompense for the hard times they had given me in the past.

Eudocia brought the wine, emerging from the back room bearing a flagon, pausing for a moment to pull the curtain shut behind her. It was a simple act, but done with such grace that everyone in the room stared at her. As she advanced towards us, carefully cradling the brimming flagon, Michael and his friends were struck dumb. Eudocia was as tall as any of them, and there was something boyish about her straight back and square shoulders. In old Sparta, where girls joined equally in all the games, she might have outrun the fleetest youth, or outwrestled the strongest. But her face and figure were as beautiful as any Michael could have seen, and he and his friends gaped meekly as she drew close. She poured carefully, leaning across the table, looking intently at each of the youths as she served him. She smelled fresh and clean. Her hair glowed in the lamplight. As she worked her way round the table, leaning between them and filling their cups, they stared at her, looking greedily at her naked arms and unveiled face. And when she went away they gazed silently into their wine cups.

It would not be much of an evening, I thought, if they carried on like that. I remembered a game that young idlers had sometimes played, and suggested it to the six youths. They each had to recite a tongue-twisting nonsensical verse, swigging wine at appropriate places, downing a whole cup if they slipped up. I demonstrated, making sure that I gave them a laugh by muddling the words, and they quickly took to the game. Michael was particularly bad at it, and had soon drunk four or five cups, egged on by his gleeful comrades. The other drinkers watched for a while, but they were soon bored by the boys' antics and returned to their own amusements.

Michael, I saw, would have been handsome had he looked a little less foolish. His face was smooth and regular, his hair curled and well cut, his beard as yet no more than a few wisps of hair. He was absorbed in the game, but not so much that he failed to notice Eudocia. Each time she came near, the youths grew quieter and less confident. Michael tried to catch her eye, though he was not brave enough to speak to her. And here I must confess to one of my failures. Though I saw their glances clearly enough, I failed to notice that something was kindled on that day. The sparks that flashed between their eyes lit a fire that lasted for decades and consumed several lives. But who could have known that then? Who could have guessed what taking Michael to the tavern would lead to?

The tavern was hot, its air stuffy. I had drunk some wine as a forfeit. Despite my responsibilities, I may have nodded off for a moment. The next thing I was aware of was a great roaring like the sound of a furious beast. It was a noise from a nightmare, the cry of a gigantic creature trapped in an echoing cave, enraged by wounds or fire. I blinked my eyes open, and looked around to see where the uproar was coming from. Perhaps I had dreamed it. Then the curtains to the back room parted and Inger burst in. His hair and beard formed a tangled nest in which his pink face nestled. He was barefoot, and naked to the waist, his lower half clad in tight trousers, his belly bulging over a broad belt. Mjollnir dangled round his neck on a leather thong. Hanging loosely in his hand was a drinking horn, which he had clearly drained earlier.

Michael and his friends looked up blankly, their game interrupted. The bodyguard moved almost imperceptibly, just resting his hand on his sword hilt.

Inger lumbered further into the room, brandishing his drinking horn like a weapon, raising it so high that it almost hit the low-beamed ceiling. He bellowed again, calling for wine. I caught Eudocia's eye. For a moment she looked scared. She was on the far side of Michael's table, a wine jug in her hand. Inger lurched towards her, calling again for wine. She hesitated, cradling the jug against her apron, looking at Inger pleadingly. She spoke a few words to him in soft, lilting Norse. For a moment the two of them stood on either side of the table, the young gentleman gaping up at them, the other drinkers looking on expectantly. Then Inger lurched again, thrusting out his drinking horn.

As soon as Inger's arm brushed Michael's head the body-guard was on his feet with his sword drawn. The Turk was smaller than the Rus, but he was armed and sober. He stepped forward nimbly, his curved sword pointing straight at Inger's neck. That crescent of polished steel, so near the young emperor's head, held the whole of my future balanced on its point.

Inger looked puzzled. He swayed backwards and forwards a few times, furrows crossing his broad brow. His naked chest heaved as he took in great draughts of air. Very gently, his hand moving like a questing snake, he touched Mjollnir. His finger stroked the silver shaft of Thor's hammer. Then he moved, more suddenly than a thunderbolt. He jerked his body back, raised his left arm and, using his iron-bound drinking horn, parried the bodyguard's sword. With his right hand he swiftly grabbed the Turk's wrist and yanked it sharply downwards. The sword fell with a clatter onto the tavern floor. Inger placed a bare foot firmly on the blade and glared defiantly at the Turk.

"No sword now," he bellowed. "I fight you!"

There was a scraping of benches as the regulars drew back for a better view. Michael and his friends grabbed the chance to scramble out of the way, taking refuge among the regulars. Only Eudocia and I still stood in the centre of the room, within reach of the two barbarians. They did not look well matched to me. Inger towered over the wiry Turk, who gazed with astonishment at his fallen sword and the broad foot that pressed down on it. I had seen what Inger could do in battle. If there was a fight, drunk or sober, he would crush the disarmed Turk easily.

"I fight you," Inger repeated.

I could not allow them to fight. What would happen to me if an imperial bodyguard was killed or injured?

"Eudocia," I said. "We must stop them."

She reached out and took her father by the arm, gently drawing him away from the Turk. I was surprised at Inger's meekness. He was like a fierce dog calmed by a pat on the head. But he had forgotten the sword, which still lay on the floor. Without thinking, I swooped, grabbed its leather-bound hilt and threw it into a corner. The Turk lunged at me, but I dodged round behind Inger and Eudocia, who was whispering urgently in her father's ear.

"Can you stop him?" I said.

"I can stop him fighting," she said. "But only if the other man meets his challenge."

"What challenge?"

Before Eudocia could answer, Inger slipped from her grasp and stepped forward. "We drink!" he shouted. "You drink. I drink. Who drinks most wins."

A great cheer went up. The seafaring regulars, the pigs' tail stew eaters, Michael and his friends, all roared with joy at the prospect of a drinking match. Before the Turk could say or do anything they leapt into action, dragging benches into a circle, pushing the two barbarians forward, jostling for places with a good view. The young gentlemen forgot their fears and snobbery, and sat at the same benches as the fishermen and sailors, calling out the same dares and challenges, their faces filled with the same unfeigned anticipation. The craftier regulars made bets with Michael's friends, who staked all they had on the Turk.

I had no idea whether the Ferghanese were drinkers or not, but I was not betting. The money I carried was all reserved for paying the bill at the end of the evening, and I could see that the bill would be large. The nieces brought fresh cups and flagons, made sure that everyone was served, then the contest began. There is not much to be said about a drinking contest. As a sport, it has few rules or niceties. A niece stood by each man and filled his cup. Eudocia held a tally stick, which she marked with a kitchen knife.

"Skoal!" Inger said as he raised his cup. The Turk merely grunted, but the contest began, and the two men drank, raising their cups in unison and draining them quickly. The first dozen cups were disposed of easily. The next dozen were drunk almost as fast. Inger was enjoying himself, and smiled broadly at his audience. The Turk was as impassive as ever.

New bets were made, not on who would win, but on how much the winner would be able to drink. The regulars started to copy Inger, calling out "skoal!" whenever he did.

As they began the third dozen, Inger's face turned so red that he resembled a fire burning up the wine rather than a man drinking it. The Turk's face grew paler. He loosened his silk coat and threw it off, dabbing at his sweat-beaded brow with one of its sleeves.

Inger celebrated the thirtieth cup with a song about an eating contest between Loki the trickster and an all-consuming giant, which he bellowed at the top of his voice. The song was followed by a brief truce while the two went outside to piss. When he took his place again the Turk did not look well. He sipped his thirty-first cup slowly, forcing the wine down as though it was one of Leo's bitter concoctions. Inger raised his thirty-second cup cheerfully, tipping it at the regulars. When they all shouted "skoal!" he drained it.

The Turk stared at his drink, swaying backwards and forwards slightly, his Adam's apple bobbing up and down uncontrollably. The spectators looked at each other eagerly. One or two tried to renegotiate their bets. Then the Turk clutched his throat and fell forward, waves of rich red vomit spewing over the table in a torrent. He jerked up and down, heaving and retching, spraying half-digested meat over the spectators, gentlemen and seafarers alike.

Inger leapt to his feet with a great roar of triumph, calling for another cup of wine. There was a cheer from those who had won their bets. The Turk jerked upright again, his face greenish and contorted with anguish. He tried to stand, his arms flailing uselessly as though underwater, but before he was halfway up, fresh waves of vomit gushed out of his gaping mouth. Benches toppled as men scrambled to get out of the way. The Turk fell backwards, dead drunk.

I decided that, as far as my charges were concerned, the evening's entertainment was over. But how was I going to get them back into the boat? And what about the bodyguard? He was worse than useless to me now. While the nieces threw water over his face I mingled with Michael and his friends, politely suggesting that it might be time to return to the palace. But they had bet on the Turk, were being pestered to pay their debts, and took no notice of me. Michael paid up happily. A gold piece or two made no difference to him. But a couple of his friends argued, complaining that the contest was not fair.

"Please gentlemen," I said, raising my voice as much as I could. "It really is time to go."

But they ignored me and continued their quarrels. I turned to Eudocia. "How can I get them to go?" I said. She looked at me almost pityingly, then stepped confidently into the centre of the room. She took a deep breath, making her breasts rise impressively under her wine-stained apron. Then she spoke.

"Listen to me boys!"

It was no feat of rhetoric, but Michael and his friends listened. The seafarers ceased pestering them for money. All of them stopped what they were doing and turned towards her. She stood there, tall, blonde and beautiful, surveying the room with her clear blue eyes.

"You've all had a good time," she said. "There's no need to worry about money." She glanced at me, and I nodded. "The drinks are free," she said. A ragged cheer went up from the regulars. She looked at Michael. "Now boys, your friend is lying on the floor. You're not going to leave him like that?"

Michael shook his head, a foolish expression spreading over his face.

"Come on," Eudocia said. "Let's pick him up and carry him back to the boat."

The youths obediently shuffled forward. Under Eudocia's direction they manhandled the Turk out of the tavern, got him down to the shore and into the boat. I collected his coat and sword, paid the nieces, and walked gratefully out into the chilly night.

The Chaldean Oracle
[AD 855]

"A triumph," Bardas said. "Couldn't have planned it better myself. To think you pretended you didn't know what to do!"

Photius smiled modestly and laid his dish down so that a servant could take it away. "I am glad it went well," he said.

"You know more about how to have a good time than you let on," Bardas said. "Michael can't stop talking about it. That's unfortunate, in a way, as Theodora is bound to hear all about it before long. She'll marry Michael off to some pure little virgin then. But it's done him the world of good. He's keen to go back, and meet this girl again. He's really taken a fancy to her."

"Girl?" Photius said. "What girl?"

Those were difficult times for me. I had just rediscovered Eudocia, and wanted nothing better than to spend more time with her. Seeing her again had made me realise what I truly lacked. She was my family. I had helped rear her, protected her from the nieces' jealousy, found solace in her unconditional love. When I bathed and swaddled her, she had not cared that I was a slave and a eunuch, had not even understood that I was inferior. And yet, provoked by the nieces, tempted by Constantine, I had abandoned her.

Having found Eudocia again, my fate was to hand her over to Michael. He was a spoiled, weak-willed youth, whose word, when he knew what it was, was my command. And if I thought for a moment of disobeying him, I had Photius and Bardas to answer to. Obedient, I took Michel back to the tavern often, and got to know the Golden Horn, in all its moods and seasons, as well as any waterman. Michael usually put me ashore and took Eudocia out on the water. They spent hours together, concealed under the boat's awning, unseen by anyone but the crew, discovering what love is, and what lovers do. I brooded, strolling along the shore, sitting beneath the plane trees, wondering how it would all end.

To be taken up by an emperor, even a young and powerless one, was unimaginable good luck for a girl like Eudocia. But I knew that it could not last, and so did she. After the first few weeks, Michael's attentions made her sad rather than happy.

"Zeno," Eudocia said, while Michael was at the waterside instructing the boatmen, "you do care for me, don't you?"

"Of course I do. You are like a like a sister to me."

She looked disappointed. "Only a sister? Don't you love me?"

"You know what I am, and what I lack."

"What you lack? You've got a heart, haven't you?"

"I have, and I love you as much as it is possible for me to love anyone."

She took my hand and stared at me directly. "You wouldn't want me to be unhappy, would you?"

Her eyes were as blue as a cloudless sky, but there was sadness in them. They brimmed with moisture, as though they were pools reflecting the sky, or as though a clear sky could suddenly give forth rain. But I am muddling my metaphor. That is the effect she had. Her gaze could undo reason and sap the will.

Eudocia's eyes were not evil. No one could believe that. But there was a magic about them that was hard to resist.

"No," I said. "I would hate you to be unhappy."

"I'm afraid," she said, gripping my hand harder. "I think Michael will get tired of me."

"Has he said anything?"

"No. But look at me." She withdrew her hand from mine and tugged impatiently at the simple clothes she wore. Michael had not thought to give her presents or money, or even a new dress. He had just dallied with her. "And look around," she said, gesturing vaguely at the unwiped tables and greasy, food-spattered floor. A couple of dozing drinkers stirred slightly, then slumped even further against the grimy wooden wall. "I am just a servant," she said. "Working in a tavern. How can Michael love me when I live like this?"

"You are beautiful," I said.

"There must be beautiful women at the palace."

"There are," I said. "But not like you. Their beauty is all silk and jewels and make-up."

"I want to be like them. I want to wear silk and jewels and live in a fine house with servants. I want to be a lady. Then Michael will love me properly."

"I am sure he loves you already."

"So why doesn't he give me what I want?"

"Have you asked him?"

"No! Of course not. He'd hate me if I asked for anything."

"But you want it anyway?"

Eudocia took my hand again. "Don't be like that," she said. "I only want to be happy. And I can be, if I can get away from here and live like a lady." A few tears trickled down her cheeks. "You can help me."

"How?"

"You know all those people in the city. All those gentlemen. They could help. They could get me away from here."

Hearing Michael's step outside, she dabbed her eyes with her apron then went out to meet him. I poured myself a cup of Monemvasia and pondered.

I found Theodore haggling with a book dealer in a little shop close to the church of Saint Gregory. He concluded his business, then led me into the church, which was dark, neglected and reassuringly empty. While I talked, he leaned against a pillar, one foot resting on its pedestal, his leather book-bag cradled in his arms. With his wild hair, jutting beard and grubby coat he looked like an unworldly scholar. Yet he appeared to know everything that went on in the city, and hinted that he had the power to influence events.

"What does the imperial family want most?" Theodore said, when I had explained what Eudocia had asked of me.

"Power?" I suggested.

"No."

"Wealth?"

"No." His tone was condescending, but having decided to ask Theodore's help I was obliged to overlook that. "What they want most," he said, "is sons. And Michael is just the age when princes get married. They'll be looking for a wife for him."

"That's what Bardas said. I suppose that's what Eudocia is afraid of. When Michael marries that will be the end of their affair."

"Unless he marries her."

"Michael marry Eudocia? I don't think even she hopes for that. She just wants to live like a lady and be loved by him."

"Why shouldn't he marry her? Emperors have married all sorts of women. Justinian married a circus performer."

"They won't let him. The empress is too pious."

"Then we must find a way round her."

"How?"

Theodore reached into his bag and drew out a book. "With this!" he said. "The *Chaldean Oracle*. I see from your puzzled expression that you are not familiar with it. It is an ancient text, full of prophecies." He dangled the book in front of me, opened its pages, briefly showed me its contents. "What do you see?" he said, pulling the book away from me.

"It looks like verse."

"It does, doesn't it? But ordinary readers would find little sense in it. Fortunately I have become an adept, and when I consult this volume I see the future."

"Is there anything in there about Michael and Eudocia?"

"Are you asking for yourself?"

"I am asking for her."

"Are you sure? It makes a difference, you know. Before consulting the oracle one must be absolutely sure what one is asking and why. And on whose behalf. An ill-considered question could have disastrous results."

"Do you really believe in this book?"

"I have found it invaluable."

"And it can help Eudocia?"

"It can help us all, if we ask it the right questions."

"What do you suggest?"

"Isn't it obvious? We should ask the name of the woman who will bear sons for Michael."

"Go on! Ask it now!"

Theodore stepped away from the pillar and looked cautiously around the church. It was still empty. "Zeno," he said. "It is not as simple as that. I am confident the book will give us the right answer. It always does. But what use is that? If the prophecy is to be effective it must be done in public, in front of someone important, someone who can make the prophecy come true."

"The empress!"

"Do you have access to Theodora? I thought not. Under the circumstances, our best choice would be Bardas."

"But Bardas has no influence. The empress won't even let him into the palace."

"Exactly! That is why he is the best choice. He craves power. If you want Eudocia taken out of her tavern and made into a lady, you must persuade Bardas that advancing her will help him win power. With my help, and the *Chaldean Oracle*, that should be easy."

Theodore put the book in his bag. I could not decide whether he really believed in its oracular powers, but I had learned that he was willing to give advice, and anxious to be thought an expert. He went on, explaining how the book was to be consulted, what questions were to be put, and what kind of answers it was likely to give. My part was to warn Theodore when Bardas was expected at my master's house, and to concoct a pretext on which the oracle could be consulted.

Theodore was so helpful, so keen to get every detail right, that I wondered whether I had misjudged him. I was on the point of thanking him when the reason for his enthusiasm became clear.

"You will have to do something for me," he said.

"What?"

"You must press my case with Photius."

"What case?"

"The case for appointing me rector of the university. Bardas has put up the money, Photius is advising him, but they haven't chosen the staff. The whole thing was my idea. They should put me in charge of it."

"You could speak to Photius yourself."

"It would be better coming from someone else. He trusts you, I know he does. And Bardas trusts him."

As I left the church and walked up the narrow street I had more doubts than before. Would Theodore take advantage of my dilemma to advance himself? Probably. But I had no other plan, and no choice but to trust him. I could not let Eudocia be unhappy.

Theodore arrived at my master's house apparently by chance, just as dinner had been cleared way and Bardas was bemoaning his lot again. Bardas was not particularly pleased to see him. Photius, ignoring the coolness between them, settled Theodore on his couch and asked me to serve him wine. For a week or so, I had been pestering my master with talk of oracles and prophecies. My curiosity was not feigned. I wanted to know whether there was any truth in such things, whether adepts like Theodore really could see into the future.

"God grants some men glimpses of things to come," he said. "And the devil leads others astray by showing them what they desire."

I might have taken more notice of those words, had I not been so intent on getting Eudocia what she desired. By the time Bardas came to dinner my master's head must have been buzzing with signs, portents and prophecies. After quaffing a cup or two, Theodore casually mentioned the book he was carrying.

"The *Chaldean Oracle?*" Photius said. "Of course, I have heard of it. But I confess I have never read it."

"Read?" Theodore said. "It is not a book to be read. It must be consulted, and by someone who knows how."

It was cold outside, and there was a brazier in the room. The glow from the coals gave Theodore's shaggy face a demonic cast. I feared that Photius would scoff, but he raised no objection when Theodore offered to demonstrate the book's power. I brought him a lamp and a tripod table. He set the book down, opened it apparently at random and stared at it. He breathed deeply, ruffling his whiskers, and rocked backwards and forwards, his shadow growing and shrinking on the panelled ceiling. Then he began to speak in a high, whining voice like the wind forcing its way through ill-fitting shutters. There were no words at first, only jumbled syllables. When words came, they meant nothing. But gradually fragments of sense emerged. There were some names, which meant nothing to me, but made Bardas stare with wonder. There were some phrases about power and justice. Then Theodore mentioned Michael.

"He must be given wise counsel," he said. "When he rules, he will raise up those who have counselled him, those who have helped him."

Bardas looked sour. Before Theodore came, he had been complaining again of the bad influence of Theoctistus, the eunuch Logothete who controlled the court.

"Michael will marry," Theodore said. "He will marry and have sons. They will rule after him. A great dynasty!" Theodore clutched his brow and rocked so furiously that I feared the couch would collapse. "The Mother! She is outside the walls, beyond the city. She must be found! Her name . . ." With closed eyes he held a clawed hand over the book. "Her name," he whispered, "will be Eudocia."

Bardas was so impressed by Theodore's performance that he quickly installed Eudocia in a house near the palace, providing her with money to live on, and servants to look after her. The house, like most such houses, was unremarkable from the outside. The rich like to live behind high, plain walls, keeping their wealth from prying eyes. But inside, the house was almost as luxurious as my master's. Eudocia's rooms were elegantly decorated, with rustic scenes painted on the walls, and carved and inlayed furniture standing proudly on the polished marble floors. Servants received me deferentially, as though Eudocia and I were both important people, and led me to her chamber.

Eudocia's hair had been curled and plaited, piled up into an elaborate golden confection.

"Do you like it?" she said, smoothing the folds of her softly pleated silk dress. There were other dresses strewn all over the room: shining silks, fine Egyptian linens, furs from the far North, sheer veils and delicately made shoes. There were samples of fabrics, jewellery and perfumes, sent by eager merchants all too aware of Eudocia's new status.

"The dress is beautiful," I said. I had never seen one like it. It fell in creamy billows, almost to her bare feet. Her pink nipples were quite visible through the thin fabric, which quivered with every breath. If respectable women ever wore dresses in that style they did so only in the women's quarters, or concealed under the veils and mantles they wore in public.

"Will Michael like it?"

"He is sure to."

She reached up to her shoulder and fiddled with one of the ties of her dress, but before she could unfasten it her servant girl dashed forward and did it for her. The dress fell to the ground with a rustle. She was naked.

I had not seen her naked since she was five years old.

Eudocia was so unlike her mother, and so like Inger. It must be as Leo the philosopher taught me, that a woman's womb provides only the place in which a man's seed can ferment into an embryo. Leo, like other scholars, like most men, regarded women as imperfect, inferior, unfinished. Even their souls were not fully formed. Yet Eudocia, standing naked before me, was the most perfect thing I had ever seen. Her breasts were as white as milk. Her belly gleamed like Parian marble. The skin of her thighs was so delicate that blue veins showed through clearly. She was like the ivory statue carved by Pygmalion. According to legend, the sculptor fell in love with his creation and prayed for it to be filled with life. I expect the story ended unhappily, as such stories often do. I cannot remember the ending, and have no books about me now. I prefer not to draw attention to myself by wandering the city in search of libraries or booksellers. I have left the scholarly life behind, and do not wish to resume it.

Whatever the truth about that old story, Eudocia was no statue. Despite being only a girl in years, she was a woman. No one seeing those full breasts, her broad hips, the bush of reddish hair at her groin, could doubt that.

As I gazed at her, I realised that I too was not a statue. I had feelings. I noticed a strange stirring in my innards, an errant beat of the heart, a prickling of the skin, even a twitching of my little member. How can I explain those unexpected sensations? Can beauty alone stir the admiration of a sexless creature like me? I was not so stirred when I shared a bed with her mother. On those cold nights at the tavern I felt warm and needed, but no more than that. When I bathed the infant Eudocia I felt nothing but brotherly love. Seeing her grown to womanhood and naked, I felt unwonted and unseemly desire.

"Bring me that one," she said, pointing to the heap of clothes on her bed. Her voice, so clear and strong when commanding drunken revellers, sounded weak and uncertain. Nevertheless, the maidservant darted forward, divined which garment Eudocia wanted, and brought it to her. I waited while she helped Eudocia into the new dress, then held up a mirror. Eudocia admired her image calmly in the polished silver disc, sighed, then sent the servant away.

"Why can't I see him?" she asked.

"You do see him," I said. "I know he can't come here every day. But you've got what you wanted. Look at this lovely house and all the beautiful things in it."

"I don't want all this. I want Michael."

"You must understand that he has his duties."

"It's his mother's fault. She keeps him busy all the time at the palace. Her and the eunuchs. They make him dress up in stupid costumes, then lead him round the palace singing and chanting. He has to sit for hours on a throne and let important people come and look at him. He can't even move his head unless they tell him to. He has to listen to people telling him what's going on. He signs everything they give him, but he's not allowed to read it. And when he's not doing that they make him go to church and listen to some old eunuch

118

preaching about sin. His mother makes him do it. Why can't they get rid of her?"

"Theodora is popular with the people. They love her for restoring the icons."

"What do I care about that? I want Michael, and I see him less now than before."

Reversals
[AD 856]

Theodore had disappeared for a while after making his prophecy. I assumed he was in the East, on a monastic book-buying tour. When I next met him, apparently by accident, in the street near Eudocia's house, he wore a large wooden cross, which dangled loosely beneath his beard. It looked a little ostentatious, especially in contrast to his usual unkempt clothes.

"Why are you wearing that?" I asked, as he fell in beside me.

"I have got myself ordained as a deacon."

"A deacon?"

"It is not much, I agree. But it is only a first step. Who knows where it will lead?"

"But why the priesthood?"

"I have to advance myself somehow," he said, helping himself to a sweetmeat from a monger's display. The monger glared at him, but Theodore smiled sweetly and made a gesture vaguely reminiscent of benediction. "Bardas wouldn't put me in charge of the university," he said, as we walked on. "For some reason he preferred Leo. I am surprised Photius didn't feel able to recommend me."

"I put your case. You know I did."

"Yes. But I wonder how persuasive you were. It is important to return favours, you know. Men like Bardas can afford to be ungrateful, but can you?"

"I've done my best to help you, but I have new duties now."

"Ah, yes! And how is the lovely Eudocia?" Theodore smiled unpleasantly. "Happy, I hope?"

"I believe so."

"She ought to be delighted. Bardas must have spent a fortune to set her up like that. But he is something of an expert at managing mistresses."

"So I hear."

Theodore's step faltered. "Now tell me," he said. "What, exactly do you do at her house?"

"I teach her how to be lady."

"And you know all about that?" Theodore's tone was mocking. Like other men, he liked occasionally to sneer at eunuchs.

"No," I said. "My task is to teach her the rudiments of literacy, how to speak well, and how to pepper her conversation with well-chosen phrases from ancient literature. Her servants are teaching her the other things she needs to know, court etiquette, a ladylike manner, how to dress, and so on. I couldn't teach her any of that."

We had reached the end of the street and were about to emerge into a large square. Theodore halted and gripped my arm. His face was strangely agitated. "They'll be teaching her the secrets of womanhood as well?"

"What secrets?"

"The secrets of the bedchamber," he said, licking his lips. "How to please a man, and how not to conceive. Any mistake of that sort would be the end of her."

"You predicted she would bear Michael's sons."

"Of course, and so she will. But not too soon."

"You are sure he will marry her?"

"The oracle does not fail. Eudocia will be Michael's wife. I hope *she* will be grateful."

I heard the reproach in Theodore's voice, and felt the grip of his bony fingers on my arm. I tried to pull myself away, to get out into the bustling square. But Theodore held on to me.

"What is the state of her faith?" he said.

"Her faith?"

"Has she been fully instructed? Is she thoroughly orthodox?"

"I expect so."

"You don't sound sure. It is important, if she is to marry Michael. If there any gaps or defects in her faith, you must tell me."

"Why?"

"So that I can correct them."

To escape from Theodore I had to repeat my promises to help him. Questioning Eudocia, I found that she knew more of Inger's gods than she did of orthodoxy. I did not tell Theodore. The thought of him worming his way into her chamber, seeing her in those sheer silk gowns, all on the excuse of reinforcing her faith, disgusted me. And I was puzzled by his ordination. To be accepted into the priesthood he must have dealt with the Ignatians, who would surely have rejected him as a friend of Photius. Then I realised that, despite his promises, Theodore had not actually taken part in the public mockery that followed Ignatius's sermon against the false heresy he had helped devise.

There was much rejoicing in the city when the Empress Theodora announced that Michael, having come of age, was to marry. The bride-to-be was a girl from the provinces called Eudocia Decapolitana.

Bardas was furious.

"I was right not to trust Theodore," he said. "He tricked me!"

"I am sure he meant no harm," Photius said. "He just spoke the words the oracle inspired in him. And the oracle was correct, everything is happening just as it predicted."

"But we thought it meant our tavern-girl."

"Oracles are like that. Take Oedipus, for example. The Delphic Oracle said . . ."

Bardas glared at him. "It was a trick, I'm sure of it. Someone wanted that tavern-girl set up in luxury. And if it wasn't Theodore, then who?"

I lurked in a corner, unwilling to show myself, hoping that Bardas would never learn whose idea it had been to turn Eudocia into a lady.

"Will you turn her out?" Photius asked.

Bardas thought for a while. "No," he said. "I will keep her on. And I will make sure she gets the best of everything: clothes, jewels, perfumes, whatever it takes to make her irresistible to Michael."

"But he will be married soon," Photius said.

"That's never stopped me."

"And you don't intend to stop him?"

"Of course not. I can just image the sort of dull little virgin my sister will have chosen for Michael. He'll want a bit of fun on the side. And the more of that he gets, the more grateful he will be to me." Bardas paced up and down a few times. "There was another part to that prophecy," he said. "Something about Michael raising up those who have given him good counsel, and those who have helped him. Well, I intend to make sure that's me."

My master's brow furrowed. His mouth opened, then closed. He did not say anything.

A few months after the wedding, Bardas announced that he was going to inspect the university. He had got nothing from his investment in Eudocia, and was still excluded from court. He was determined to pose as a civic benefactor by inspecting his scholars as they toiled in the fine building he had provided, just beside the palace walls.

He arrived in the most elaborate ceremonial robes, of a kind I had seldom seen before. Over a richly brocaded coat, he wore a flowing, sleeveless over-mantle of shimmering blue silk, embroidered with all manner of golden foliage. His servants wore gaily-coloured tunics, and even his bodyguards were dressed in parade uniforms of red and blue, with scabbarded swords swinging loosely on bright baldrics. The whole party looked as though they had wandered off from an Imperial procession.

Photius had also dressed up, though not as grandly as Bardas, and waited in the portico, anxious to please Bardas, and to justify the money he had spent. Leo and the other teachers, all wearing the homespun garments of unworldly philosophers, paced in front of their students, all delivering well-rehearsed lectures which they hoped to bring to a peak of eloquence just as Bardas arrived. But Bardas was not much interested in the classes. After walking briskly from room to room, paying no more attention to the teachers or pupils than he did to the marble floors and pillars, he suddenly demanded to see the head porter.

"But why?" Photius said. "He knows nothing of our work."

"Just send for him, will you?"

Seeing my master's puzzlement, I did as Bardas asked, and found the head porter lurking in a storeroom. I dragged him into the main reception hall, where Bardas and my master waited beneath an ornate dome. The porter flung himself at Bardas's feet, kissing the hem of his silk robes.

"Get up, you fool," Bardas said, almost kicking the porter's head away.

"Your highness," the man said, scrambling to his feet. "How have I offended you? It wasn't the lamp oil, was it? I couldn't help it. I swear the merchant swindled me!"

"Shut up. I want to know where the door is."

"What door, your highness?"

"I was told there was an old iron door that leads through the walls, into the palace gardens."

"An iron door, your highness?" The porter looked relieved. "I know where that is."

"Then take me to it!"

Leaving the rest of us standing under the dome, Bardas followed the porter, his robes billowing out behind him. His bodyguard dashed after him. Moments later we heard a tremendous hammering, then a prolonged creaking, then a crash like thunder.

"Of course," Photius said, "it was very wrong of Bardas to kill Theoctistus. I am sure he realises that now. But it must have been very annoying to be told that he could not see Michael. His own nephew! Where is the justice in that? And to be told it by a eunuch, even if he was the Logothete. No wonder he drew his sword and cut Theoctistus down. I am glad I was not there to see it." Photius shuddered. "But the fact is that men of action like Bardas sometimes get carried away. He could hardly be so successful in war if every time he was confronted by an enemy he stopped and thought before striking. And

Theoctistus was an enemy. There is no doubt about that. He was the enemy of moderation and compromise."

"Constantine liked him," I said.

"Constantine likes everybody." Photius allowed a faint smile to displace his earnest frown. "We must not forget," he said, "that Theoctistus was a friend of Ignatius. And Bardas is not."

"Will Bardas depose Ignatius."

"He could." My master's smile grew wider. "He has the power, now that Michael has made him Caesar, and sent Theodora to a nunnery, there is nothing to stop him. But I doubt that he would. Not without a very good reason."

An ordinary man might have abandoned scholarly pursuits when raised up to high office. But Photius did not, even after Bardas appointed him as chief secretary of the imperial chancery. It was an administrative post, but it gave my master free access to the palace, and he quickly became the leader of the moderate faction among the courtiers. Some of them were wary of Bardas. They feared his immorality, ambition and ruthlessness. But they trusted Photius who was a scholar and a gentleman, and not given to risky and unpredictable action.

My master was determined to prove himself the most learned man of the age. Soon after taking up his new post, he began the work he hoped would win him that reputation. It was an annotated catalogue of every book he had ever read, and a few, it must be admitted, which he had not. It included all subjects: theology, both orthodox and heretical, philosophy, history, geography, medicine, the great literature of the ancients, and even a few fanciful romances, as well as dictionaries and manuals of rhetoric. For reasons that I have already explained, the only books Photius missed out were those that everyone knew: Homer, Plato, Aristotle, and the Attic tragedians. My master had a prodigious memory, and could recall the substance of books he had read years earlier. Almost every day, after he had returned from the chancery, and before he dined with his friends, he dictated notes to me, which I wrote out neatly the following day. To make the catalogue more impressive, Photius quickly read new books brought to him by Theodore, or borrowed notes made earlier by Constantine.

The first book we tackled was the commentary on Dionysius the Areopagite that Photius bought from Theodore. It was written by a Greek monk living in Italy, who championed the Dionysian texts, claiming that they were true and genuine.

"The monk is wrong," Photius said. "As monks often are. His error would be obvious to anyone who knew history. Ideas do not occur randomly. Nor are they revealed, once and unchangingly. Ideas develop, one following another. And anyone who has studied the history of ideas, as I have, can place a text in its true era. How could the Areopagite, a contemporary of Saint Paul, know and quote the writings of the Cappadocians? It is impossible, unless he had miraculous knowledge of things to come. The texts are clearly forgeries, and the false Dionysius, whoever he was, must have written them between the time of Saint Basil and our own age. It is a shame, as there is much to commend in his ideas, despite their neoplatonist taint, and the monk's commentary is of some value."

I recorded my master's views, and we went on to other books, sometimes dismissing them in a line or two, sometimes devoting several pages to a summary of their contents. By the time we finished, we had listed and described three hundred books. I do not believe that even Leo the philosopher, who knew more than my master about some things, had read as much as that. Nor did Leo have the will and energy to compile everything he knew into a book, despite his plans to elucidate the Secrets of Love.

Photius arranged to have copies of his catalogue made, so he could give them to all his friends. "Future generations of scholars will be grateful to me," he said. "If there are any scholars in centuries to come. I would not claim, like the Areopagite, to be able to see miraculously into the future. But I sometimes fear that all my work at the university will be in vain, that zealotry will drive out scholarship altogether, that there will be a long dark night when man knows nothing. It is a melancholy thought, but I have done my best. If men remember anything of this age, they will remember my name."

I hope he is right. My master deserves to be remembered, despite his faults and mistakes. And if he is wrong, I hope these memoirs will help preserve his memory. I have not written this book to glorify myself, as readers will surely realise. Without Photius I would be nothing.

Soon after completing the library catalogue, Photius was sent on a mission to the court of the Caliph, and I went with him. We were away for months, endured many privations, and saw many wonders, including the famous city of Baghdad. Despite being recently built, it was already half ruined and partly abandoned, the court having moved elsewhere. As Photius said, the Saracens are an odd people, mistaken about almost everything. It was a relief to return to Constantinople, the greatest city in the world.

I visited Eudocia as soon as I got back, keen to tell her all I had seen in the East, and found that her house was being refurbished. Shutters and grilles swung open, dust billowed from the windows, and rubble and timber lay in heaps in the street outside. The guards, weary of checking the coming and goings of artisans sent from the palace, allowed a mere eunuch like me to pass without question. Eudocia received me in her bedchamber, which was piled high with dusty furniture moved from other parts of the house.

"They might have given me somewhere else to stay," she said, frowning at the disorder that surrounded her. "But Bardas doesn't like me to leave this place."

"Does he give you orders?"

"Michael may be the emperor now, but Bardas is in charge. He runs the palace, and the treasury. He's paying for all this." She sighed. "But I suppose it's not too bad. He lets Michael enjoy himself. He comes to see me more often."

"So you are happy?"

"I suppose so."

"You sound uncertain."

"I thought I might do better."

"You didn't think he would marry you?" I had never mentioned that possibility to her. It would have been too cruel. Nor had I told her about Theodore's prophecy. I wanted her to think she was favoured because she was loved, not because others thought they could use her. "Did Michael say he would marry you."

"No," she said. "But I hoped."

"You've got what you wanted. Or what you told me you wanted."

"Yes, Zeno. And I haven't forgotten that you helped me get it."

Her servants brought a meal, which we ate, sitting side by side on a couch. It was simple fare, some smoked fish, white bread, a salad of stewed vegetables, a little cheese, and a jug of wine, which we drank watered. Only the spiced honey cakes we ate for dessert added a touch of luxury. I wondered whether Eudocia was already nostalgic for the life she had left behind. But who would want to return to Inger's drunken rages and the nieces' constant tormenting? Perhaps she had no control over the food that was served in her house. She was younger than most of her servants, and they would take their orders from Bardas.

While we ate, I told Eudocia of the wonders and mysteries of the East. She listened politely, distracted by the servants, who served that simple meal with far more ceremony than was needed, coming and going with unnecessary vessels and implements, closing shutters, arranging cushions, filling lamps and lighting them.

"Is it true," she said, wiping sweet crumbs from her lips with a pale finger, "that the Saracens have dozens of wives? And do they keep them prisoner?"

"They never leave their quarters."

"I sometimes feel a prisoner here. But I get out sometimes. More often than they know. The guards can be persuaded."

"Saracen women are guarded by fierce eunuchs. I doubt that they could be persuaded."

"You are not fierce," she said, looking straight at me with her clear blue eyes. "You are as soft and pretty as a woman."

"Not as beautiful as you."

"Are Saracen women pretty?"

"So I hear."

"Didn't you see for yourself?"

"Of course not! They wouldn't have let me in."

"But eunuchs can pass anywhere."

"Not there. And not me. I am not mutilated enough for the Saracens' liking. Their women would have thought me almost a man."

"Really?" she said. She let her hand fall softly on my leg. "I think those Saracen women would have liked you, if you had got into their quarters. Could you please a woman, if you wanted to?"

"There are ways, I believe."

"Have you tried?"

How could I tell her that I had pleasured her mother? The thought confused me, made me think that I should not be in Eudocia's chamber, that she ought not to tease me so. Had she learned it from the nieces?

Before I could think of an answer to Eudocia's question, a servant came in to clear up. As she picked up the empty cake dish she leaned over Eudocia and whispered in her ear.

"He's here!" Eudocia said, sitting up straight.

"Who?"

"Michael. You'll have to go."

I looked around the cluttered room. I could see no door but the one I had entered by. "Where?" I asked.

"There!" Eudocia pointed to the corner, where some rolled carpets were propped up against a carved chest. "Hide there."

I dived into the corner, getting myself out of sight just as Michael entered the room. As I crouched behind the chest, my heart pounded so loudly that I feared Michael might hear it. But he, I realised, was too busy talking to be interested in anyone else. In a weak and whining voice, he was complaining, moaning about something that he was being made to do, or not do, by Bardas. As quietly as I could, I sat upright and peered over the top of the chest.

"It's not fair!" he said, slumping onto the couch.

"Of course it isn't," Eudocia said, sitting down beside him. "But you're here now. Let's make the most of it, before you have to go back."

She cupped his face in her hands, then leaned forward and kissed him on the mouth. He squirmed sulkily, sinking deeper into the cushions. "Don't be like that," she said. "Let me make you happy."

Michael started to complain again, and Eudocia silenced him with a kiss. It was my turn to squirm. I had no wish to see the two of them making love. I had tried not to think of that when ferrying Michael to the tavern. I could not bear to think of Eudocia debasing herself.

Filled with a sudden loathing, I longed to leap onto the couch and tear the two of them apart. But Michael was the emperor. He could have me killed if he wanted to. I was only a eunuch and a slave. There would be guards outside, who would strike me down just as ruthlessly as Bardas had struck down Theoctistus.

I subsided feebly behind the chest. I tried to shut my eyes, to ignore what was going on, but I could not. I had to watch, whether I wanted to or not.

Michael remained recumbent, determined to make no effort. Eudocia climbed on top of him, then reached up and unfastened her head-dress, allowing her blonde hair to tumble over her face and shoulders. Michael giggled when her hair brushed his face. Encouraged, Eudocia lifted the skirts of his long tunic and felt beneath them. She tried to hoist the tunic higher, searching for something solid under the silky folds, but Michael resisted. "You first," he said. "Undress for me."

It was a command, but not a very forceful one. I sensed that he was not sure what he could ask for, was afraid of being refused or made a fool of. Eudocia did as she was told, unfastening her shoulder-ties, allowing her softly pleated dress to slip almost silently to the floor. Her naked body glowed like alabaster in the lamplight. Surely Michael would not be able to resist her beauty? I am sure that I could not have resisted it, had I been a whole man. And I am sure I would have made a better job of bedding Eudocia, had she not been like a sister to me. I had seen the act performed often enough, in all its permutations.

But Michael, I suppose, had not. He was not much more than sixteen. He was married, but recently so, and his wife, being noble and respectable, would have known nothing of the arts of love except what he could show her. He lay there looking at Eudocia, drinking in her beauty, gazing at her firm breasts and strong thighs, but doing nothing. Seeing how passive he was, I realised that he could not have shown his wife much. I wondered whether his marriage had even been consummated, and whether, despite Theodore's prophecy, he would produce sons to inherit the empire.

Eudocia knew what had to be done. Whoever instructed her had taught her well. She climbed onto the couch again, kneeling astride Michael. Reaching beneath the folds of his tunic, she found his semi-tumescent member and coaxed it into life with a few deft strokes. When it was firm enough she guided it into her, sinking on top of it until it disappeared beneath her bush of golden hair. Then she began to rock, gently sliding backwards and forwards, moaning softly.

It was over very quickly, as is often the case, I believe, with inexperienced youths. With a jerk and a whimper, Michael slid from under her, almost falling from the couch. After lying still for a moment, he struggled to his feet and rearranged his clothing. Eudocia stayed on the couch, pulling her discarded gown round her radiant nakedness. I thought Michael would leave then, giving me a chance to emerge from my hiding place. But he did not. Instead, he began to pace the room, resuming his complaints about life at the palace and the burdens that were being heaped on him.

It was some time before he left, and when I emerged from my hiding place I found it difficult to look Eudocia in the eye. Had she known Michael was visiting? Did she want me to see them making love? Was she trying to provoke me, to make me love her more?

Games
[AD 857]

Sixteen horses emerged from the cloud of dust that shrouded the far turn. They thundered towards us, four chariots hurtling behind them, their drivers lashing furiously with long whips. There was a sudden jolt as one chariot touched another. Wheel juddered against wheel. Sparks flew from clashing hubs. The two drivers turned on each other, each trying to drive the other away with savage whip-cuts.

The men around me went wild. In an instant, grooms, servants, nobles and barbarians all forgot their rank and became a mob. They jumped with joy, waved their arms, threw hats and scarves into the air. They shouted the names of men and horses, and of four colours: blue, red, green, white. As the horses galloped closer the men surged forward. I hung onto my master, trying to stop him from being dragged onto the track. A torrent of men swirled around us, pushing, shoving, grabbing, stamping. Photius flinched at every touch. I held him firm while the crowd flowed and ebbed.

The two chariots struck each other repeatedly. Bits of rail splintered and broke off. Then, with a tremendous crash, the green chariot overturned and shattered, sending its driver flying into the air. He rose up, twisted, struggled, cried out, but he was entangled. His reins snapped tight, jerking him down to the ground and into the path of the red team. There was nothing the red driver could do. His horses crushed the fallen man, their hoofs trampling his body to a pulp.

The race did not end. The body lay where it was while the remaining teams continued, the drivers lashing their horses as relentlessly as before.

"Isn't this dull," Photius said. He tugged his clothes into place, and looked longingly at the imperial box, unreachable on the far side of the racetrack. In that pillared pavilion there were shady rooms furnished with couches and cushions where spectators might sit in comfort. Every so often the smell of roasting meat wafted towards us, revealing that cooks were toiling in the kitchen, that a feast would soon be ready. But we were not even allowed a cooling drink while the races were running.

"I have never understood the attraction of the Hippodrome," Photius said. "What could be worse than waiting for hours while teams of men and horses gallop endlessly round a dusty racetrack. Who could possibly care which of four muscular oafs goads his team to the finishing line first? The factions are all the same to me."

The race was over. The mob broke up and turned back into men. The winner was congratulated, servants attended to their masters, grooms dealt with the dead man and injured horses.

"Michael and Bardas are enjoying it," I said.

"So I see. Michael is becoming quite overexcited. It is unseemly, especially in front of the barbarians."

The Bulgar ambassador was a short, bow-legged man, much like the nomads I had seen as a boy in Tmutorokan. Unlike his retinue, he was dressed in the Roman style, only an excess of jewellery showing that he was a barbarian and a pagan.

"How can I be expected to do business with a man like that?" Photius said. "His natural savagery is stirred up by all this noise and violence. How can I possibly sound him out? This is hardly the time for a calm discussion about Khan Boris's policy towards the Franks and Slavs, or the likelihood of the Bulgars' conversion. What was Bardas thinking of?"

The racing had been going on for hours. It was a private meeting, held by Bardas to entertain the Bulgar ambassador. The benches, which would normally have held forty thousand spectators, were empty. There was no ceremony, and none of the clowns, jugglers, acrobats, dwarfs, or wild animals that would have filled the intervals in a public meeting. The day was devoted solely to racing, and to the expert appraisal of men and horseflesh. Time after time, horses thundered down the straight, veered round the great curve at the far end of the track, then galloped back to the start. Whether the race was a sprint, or went on for many laps, the excitement did not abate, except for Photius, who looked increasingly desperate as the afternoon wore on. His attention was drawn to the antique monuments that lined the centre of the track, stretching from one turning post to the other.

"Look," he said. "The Colossus of Constantine, the Serpentine Column that was brought from Delos, the statue of Hercules, Egyptian obelisks aplenty, ancient statues salvaged from all over the empire. It's a history lesson in stone and bronze. But what do we do? We race horses around it!"

Before I could think of an answer, Bardas came over to us, mopping his brow with a sky-blue silk scarf. I did not feel comfortable when he was near me. He was a murderer, had killed a eunuch, and was easily provoked to rage. And I had conspired against him with Theodore.

"Will you make a bet?" Bardas said, smiling at my master.

"I am not much of a judge," Photius said. "I have already lost several gold pieces."

"Surely you'll bet this time. Michael will race for the Blues."

"In person?"

"Of course. I'm backing him. Surely you will wager something on the Greens?"

Photius sighed, agreed, and watched while Michael was led to his chariot by a crowd of cheering supporters.

"What folly!" Photius muttered. "I can't see how this sort of thing is going to improve Michael's character. I know Bardas wants to make a man of him, as he puts it. But driving a chariot is slaves' work, or always used to be. In any case it is ignoble. Charioteers may be feted like heroes, but history does not judge performer-emperors kindly. Elagabalus drove chariots. Nero acted and sang. Commodus fought as a gladiator. Remember what happened to them?" I said nothing, but Photius leaned towards me and spoke almost in a whisper. "All were assassinated."

I, too, had read the histories in my master's library. "Those emperors," I said. "Nero, Commodus and Elagabalus. They had something else in common. Something that made them unpopular with the Senate and army. They all loved men at least as much as they loved women."

"You are right," Photius said. "Michael has a mistress as well as a wife, so perhaps things are not so bad. The emperors who ruled in Rome were a depraved lot. There must be something in the air of that city, something enervating, that inclines men to vice. How much better off we are since the empire has been governed from Constantinople."

While Michael raced, Photius inspected the racetrack's monuments even more earnestly than before. I was no more interested in the races than my master, but I think he underestimated Michael. He handled his team well. They ran straight, turned well, did not bolt or crash, and I saw no signs that the other drivers had let him win. The boy was brave, and had acquired a skill which, if ignoble, was at least manly. He had escaped from the influence of his mother, and made himself popular with other men, just as Bardas had hoped. If he carried out his ceremonial duties properly and led the army successfully, he would be popular with the people. As long as there were no public displays of Michael's charioteering, the social order would not be threatened.

The meeting had reached its climax with Michael's victory. Photius paid his gambling debts and looked longingly at the imperial box, where servants were busy setting out tables. The crowd began to break up, but the Bulgar ambassador, angry at having lost money by backing the Greens, proposed a further contest. He summoned a slave from his entourage, and, boasting loudly in the barbarian manner, claimed that he was a champion wrestler who had never been defeated. The slave was huge, well over six feet tall, with arms as fat as Thracian hams, and an ugly, misshapen face that looked as though it had been pummelled by a butcher to make it tender. He took his tunic off and swaggered about on the dusty track, puffing out his scarred and tattooed chest, flexing his muscles. I could see that the Bulgar giant would be hard to beat. Even Inger might not have defeated him, and he was the toughest fighter I knew.

Suddenly, Photius was interested. "This cannot be allowed," he said. "We cannot let a pagan barbarian defeat us merely by boasting. Someone must fight the Bulgar."

The tavern was far away, and Inger was almost certainly too drunk to fight. In any case, honour required that the contest was won by a Roman rather than another barbarian. The courtiers huddled together, anxiously suggesting names, then rejecting them. Bardas looked angry. Michael looked foolish. The Bulgar ambassador looked triumphant.

Then a nobleman named Theophilus stepped forward. He was a distant relative of Bardas, and well known at court, though he was sometimes laughed at for his small size and fussy way of dressing. "Your highness," he said, in a weak, quavering voice. "I have a man who will fight the Bulgar."

"Who?" Bardas asked.

"My groom."

"Your groom? Not one of those handsome fellows who always follow you around? We all know about the beauty of your menservants." Bardas laughed. "They may look the part, but I doubt if any of them could fight."

Theophilus held his head up high, but he still barely reached Bardas's shoulders. "I can assure you, your highness, that my man Basil will fight that Bulgar, and beat him."

"You are a little fellow, but you make big boasts. Let us see this man of yours."

When Basil was brought from the crowd he proved to be very handsome, with a broad, regular face, brown eyes, chestnut coloured hair, and a smooth, unblemished, golden skin. He was in his early twenties, a few years younger than I was. When he stripped off his tunic he showed a broad chest and a fine set of muscles. But he was not nearly as big as the Bulgar, and if he dared to fight him it was obvious that he would be crushed. Bardas looked disappointed, almost contemptuous. But no other contenders came forward.

"Just give the word, your highness," Theophilus said. "And Basil will fight for the empire."

"Very well," Bardas said, coldly. "Let him fight."

Basil smiled, impudently looking directly at Michael. The

young emperor was not put out. On the contrary, his face filled with a slavish expression that reminded me of the time he had first seen Eudocia. And he was not the only one. When Basil smiled, almost everyone present was entranced. Nobles, courtiers, senators, servants, slaves and grooms, all except Bardas gazed at him with open admiration. As the sun beat down on his golden skin he was surrounded by a nimbus, like those that indicate saintliness in icons. It was not holiness that shone from him, but strength, assurance and manliness. Basil was an unspoken reproach to me. He was everything I was not.

If only Basil's nature had been as admirable as his person. How different my story would be! But who could have known that a mere manservant would achieve so much? His fate convinces me that we are not watched over by one Almighty God, but by a horde of lesser gods. And there are demons too, sometimes in the form of men, tempting us, leading us astray, persuading us that what we desire is not so wrong, that the harm we do is no harm at all, but indistinguishable from good. How else can we account for the failure of virtue to triumph, and the constant reversals that thwart our best intentions?

Servants came from the imperial box and sprinkled water over a section of the racetrack to lay the dust. After a brief but arcane discussion between Bardas and the ambassador, the two fighters squared up, bare-chested, wearing tight trousers and wide belts. As soon as the signal was given, the Bulgar lurched forward. He slammed into Basil, driving him backwards with his fat belly. Basil staggered, stumbled, and almost fell. There was a cheer from the Bulgars while he struggled to regain his balance. When the giant turned to acknowledge the cheer, Basil struck. He lunged, twisted, locked both hands together and slammed his elbow into the Bulgar's chest, hitting him just below the ribs. The blow would have felled a normal man, but the Bulgar giant merely stepped back and looked down at his opponent, shaking his head with mock puzzlement.

The two men advanced again, and gripped each other's

belts. They stood, belly to belly, grimacing like madmen, straining every muscle, each trying to heave the other off the ground. It was obvious that, however strong he was, Basil could not succeed. Yet he played with the Bulgar, bending and twisting, feinting and retreating, forcing him to waste his strength. Veins twitched, and sinews stood out like cables. Sweat streamed off the two men, making their muscles glisten, soaking into their trousers, sticking thin cloth to firm buttocks and tensed thighs. Michael, Bardas, the ambassador and his retinue, all stood silently, taking in every detail of the fight. Even Photius watched with attention.

It seemed the bout would go on for ever, and that neither man could win. The Bulgar was too strong and Basil was too clever. Bardas looked tense. Even a draw would disgrace the empire. And if Basil lost, the ambassador would go back to his Khan saying that the Romans were weaklings and could easily be beaten. Some of the grooms and servants fumbled inside their tunics, touching talismans and muttering imprecations. The ambassador's men answered with pagan incantations of their own. The wrestling match was turning into a battle between faiths. I heard a voice beside me, turned to look at Photius, and saw that he was muttering a prayer. I had never heard him do that before. He knew everything there was to know about the orthodox faith, but seldom practised it.

Suddenly, the Bulgar leapt back from Basil and ducked down to scoop up a handful of wet dirt. That was how the god of the Bulgars had created the world, from a handful of mud. But the pagan wrestler was intent on destruction, not creation. He flung the dirt at Basil, aiming at his eyes. But Basil was too quick. He dodged, dashed forward and, before the Bulgar was up, grabbed him by the neck. He used both hands, pressing his thumbs deeply into the Bulgar's throat, gripping his fat nape with hooked fingers. The Bulgar was caught half crouching, unable to rise. He clutched feebly at Basil's hands, then his arms went slack, falling uselessly to his sides. His eyes bulged, and flecks of foam formed around his lips. His legs buckled and he dropped to his knees. We saw then that we had underestimated Basil. He was immensely strong. The huge Bulgar hung in his grip as limply as a child's doll.

Basil looked up and entranced the crowd with another of his broad smiles. He adjusted his grasp slightly, allowing the Bulgar to struggle up from his knees. Then, with an ease I would have thought impossible had I not seen it myself, he crouched, hoisted the Bulgar across his shoulders and flung him to the ground.

The crowd surged forward, nobles and servants mingling without ceremony. Basil was lifted into the air by his fellow grooms, who carried him round the Hippodrome on their shoulders, shouting and chanting as they went. He was not just the winner of the bout, or even the hero of the day. He was the defender of the empire's honour, and of its faith. The Bulgar ambassador was speechless with anger, and could only stare incredulously at his fallen champion. When the grooms staggered back to the starting line Basil was lowered to the ground and stood proudly before the young emperor.

"Theophilus!" Michael said. "I want this man for my stables. How much do you want for him? Name your price."

"Your majesty," Theophilus said, his voice barely audible above the exultant chatter of the crowd, "it would be an honour to present him to you. I beg of you, consider him yours."

When the nobles went into the imperial box to dine, Basil went with them, and was given a place of honour and supplied with the finest food and wine. The Bulgar ambassador sulked throughout the feast, refused to talk to Photius, returned to his country as quickly as possible, and soon afterwards persuaded Khan Boris to sign a treaty with the Franks.

The next time I visited Eudocia she was dressed in a simple, unglamorous woollen gown. Her golden hair was covered by a plain veil. She looked as though she was in mourning.

"Michael won't come to see me," she said, when she had dismissed her maidservant.

"I know he cannot see you as often as you would like," I said. "Now that he is married."

"Michael doesn't love his wife. He never goes to her bedchamber."

"He has to keep up appearances."

"He didn't stop coming to see me after the wedding. But he's stopped now."

"I expect he is in training. Bardas is planning an expedition against the Paulicians. Michael will have to play his part."

Eudocia tugged at her veil, twisting it between her fingers. "I know what Michael is up to," she said. "He is learning to wrestle."

"It is good training for a soldier, or so I believe."

Eudocia's blue eyes met mine. I felt guilty, yet my excuses and evasions were intended to protect her feelings.

"He is being taught by a groom," she said.

"You know about him?"

"Basil? Of course I do. Now, tell me what you know."

I had to think quite carefully about what to tell Eudocia. I did not want to alarm her, so I described what everyone knew, the wrestling bout in the Hippodrome.

"They say this Basil is an illiterate peasant," she said.

I did not remind her that until quite recently she had been serving in a tavern. "Very likely. But he is a good wrestler, and I am sure Michael will learn something useful from him."

"Do you know they wrestle naked?" she said. I looked around anxiously, wondering whether anyone was listening. Ridiculing the emperor was not wise. "You don't need to worry about the servants," she said. "They are loyal to me, and they tell me things. That's how I find out what is going on at court."

"They may exaggerate, or mistake gossip for the truth."

"They were quite clear about the naked wrestling."

"That is the antique way," I said. "The Spartans did all their sports naked."

Eudocia looked at me sadly. "Is that what it says in those old books you read?"

"Yes."

"There are all sorts of rumours about this Basil. They say

that he wasn't just Theophilus's groom, that he was a special friend."

"Sometimes servants become friends. I like to think that I am more than just a servant to Photius."

"They say that before Basil met Theophilus, he was very friendly with another man, a priest called Nicholas, who gave him money."

I had heard those rumours too. Nicholas was supposed to have found Basil sleeping rough in the porch of a church, after he had walked to Constantinople intent on making his fortune. The priest was impressed by the peasant's beauty, and took him into his house. But I saw no reason to worry Eudocia with more details. "Priests can be generous," I said.

"Basil had another friend as well. A man called John, the son of a rich widow. The widow gave Basil money, and John and Basil swore vows of eternal friendship."

"There is nothing wrong with friendship."

"You don't understand, do you? Michael is wrestling naked with a man who sells his friendship, who has been almost a wife to other men."

I thought of examples of great male friendships from history and literature. There are many of them, but I knew they would not impress Eudocia. Then I remembered another bit of gossip. "I happen to know that Basil has a wife. A peasant girl from Macedonia."

"I know about her," Eudocia said. "She's called Maria. And she's pregnant. And Basil has abandoned her." She burst into tears, and I had to take her in my arms and comfort her, feeling the unfamiliar softness of trembling female flesh. "Basil is going to take Michael away from me," she sobbed. "I'll be sent back to the tavern."

As I walked away, wandering the narrow streets north of the palace, I wondered. Was Eudocia right? Would she be stripped of her fine clothes and jewels, sent away from her comfortable house? I could not bear to think of her washing pots, serving wine, living in squalor again.

Bardas paid Eudocia's allowance, and he did it as much to

spite his sister as to keep Michael occupied. But Theodora was powerless, confined to her quarters. Bardas had no further need to spite her. And if Michael really had tired of Eudocia, Bardas might well end his support for her. But it might be worse than that. Eudocia knew the secrets of the imperial family. And Bardas was a murderer.

I had let Eudocia down, failed to protect her, failed even to tell her the truth. I almost turned back and rushed to her house again. Yet what could I have said to her?

The rumours were true. Michael and Basil had wrestled naked. And it was partly my fault.

Photius, despite his boredom at the race meeting, had seen an opportunity to flatter the young emperor, and had compiled for him a selection of equestrian literature. Naturally, he had left the actual copying to me, and I did much of the selecting too, finding accounts of horse-taming, racing and charioteering, all drawn from the antique books in my master's library. The work was not difficult, as most of the passages were drawn from Homer, who is, after all, the only poet youths like Michael can be expected to have heard of. When the book was finished and Photius had added a dedication in his own hand, he sent me to deliver it.

Michael was already so enthusiastic about racing that anyone wishing to do business with him was usually obliged to look, not in the palace, but in the warren of stables, cages, workshops, tackle rooms, feed stores, mews, and servants' hovels, that clustered round the Hippodrome. My master's name got me past the guards and into a straw-strewn exercise yard where I found Michael and his friends. I had learned a few passages off by heart, and was ready, if asked, to recite the description of the chariot races that Achilles staged at the funeral of Patroclus. However, it was obvious that the emperor was not in the mood for listening to poetry.

I arrived just as Basil had slipped off his tunic and was standing in the centre of a circle of young men. Basil had been impressive when he faced the Bulgar. He was even more so surrounded by youths of Michael's age. Though he was a peasant and they were mostly nobles, Michael's friends were in awe of Basil. They watched admiringly while he went through an athletic routine, bending and stretching, flexing and rippling his muscles. When he finished, Basil offered to fight any of them.

There was a lot of boasting and bantering, but no one came forward. Michael's friends urged him to offer a prize, and something for the loser, to make a beating worthwhile. One of them, a fat youth called Gryllus, plucked at Michael's sleeve and whispered in his ear.

"I will do better than offer a prize," Michael said, stepping into the circle. "I will fight Basil myself."

His friends cheered, sycophantically predicting that he would win easily. Some of the richer ones made large bets, willing to lose money to flatter their emperor. I stood at the fringes of the circle, clutching the book, thinking that I ought to have included in it a later episode from Patroclus's funeral games, a passage describing a wrestling match between Odysseus and Ajax. Those two heroes fought to a draw, an unlikely outcome in Basil and Michael's case.

Michael allowed his tunic to be removed, and stood in his drawers while a servant anointed his skin with perfumed oil. Basil, too, was oiled, and the pair were about to square up when Gryllus spoke again. "Wait!" he said. "What about the rules?"

"Rules?" Michael looked puzzled.

"Your majesty cannot fight by the same rules as Bulgars and peasants," Gryllus said. "You must fight by the noble rules of the ancients."

Michael looked doubtful. "Must I?"

A crafty smile spread across Gryllus's fat face, making him look quite swinish. "Yes. You must fight by Spartan rules. They are the most noble."

"Yes," Michael said. "I must only fight by noble rules. How did the Spartans wrestle?"

"Naked."

Some of the onlookers laughed. Michael's face went red. I thought that would be the end of Gryllus's joke. But

143

Michael's expression changed, becoming oddly intense. "Is that true?" he asked.

"Of course, your majesty. Ask anyone." Gryllus surveyed the circle of onlookers, some of whom tried to shuffle out of the way. He saw me. "You!" he said. "The eunuch. I know you. You're a scholar, aren't you?"

"Of a sort."

"You're carrying a book. That makes you a scholar. Now, tell us, did the Spartans wrestle naked?"

I clutched the book tightly, hoping Gryllus would not ask me what it was about. "I believe so," I said.

Gryllus looked triumphant. "There!" he said. "The scholar believes it, so it must be true. The Spartans wrestled naked."

A great cheer went up. I crept backwards over the straw-strewn ground, trying to make myself inconspicuous. Michael untied his drawers and stepped out of them. Basil followed his example.

Michael was not bad looking. It was his foolish expression and weak deportment that let him down. When he stood up straight and looked serious he was quite handsome. But Basil easily outshone him. He was a few years older than the emperor, and a good six inches taller. His shoulders were broader, his neck thicker, his muscles firmer, his expression, despite his peasant origins, more noble.

Gryllus, appointing himself referee, gave the order and the bout began. It was almost gentle at first. The pair circled each other like rustic dancers, shaking their arms and stamping their feet. A tactful man would have let the emperor win, but Basil was not tactful. Proud of his strength, he began to wrestle in earnest, easily gripping Michael and pulling him this way and that, encircling him with his huge arms, lifting him effort-lessly from the ground. Even so, Basil did not fight as grimly as he did with the Bulgar. Each time Basil overpowered Michael he stepped back, allowing his opponent to recover. Michael looked as though he was enjoying the fight, even though he lost every round.

The onlookers shouted advice and encouragement, jangled their purses, reminded Michael that they had money riding on the result. He stepped forward calmly, then lunged at Basil more fiercely than he had before. He got in a blow to Basil's shin before Basil enclosed him in a final embrace. They swayed and staggered, then fell to the ground. Michael lay face down, his chest heaving. Basil lay on top, twisting the emperor's arm. Michael soon yielded, and the two of them struggled to their feet, naked and sweating, covered with dust and straw. Michael grinned, apparently happy to have been defeated by Basil, even in front of his friends. Basil's expression was harder to make out. He was holding back his feelings. Servants rushed forward with Michael's clothes. But in the brief moment before he was dressed, I saw that Michael had become aroused. His penis, swollen and heavily veined, stood out from his body like a brass gnomon. Not for the first time, I wondered what it must be like to be attached to such an unruly member. Can an uncut man be truly in command of himself? I think not. The penis is a tail that wags the dog.

There was no doubt about it. Michael was aroused by the touch of another man's flesh. That was the truth I dared not tell Eudocia, the truth that threatened her happiness, and mine.

It was Ignatius, my master's zealot enemy, who saved the situation by distracting Bardas from Michael's antics. Quite unexpectedly, and for no obvious reason, the desiccated old eunuch got into the pulpit of Hagia Sophia and denounced Bardas for committing adultery with his daughter-in-law. Of course, the accusation was justified, but it was hardly politic. Soon afterwards, Bardas discovered a plot against himself, accusing his sister Theodora of trying to poison him. Michael condemned his mother to be tonsured and sent to a nunnery, but Ignatius refused to take part in the humiliation and banishment of his greatest ally. Bardas deposed Ignatius and sent him into exile. He then invited my master to become the next patriarch.

"It's the last thing I want," Photius said. "I am a scholar not a churchman. I have devoted my life to books and learning, not to acquiring power. Choose someone else, please!"

Power
[AD 858]

"It was very moving," Photius said, when he came back from the cathedral on the evening of Christmas day. "They dressed me in the finest vestments, but my robes were nothing to what Michael wore. The imperial costume is ancient in origin, and every garment has a meaning, every thread and jewel a significance. It is a history lesson in silk and gemstones!"

"I wish I had been there," I said. And I meant it, too. My master's sudden elevation to supreme ecclesiastical power had made me think about God. I did not know whether He was one or many. Perhaps He merely seemed to be one. After all, a multitude can act as one when it coalesces into a mob. That would account for the randomness of God's acts. It was very odd of God to ignore the sins of Bardas, to cast down the puritanical Ignatius and raise up Photius, who had mocked Him with false doctrine. It was like the behaviour of the Hippodrome crowd, who cheer a favourite to victory, but abandon him when he loses. Whatever the truth about God, my master would be serving Him, and I would have liked to be in His house and watch the ceremony.

"I am sorry Zeno, but it was not possible. Things have changed. From now on I must observe protocol and perform all ceremonies punctiliously. No irregularities can be permitted. Speaking of which, I was telling you about Michael. He was very impressive. In purple and gold, his flesh almost invisible behind a mass of silks and jewels, he looked more than human. He shimmered as though filled with unearthly light. There was something sun-like about him, a hint of the divine. And that is fitting. He is God's representative on earth. He will rule the empire, just as I will rule the Church. And I am sure he will rule it well. True, he is only a youth. How old is he now?"

"He is eighteen," I said.

"That is an advantage, especially when he has such good

advisors. He is sure to turn out well if he continues to listen to Bardas. And to his new patriarch. I hope he will listen to me too."

"I am sure he will."

"I feel transformed," Photius said. "It has been an ordeal, these last few days, though not an unpleasant one. To think that I was a layman only a week ago! But there was something beautiful about the ceremony. Each day a new stage of ordination. I felt like a soul ascending the levels of enlightenment. And today I reached the highest stage of all."

Reclining on a couch in his beloved library, still wearing the underlayers of his patriarchal vestments, Photius went on, telling me how he felt, and what each stage of the ordination meant to him, citing the false Dionysius, who described in Platonic terms the approach of Man's soul to the Divine. When he finished doing that, he repeated and elaborated the hopes he had for Michael. According to my master, the empire was entering a Golden Age when it would be governed by the Wise, the Good, and the Brave.

I sat at his feet and let him talk on, not believing all he said, but knowing that it was important to listen. Eventually he stopped talking about himself and said that he had an announcement to make.

"In view of the great honour that has been thrust upon me," he said, "I have decided to free you."

"Free me? But where will I go?" The thought of being thrown out horrified me. I had grown used to the comforts of my master's house, and had no wish to go back to my old life, even if such a thing were possible.

"Nowhere," he said. "I am not going to send you away. On the contrary, you are to stay here in this house, and work for me, but as a free man."

I was suspicious. "Why?" I asked.

"Because my circumstances have changed. As patriarch, there will be places I cannot go to. And things I cannot do or say. You must be my eyes and ears. And my mouth."

"I already act as your eyes, ears and mouth. Why do you want to free me?"

Photius looked disappointed. "Must I explain everything? It is, as I have already told you, a gesture of magnanimity. One that becomes my new rank. It is in accordance with the view, expressed by some but not accepted by all, that priests ought not to own slaves. But I must confess that freeing you may bring me some advantage. When you are no longer my slave, no one will associate your activities with me. You can act freely, in any part of the city, or the empire, for that matter."

I remembered a phrase Constantine had used when describing the lesser god of the Bulgars. That pagan deity, who shaped the world from a handful of mud, was not so much a devil, Constantine had said, but more of a workman employed to do a dirty job by a fastidious master. Was I to be such a workman? What tasks would Photius find for me? He had enemies. The zealots were still strong, even though Ignatius was exiled. No doubt others would turn against my master when they saw what power he wielded. But what choice did I have? The next day my master summoned a notary and went through the ceremony, ending my state of slavery, which had begun almost twenty years earlier.

Eudocia was cheered by my new status, and by the realisation that Michael had not abandoned her. He spent time with Basil, at the Hippodrome, or in the country, hawking and hunting. But he visited Eudocia often enough to keep her happy, and Bardas carried on paying for her to live in the house near the palace.

"You are a very important person now," she said, kissing me on the cheek. She sat me beside her on a silk-draped couch, and poured us sweet wine from a Syrian glass jug.

"No," I said. "Just a free man."

"You are a friend of Photius."

"I'd like to think so."

"Well, he's important, isn't he? Now he's patriarch he comes next after Michael."

"And Bardas."

"He's still very important, and you're his friend, so that makes you important too."

148

"Perhaps."

"Don't be so modest," she said, giving me another kiss.

Inwardly, I was not so modest. I had not done so badly for a boy from Tmutorokan. In fact, I had an enviable life. As well as being free, and the confidant of Photius, I lived in comfort, knew some of the wisest scholars and philosophers, and had read as much as any of them. And I was still not yet thirty. Unlike some eunuchs, I had achieved all that without being obliged to submit to what Photius called unnatural lust. But I knew that there would be a price to pay, and I did not want Eudocia to think me proud.

"We've got what we wanted, haven't we?" she said. "I'm living like a lady, and you're living like a gentleman."

"It's true, I live in a fine house. I have the run of it while Photius is at his official residence. But I have to keep an eye on everything, to look after the library, hold the keys to the store-rooms and cupboards, and make sure the servants don't take any liberties."

"You don't like them, do you?"

"The servants? No. They beat me once, when I first went to the house."

Eudocia took me in her arms and hugged me. "You poor thing," she said. "I can't bear to think of them being nasty to you.

"I won't let it happen again."

"If they give you any trouble, you come to me and I'll tell you what to do. I've got my servants under control."

"I will."

"You will still come to me now that you are free?"

"Of course I will. I'll come more often."

"I mean it," she said, giving me another hug. She was very strong. I could imagine her giving her servants a beating if they displeased her. "I'll pine away if you don't."

"I'll never desert you," I said.

"Shall we drink to that? To never deserting each other?" She raised her cup, and I raised mine. "Skoal!" she said, and we drank.

★

As I came and went, I was beset, not by my master's enemies, but by would-be friends, who hung about the house at all hours.

"Who are those men?" Theodore asked, after struggling through the crowd. "I am sure they did not come here to admire the statues in the courtyard, or the flowering shrubs. It is hardly the time of year for that."

"They wanted to ask me some questions."

"And favours, I daresay."

"Perhaps."

"Did they offer you money?"

"No."

"Really? Well, they will. You can expect it now that Photius has been elevated. All sorts of men will come here asking you for favours. They will want a word in your master's ear, a petition pushed to the top of the pile, advancement for a relative, things of that sort."

"I couldn't help them. I told them that."

"They will be back with bribes."

"I wouldn't take their money."

"Very laudable. But if I were you, I'd take whatever was going. You don't have to do what they ask. How would they ever know? But if you did help them out, you could make a fortune."

"I will not betray my master," I said. And I meant it. What did I have to gain from it but a few grubby coins?

I have no ambition. What can a eunuch hope for? My kind can only serve others and bask in reflected glory. Photius had achieved the highest office possible. All I had to do was serve my master while enjoying the comforts his elevation ensured.

Or so I thought, until I was summoned to the palace.

I had often collected Michael from the gate in the sea walls, but I could not claim to know the palace well. It is quite possible that no one did, not even the eunuchs who ran it. The palace is not a single structure, but a collection of reception rooms, pavilions, barracks, stables, workshops, guard-houses, offices, storerooms and churches, as well as the imperial family's living quarters, all enclosed by high walls that run down to the Marmora shore. To the west is the Hippodrome, a massive bulwark against the tumult of the city. To the north is the Senate, the cathedral of Hagia Sophia, and the residence and offices of the patriarch. The senators and nobles, attracted to the palace like ants to honey, all try to live as close as possible to that quarter.

The palace is a city within a city, parts of it centuries old, its sloping site well planted with trees and gardens, cooled by pools and fountains, and decorated with ancient statues and columns. If there was ever a plan, it had long been abandoned. Each emperor, if he reigned for long enough, added something, clearing away what was obsolete or unfashionable, squeezing new buildings into whatever space was available. Michael's father had built several reception halls, the grandest of which housed the mechanical wonders designed by Leo the philosopher. To impress barbarian ambassadors, Leo had devised roaring lions, singing birds, and a throne that rose from the floor to the ceiling in an instant, all made of gold and propelled by mechanisms found in ancient philosophical books. Having seen Leo's steam-driven sphere revolving as though by magic, I could well imagine the awe of an ignorant foreigner faced with moving statues.

The palace was not all wonders and treasures. Beneath the slopes and terraces are cellars, cisterns, tunnels and dungeons, some of them, it is rumoured, walled up and forgotten. But I will tell of them when the time comes.

The eunuchs were waiting for me in one of the lesser reception rooms, in a part of the palace that had fallen out of favour with the imperial family since the alterations and improvements made by Theophilus. Cyril, who had summoned me, led me through the first of the triple doors.

"You know who I am?" he said, looping his arm through mine. His grey hair was dyed a bluish colour and swept up over his head like a pigeon's wings. His face was dusted with white powder, and there was something unnatural about the redness of his lips and cheeks.

"The chief eunuch?"

Cyril's jowls quivered as he laughed at my answer. "No," he said. "The chief eunuch is quite another person, if indeed anyone can claim that title. You won't see him here. I am the chief of the guild of palace eunuchs. Not the same thing at all."

He continued to chuckle as he led me through the last door into the hall. Its marble walls were hung with silks and tapestries, some of them embroidered with flowers and foliage, others depicting indecent scenes from ancient myths. The space beneath the central dome was furnished with couches arranged in the customary semicircle. The eunuchs evidently aped their masters in their antique style of banqueting.

"You look very drab," Cyril said, running a plump finger down the front of my best tunic. "We'll have to do something about this."

I looked around the hall. The other eunuchs wore jewelled collars that glittered in the lamplight, and elaborate costumes of a type more appropriate to women than to men. But I might have expected that. Eunuchs, as I had helped Leo to prove, are neither one thing nor the other.

"You must have a robe of honour," Cyril said, gently leading me into a side chamber. A boy appeared and began to take off my coat and tunic.

"You're a pretty young thing, aren't you?" Cyril said.

I flatter myself that I was rather good looking as a youth. Eudocia used to say that I was as pretty as a woman. In fact, I believe I am still quite handsome, despite the great age I have reached. I have avoided the usual curses of the eunuch's condition. I am not one of those gross, swollen eunuchs, like Cyril, or one of the dried-up, wizened ones like Ignatius. Nor has my skin collapsed into a mass of creases like an empty sack. However, if my face has retained a youthful softness, it has been said that my nose is a little sharp, a tendency that has been accentuated by age. Seldom troubling to view my face in a mirror, I cannot tell.

Whatever the truth about my appearance, I did not care to have it commented on by Cyril, still less to have him staring at me while I undressed. He looked at me for a little longer, then clapped his hands, causing another boy to arrive with a bundle of rustling silk. He unfolded a court robe and draped it around me.

"That's better," Cyril said, tucking and tying some of the looser bits of my costume. His voice was soft, and gently mocking. "You're one of us now."

Cyril led me to the central couch. I sat perched on the edge, not sure what to do. I had observed such banquets before, though on a smaller scale. But I had been a servant then, a server of wine and overhearer of gossip.

"Relax," he said, patting the space beside him. "Recline. And why not? We are the masters here." He gave another of his jowl-quivering chuckles. "We are the masters everywhere, though we don't always like it to be known. Better to let the beards think that they are in charge."

Turning his attention from me, Cyril made a short speech of welcome, reminding the guests of their duty to enjoy themselves. Then he clapped his hands, signalling that the feast was to begin. The servants were muscular young men dressed in short tunics like charioteers, their waists and shoulders belted with leather straps. They displayed a good deal of bare flesh, sun-bronzed and slick with oil. Cyril watched them eagerly as they bustled between the couches, bending low to serve the food, stretching out to fill the gleaming goblets that stood before us on little tables.

"Have some oysters," Cyril said, when he had made sure my goblet was full. A servant stepped forward with a heavily loaded dish, which he balanced dextrously while holding an oyster up to my mouth. He tipped it, I swallowed the slippery mass, and another man stepped forward with a napkin to dab my mouth. Clearly, I was an honoured guest.

Summer oysters have a peculiar flavour, a rich, salty creaminess that is not to everyone's taste. It is, as Leo the philosopher once explained to me, a consequence of the breeding season, a time when their shells are full of male and female seed, which combine and grow into new oysters. Are female oysters inferior to the males? Or are all such creatures hermaphrodites? I do not know. But I ate my allocation of oysters, allowing their mingled seed to enter and mingle with my flesh.

A servant brought me some crisply fried sea-anemones, which were popped into my mouth one by one. I felt like a nestling bird being fed by its mother. A bowl of pickled sea cucumbers was placed at my side as a relish, and I was allowed unaided to eat from a dish of sliced bulls' testicles sauced with honey, almonds and fermented fish. The best I can say about them is that they were more edible than the peppered sows' vulvas I ate on another occasion.

After that, there were spiced cakes, fried sweetbreads, coddled eggs, cockscombs in honey, whitebait, bloated goose-livers, glistening sausages, truffled faggots, green-boned garfish, plump squabs, and many other dishes, all served with wines finer than any I had ever tasted. I realised then that I was an amateur at dealing with wine merchants. I had secured for Photius better wines than he had had before, but none as good as those the court eunuchs drank.

All around me, men sliced, spooned, poured and served, while eunuchs licked, sucked, chewed, and swallowed, engulfing dish after dish, filling themselves with every sort of flesh. While I struggled to keep up with them, Cyril looked on approvingly, though not without stuffing himself with far more food than I could ever have managed. He was particularly keen on the bulls' testicles, despite their pungent sauce, and had the servants bring him several helpings.

"Do have a figpecker," Cyril said, offering me the dish of small roasted birds himself. When I hesitated he popped one into his mouth and crunched it up whole, brushing the charred feet from his chin with fluttering fingers. "The liquefied innards make a delicious sauce," he said, licking his greasy lips. "What fragile creatures they are. Rather like some of us. Not me, of course." He patted his plump silk-clad belly. "I am far from fragile." He reached out and took my hand, pressing his slippery fingers against mine. "I am thinking of you," he said, twisting round clumsily on the couch so that he could look at me directly. "You could easily be swallowed up whole. If you are not careful."

There was a pause while some of the dishes were taken away and servants went round again with napkins and finger-bowls. Then the main course was brought in. It was a huge pie on a silver tray so big that it took four men to carry it. When its crisp golden pastry was broken open, to much applause, its contents were revealed to be a mixture of sows' wombs and udders, stewed in an almond and saffron sauce. I could hardly eat another thing, but I nibbled politely at some sauced crust while Cyril swallowed pie and filling like the all-devouring giant of Inger's stories. Unlike the giant Logi, Cyril was anything but fiery in his nature. On the contrary, he was cold and clammy, loose and sack-like, little more than a soft stomach waiting to be filled. Most of the other eunuchs were just as greedy, and hardly any of the pie was left for the servants. But even that was not the end of the feasting, as innumerable trays of sweet and fancy dishes circulated the room, accompanied by even sweeter wines.

"Now, Zeno," Cyril said, nibbling at a sugared fig. "There are some things I must say to you, and I hope you will listen very carefully. It is important that we all see eye to eye about things. We can have no dissenters. Nor can we have people acting on their own behalf, doing things without our knowledge or consent. And we can't have eunuchs talking, giving away our secrets. Our comfortable arrangements would crumble if men like Bardas understood too much of what goes on. You agree with us, don't you?"

I nodded, in a manner that I hoped was non-committal.

"I knew you would understand," Cyril said. "That is why we brought you here, to explain certain matters. Your master, for instance."

"He is no longer my master," I said. "Photius has freed me,"

"Of course. The beards often try that trick. But have you freed him? That is the question. You can't break the bond between a beard and his eunuch just by mumbling a few words over the prayer book. The bond works both ways. Because of all the secrets he knows, a servant has a hold over his master. And it would be foolish to waste such a hold. Don't you agree?"

I agreed, though I did not intend to use whatever influence I had over Photius for Cyril's benefit.

Cyril clapped his hands, indicating that the banquet was over. The servants took away what remained of the food. Replete, we lay back while a muscular young man wiped our faces and hands. After another servant had reapplied powder and colour to his face, Cyril turned to me and spoke with an unexpectedly hostile tone.

"We know what you've been up to," he said. "Interfering in affairs of state that are not your business at all. You even had a hand in the murder of Theoctistus."

"That was Bardas. It had nothing to do with me."

"Really? You recklessly introduced our young emperor to that girl, distracting his attention while Bardas plotted to creep back into the palace. The first thing he did was to kill Theoctistus. Yet you say you had no hand in the death of the most senior of all the eunuchs."

Cyril's accusations were alarming. I had not dreamt that anyone watched me so closely. Yet there were things he did not seem to know. He had not mentioned Theodore or his prophecy.

"I didn't know what Bardas would do," I said. "How could I have any influence over someone as powerful as him? And as for Eudocia, I was only doing what I was told."

"How very reassuring. I am glad to hear that you can follow instructions."

Before Cyril could speak again, two dancers tumbled into the centre of the room and stood before him. He raised his hand, indicating that they should wait. "You must remember," Cyril said. "That we, the eunuchs of the palace, control all access to power. Nothing must be allowed to happen without our permission. Our wealth and privileges depend on unity. Sometimes our lives depend on it too. Do not even think of taking bribes. We have strict rules about that sort of thing. You will remember that, won't you?"

I nodded, and Cyril smiled. "But enough advice!" he said. "I am sure you have seen enough here to know where your best interests lie."

Cyril clapped his hands and the dancers began a lascivious performance involving much writhing of oiled bodies and intertwining of limbs. Both were slim and young, with long dark hair. As they squirmed and coiled, the lamplight caught their glistening flesh, but I could not tell what gender they were.

"Flexible, aren't they?" Cyril said. "An example to us all."

I mumbled some sort of agreement, but was hardly able to take my eyes off the dancers. What few clothes they had been wearing to start with were soon shed, and they cavorted before us stark naked. I saw then that they were of opposite genders, and that the male one had been aroused by his slithering contact with the female. He turned away from his partner, and stood before us, proudly displaying his erect member.

According to Aristotle, or so Leo once told me, men with large penises are less fertile than other men, as their seed has further to travel and grows cooler and less potent on the way. That dancer's penis was the largest I had seen, and it throbbed with youthful readiness. With a rustle of silk, the court eunuchs leaned forward in their couches. Cyril licked his newly-reddened lips, then fumbled in the breast of his robe of honour. He tugged out a silk handkerchief, held it high, then, like an emperor starting a chariot race, dropped it onto the marble floor.

The girl fell to the floor as quickly and limply as Cyril's handkerchief, then sprang up again, rapidly rolling over several times before landing deftly on her back. After a little terpsichorean twitching and quivering, she opened her legs, spreading them wider than I would have though possible, offering her most private parts for the delectation of the eunuchs. They were not much interested in what she was displaying, but were still watching the youth, whose erection was twitching with eagerness. He knelt before his partner, she arched her back, and with a swift movement he slipped inside her. Thus connected, they resumed their dance, locking their limbs together, rolling over each other, rising from the floor and falling back onto it, all without breaking their slippery rhythm.

I had never seen the sexual act performed so enthusiastically, even when Leo was testing his aphrodisiacs. Nor had I
seen it performed so publicly. I studied the dancers philo-
sophically, just as Leo studied the two whores I had hired for
him. I knew those dancers could have no effect on me, and so
it proved. It was only when they had finished, and lay panting
on the marble floor, that I looked again at Cyril and saw that
he too was panting, and drooling, and fumbling with his robe
of honour, which he was attempting, with trembling fingers,
to untie.

The dancers, their faces blank with exhaustion and expired
lust, gathered their discarded garments and crept out of the
room. The muscular young servants reappeared. Cyril
beckoned the biggest and strongest of them, patting an empty
space on the couch between us. The servant helped Cyril
unfasten his robe. After much tugging and heaving, the heavy
silks slithered to the floor, revealing mounds of creased
flesh, in places as white as a Vlach goats' cheese, elsewhere
blotched and bruised like figured marble. The servant rolled
Cyril over so that he lay on his ample belly, then lifted his
short tunic to reveal that he was as erect as the young dancer
had been.

What a strange scene that was! And how puzzled Leo
would have been! Cyril was a eunuch like me, yet he was
overcome by lust. Castration had not made him sexless, it
had turned him into a woman. Yet I was sure that no
woman as old as he was would have desired a man, and that
no woman as repulsive as him would have found one.
Nature has decreed that a whole and vigorous man will be
aroused by the sight of a young and beautiful woman. That
is necessary for the propagation of humankind, though the
degree, urgency and frequency of such desires is puzzling.
But why should one man desire another, or a eunuch? And
how could the muscular young servant who stood over
Cyril have been aroused by the slack folds of mottled but-
tock flesh that lay quivering before him like a mass of rising
dough?

I have heard it said that among the countless inhabitants of

Constantinople, devotees of every form of pleasure can be found. Yet I cannot believe that nature alone can have inclined the young servant to desire anything as repulsive as the old eunuch. Perhaps he was motivated by the promise of a reward, or by the threat of punishment, or by some notion of duty or honour that prevailed among court servants.

I did not think any of those thoughts at the time. Instead, I perched on the edge of the couch, trying to keep as far away as possible from Cyril's trembling buttocks, wondering how I might escape from that chamber of inexplicable desires. Whatever impelled the servant, he acted with enthusiasm, pressing himself on Cyril and plunging his erect member into the eunuch's yielding flesh. To my left, on the next couch, another court eunuch engulfed an engorged member with his artificially reddened lips, devouring it as though barely satisfied by the banquet. Elsewhere, Cyril's colleagues were shuffling out of their encumbering robes and lying face down on couches. All around me in that grand reception room, unmanned men, creatures who claimed to wield true power, were offering themselves to their servants, submitting to degrading and baffling pleasures.

Before I could decide what to do a servant appeared, dressed like the others as a charioteer, and began to undo my robe. I tried to resist, but he was far too strong. In a moment he stripped me naked and threw me face down on the couch like a victorious wrestler. Cyril's face, flushed, jowly, smudged and sweaty, was uncomfortably close to mine. As the servant forced himself inside me, I felt a pain that tore at my innards and brought back the terror of the castrator's knife. I relived the moment on the island in the Black Sea, when the Rus cripple crouched over me ready to deprive me of my manhood. I tried to think of nothing, to feel nothing, to become nothing.

After a fiercer thrust than before, I felt a spasm, and the servant's seed, like that of the oysters I had eaten, entered into me and mingled with my flesh. I must have groaned in protest. Cyril turned his head, raising it slightly from the cushion it was pressed against. He opened his drool-smeared mouth.

"Not too full are you?" he said.

If that was pleasure, I decided, they could keep it. And if that was what Cyril considered a reward, I would defy him all the more resolutely, for fear of being rewarded again. But it struck me, as the pain wore off, that Cyril knew very well that I had not shared his pleasure. If I continued to defy him he was quite likely to invite me to the next of their little receptions, where I might be painfully rewarded again.

Yet, I wondered, did Cyril and his kind really run the palace? I had heard Bardas talking as though the eunuchs controlled everything, but that was when he was embittered and excluded from power. And whatever Cyril hoped for, I had little opportunity to influence Photius. He was too busy at the cathedral, and at the palace, ruling the Church and helping Bardas rule the empire.

Gog & Magog
[AD 860]

The fishermen had landed a catch that morning, but no one was buying the heaps of sardines, silver bass and bream, striped mackerel, or baskets of tiny anchovies. No one was buying vegetables either, or fruit, or any of the other things that were piled up on offer at the quayside. When I saw the longships riding proudly in the choppy waters of the Bosphorus, I knew why.

I recognised the square sails, high-curved prows topped with carved beast-heads, and the round, painted shields mounted on the gunwales. I remembered the killing, looting and burning. I experienced again the pain and terror I had felt as child. The Rus had come. But not just in one ship, with a little loot for sale. They had come by the thousand, manning scores of ships, armed and ruthless, to the city they knew as Micklegard. And they had arrived when Michael and Bardas had just set off for the East, accompanied by most of the army and imperial fleet.

The city was defenceless.

Leaving the idlers to point and stare, I raced up the hill to the patriarch's residence. As soon as I reached the forecourt, I stopped, amazed. Usually there were a few petitioners waiting by the doors, and sometimes on holy days the faithful waited to be blessed as Photius proceeded to the cathedral. But on that day the patriarchate was besieged by a great crowd of monks, all wailing and chanting.

"Ezekiel has prophesied this!" one of the monks cried. "And it shall come to pass that when Gog and Magog shall come against the land of Israel, said the Lord, my fury shall rise up within me."

"The tribes of the North have come to chastise us."

"And when the thousand years are expired, Satan shall be loosed out of his prison, and shall go out to deceive the nations which are in all four corners of the earth, Gog and

Magog, to gather them to battle, the number of whom is as the sand of the sea."

"The reign of the righteous is over."

"The false patriarch has failed us."

"He has led the city into sin and error."

"Bring back Ignatius. End his exile."

I pushed through the protesters until I was able to talk to one of the doormen, but it was only with some difficulty that I was able to persuade him to let me in.

Inside, almost filling the main reception room, was another crowd, composed of city worthies and officials. Some had put on their ceremonial robes, though most had rushed to the patriarchal residence as they were. All looked anxious. At their centre, gathered around a map of the city that had been unrolled on a wide table, were the prefect of the city and his deputy, the captain of the guards, and a few other holders of high office. Presiding over them all was Photius. He was an impressive figure, still handsome at forty, and calm, commanding and dignified. I struggled through the assembled worthies until I was near the front. I tried to catch my master's eye, but he gave me no hint of recognition.

"Now, gentleman," he said, turning back to his colleagues. "We have established the course this fleet is taking."

"They tried the Golden Horn," the prefect said. "But we got the chain up in time. Now they are heading along the Marmora coast."

"Where will they attack?"

The prefect looked blank. He fiddled with the trimmings of his official robe. His deputy spoke up.

"All the harbours are secure, sir. They cannot land inside the city. They will have to sail on until they are beyond the land walls. Perhaps they will land near the Golden Gate."

I could not stay silent. "Sirs," I said, bowing deferentially. "Forgive me for interrupting you, but I have some information."

The worthies stared at me. I was a nobody, and had spoken out of turn. Photius looked up, but still he would not recognise me. It was the prefect who spoke.

"I trust you have not come to tell us the city is about to be attacked," he said. "We know that already. That is why we are here."

"Sir, I know who they are. I know their ships. They are the Rus."

"Rus?" the prefect said. The crowd of worthies reformed itself around me, shutting me out with backs and shoulders, silently condemning me to the obscurity I deserved.

"Barbarians from the North," the prefect's deputy said. "There have been reports about them in recent years. Every so often they sail down the rivers of Khazaria, stirring up trouble among the Slavs, raiding the Black Sea ports, that sort of thing. About twenty years ago . . ."

There was an interruption. A soldier succeeded in struggling through the crowd. He thrust a document at the captain of the guard, who read it hurriedly. "From the North?" the captain said. "This reports say they came from the West. There have been raids in Thrace. And on the islands."

There was a brief argument in which the origins of the ships were disputed. Fingers were pointed at the map, reports were quoted and numbers compared.

"Are you suggesting," Photius said, "that there are two fleets, one from the North, the other from the West?"

"It seems so."

"How can these barbarians have organised a simultaneous attack, arriving just as the city is at its weakest? The idea is absurd. Bringing a fleet from beyond the Black Sea is a feat in itself. But a western fleet would have to sail halfway round the world, dodging the Franks and Saracens, and arrive here at exactly the right time. Not even the imperial navy could achieve that."

Photius fell silent and looked at the map again.

"I do not particularly care where these barbarians came from," he said. "Or how they got here. The question is, what is to be done about them. How can we defend ourselves without men or ships?"

"My men will guard the walls," the captain of the guard said.

"How many are there?

"Several hundred."

"To guard ten miles of walls?" Photius said.

"I can mobilise the guildsmen," the prefect said.

"I am sure they will be very useful," Photius said, "if these barbarians want to buy some silks, or pick up a little jewellery, or restock their ships with provisions before they depart. But as for fighting . . ." Photius stared at the map. He ran a finger along the curve of the city's eastern shore, tracing the line of the sea wall as it ran round the palace. "What size is this barbarian fleet?"

"My estimate is two hundred ships altogether," the prefect's deputy said. "Each manned by . . ."

"At least two dozen men," I said, pushing myself forward again. The city worthies all glared at me. "I know what I am talking about," I said, elbowing a senator aside. "I was captured by the Rus. I have sailed with them. I know their ships and their ways. And I know something else as well. That is what I came here to tell you. There is a Rus living in the city, or not far from it. He might be of use."

"Who is this barbarian?" Photius said, forgetting not to know me.

"He is called Inger," I said. Then I realised that I could not explain who Inger was without mentioning Eudocia, which would not be wise. And I had not worked out what use Inger might be. I had rushed into the patriarchate without any sort of plan, and risked embarrassing my master.

The prefect glared at me. "The city is full of barbarians and provincials," he said. "There are far too many of them, and they can't be trusted."

"Quite," Photius said. "I suggest that we take steps to recall the army and fleet. Are the beacons ready?"

"What beacons?"

"The ones devised by Leo to bring news of invasion from East to West. I presume they will work in reverse. Perhaps you would make arrangements to have them lit. And speaking of fires, are there stocks of naphtha at the arsenal? Even a few ships equipped with flame-throwers might be enough to scare off simple barbarians." Photius looked round the table at the assembled worthies. "If all of you go to your tasks and organise men and materials, I will go to mine and mobilise relics and icons. Between us, with God's help, we may be able to save the city." He paused for a moment, looking earnestly at each man. "Now, if you will excuse me, I must compose a sermon."

I was swept out of the room by an ebbing tide of chattering officials. Even as I struggled to resist the flow, I realised that I had made a mistake. Photius had reminded me by his cold tone and abruptness that I should not have approached him in public. Whatever I did with my knowledge, whatever action I took, was nothing to do with him, even if it was done on his behalf.

Outside, the wailing monks were still there.

"Son of man, set thy face against Gog," one of them intoned.

"I will send a fire on Magog," another replied.

At Photius's house the servants were in a panic. Some of them were praying, others drinking. Some had gone to man the walls with the guards and guildsmen, or had simply run away. A few were hiding valuables, though whether for their own or their master's benefit, I do not know. I attempted to restore order, but the servants took no notice. My authority had always been tenuous, and in that crisis it vanished altogether.

I retrieved a strong-box full of money from its hiding place and shut myself up in the library, meaning to guard the books, if I could achieve nothing else. I dragged a couch in front of the door and lay on it. The heat of the night was oppressive. It would have driven me outside, to sleep in the courtyard or on the roof, if it were not for the danger. I could hear the servants creeping about the courtyard, whispering to each other, sometimes shouting, occasional trying the library door. Noises from the city drifted in, hinting at the disorder outside. The Rus might win the city with fear, without actually attacking it.

I slept a little, and in my nightmares I saw fire-topped

towers, red-faced giants clad in chain mail and wolfskins, smoke drifting over looted markets, raped women and hanged men. I heard the clash of swords and axes, the crackle of blazing brushwood, the cries of the dying, the rough songs of victorious Rus. Lying in that dark airless library, I almost felt the heat of the ships that burned in my dreams.

Eudocia received me in bed, though it was almost noon. A pet monkey that Michael had given her lay curled up on the silk sheets, oblivious to the city's danger or the mood of its mistress.

"So?" she said, when I told her about the Rus fleet. "What do you expect me to do about it?"

"I thought you might come with me to the tavern. I hoped you might persuade your father to help us."

"What can he do against hundreds?"

"They are his people. Yours, too, in a way. He might persuade them not to attack. Come with me, please. There's no time to waste."

"I'm not setting foot outside this house," she said, pulling the sheets up over her half-exposed breasts. "I'm not even going to get out of bed."

The monkey readjusted its position, looping its hairy arms round Eudocia's white neck.

"But the city is in danger," I said.

"That's hardly my fault. Michael should be here defending us. Did I make him go off to fight the Saracens? No, I begged him to stay. But he doesn't listen to me now. He only listens to Bardas. And to Basil. We mustn't forget him. Do you know what I've heard? Michael wants to adopt Basil as his son. His son! It's ridiculous. Apart from the fact that he's an emperor and Basil's a peasant, Basil's four years older than him."

Though Eudocia's hair was tousled and her eyes red and puffy, she was more beautiful than ever. It was hard to believe that Michael was neglecting her.

"Michael might be pleased if you helped," I said. "He might be very grateful"

"He doesn't care. I'm staying in bed."

★

166

During the morning a rumour spread that the invaders had broken the chain and forced their way into the Golden Horn. The story proved false, but the boatmen were most unwilling to take to the water. I had to pay many times the usual rate to persuade a crew to row me to the tavern, and as soon they dropped me on the shore they rowed away, leaving me stranded.

The tavern's regulars were not panicking. They were drinking. And Inger was drinking with them, singing, shouting, pouring wine, urging all present to drink as much as possible. It was as though he had heard what the monks were saying, expected the end of the world, and was determined to be as drunk as possible when it came. If Inger had once been bear-like, he was a mangy beast by then. His once-golden hair was grey and thin, his beard tangled and filthy. His broad shoulders were hunched, and his muscles had wasted and softened. But his voice was still strong, and he used it to dominate the room.

I looked for the nieces, hoping they might help me, but they had gone. I tried to talk to Inger, but I might just as well have been a fly buzzing past his ear for all the notice he took. There was no chance of making him listen to me. But some of the regulars took exception to my pestering their host. They threw me out, though not before taking some money off me to pay for their drinks, or so they said.

I wandered down to the shore and sat on a fishing boat, remembering the stories Inger had once told me. He had longed to go back to the North. Now his fellow countrymen had returned. How could they have done it? How could they have sailed round the world in two huge fleets, braving un-known seas, enduring storms and calms, defying the empire's enemies, arriving at Constantinople strong and ready to fight. They were heroes, if not giants, and they promised a great battle that would end our world. Ragnarok, the Rus called it. The day of doom. If the Rus broke through the triple walls, untold Christians would be slaughtered, the most beautiful city ever built would be ransacked, and everything in it destroyed. Churches, houses, palaces and libraries, all would go up in flames. After that, men everywhere would sink into a twilight of ignorance, just as Photius feared.

The southern sky was the colour of blood. The Rus must have set fire to the suburbs on the Marmora shore. If they followed the land walls, they might reach the tavern in a couple of hours. I hoped the prefect had found some means of diverting them. I paced, sat, dozed a little, until the sky grew red in the east, and the sun rose above the slack waters of the Golden Horn.

A figure appeared out of the dawn, walking towards me along the shore. It was tall, cloaked and hooded. I could not tell whether it was a man, woman or eunuch. When it reached me the figure threw back its hood and unwound a veil. It was Eudocia.

"I told you I'd never desert you," she said. "We drank to it, remember?

"You came here alone?"

"The litter-men wouldn't carry me beyond Blachernae. I'll have them whipped later. If I can find them."

Inside the tavern, Eudocia took charge as though she had never been away. She kicked the sleeping drunkards, shouted at them in her shrillest voice, waking them and sending them on their way. She threw water over Inger's face, then dragged him from the floor. She washed him, combed his hair and beard, and dressed him in clean clothes. It was strange to see her, grown to womanhood and dressed like a lady, working like a servant again. She knew where everything was, found the food and clothes we needed, and got them ready without complaining. Inger did not seem surprised by the reappearance of his daughter. He ate the gruel she had made and called for wine so he could start the day properly.

"Not too much, father," she said, reluctantly offering him the jug. "You must do something important today."

"What?" he said. He took another swig of wine, then a gap-toothed smile spread across his face, dividing his unkempt whiskers like a ravine. "I know," he said. "You get married."

"No," she said, sadly. "It is not that. The city is being attacked."

Inger looked puzzled.

"The Rus have come back," I said. "Everyone was talking about it last night."

"Last night?" Inger had forgotten the last few hours. I told him about the Rus fleet, talking a mixture Greek and Norse, with Eudocia supplying the words I did not know.

"My people are here?" Inger said, when he had finally understood. "I go to them."

"You must tell them not to attack us. Tell them that trade is good, that peace is better than war, that the walls are too high, that the army is on its way back, that the fire ships will burn their fleet. Tell them . . ."

"I know what to tell them," Inger said.

He gripped Mjollnir, the silver hammer that always hung round his neck. Then, trembling from the effects of years of drunkenness, he opened the chest that stood by his bed and took out his armour and weapons. The mailcoat was a little rusty, but there was no time to clean it. We helped him into it, easing the heavy iron folds over his broad shoulders. He strapped a belt round his thick waist and hung his sword from it. I polished his helmet with an oily cloth, and when he put it on, he became a warrior again. Despite the weight of his armour he stood straighter, and, with his blue eyes flashing from behind an iron nose-guard, looked fiercer.

Inger rummaged in the chest and pulled out a small bag, which he hung round his neck. Finally, he picked up his battle-axe, smoothed its dull blade with the flat of his hand, then raised it onto his shoulder.

He stepped outside and walked away from the tavern and the plane trees that shaded it. When he got into the open he did not look back at the place where he had lived for twenty years. Instead, he sniffed the air, looking south to where smoke rose above the wooded horizon. Then he turned and looked at Eudocia.

"You come to our people?" he said.

Eudocia followed Inger's gaze, watching the columns of

smoke that showed where the Rus had raided. She looked away, back to the mist-shrouded waters of the Golden Horn, to the tall trees that grew along its banks, and to the city beyond them. I looked at her anxiously, wondering what we should do.

"We'd better go with him," she muttered, catching my look. "He might not make it on his own."

"It's a long walk," I said, looking at her delicate sandals. "Maybe four or five miles to the other shore."

"I'll make it," she said. "Barefoot, if necessary."

Eudocia took her father's arm, looked into his bloodshot eyes, and led him gently forward.

The land rose gently for a couple of miles. We followed the slope, keeping the city walls well to our left, steering clear of villages and suburbs, watching out for any Rus raiding parties that might have strayed inland, or for prefect's men who might mistake us for the enemy. We halted at the high point of the land, from which we could see the Sea of Marmora. Inger sniffed the air in his characteristic way, raising his nose high and sweeping it through the air, snuffling loudly like a questing hound. It was as though he could tell by its scent how fresh the drifting smoke was, and whether the fire that caused it had burned timber, crops or human flesh. Perhaps he could, or had once been able to. It was unlikely that his sense of smell had survived years of idleness and overindulgence at the tavern. After gazing for a while at the smoke-smudged horizon Inger hoisted his battle-axe and set off again.

We reached the first village and found it devastated. The dozen or so houses were roofless and burned out. Charred corpses lay beneath the smoking timbers. Others, gashed and gutted, deprived of heads or limbs, were scattered among the ruins, lying in the gardens they had tended. There cannot have been much to steal in a place like that, but the Rus had spread terror anyway, hoping to flush out what there was. I kept my eyes on the path, and tried not to look too closely at the bodies.

Near the shore was a half-ruined church. Having seen the

170

burnt-out cottages, I had no wish to enter it. But Inger rushed in, and it did not seem safe for us to linger outside. Sure that I could hear shouts in the distance, I took Eudocia's arm and led her through the shattered doors. In the centre of the small nave, hard to make out in the dim light, was the naked body of a man. He lay face down on the dusty floor, a tangle of ripped and bloodstained robes scattered round him. Something red, a stole perhaps, had been thrown over his back. It was a pathetic gesture, as though someone had thought the body could be given a little dignity by that inadequate covering.

"A priest," Eudocia said. "Is this what the Rus do? Is this what our people are like?"

Inger ignored her and strode towards the corpse. I gripped Eudocia's arm harder and tried to drag her away, but she resisted and pulled me closer to the dead priest. Reluctantly, through half-closed eyes, I looked at the pallid flesh and fouled vestments. Inger reached out with his right foot, and prodded the corpse.

The priest twitched. A muffled, gurgling groan came from his half-hidden mouth. I opened my eyes wider, allowing myself to see what my reason had denied. The red thing on his back quivered and frothed. Blood trickled from its edges. It was not a stole. It was his lungs. His back had been hacked open. Torn flesh and broken ribs lay among the tangled vestments. The priest's lungs had been pulled from his body and spread out like wings. And he was not dead.

I shut my eyes. My stomach heaved. Had I eaten anything that day I would have vomited it up. Eudocia held me while I bent and retched.

When I opened my eyes again Inger was looking calmly at the mangled body. "Blood Eagle," he said, stroking Mjollnir's shaft. "A bad way of death."

"But he's not dead," Eudocia said. "You can't leave him like that. Finish him off."

"No," Inger said. "He is sacrifice."

"Kill him. Use your axe."

"No. It is not our way. His death is for Odin."

Inger strode out into the sunlight, leaving Eudocia to

comfort me. I tried not to look at the body. How could I have forgotten the bloodthirsty sacrifices of the Rus, and the cruelty and capriciousness of their gods? What had made me think that Inger, or anyone, could reason with them? I clung to Eudocia, wondering why I had been so stupid as to venture out of the city while it was being attacked by barbarians.

Then, as though summoned by Odin's name, a gang of Rus burst through the church door. There were seven or eight of them, all big men, mail-clad and heavily armed, their clothes filthy and blood-spattered. Beneath heavy iron helmets their faces were contorted with battle-rage. They let out a great roar when they saw us. I knew from the look in their eyes that they had taken us both for women, and were ready to have their fun with us. They raised their weapons and rushed towards us. At that moment, everything went black and I fell to the ground.

A vote
[AD 860]

I hope you will not think me too much of a weakling, or that such feebleness is typical of my kind. I was tired, had not eaten since the previous day, and had just seen the most terrible sight. And I did not relish being raped by gigantic barbarians, however much Cyril and his friends might have enjoyed it. It is true that Eudocia did not pass out. Perhaps, despite what philosophers say, women are tougher than men.

When I came round, Eudocia was bending over me, mopping my brow with her veil. "You're safe," she said.

I looked around anxiously, but the church was empty. "Where are the Rus?"

"They went away."

"They didn't attack?"

"They stopped when I told them to."

"You stopped them?"

"I spoke to them in their language. They were surprised."

"You saved us."

She mopped my brow again. "I just spoke to them. I told them who I was. They've gone to find my father."

"They knew him?"

"They knew his name."

I did not have time to reflect on what might have happened to us if Inger had not been there, or if Eudocia had forgotten how to speak Norse. My ears were filled with a familiar but half-forgotten sound. From outside the church, softly at first, then loud, growing harsher with each blast, came the discordant lowing of a great oxhorn.

"The cripple!" I said.

"Who?"

Eudocia gently mopped my brow. Evidently she thought I was babbling.

"The man who cut me. He must be here."

Eudocia helped me up and led me outside the church. The

173

sound of the oxhorn came from above us. I craned my neck, and saw that the hornblower had scrambled on top of the porch. He was no cripple.

What would I have done if it had been him? What could I have done? I do not know, but for a moment my heart filled with anger, and with an urgent desire for revenge. The feeling blazed in me for a moment, driving away fear, then died.

Beyond the church, on a patch of flat land shaded by a few small fruit trees, Inger stood, surrounded by a gang of Rus warriors. Most of them were young, tall, finely dressed men, who made Inger look stooped and shabby. They all looked the same, as though picked for height and handsomeness. But one man stood out. He was as old as Inger, but stood straighter. His beard was almost white, but it flowed like spun silk over the folds of his spotless cloak, mingling with the shining links of his long mailcoat. Holding a gleaming iron helmet as though it was an orb, he watched the others through calm blue eyes. There was cruelty in his gaze, but also wisdom. Whoever he was, he had not wasted his days with drinking and sleeping.

The man saw us, and touched Inger's arm. Inger spoke to him, then beckoned us forward. I was reluctant to go, but Eudocia took my arm and would not let go of it. When she smiled, the young warriors parted to let us through, but they stared at me, doubtless wondering what kind of creature I was.

Inger gestured at the white-bearded man. "Rurik," he said, "He is my lord."

Did that mean Rurik was a king? Whatever his rank, he radiated power, in a way that Michael did not. I bowed politely, and so did Eudocia.

"I tell him you help me," Inger said.

Rurik muttered a few words, and looked at us briefly with his cold eyes. Then he turned away to watch the summoning of his men.

All around us they were gathering. Men clambered out of beached boats and strode up the shore, emerged from ruined houses or wrecked orchards, trudged across fields and marched along roads. Many of them drove beasts, carried sacks, or dragged captives. And as they gathered they called out, men of each crew seeking each other, coming together, finding comrades and kinsmen. Wave upon wave of men advanced, drawn by the oxhorn, singing and shouting, banging their shields. Soon we were surrounded by hundreds of red-faced giants, clad in mail and fur, armed with swords, spears and axes. The tide of men broke on the slopes below the church. The Rus horde, the crew of the two great fleets that had encompassed the world, came together.

As the oxhorn's last notes died, warriors lowered their weapons, dropped their shields, stood, or sat on the grass, waiting to hear what their leaders would say. Like them, we could do nothing but wait.

Rurik spoke first. His voice was calm, deep, reassuring. The Rus listened, and nodded their heads wisely.

"Can you understand him?" I asked.

"He is telling them that they must decide," Eudocia said. "They must choose whether to attack the city or go home."

When Rurik had finished, he brought Inger forward. The old drunkard stood unsteadily, looking down at the sea of warriors. In his shabby clothes and rusty armour, he was a veteran, twenty years older than most of them. But they remembered him, perhaps told stories about him, back in the North. They would know nothing of his drunken idleness, only that he had had adventures, and knew the city they hoped to capture.

Inger hesitated, looking uneasily at his audience. He took a deep breath, then let it out again without speaking. I feared that he had forgotten what to say, was no longer fluent in his own tongue. I muttered a prayer to whatever gods were listening, hoping they were kinder than Odin, begging them to make Inger eloquent. He reached up and touched Mjollnir's shaft, rubbing a fingertip on the tarnished silver. Thor must have sent him words and filled him with the courage to say them. Inger spoke slowly at first, and haltingly, but with the god's help he stood taller, held his head higher, looked nobler. His wine-roughened voice sounded clearly. He spoke as one man to another, in the language of his people, using words I could barely understand. I watched the mass of eager faces, trying to divine what those warriors were thinking. The Rus were brave and ruthless. They had sailed round the world to reach Constantinople. Yet they were men, who felt pain, were dirty, bloodstained and sweaty. And they knew doubt, as I could see in the furrowing of their brows and the grim set of their mouths. They had seen Micklegard and its many-towered walls. They knew how hard it would be to capture. They had some loot, and would win more on the way home. They listened respectfully to Inger's story, and to his advice. When he finished there was much sage nodding among the Rus.

Rurik spoke again, putting a question to his men. The oxhorn sounded again. Its blast pierced my ears, echoed from the gutted church, reverberated over the beached ships, the wrecked villages and empty countryside. They must have heard it in Constantinople, beyond the ill-manned walls.

The Rus grabbed their weapons and leapt up. Their reply to the horn-blast was a quick, rhythmic, steely hammering of sword on shield-boss. It was terrifying, the most warlike sound I had ever heard. Surely it presaged the destruction of the city? The noise alone was enough to bring the walls down.

Then, when I feared their thundering could get no louder, it stopped. There was a brief, startling moment of silence, and the Rus horde let out a great cry.

In one tremendous, rumbling voice, they spoke.

Rurik smiled grimly, then put his helmet on, lowering it gently like a crown. He picked up his brightly painted shield, put a hand on his sword-pommel, and set off down the slope to be among his men.

Inger strode towards us, looking elated. After years of drunken exile, he had met his lord, addressed his people, been listened to respectfully. He was important again. "They go," he said. "Micklegard too strong. My people know that now. They finish raid. Move on. Go home. I go with them."

Inger and Eudocia stood for a moment looking into each other's eyes.

"You come?" he said.

Eudocia looked at the departing Rus. She was unhappy as Michael's neglected mistress. Would she be happier in the icy North, warming the verminous bed of a shaggy warrior? Had I led her out of the city, exposed her to danger, been saved by her, only to lose her forever?

"No," she said. "I will go back to the city. It is where I belong, now."

Inger let go of his daughter's hand and looked at her sadly. Then he flung his mailed arms around her, hugging her so fiercely that she was almost crushed.

"Shall we go back?" I said, pointing the way to the city. I felt a strong urge to get away, to be safe inside the high walls.

"Wait," Inger said. "I give you something." He reached into the bag that hung round his neck and drew out a small wooden figure, which he gave to his daughter. She held the carving up, inspecting its grinning face and huge phallus.

"One day you be married," Inger said. "The god Frey bring you sons. Many sons." He frowned, perhaps remembering that the fertility god had brought him no sons and only one daughter. I suppose that is the way of things with gods, especially Rus gods, who love playing tricks. I sometimes wonder whether the Christian God is not the same. Being both human and divine is nothing. All gods can do that, turning themselves into anything they like, whether human or animal. But impregnating a virgin, creating the devil and letting him lead us into temptation, sending His son to expiate sins He made us willing to commit, splitting Himself into three and requiring us to believe them One, incorporating Himself in bread and wine, are all good tricks, and have sown much confusion among the faithful.

"Are you going to take it?" I asked, wondering what Eudocia would do with a pagan idol in a city that had only recently reconciled itself to Christian images.

"Yes," she said, wrapping the wooden god in the fold of a

silk scarf and tucking it between her breasts. "It will bring me what I want."

Inger rummaged in his sack again, and drew out another idol, the ivory figure of Thor. He held it out to me. "You take," he said.

I hesitated. As deities go, Thor is not particularly powerful. Nor is he mysterious. He is like a man, but more so, with human faults and appetites. Perhaps that makes him a suitable god for a creature like me, who is like a man but less so.

"Go on," Eudocia said. "Take it."

I held out my hand and took the hunched, wine-stained god.

"Keep him well," Inger said. "Thor guard you both."

I tucked the idol inside my tunic. I thought I saw tears in Inger's eyes when he shouldered his battle-axe and strode down the slope to the ships. Eudocia was certainly crying. Her golden hair was dishevelled, her face smudged and her silk dress stained with dirt and rust. I put my arm round her waist. She put her arm round mine, and we walked to the city like a pair of lovers.

The Golden Gate was firmly shut, and no one was being allowed in or out. I found a postern and rapped loudly on it, urging the gatekeepers to open it, which they swore was against all orders and more than their lives were worth. In the end I had to bribe them, using the last of the money I had taken from my master's strong-box. Once inside the city we realised that something important was happening. The people were lining the streets, leaning out of windows, even perching on walls or in the branches of trees. Children carried bunches of wilting flowers, and green branches and gaudy cloths hung from all the houses. Surely it was too early to be celebrating a triumph?

From that southern corner of the city it was several miles back to Eudocia's house, though not as far as we had already walked. I hesitated, not knowing whether to find a litter for Eudocia or escort her home myself. But how could I pay for a litter when I had no money left? Then, unexpectedly, I saw Photius. He was at the centre of a small group of richly dressed nobles. As they processed slowly beneath the inner-most of the three great walls that guard Constantinople, others followed them, priests and monks, all looking grave and pious, not wailing or complaining, but chanting hymns in honour of the Virgin Mary, Mother of God and Protectress of the city.

"Look," Eudocia said. "It's Michael. He's back."

She was right. Summoned by Leo's beacons, Michael had returned, and he walked beside my master, though he was so elaborately clothed, painted and bejewelled that I could hardly recognise him.

Eudocia tugged at her veil, making sure that her face was fully hidden. I raised my hands, covering my face as though in awe or contemplation. Peeping through my fingers, I saw that my master was carrying a cloth of some kind, musty-looking and much folded. When the procession drew near, the people around us suddenly threw themselves to the ground. We did the same, lying prostrate before the emperor and patriarch. As I lay, I felt Thor pressing into my flesh, reminding me that more than one god watched over Constantinople that day. Photius raised the cloth, holding it above his head, allowing it to flutter in the breeze.

"The Sacred Veil," someone muttered. "The Robe of the Mother of God."

They had brought it all the way from Blachernae, in a procession that matched our march beyond the city walls. As the relic passed, people prayed and called out, begging the Virgin to save the city from the ogres Gog and Magog and their demonic legions. They blessed their emperor for return-ing to them, urging him to send the navy against the barbarian fleet. They did not mention Photius, either to praise or blame him, but he played his part well, wearing his glittering vest-ments with dignity, displaying the holy robe with suitable reverence, praying and chanting with the monks and priests. Some people got to their feet and joined the procession, fol-lowing it down to the Marmora shore, where the robe of the Virgin was ceremonially dipped into the sea.

★

179

When Photius returned to inspect his house, I tried to tell him about my adventure with the Rus, but he was not interested.

"There may well have been a miracle," he said, "I'm not claiming there was. That's not for me to say. But you can't argue with the facts. And the fact is, a wind sprang up when I dipped the Virgin's robe in the sea. It was not much of wind, I admit, but any wind can inconvenience ships, if it blows in the wrong direction. In any case, a wind need not be physical. It can be spiritual. So when people speak of a miracle that drove the Rus away, they may mean that the pagans were driven away by the Holy Spirit. That would be perfectly reasonable, from a theological point of view. Something drove the Rus away. That is certain. Of course, I cannot claim the credit for a miracle myself. Miracles come from God. But I daresay the people have stopped calling for the return of Ignatius." Photius turned to me anxiously. "What do you think, Zeno? You are supposed to be my eyes and ears."

"You are right. Something drove the Rus away. And no one is giving the credit to Ignatius."

"Ignatius!" Photius said with a grin. "It was stroke of luck that the Rus raided Terebinthos on the way home. They nearly killed the old fool when they sacked his monastery."

"People are saying that Ignatius could do nothing to stop the Rus, but that you did. I have not heard anyone calling for his return since then."

Photius looked pleased with himself. He already knew what I had told him, but he was not unique in needing to hear himself praised.

Deplorable follies
[AD 860]

A few months after the Rus raid, on an autumnal evening cooled by chilly winds from the Black Sea, I waited at the Hippodrome stables for the emperor Michael and his friends. It was the first time I had been asked to attend him there, and I was not at all sure what to expect.

"Is he here yet?" I asked the stable-hand who let me in.

"His majesty? He's around somewhere. Inspecting the new buildings, most like. By the time he's finished, the stables will be better than a palace. Marble everywhere. He likes to see how it's going before he comes here to meet his friends. He likes to look at the horses, too, and check the chariots and harness, to show what a good judge he is. He's always got a good word to say to those of us that look after it all. A present, sometimes."

Simpering, the stable hand held out a grubby hand, showing me the dung-encrusted rings that encircled several of his fingers. I dreaded to think what he might have done to earn those presents.

I sat and waited on a bale of straw. In my youth I might have felt comfortable there. At one time, the squalor, smells, and rough company would not have troubled me. I would have looked around the place, got the measure of it, and worked out how to take advantage. But living among scholars and gentlemen had softened me. And the Rus raid had alarmed me, revealing how fragile the good life was. It had shown me how much I loved Eudocia, how I feared losing her. The last thing I wanted was to betray her by encouraging Michael's foolishness. But I had no choice.

When Michael arrived he was dressed like a stable hand, in a short tunic that showed his legs, and riding boots of soft but worn-out leather. His friends, Basil among them, were similarly dressed, though for most of them their humble and grubby clothing was not a disguise, as they had come straight from their work in the stables.

"Zeno," he said, surprising me by remembering my name. "Where are you going to take us?"

"To a little place I have heard of," I said. "Beyond the Harbour of Julian."

"Will we like it?" Michael said, wrapping himself in a coarse woollen cloak that had been offered to him by one of the grooms.

"I hope so."

"I hope so, too," the emperor said. There was hint of menace in his voice, but it was no more than a hint. It was sign of his lack of confidence that he even tried to scare us. He was, as we all knew, the emperor, and could do what he liked.

I led Michael and his friends, most of them ten years younger than me, to a part of the city where the streets are narrow, dirty and ill lit. After a little wandering, which made me feel very uneasy, we found the waterfront tavern I had been told about. The owner, a scrawny fellow with a pock-marked face and patchy beard, was happy to seat us near the door and offer us the finest efforts of his cook.

"We'd like some fish," fat Gryllus said.

"Fish!" The tavern-keeper was indignant. "What do gentleman like yourselves want fish for? It's not a fast day."

Michael seemed to like being rebuffed, but Gryllus persisted. "Surely you serve fish," he said. "We are right by the harbour."

"Exactly! And if you knew what went into the harbour, you wouldn't want fish. Nasty, stinking, watery things! Fish are only fit for monks and women."

"What have you got?"

"Offal. I recommend it."

"I don't think so."

"You don't understand me gentlemen. When I say I recommend the offal, what I mean is, that's what there is. You can have trotters, tripe, ears, snouts, sweetbreads, lights or liver."

Michael, ignoring Gryllus's reluctance, ordered stewed tripe and lupin seeds, the cheapest food you can buy, and made us all eat it. We drank sour wine the colour of straw, and listened to Michael praising the fare as exactly what he liked best and could never get in the palace. He probed the tripe with the tip of his knife, watching it quiver and ooze. "This flesh," he said, "is almost thrillingly flaccid."

Gryllus joined in the joke, if it was one, forgetting he had demanded fish, praising the food more extravagantly than Michael, urging him to dismiss the palace cooks and replace them with men hired from taverns, greedily eating whatever the rest of us left.

I was glad Michael enjoyed the meal, and that he took so long over it. But I knew we had not gone to that place just to eat. The tavern-keeper knew it too. He lingered while we ate, watching over us carefully. When we finished he addressed us, fixing his gaze on Gryllus, whom he took to be our leader.

"Sirs," he said. "I've got some boys out the back. Darkies, they are. Fresh from Africa. They're not mine, you understand. I'm just minding them for a friend." He attempted a wink, making his face even uglier. "It seems to me that you young gentleman might be in need of entertainment, and these Africans might be just the boys to give it to you."

"May we see them," Gryllus said, relishing his role as supposed leader.

"Just come this way."

Michael, Basil, Gryllus and I followed the tavern-keeper, leaving the rest of the party to drink more wine. We were ushered into an ill-lit back room and invited to sit on broken-backed couches. When the tavern-keeper clapped his hands a trio of dusky youths stepped from behind a curtain.

"Are they eunuchs?" Michael said. He sounded disappointed.

"Oh no, sir!" The tavern-keeper gestured to the youths, who lifted their tunics, proving that they were uncut. Michael and his friends leaned forward, peering at dark genitalia in the dim light.

"Why are they smooth-chinned?" Michael asked. "They are old enough to grow beards."

"They shave their faces," the tavern-keeper said. "It's the

fashion in Africa. Or so I'm told." He leaned forward and whispered loudly. "They're queer folk. You should see what they eat." He leered. "I could tell you stories . . ."

"Never mind that," Michael said. "Leave them with us."

When the tavern-keeper had withdrawn, Michael patted the couch beside him and beckoned to one of the Africans. The youth sat meekly beside the young emperor. The others, unbidden, sat beside Basil and Gryllus. There was an awkward silence. Michael looked at his African, gazing at his dark skin, curly hair, and flat features. He had seen Africans before. There were black eunuchs in the palace. But there he had to behave himself, follow the rules, pretend not to notice the servants, however interesting he found them. In disguise, on the loose in the big city, he could do what he liked.

Michael looked anxiously at Basil, who knew exactly what to do. He seized his African and flung him over his lap as though about to deliver a spanking. The African cried out in some unknown tongue, and squirmed playfully, encouraging his short tunic to rise above his bare buttocks. His skin gleamed darkly in the lamplight.

Michael made no move. He watched Basil fondle the African for a while before he spoke. "Basil," he said. "Will you be my champion?"

Basil smiled grimly, then pulled off his tunic and slipped out of his undergarments until he stood before us naked. I had seen him naked before, when he wrestled with Michael. There had been something ceremonial about the way they squared up, circled round each other, attempted grips and locks, almost as though they were dancing. But there was nothing gentle or courtly about what Basil did that evening.

The African undressed too. His chest was criss-crossed with scars. They did not look accidental, but hinted at savage pagan rites. No doubt the tavern-keeper could have told us a story about them, chilling our blood with the barbarity of the hot South. Basil reached out and touched the scars, raking at them cruelly with hooked fingers. When the African flinched, Basil reached down and grabbed him between the legs. He tugged at the youth's dark penis, bringing it quickly to life, then stepped back. Basil was taller than the African, and broader. His penis was stiffening, rivalling the African's for length and firmness. He pulled the African towards him, roughly slamming their two bodies together. Briefly, a white penis fenced with a black one, both full and eager. Then Basil turned the African round, threw him onto the couch and climbed on top of him. He knelt over his victim, proudly displaying his erection. Watching him, Michael and Gryllus groped beneath their tunics, disarranging their underwear to reach their own tumescent organs.

Basil reached out for one of the lamps and brought it up to his mouth. He blew out the flame, then tipped the lamp over the African, spilling the oil over his black rump. The African groaned, but did not move. Basil lowered himself, fitting his erect member into the slot between the oiled buttocks. The couch creaked as he eased himself back and forth, and nearly collapsed when he suddenly changed direction and thrust himself deep inside the African.

What, I wondered excited Basil? Was it simple lust, such as drives all whole men? Did he enjoy being watched? Or was he stirred by ambition, by the power he might win by pleasing the emperor? His face showed only grim determination as he drove deeper and deeper into the helpless African. During the final paroxysm, when the two bodies shuddered together, I saw a look of triumph in Basil's face. It was the face of a victorious wrestler, a winning charioteer, someone who has beaten all his enemies.

Gryllus was trembling with excitement. "Bring me a pot of honey," he said, snapping his fingers loudly.

"Honey? Where am I to find that?"

"Don't ask me. Just do it."

I was not his slave, or anybody's. But just at that moment I welcomed the chance to escape. I slipped from the room and found the tavern-keeper, who smirked when he heard my request. It cannot have been all that unusual, as he had what I wanted behind the counter. I took the jug he gave me and carried it to the back room. When I pulled the curtain aside, the scene had changed. Basil was slumped on a couch, the African curled up at his feet like a faithful dog. Michael was naked, and lay face down, with his own African poised over him. Gryllus had lifted up his tunic, and was trying to interest the third African in whatever it was that nestled among the folds of fat around his groin. Seeing me, Gryllus grabbed the jug and upended it, pouring the contents over his stumpy penis. He reached out, gripping the African by the ears, pulling him down, encouraging him to lap up the sweet honey.

I looked away, but what I saw was worse. Michael, young ruler of the greatest empire in the world, was allowing himself to be penetrated by a black slave. All around me, moist flesh slapped and slithered, couches creaked, and grunts of pleasure escaped from parted lips. I saw and heard it all, but understood nothing. How could Michael prefer that African to the fair and lovely Eudocia? And how could I face her after what I had seen?

It was Cyril, of course, who made me lead Michael round the city and spy on what he did. There was no banquet when he gave me my orders. Instead, he received me in a small cell, at the end of a large room full of clerks and functionaries. I suppose he received me there to demonstrate his industriousness, or to show me the everyday reality that lay behind the show and ceremony of the palace.

It was not a pleasant place. Men and eunuchs worked elbow to elbow, ignoring the hubbub around them, frantically scribbling, with sweat running into the ink and staining their work. Some were arguing loudly, demanding information or action, pointing out mistakes others had made, or proclaiming their own superiority. The place was so hot and crowded that it seemed a sort of hell, populated by demons wielding pens instead of pitchforks. The chief of the guild of palace eunuchs did not rise when I entered his cell, but sat at his desk while I stood before him like an insubordinate junior.

"You have not sent me many reports," Cyril said, pretending to search the documents on his desk. He was not dressed in ceremonial style. His tunic was only modestly decorated, and his grey hair was lank with sweat. "In fact, I do not think you have supplied me with one useful piece of information since our last talk."

"I am sorry," I said. "I must have misunderstood. I thought you were going to ask something of me, but I have heard nothing."

"Really!" Cyril wiped his brow with the back of a pudgy hand. His unpowdered cheeks were netted with fine veins. His tunic was so damp that it clung to him, revealing the contours of his womanish breasts. "I thought I had made myself clear," he said. "You are to further our cause in any way you can, and I expect you to use a little initiative, not just to wait for instructions. Do you think we palace eunuchs got where we are just by waiting for instructions? No! We are like bees, all working together for the good of the hive. And as you know, every hive has its queen."

I did not bother to point out that, according to Aristotle, a hive is ruled by a king bee. Pedantry is never advisable when one is at a disadvantage. It struck me that Cyril may have come from rustic stock, among whom ignorance of natural philosophy is only to be expected. Outside his cell the clerks and functionaries continued to shout and argue. I wondered how anyone could put up with those conditions all day and every day, and realised how lucky I had been to avoid such drudgery.

"As it happens," Cyril said. "An opportunity has arisen. Your chance to help us has come. You are probably aware of our emperor's habit of wandering the city?"

I had not, at that stage, witnessed Michael's antics myself. But I had heard the rumours. The emperor and a few of his young favourites had been seen roaming the streets near the palace in plain clothes. Thinking himself unrecognisable, Michael visited shops, lingered in markets, hid at the back of churches to see how the people worshipped, listened to their gossip to find out what they thought. Sometimes he would see someone he liked the look of, a pretty girl or boy, an old soldier, or even a simple housewife. He liked to follow them home, go into their houses and talk with them. More than once he made some humble family share their dinner with him, eating their coarse bread and thin stew while his friends looked on bemused. They preferred dining with charioteers, who were generally rich enough to provide a proper feast, and worldly enough to share their tastes.

However, most alarming for functionaries like Cyril were the occasions when Michael wandered off in the middle of an official procession, and the eunuchs and courtiers had to follow him, nodding and smiling as though a stinking back street was part of their usual ceremonial route.

"I have heard that his majesty takes an interest in his subjects," I said.

Cyril smiled. "Very tactful. His odd habits might be seen in that light. What could be more noble in a Christian emperor, some say, than crossing the thresholds of the poor and breaking bread with the humble. But you know better than that. It was you, was it not, who led him on his first excursion to a tavern."

"It was me," I said. "But . . ."

"You were only following orders. If you had had our interest at heart, you might not have followed those orders quite so assiduously. His majesty's friendship with all those low types has not been without its unfortunate consequences. However, now is your chance to make amends. The emperor has requested your company."

"My company? I am sure his majesty does not remember me." I had stood near the emperor often enough when attending Photius, without noticing any sign of recognition. To him, as to any other great man, I was as invisible as all other servants.

"You are right. He had forgotten your name, and had no idea where you came from. But he remembered that it was a young eunuch who first took him to a tavern. And luckily I knew exactly who you were and where you could be found." Cyril paused, and drank some water from a beaker that stood beside his desk. He did not offer me a drink. "How odd," he said, "that such a young man should already be nostalgic! It seems that the homes of charioteers and the streets near the palace are not exciting enough for him. He wants to recapture the first pleasures of his youth by visiting rough taverns and simple cookshops, not to mention brothels and other disreputable entertainments of the kind that appeal to the beards. How simple they are! They can be led by their pricks."

Cyril laughed at that thought, his jowls quivering like a bowl of pig's-head brawn. "And it's not only sex. His taste in food is terribly perverse, if you ask me. He could have the rarest meats, the richest sauces, the most expensive ingredients brought from anywhere in the world, all prepared by the finest cooks in the city. He could eat as well as we eunuchs do, better if he wanted to. But he prefers to eat what the poor eat, and I am sure even they wouldn't eat it if they had the choice. Where's the pleasure in coarse bread, or a bowl of boiled vegetables? Who could actually enjoy such food?"

Cyril looked dismayed at the thought of such unsophisticated fare. Again, I wondered whether he was the son of some peasant family, castrated and sent to the capital to make his fortune and enrich his relatives. It was a common enough practice, and one that might explain his overeager espousal of a style of luxury that those born with money might think vulgar.

"Anyway," he went on, "Michael's renewed enthusiasm for low-life has one advantage. It keeps him away from that mistress of his. Bardas supports her, and he is the enemy of all eunuchs. I don't like the idea of her whispering in our emperor's ear, filling his young mind with hateful thoughts."

"I don't think she concerns herself with things of that sort."

Cyril looked at me oddly. Had I said too much?

"That reminds me," he said. "I know how you persuaded Bardas to set her up in luxury. Your friend Theodore faked a prophecy."

"The prophecy was quite accurate, in a way."

"Why split hairs? The question is, what would Bardas do if he found out. I think I can guess. Can you?"

Ever since he murdered Theoctistus, Bardas had scared

me. I knew he would kill me without a qualm if I angered him.

"Yes," I said. "I can guess."

"Of course," Cyril said, "revealing the truth would not just put you in danger. I don't think the emperor's mistress would last long if Bardas knew how he had been tricked. But I will keep silent, for the time being. If you help me."

"I will help you," I said. What choice did I have? I would have risked my life to preserve Eudocia's happiness, but I could not risk her life too.

"I knew you would." Cyril smiled. "Whatever we may think of his tastes, his majesty the emperor has decreed that you shall lead him to the low pleasures he seeks."

"But I know nothing of such things."

"That is not what the emperor thinks. According to him, you are an expert in every pleasure the city can offer."

"I can assure you I am not."

"Then you had better become an expert, and quickly. You will be summoned to the Hippodrome stables. I don't know when. It could be today. It could be next month, or any time. But whenever it is, Michael and his friends will be expecting you. They will want you to take them somewhere special, where the most repulsively ordinary meal may be enjoyed, as well as any other pleasures they may want. I leave the details of that to you." Cyril waved a limp hand to indicate that I should leave. But before I was out of the door, he called me back. "There is one more thing," he said. "You must report back to me. I want to know everything."

The only person I could think of who might possibly know anything about low-life pleasures was Theodore. It was fitting that he should help me again. Though disappointed that Bardas chose Leo the philosopher to head the university, Theodore had eventually accepted a teaching post there, and I found him giving a lecture on geography to a small group of would-be functionaries. I sat in the shade of the colonnade, a little apart from Theodore's pupils, waiting for him to finish and wondering why anyone would want the life of scribbling and arguing I had just glimpsed. I suppose ambition drives people to endure anything, even a dull lecture on the nations of the North, given on a sweltering afternoon. The details, I noticed, were drawn from a romance called *Wonderful Things from Beyond Thule*, which Theodore had sold to Photius some years before.

"Why ask me?" Theodore said when I put my question to him. What would I know about the pleasures of the flesh? Have you forgotten that I am a priest?"

I had forgotten his ordination, and his robes, though once black, were so ragged and stained that they revealed nothing of his priestly status.

"You were not always a priest," I said. "And you are surrounded by students. Surely you must know of some places where young men might enjoy themselves, if only by repute."

"Everyone knows where the brothel is. It is marked by a statue of Aphrodite."

"Yes. And everyone knows that it is watched by the prefect's men, who note who goes there and what they do. I need to know about unofficial establishments, places where pleasure can be taken unobserved."

Theodore admitted that he had heard of such places, and grudgingly told me where some of them might be found. But he could not resist posing as an expert, whatever the subject, and with a little prompting and flattery from me, he was soon revealing more. I listened eagerly while he described taverns and cookshops that doubled as brothels, places where students mixed with poor people and foreigners, enjoying pleasures not to be found in the prosperous quarter near the palace.

The Labyrinth
[AD 861–4]

I hope you will forgive me if I do not describe this part of my life in detail. It is not a period of which I am particularly proud. With Theodore's help, I had guessed Michael's tastes all too accurately. He found everything to his liking on that first outing, and insisted that I took him out again. Cyril gave me no chance to refuse. My only choice, had I wished to defy his orders, would have been to flee the city and abandon everything and everyone I loved. From then on I was obliged to neglect my master, to deceive Eudocia, and to accompany Michael on his wanderings round Constantinople.

Our outings usually began at the Hippodrome, which Michael could reach easily from the palace. After assembling in the stables, we set off beneath the stern gaze of antique statues, which looked down on us from every corner, reproaching us with the nobility of their carved expressions, seeming to see though the feebleness of our disguises. Even dressed in borrowed rags and smelling of sweat and horse-dung, Michael was still instantly recognisable, and it took an effort for the people we encountered near the palace not to fling themselves on the ground as we passed. It was the same in taverns, where he insisted on paying with gold pieces, a habit that made it obvious he was not the groom or stable-hand he pretended to be.

We quartered the city, looking for low haunts and perverse pleasures. I did not enjoy those outings. In some of the places we went to there were painted eunuchs, who indulged in obscene buffoonery of all kinds while the emperor and his friends watched. I never acknowledged them. Those debased creatures had lost more than their balls. They had lost their self-respect. Oh, I know what you will say! You will point out that I was hardly behaving with dignity myself, that I had given in to everyone, and was doing their will whether I wanted to or not. But there are secret places in the heart which can be kept pure even when everything about us is base. Photius was good at that, refusing to acknowledge anything that threatened his dignity. I tried the same trick, letting things go on around me, while not admitting to myself that I was involved. I held on to my pride, just as Theseus held on to Ariadne's thread, knowing it would lead him out of the Labyrinth.

I affected a scholarly detachment, studying the follies and debaucheries of those young men just as Leo studied the two whores I had hired in order to elucidate the Secrets of Love. Why, I wondered, did Michael have such peculiar tastes in food? I am, as I may have remarked before, no great eater. But it seems to me that what we do eat should be good, if not extravagantly so. Michael showed a marked taste for offal, and demanded to eat ears, lips, tails, snouts, innards and nether parts. According to Leo the philosopher, such parts, or some of them, have aphrodisiac properties. If Michael knew that, he did not say so, though he often remarked that offal consists of the portions of animals not normally served at palace banquets, and his enthusiasm for it may have been no more than gastronomic contrariness. But it may also have been linked with his sexual tastes, which also concerned nether and inner parts. What he liked best, I had learned, was to be entered by another, to be treated like a boy or a woman, surrendering his power and dignity to some rough commoner. Why should a man with a noble wife and a beautiful mistress have wished to slake his lusts among men, specially uneducated men whose idea of entertainment was obscene horseplay? Perhaps, like offal, such men were beneath him, and therefore to be desired.

And what of Basil? Being a peasant, he can hardly have found such simple entertainments a novelty. Did he really share Michael's tastes? Or was he dissembling, seeking favour by pretending to like what the emperor liked. He would not have been unique in that. But he was more careful than the others, and managed to keep his true feelings to himself. I often watched his broad, handsome face without being able to guess what went on behind it.

★

After a while, even Michael tired of our outings. He came to the stables dressed in his courtly robes, which dragged in the dung-strewn straw. "I am bored," he said, waving a jewelled hand at the rest of us, who were wearing our usual disguises. "Where is the fun in pretending to be poor? Everyone sees through us anyway, so what's the point of dressing as grooms and stable hands?"

"Your majesty," I said, "you can hardly come with us dressed as you are."

Michael looked down at the stiff folds of embroidered silk that encased his body. "Perhaps not," he said. "But we must think of something new. Disguises that will be fun, and stylish."

One of the grooms, whose clothes were not a disguise, suggested that we dress as ordinary men, neither rich nor poor. Michael looked contemptuous. "Where's the fun in that? It would be just as boring as pretending to be poor."

Silently, I agreed with him. I was sick of pretending to be what I was not, of betraying Eudocia and keeping secrets from Photius. If none of us came up with any suggestions Michael might return to the palace, and his duties. But Gryllus was too stupid to realise that.

"I know," he said. "Vestments."

Michael smiled. "You mean we should dress as priests?"

"Not just as priests. Some of us can be bishops. Monks too."

"What an excellent idea! You had better be a monk, Gryllus. You should be able to find a plain habit in your size."

Gryllus bowed comically, emphasising his girth. "Your majesty must be a bishop," he said.

Michael thought for a moment, his brow furrowing. "No," he said. "Zeno must be a bishop. After all, he does lead our little outings. I will be a priest. Not an ordinary one. I will have to think what sort. Basil, you can be some sort of Armenian priest. They are heretics, I think, but that doesn't matter. The rest of you can improvise. The next time we meet, I want you all to look ecclesiastical."

★

194

I got my vestments from Leo the philosopher, who had once been bishop of Thessalonica. I found him in his rooms by the university. He was seventy, and his white beard flowed like a foaming river. He might have tucked it into his belt, had such an affectation appealed to him. But he was dressed, as always in patched and dirty robes, an ancient fur hat perched on his head. He was puzzled by my request for his old vestments, and I had to explain more than I had intended about the emperor's antics.

"He sounds like a man possessed," Leo said. "A man driven by demons of lust. He is what the Manichaeans deplore, a man whose vegetal soul is overwhelmed by fleshly desire to such an extent that his rational soul is extinguished. He is half man, half beast."

"A Minotaur?" I said.

"Perhaps. What a pity it is too late for me to study him. What a chapter he would have made for my book on the Secrets of Love."

"Have you finished it yet?"

Leo looked at me reproachfully. "Can we ever finish a life's work?"

Though old and musty, Leo's vestments had once been splendid, and still gleamed with gold thread when cleaned up. But as a disguise they were hopeless. Leading a party of rowdy monks and clergy round the taverns and brothels of the city, I attracted far more attention than before. It was even worse when the emperor added a little ceremony to our simple meals, pretending to bless the bread and wine, giving a little of each to all present and muttering the words of the Eucharist.

We had some respite from those outings when Michael went East to fight the Saracens and heretics. I doubt whether he knew much about tactics and strategy. He lacked the patience for that sort of thing. But Bardas knew everything there was to know about warfare, and under his guidance Michael led the imperial army to some great victories.

I took advantage of Michael's absences to attend Eudocia and my master. I tried to tell Photius what was going on. I knew I had a duty to him, and that Michael's follies might one day have serious consequences. But my master, having heard the more innocuous rumours, refused to hear any more.

"It is not unusual," he said, "for kings or emperors to wander their realms dressed as ordinary citizens. The histories are full of such stories. You really ought to make better use of your time, Zeno, and study some of the works in my library. I have left you in charge of it, after all."

As Photius knew well, the histories in his library contained the stories of Nero, Commodus and Elagabalus, emperors brought down by their excesses. But those were not the examples he chose to remember.

"Harun al-Rashid was famous for wandering Baghdad in disguise," Photius said. "And Michael's father, who admired the Caliph, followed his example. Theophilus liked all things oriental. He was a zealous iconoclast because Islam abhors all images. His additions to the palace were fanciful and elaborate in the oriental style. The mechanical beasts in his reception hall were inspired by similar ones in Baghdad."

"I thought Leo invented them."

"Leo is a very wise and clever man," Photius said. "But we don't have to accept everything he tells us. We should always be selective in what we believe, and what we listen to. I see nothing to worry about in these rumours. If Theophilus copied the Caliph by wandering Constantinople in disguise, who can blame Michael for wanting to see the city he rules and understand how his subjects live? It is true that Theophilus was sometimes laughed at for the feebleness of his disguises, but perhaps that tells us that he wanted to be recognised, and wished his people to know what he was up to. For all his faults, Theophilus was respected for his willingness to meet the people and hear their petitions. No doubt Michael is merely following in his father's footsteps."

"Michael is not like his father," I said. "He cares nothing for the East. He only goes there because Bardas tells him to. He wanders the city for fun, because he is bored with power."

"Zeno, I am shocked. You should be more respectful when speaking of our emperor. It is clear that you do not know him as well as I do. He is a fine young man who defends the empire because he loves it. Yes, he was wayward in his youth. But he has changed. He plays a full part in the life of the Church. Perhaps if you came to the cathedral more often you would know how pious he has become."

"But he isn't! The people are saying . . ."

"The people! What do they know? You might think they would be grateful to me, after the miracle with the Robe of the Virgin. But no! They accuse me of not taking my patriarchal duties seriously. It is absurd! They say I recite antique pagan verse instead of the liturgy. Verse, of all things! If they knew me better they would know how much I dislike poetry."

"I must tell you about Michael . . ."

"Ignatius is behind it. The common people would never think of something like that for themselves. Ignatius has always hated literature. Profane writings, as he calls it. But he might have accused me of reciting something I actually like!"

"If only you knew . . ."

But it was impossible. If Photius would not listen, how could I tell him that Michael was turning into a fool and a wastrel? And in truth, my master had enough to think about. When he wrote to Rome announcing his appointment as patriarch he assumed the letter was a formality. He did not know that Ignatius's followers had already denounced him, and that the pope would question his accession. When the pope sent commissioners to Constantinople to investigate the case, Photius spent a fortune in entertaining them, sending them back to Rome with expensive gifts. He certainly cannot have expected that, just a couple of years later, the pope would formally depose him and restore Ignatius.

"It is just as I have always thought," Photius said, glaring at the pope's elaborately inscribed missive. "There is something enervating in the air of Rome. Pope Nicholas is subject to the same follies and errors as the old emperors. The Church can no more be governed from Rome than the empire could. Did not Constantine the Great found the Second Rome here in Byzantium for precisely that reason?"

Photius rambled on for a while, setting out in detail the

rival claims of Constantinople and Rome, always to our city's advantage, as though lecturing at the university. I watched him without really listening, noting that his beard shook as he grew more agitated. In keeping with his status, he had let his beard grow long. It hung down his chest, spreading over his brocade coat in thick curls. Such shagginess was not to his taste, but is expected of a patriarch, unless the holder of that office is a eunuch, as Ignatius was. Perhaps the inability of eunuch priests to signal holiness by growing a beard explains their tendency to excessive zealotry. I do not know whether popes cultivate beards, though many westerners shave themselves as smooth as the eunuchs they affect to despise.

"It is absurd," Photius said, "for the pope, any pope, to claim that he has the right to depose me. But Pope Nicholas is ignorant of civilisation. Because I was a layman, he thinks I cannot be a churchman. In the West, it seems, only priests are educated. He does not understand that in Constantinople there are educated, secular men who understand the sacred as well as the profane. I, of course, am one of them, perhaps the greatest. That is why I was chosen."

"Does the pope's opinion matter?" I asked.

"Of course not. How many legions has the pope? Will he send a navy here to attack Constantinople like the Rus? Will his men drag me from Hagia Sophia and carry me off to Rome? Will they bring Ignatius and install him in my place? I think not." He stared scornfully at the papal missive. "It is about time the bishops of Rome accepted their true position. Rome is a backwater, a province so unimportant that the empire abandoned it long ago. Michael decreed that I should govern the Church, not some ignorant barbarian in the West. There is only one true emperor, and one universal empire, whatever the Franks claim. Michael may be young, but he is well advised, and must be obeyed. If Pope Nicholas will not accept my legitimacy, then I will depose him. And excommunicate him. That will teach him to meddle in my affairs."

He flung the letter to the ground and began to pace the room angrily. I picked up the letter and quickly read it through.

"There is a way out," I said. "The document mentions several dioceses in Illyria. According to the pope, they belong rightly to Rome. If you were to transfer them . . ."

"Exactly! The pope would sell me my own office for a handful of bishoprics. That shows how unprincipled he is."

"It might be worth it. Illyria is not important."

"But it is!" Photius said. "It is very important indeed. And not because it was granted to one part of the Church or another by some long-forgotten emperor. It is the future of the Church that is at stake, not its past. The future lies with the barbarians, with the people of the North who have not yet been converted. What a pity that Constantine was unable to persuade the Khazars away from their Jewish faith. The Jews are the most obstinate people in the world. Nothing will persuade them that they are wrong. I suppose we must be grateful that Constantine managed to get some prisoners released. And for the fact that the Khan prefers fighting the Saracens to fighting us. But for the time being, we must leave the Khazars in error. The pagans must be our true target."

My master's voice grew louder, as though he was trying to fill the domed nave of Hagia Sophia and inspire a congregation. "We will convert the Slavs and Bulgars, perhaps even the Rus, if we can find out where it is that they come from. We will send the Gospel over inaccessible mountains, through dense forests and dismal swamps, to the icy wastes of the far North. And Illyria is the beachhead from which the missionaries will advance. Constantine is planning it already. He will start with the Moravians, then other Slav tribes, then the Bulgars. If we bring them into the Eastern Church, what a blow that would be to Rome's ambitions!"

Photius had once mocked Constantine's missionary enthusiasm, dismissing the Slavs as irredeemable barbarians. But he was not patriarch then. Converting the Slavs and Bulgars would clearly win him much more power than the pope could possibly take away from him. His empire, though spiritual, would be greater than Michael's. "It would be a triumph for you, too," I said.

A Triumph
[AD 865]

Eudocia and I watched the Triumph from her house. Though it was not quite on the parade route, her servants decorated it, opening shutters, removing trellises, and hanging rugs and green branches out of the upper windows. Anything less would have been unpatriotic. I had already seen some of the preparations. The citizens were dressed in their finest clothes, and streets were strewn with flowers and scented herbs. Merchants had set out extravagant displays, decorating the streets and advertising their wares. The Greens and Blues had assembled their choirs and practised acclaiming the emperor. There were troops of soldiers in dress uniform, their burnished breastplates gleaming brightly in the sunlight. Some of them enthusiastically goaded droves of Saracen prisoners, who were chained together at the ankles or mounted backwards on donkeys as a sign of their ignominy. The public must be given the opportunity to jeer, as well as cheer. Most impressive of all, and very necessary for an emperor whose extravagances consumed large quantities of money, were the wagons loaded with loot from the East. However, the loot, I happened to know, was not as impressive as it looked, being made up of thin layers of gold coins, glittering jewels, silken fabrics, carpets, and other valuables, scattered lightly over sacks filled with sand or straw.

When we heard the trumpets, we all leaned out of the windows and tried to catch a glimpse of the procession of soldiers, eunuchs and dignitaries as it passed along the main avenue. Somewhere among them were Michael, Bardas, Photius, and everyone else of note, all dressed in their finest clothes, carrying standards, silk banners, garlands, the holiest icons and relics. There was to be a thanksgiving service in the cathedral of Hagia Sophia, and a mass acclamation in the Hippodrome, much giving and receiving of presents and rewards, and banquets in the palace and throughout the city.

Eudocia's servants had dressed up, and expected a day off in honour of the emperor's victory over the Saracens and heretics. But I could see that Michael's triumph brought no happiness to his mistress.

When the last stragglers had passed, and there was no prospect of seeing anything else, the servants went downstairs and ate the feast they had prepared. Eudocia did not follow them.

"What is wrong?" I asked.

"I am to be married," she said.

"But how?" Theodore had always insisted his prophecy was accurate, even after Michael married the wrong Eudocia, but I did not see how it could be fulfilled in the way we had hoped for. "The empress is still alive and well," I said. "Surely . . ."

"I am not going to marry Michael." She sniffed, and raised a hand to her tear-filled eyes. "I am to marry Basil."

"Basil?"

It was unthinkable, impossible, as baffling as any of my master's abstruse theological paradoxes. I had watched Basil do things I dared not tell Eudocia, could not have described to her if she had begged me to. He had been married, and perhaps still was, but no one seeing him roistering with Michael would have guessed it. I did not know whether Basil was driven by desire or ambition. But I had seen him plunging eagerly into the foulest of places, seeking perverse pleasures, consorting with slaves and Negroes, dragging Michael down into depravity. I knew his shame because I had shared it. How could my Eudocia marry a creature like him? And how could I tell her why she should not?

"But I thought you hated him," I said. "You always said he took Michael away from you."

"He did. But now he will be giving Michael back to me."

Eudocia's words made no sense. "You can't marry Basil."

"I have no choice. Michael has decreed it."

"Why would he give you away?"

"Because he is bored of visiting me in secret. He wants to get me into the palace. He's going to give Basil some new job.

I don't know what it is. But afterwards we will all live in the palace together, and Michael can see me as often as he likes."

"Even though you will be married to Basil?"

"It won't be a real marriage. I'll still be Michael's mistress."

"Has Basil agreed to this arrangement?"

"Do you think I have spoken to him? Why should I care what he thinks? He will go on doing what he likes, and so will Michael. I am just a plaything. I should have gone North with my father."

I was still wondering what Eudocia's news meant, and what I should tell Photius, when Bardas arrived at the house. His face was burned almost black by the Eastern sun, but I could see anger flashing in his eyes, and in the way he paced the library, fuming at Michael's latest plans, saying things he could not say at court, or to his family.

Eventually he sat down and Photius tried to calm him.

"Surely it is fitting," my master said. "Basil is a peasant, and she was a tavern girl."

"I hope she is better than that now," Bardas said. "I've spent a fortune on her. If she hasn't been turned into a lady by now, I want to know where all my money's gone. It was your eunuch, wasn't it, that trained her?"

I shrank into the background, as was my custom when Bardas came to my master's house.

"He had a hand in it," Photius said, looking around the room. "Zeno, come here and tell us what you think. Is Eudocia any better than a tavern girl?"

Reluctantly I emerged from the shadows and bowed respectfully before Bardas. "Yes sir," I said, shaking a little as I addressed the Caesar. "I have done as you ordered. And I can confidently report that my efforts have been successful. Eudocia is just like a lady."

"What a waste! I set her up in luxury to keep Michael occupied, not so he could hand her on like an old cloak or unwanted sword."

"I feel sure that this is good news," Photius said. "Michael is shaking off youthful folly. He is marrying his mistress to his favourite so he can do his duty to his wife. The empire needs an heir, perhaps now he will produce one."

"An heir! Your friend Theodore prophesied that Michael would have sons by Eudocia. He didn't tell us which one, but he hasn't had sons by either of them."

"It is most unfortunate."

"It's worse than that," Bardas said. "I thought I'd set Michael a good example, but does he know what to do with a woman? I sometimes wonder what he gets up to with that Basil."

"Your nephew is a fine young man, I'm sure of it."

"Michael is a fool. He's not just giving away Eudocia, he wants to promote Basil to High Chamberlain."

"Surely not! That's a eunuch's job."

"Exactly. The court eunuchs got wind of it before I did. They sent a deputation led by some disgusting old creature called Cyril. They pointed out that the job can't be given to a whole man because the chamberlain has to sleep in the emperor's bedchamber."

"In that case, Basil's promotion might be a good thing. You have always complained about the eunuchs' power."

"If I had my way, I'd fit Basil for the job." Bardas said. "I'd cut his balls off!"

"The procrustean method," Photius said. "But if you did that, there would be little point in him marrying Eudocia."

"Ha! I don't care about the marriage, despite the money I've wasted. If Michael's tired of Eudocia, then good riddance to her! But Basil! I thought he would be good for Michael at first. I thought he would teach him wrestling and horse-taming and hunting. I never dreamt he would worm his way into the palace. How can I influence my nephew when Basil is sleeping across his bedroom doorway?"

"I can see that it might make things difficult," Photius said.

The two men, patriarch and Caesar, went on, lamenting the state of the empire, and blaming everyone for it but themselves. Then they sat and thought for a while, even neglecting to drink their wine. I was relieved that Bardas had not lost his temper, and that he did not seem to know the full story of Michael's nocturnal follies. But I was alarmed that he had mentioned Cyril. What would happen to me if the old eunuch revealed what he knew? If Bardas did not punish me for instigating Theodore's prophecy, he surely would for encouraging Michael's debauchery.

Could it be, as Photius suggested, that Michael really was shaking off youthful folly? Judging by his new-found enthusiasm for vestments, it was unlikely. But it was possible that Michael's tastes were changing, that he might be content to stay in the palace and have his pleasures brought to him. I hoped so, even if it meant that I saw less of Eudocia.

Then an idea came to me. Eudocia, despite her low birth, would be mixing with ladies in waiting, with the wives of nobles and senators, perhaps with the empress and her retinue. I could not bear to think of her being patronised by those women of the court. I decided to give her something that would make her seem their equal. But I only knew one man who could help me give it to her, and I did not want to ask him on my own behalf.

When Bardas left, I made a suggestion.

"If Basil is to be given high office," I said. "And Eudocia is to marry him, then perhaps she should be given noble status."

"A tavern girl!" Photius said. "Noble?"

"It could be done," I said. "A genealogy could be constructed. She might be grateful. Your influence might increase."

"My influence with Eudocia?"

"With Michael."

"But Zeno, he is discarding her."

"No, he will be seeing more of her. That is why he is marrying her to Basil, so he can bring her into the palace."

Photius looked puzzled. "How lucky we are to be celibate. Life is so much simpler."

I could not entirely agree with my master. Life was far from simple for me. But I persuaded him that it would be worth his while to flatter Eudocia, then went to consult Theodore, who was expert at discovering lost or hitherto unknown documents. He remembered Eudocia's origins.

"Her mother owned a tavern did she not? And her father was a barbarian."

"Inger was a warrior," I said. "And among barbarians, that often counts as nobility."

"Yes, and owning a house with four walls and a roof often counts as kingship. However, you have a point. We might describe this Inger as nobleman in his own country."

"She will be called Eudocia Ingerina," I said. "And if anyone asks who Inger is, we will tell them he is a Rus noble."

"A Rus? Such a barbaric name. And such an unpopular one, after their raid."

"A Scythian, then, or a Cimmerian, or a noble from beyond Thule," I said, remembering Theodore's tedious and fanciful geography lecture. "But a noble. That is the important point. And now that Inger has returned to the North, no one can prove us wrong."

"Very well," Theodore said, making a note on his wax tablet. "Now for the mother. I can't see how we can make anything out of a woman who keeps a tavern."

"She doesn't keep it any more. She has gone back to her village."

"Then the best thing will be to find Eudocia a new mother. I know a family who would be only too happy to oblige. They are noble but poor, and they live in the provinces, which is a point in their favour. I am sure they will be happy to acknowledge Eudocia as one of their clan if she is to be associated with the imperial household. They would not be in a position to provide a dowry, of course, but since the marriage is Michael's idea, no doubt he will provide something from the imperial treasury. To preserve appearances, discreet arrangements would have to be made. I would be willing to act as intermediary, when it comes to actually passing on the money. Perhaps you could recommend me."

"Perhaps," I said, though I had no intention of recommending that Theodore be trusted with money. "There is just one difficulty with this scheme. Eudocia's mother left two nieces in charge of the family tavern. They know exactly who Eudocia is and where she came from."

"Then they must be bribed or threatened into keeping quiet. If they won't co-operate, they can be eliminated. I am sure you can see to that."

Marriage
[AD 865]

Have I described how beautiful Eudocia was? It was not just her fair face, golden hair and blue eyes that made her so. It was the way she responded to others. When she spoke, her face filled with pleasure and enthusiasm. When she listened, her eyes widened with interest, her wide mouth turned up in a smile, and she leaned forward, drawing close to whoever was speaking, making them feel special. Her skin had a whiteness all of its own, paler even than ivory, as white as an alabaster carving lit by the glow of a church lamp. When she slipped off her robe and stood naked, the room filled with light as though shutters had been thrown open on a sunny day.

Yet she must have been dark in mood as she stepped into the gleaming marble bath and lowered herself into the scented water. It was her wedding day, and her eyes swam with tears. Her maidservants cried too as they threw petals over her, but that was all part of the ritual. They stepped down into the bath, letting their thin shifts drag in the water, scattering blood-red petals over Eudocia's milky skin. They crouched beside her like river-nymphs, washing her soft flesh with the finest Gallic soap, the sort reserved for the imperial family. And then, when they judged her clean enough, they led her from the bath, gently dried her, and dressed her in wedding clothes of pearly silk.

Eudocia's elevation had begun. It was her last morning in the house Bardas had provided. Yet nothing was what it seemed. At twenty-four, Eudocia was a little old to be marrying, and she could hardly claim to be pure. The ritual bath, like the white clothes, like the wedding itself, was a sham. All of it was as false as the genealogy I had devised with Theodore.

I could not bear to think of Eudocia marrying Basil, of her being dragged off to the palace like an Athenian maiden condemned to the Cretan Labyrinth. Would I be dragged after her? Would we ever escape? Or were we to be parted, never to see each other again? Whatever happened, it was my fault. I had introduced Eudocia to Michael. I had encouraged Michael's folly. And now Eudocia was being given to Basil for reasons I did not understand. Did Michael really want his wife, mistress, and favourite, all living together at the palace? How would he manage them all? What use would he put me to?

In fact things were worse even than I realised. But who could have guessed how capricious Michael would become, or how pointless the marriage would turn out to be.

When Eudocia was carried off to the church in a litter decorated with silver and ivory, accompanied by festively dressed servants, I went back to my master's house and brooded. I was not invited to the wedding. That was official business, an elaborate church ceremony, as befitted the emperor's High Chamberlain and the noble lady he was to marry. Photius did not perform the ceremony himself, claiming that a patriarch could only marry an emperor, though he presided over it and embraced the couple afterwards. Photius knew what the officiating priest did not, that Basil was already married, and had a wife and child still living in Macedonia.

The reception was to be held in the hall that housed Leo's famous mechanical beasts. I felt like an automaton as I made my way through the gates and guardrooms to the heart of the palace. I was impelled by forces outside myself, as irresistible as the springs, wheels, cogs and rods that drove Leo's creations. All it took was for someone to press a lever, and I sprang into simulated life, doing or saying whatever was wanted of me. And only a few years earlier I had congratulated myself for having achieved freedom and independence.

Perhaps all eunuchs are the same. We lose our autonomy when we lose our balls. And that is not to be wondered at. Some ancient philosophers have defined life in a way that excludes eunuchs. According to them, a living creature must be able, in addition, to moving, eating, breathing, and so on, to make more of its own kind. Something like me, that moves and speaks, but cannot reproduce itself, must be a sort of animated statue. Cyril, though no philosopher, had hinted as much when he compared eunuchs to bees. We work for others, not ourselves, with no hope of passing on any advantage we win.

"I am so glad you could come," Cyril whispered to me as I passed through the bronze doors, though he knew very well I had no choice. His minions hurried me into a vestry and draped a robe of honour round my drooping shoulders. I allowed my hair to be dressed, my face to be dusted with powder, and a jewelled collar to be placed around my neck. Though the costume brought back uncomfortable memories, I was glad to wear it and pass, as far as anyone who might know me was concerned, as just another court eunuch. For the first time I would be in a room where Photius, Michael, Eudocia and Cyril were all present. How could I face them when I had worked for each of them against the others?

The hall was just as magnificent as it was reputed to be, its triple-domed ceiling held up by marble columns of every imaginable colour, all carved with twining beasts and foliage. Cyril, having seen the place often, was more interested in the guests.

"What a crowd!" he said, taking my arm. His hair was lacquered, and sprinkled with golden dust, which fell on my shoulder when he leaned against me. "And what a mixture. Working out the protocol has been a nightmare. By rights, some of the guests have no rank at all, but courtly robes cover a lot. That's what we eunuchs are here for, to make everything run smoothly. We can work wonders when we have to. Today, there are not just the nobles and courtiers you might expect, but all sorts of other types as well. I suppose it is natural that the groom should invite some of his friends. Or perhaps they are Michael's friends?"

Cyril looked at me questioningly. I said nothing.

"What is odd," Cyril said, "is that so many of them are charioteers and stable boys. Still, they look quite presentable when properly washed and dressed, don't they? Some of them are rather handsome. I must have a word with them later. We can't let the beards have all the fun!"

Cyril led me on, or rather, leaned on me in such a way that I had to go wherever he wished. "Look!" he said, waving a silk-clad arm at a group of unfashionably dressed elderly ladies. "Eudocia's aunts, or so we are told. These provincial families are so hard to keep track of. I expect they live in a crumbling country house in some remote district with only a few old retainers to look after them. How glad they must be for a chance to come up to the city." We stopped for a moment and watched them. "What on earth made them wear their own clothes? Quite apart from being horribly old-fashioned, they ruin the colour scheme. They could easily have been found something better," Cyril said, sadly. "And isn't it odd how unlike Eudocia they look!"

"She takes after her father," I said.

"Of course." Cyril gave me a knowing wink. "The provincials seem a little overwhelmed by the decorations."

The centrepiece of the hall was an artificial tree hung with silver leaves and golden fruit. It was studded with pearls to look like dew, and every so often a slave tugged on a silken cord to shake the tree and make its hangings tinkle as though in a breeze. There were gilded birds in the branches, but I did not hear them sing. At the far end of the hall were Leo's golden beasts, mechanically rearing and roaring, just as advertised. But the courtiers, having seen them often, took no notice. Only a few of the commoners and provincials stopped and stared.

Elsewhere the hall was decorated with flowers, silver chains, wreaths of bay and olive, chandeliers, richly embroidered hangings, Persian rugs, and elaborately pleated draperies, all purple and gold. The marble floors were strewn with sweet herbs, and the apse was carpeted with rose petals. An organ burbled in the background, filling the air with sound just as the strewn herbs filled it with scent.

"And talking of provincials," Cyril said, "look over there." He pointed to a group of golden-skinned, well-built men, who looked uncomfortable in their elaborate robes. "The High

Chamberlain's relatives. Basil seems to have an awful lot of brothers and cousins. And they all seem to have found jobs, somewhere in the palace or the army. These Armenians stick together!"

"Armenians? I though Basil came from Macedonia."

"Haven't you heard his accent! His family came from the East before they settled in Macedonia. Now they are finding allies among the other Armenians in the palace. Quite a faction, they are."

Cyril understood that I wished to avoid meeting my master. When the patriarchal party passed, he drew me into the shelter of a draped colonnade so that we could watch events from there. Photius had changed out of his vestments, but wore robes that were hardly distinguishable from them, stiff with embroidery and bright with contrasting colours. From behind our pillar, Cyril pointed out the some of the more interesting guests

"There is the widow Danielis," Cyril said, indicating a short fat figure wrapped in pink silk, and as elaborately coifed as he was. Only her dark moustache revealed that she was a woman. "She gave the couple all these hangings." He pointed out the rich textiles that decorated the walls. "But she is in the trade, and fabulously wealthy by all accounts." Cyril drew me closer to him. "That is her son John beside her," he said. "A strapping young fellow, don't you think?"

John was indeed handsome. I could see why Cyril liked the look of him. If dressed like a charioteer, he might have been one of the servants who pleasured the court eunuchs.

"He's not the one there were rumours about?" I asked. "Didn't Basil swear an oath of eternal friendship with him? Some say the two of them were as good as married."

"I am sure the High Chamberlain has done nothing dishonourable." Cyril smiled. "But something must have persuaded Danielis to be his patroness. Basil has a knack of getting people to do what he wants."

Cyril nudged me, drawing my attention to a woman even fatter than Danielis, and wrapped in even more magnificent silks. "Thecla," he said. "The emperor's sister. She's put on an awful lot of weight since he let her out of the nunnery. They must have starved her in there." He absent-mindedly rubbed his bulging belly. "Excess is so unbecoming in a woman, don't you think?"

We watched Thecla, supported by two eunuchs, waddle to the apse where Basil and Eudocia sat on a couch as though enthroned. Michael sat behind and above them, on an actual throne. It did not rise up to the ceiling, as it might have done had the guests been ignorant barbarians. Beside him, on a lesser throne, was the other Eudocia, the empress. The guests filed past the imperial party in strict order of precedence, conducted by court eunuchs. Those who had not already been presented to the emperor that day had to prostrate themselves, however elderly, and there was much delay while the eunuchs helped their charges up and on.

Michael, ignoring the struggles of his humble subjects, looked around the room, enjoying the odd mixture of people he had brought together. The expression on his face, a mixture of fascination and puzzlement, was exactly the same as when he watched the wild beasts in the Hippodrome menagerie. I almost expected him to throw a chunk of bleeding meat into the crowd to see what they would do, or to order a fight to be staged between the most unlikely pair he could think of. That was the sort of thing he did at the stables, when he was bored with racing and wrestling.

The empress showed little interest in the guests. She stared vaguely down, nodding an acknowledgement when names and ranks had been announced. Her face was so stiff with make-up that it was hard to tell whether she was as plain as everyone said. It was also hard to tell whether she knew that Eudocia was Michael's mistress. Had she managed to ignore the rumours? Did no one dare tell her? Whatever the truth, it was strange to see the two Eudocias sitting so close to each other.

My Eudocia had changed into another outfit. Her gown was blue and gold, and her head-dress encrusted with pearls. She had no need of such things to make her beautiful. I felt an overwhelming urge to throw myself on the petal-strewn floor and apologise. Because of me, she was doomed to unhappiness, confined to the palace and passed from man to man like a concubine. I wanted at least to catch her eye and indicate my sympathy.

But Basil and Eudocia, I was surprised to note, were gazing at each other raptly. It was almost as though they were actually in love. Of course, some sort of performance was in order, especially with the empress sitting beside them, but I thought that they were overdoing it, and might anger Michael.

"A handsome couple," Cyril said. "Both of them tall and well-formed. Quite beautiful, really. Even her. And with an animal vigour about them that is almost disturbing." Cyril patted his hair, making sure the lacquered pigeon wings were still in place. "What an unlikely pair to be marrying here in the palace. He, a peasant, and she . . ."

"The daughter of a prince from beyond Thule."

"Exactly. What a pity her father isn't here. He might have cut quite a dash, striding about in his tribal finery. Some of the Franks and Bulgars look quite magnificent, in a primitive sort of way. Others, of course, try to dress like us. It doesn't fool anyone."

It was then that I realised. Basil and Eudocia had never really met before. They must have caught glimpses, but had never been close up, stood in the same room, actually spoken, until the day of their wedding. And now they not could take their eyes off each other.

When all the guests had been received, Michael and the empress climbed down from their thrones and led the procession to the dining room. There was much delay, and some jostling, while all the guests were got in order and marched across a courtyard. By the time Cyril and I had hurried after them, the first courses were already being eaten, and servants were scurrying among columns of inlayed green marble, beneath a gilded ceiling. All I could do was look on, amazed by the magnificence of the room, and by the abundance of gold, silver and enamelled ware that was laid out on the many tables. On the walls were mosaics depicting a grape harvest, with lifelike peasants climbing and picking, and ripe fruit made of golden tesserae. Even under the iconoclasts, there had been no ban on secular images.

Women do not usually dine on couches, so the empress sat at a linen-draped table with Eudocia and Thecla beside her, surrounded by a selection of ladies of the court. Michael and Basil reclined together, with a few of the more presentable young courtiers. On that occasion, Michael did not dare to dine with his favourite charioteers, who were entertained elsewhere. There were not enough couches for everyone, and only the most important men dined in the antique manner. Many others dined at tables, and some of us, despite our robes of honour and jewelled collars, had to grab what we could and eat it standing up.

"It is just as well," Cyril said, taking a handful of pastries from a passing tray. "If we reclined on couches like the beards, they might suspect us of having too much power. It is best to seem humble on occasions like this, and enjoy ourselves in private, don't you think?"

While each course was served, an organ played. While it was eaten, concealed choirs sang. But the music did not stop the less polished guests from talking loudly as they ate. Cyril and I took what we could and consumed it behind the pillars, like schoolboys who have stolen fruit from a market. Cyril was absorbed by the task of getting as much food as he decently could, but I was not. Several times he dashed off to rebuke a servant or eunuch, always grabbing some food on the way back.

I am no great eater. That is how I have kept my youthful figure. For me, food is like religion. It can be nourishing, and, in its endless types and varieties, interesting. But too much of it is a bad thing. One would not wish to be enslaved by it, or by any other form of pleasure. Both food and religion lead to trouble if they are indulged in.

At the high point of the meal a shoal of gigantic turbot were served, each as large as an infantryman's shield. They were of the Black Sea variety, famed for its fine flavour and bony nodules. Few fish are better than turbot, perhaps none. But the nodules, which gastronomes crunch up eagerly, are supposed to be aphrodisiac.

I have, as I have already explained, sampled many reputed love potions in the spirit of philosophical enquiry, with little effect. Yet whole men claim that their sexual desires are sharpened, and that their ability to perform the act is enhanced. But why do they want to stir up such troublesome desires? Why are they not content to enjoy simple pleasures without the derangement of their senses? Surely the ancient philosopher was right when, finding that he had in old age lost all sexual desire, he said that it was like being unshackled from a lunatic.

I suppose it was Michael's idea of a joke to have an aphrodisiac dish served at a wedding. Perhaps he hoped the feast would end with an outbreak of uncontrolled lust, in which all propriety would be swept aside. The guests all ate the turbot enthusiastically, dipping the firm flesh in sauce, shovelling it down their throats and groaning with real or simulated pleasure. Some called out for more, and ate that just as eagerly. But nearly all of them, I noticed, left the skin and nodules. That was proof, I suppose, that they understood Michael's joke, even if they did not mean to go along with it.

Michael must have intended the turbot to be the feast's climax. After a few final toasts, the bride was led away, out of the dining hall and along a garlanded colonnade, to a nearby imperial bedchamber. Most of the women left then, either to attend and prepare Eudocia, or simply to go home. Photius must have slipped away with them, as I did not see him later. I suppose a patriarch may count as a lady if he chooses to.

The men lingered for a while, enjoying a few more drinks, mingling with the charioteers and commoners who were let in from another room. There was some ribald talk, and a little buffoonery. Some guests claimed to be irresistibly aroused by the turbot, and called for dancing girls, or eyed up the prettier eunuchs. Most of them merely watched Basil and Michael, and wondered which of them would enjoy Eudocia's favours that night. The two men sat side by side, receiving and proposing toasts, smiling and laughing, but giving nothing away. When the time came to consummate the wedding Basil rose to his feet, to loud cheers. And Michael rose with him.

Of course, it was natural that the bridegroom's best friend should escort him to the nuptial bedchamber. But the speed with which the other men rushed after them was unseemly. They whooped, cheered, and shouted advice, all the time jostling to get ahead and be sure of a view into the bedchamber. At the end of the colonnade they were disappointed. A line of Ferghanese bodyguards had formed up. It was dark by then, and the colonnade was lit by torches. The guards stood impassively, their faces looking crueller than ever in the flickering light. They held their curved swords up as though in salute, each blade a gleaming crescent of deadly steel. The guards stepped smartly aside to allow Michael and Basil through, then reformed. The crowd hesitated. Some, afraid of the swords, fell back. Others, determined to see who would join Eudocia in the bedchamber, ran out of the colonnade and tried to outflank the bodyguards. But more Turks appeared from the darkness and, after a little skirmishing among the fountains and flowerbeds, drove the wedding guests back. The rest of the guards formed up, extended their swords, and silently strode forward. No one was ready to defy those fierce Turks. We were herded back into the dining room like sheep, and the doors were shut firmly after us.

There was a terrible hubbub. Some of the guests hammered on the doors or berated the servants, demanding to be let out. Others resigned themselves to confinement, got hold of wine jugs and drank what they could. A few of the commoners and charioteers were busy pocketing golden dishes and jewelled goblets.

"Did you see?" I said to Cyril. "Which of them went in? Was it Michael or Basil?"

"It is an intriguing question," Cyril said. "One that you, of all people, are best placed to answer." He smiled grimly. "I suggest that you do your very best to find out."

A procession
[AD 865]

I knew that everything would change after the wedding. It did, though not in the way I expected. Michael's follies did not end, though Basil took no further part in them. Those who took the marriage at face value assumed that Basil was spending all his time with Eudocia. Others said that marrying a beautiful noblewoman and being High Chamberlain were enough for him, that he had no further need to please the emperor. In fact, Michael had no further use for Basil. Only a few weeks after marrying his mistress to his favourite, Michael found a new favourite, an oarsman called Basiliscianus, whom he spotted among the rowers of an imperial barge. Basiliscianus was handsome, ambitious and obliging, and quickly took a leading part in Michael's crepuscular expeditions, encouraging him to go further than before.

I have already described one of Michael's Paulician masses. I could never really see the point of them. Michael and his friends were only pretending to worship the devil. They might just as well have dressed up as rustic Slavs and worshipped the moon. That would have given them the pretext for a banquet, perhaps even for deflowering a virgin or two. But only Constantine knew or cared about such things, and he was in Moravia battling with the Germans. I missed his goodness and simplicity. He, more than anyone, might have persuaded me to believe truly in the Christian faith. As I watched the antics of Michael and his cronies, I understood that all belief is sham, and all worship is travesty.

The mock masses came to an end after an event I had hoped fervently to avoid; an encounter with my master while we were all dressed in our vestments. As usual, I had been obliged to eat a little of the dung and drink some of the blood. I held them in my mouth, ready to spit them out as soon as I got the chance. That came when Michael, egged on by Basiliscianus,

217

announced that we would complete our worship with a procession. We had never done that before, but we obeyed, forming up, shuffling uneasily into our places, tidying our chasubles and stoles, hardly believing that the emperor would dare to walk through the city dressed as he was, while it was still light. But he did, leading us out of the stables, past the menagerie full of yelping and gibbering animals, beyond the high walls of the Hippodrome and across the broad square that divided it from the cathedral of Hagia Sophia. Michael ordered me to hold my chalice high, urged the dung-bearer to raise his burden, and led us, chanting, round and round the square. Two boy thurifers followed us, scenting the air with acrid smoke.

At first, no one noticed. I suppose we looked like any other religious procession. There were always plenty of them: monks upholding their privileges or showing off icons, the guardians of out-of-the-way shrines airing their relics, stylites in search of patrons, provincial bishops justifying a visit to the city, pilgrims parading flasks of oil brought back from the Holy Land, or Ignatians trying to provoke a disturbance. A procession from one church to another, taking in a few turns round the square to show off their holy objects, would be routine for any of those groups, and, except on holy days and in emergencies, the public had learned to ignore them. We might have circled the square many times without anyone noticing that we venerated dung instead of bread, had not Photius emerged from the cathedral. He too was at the head of a procession, accompanied by a small selection of the many priests, deacons, choristers, monks, and others of all ranks that both helped and hindered him in his patriarchal duties.

"It is my patriarch," Michael said. "Let us go and greet him." He strode forward confidently, making his way across the square, which is a large one, as visitors to Constantinople will know. We straggled after him, not at all sure what would happen when mock priests met real ones. I, in particular, did not want my master to see me attending the emperor while dressed as a Metropolitan of Thessalonica.

When we neared the cathedral of Hagia Sophia the pace of

the patriarchal procession faltered. Photius looked irritated at the prospect of his serene progress being hampered by provincials, petitioners, or attention-seeking zealots. I could see him studying our ill-assorted costumes, trying to work out what sort of trouble we were going to cause him.

Michael's followers, sharing my unease, huddled together, trying to hide behind each other or conceal their faces behind ecclesiastical headgear.

"Don't hold back," Michael said, frowning at his friends. "Let us greet the patriarch." Some of the group adopted humble postures, ready to bow or beg a blessing. "That won't do," Michael said. "Patriarch Photius is a friend of mine. We must greet him in a friendly manner."

When Photius saw who was leading our procession he was astonished. The emperor had no bodyguards, was not surrounded by musicians and singers, or by bands of noisy Blues and Greens. Yet he was leading a procession of some sort. It was all most irregular. Even so, Photius knew what to do. He had not seen Michael that day, and was ready, as protocol requires, to throw himself prostrate on the ground.

"Your Majesty!" he said, falling quickly to his knees. His retinue imitated him, dropping their impedimenta, hoisting the skirts of their vestments, bending stiff knees and falling forward onto the hard cobbles. Before Photius could fling himself down, Michael reached out to him and took his arm. "Stand up," he said. "There is no need for formality. We are not in the palace, and as you can see, I am not dressed in my court clothes."

The patriarchal party, not sure whether they were included in Michael's instructions, hesitated. Some, unable to stop themselves, toppled to the ground. Others, stuck halfway, clutched at each other for support, trying to stand again with dignity.

"You must come with me," Michael said, gripping the patriarch's arm more firmly.

"I am leading a solemn procession," Photius said. I could see from his expression that my master was still baffled at seeing his emperor before him instead of what he had taken to be a rival bishop. If he had noticed that I was among Michael's party he did not show it.

Michael turned to the patriarchal retinue. "By imperial order," he said, "I am calling your patriarch away. The rest of you can carry on without him."

Back in the stables Michael ordered some of the grooms to set up bales of hay in imitation of couches. When all was ready he invited Photius to sit beside him.

"What is the matter?" he asked, seeing my master's puzzled expression.

"Nothing," Photius said. "This just seems such an odd place to bring me."

"Surely you are not too proud to come here? I understand that Our Lord was born in a stable."

"Of course, but I cannot understand why your majesty should humble himself so."

"Actually, you have a point. The stables are a little untidy. Squalid, some would say." Michael looked down and delicately touched a pile of dung with a silk-shod toe. "That is why I am having the stables enlarged and improved. The masons are at work even now, cladding some of the other buildings with marble, laying mosaics, and so on. It's all terribly expensive, or so my uncle Bardas tells me. But why should I listen to him? I plan to have the fittings gilded, and the ceilings painted. What kind of pictures would please horses, do you think?"

Photius looked startled. "Meadows, perhaps?"

"Excellent! I will suggest it to the artists next time I visit the works. In the meantime, this is where I come to relax, to spend time with my friends when the duties of empire become too much. Everyone needs somewhere like this. I am sure you do. I believe you slip back to your own house from time to time, when you want to escape from the patriarchate, and share a drink with old friends."

Photius glared at me, but if anyone had told the emperor about my master's habits it was not me.

"And talking of drink," Michael said. "Let us have some wine. Reciting the liturgy is a dry job, is it not?"

"It is, and I would be glad of a drink. Wise men say 'one cup for health, a second for pleasure, and a third for a good night's sleep.'"

Wine was brought and the two of them served, and only when some of it had been drunk did Photius dare ask the question that had been nagging at him since first seeing us.

"May I ask, respectfully of course, why you and your friends are all dressed as priests."

"We have been celebrating a Eucharist of our own. A Paulician one."

Photius almost fell off the straw couch. I had to step forward to steady him. "Paulician!" he said. "Surely you are not a heretic?"

"Of course not. As everyone knows, there are no Paulicians in the empire. I have driven them all out. We have just been entertaining ourselves. Playing a sort of ecclesiastical joke."

My master's mouth opened and closed, but no words came out.

"I believe you like jokes," Michael said. "Especially theological ones. Didn't you once tease Ignatius with an imaginary heresy?"

Photius gulped some wine. "I did," he said.

"I thought so. But Ignatius was patriarch then, and you were not. I hope you have not become too pompous to share my joke."

"No, of course not."

"Good. I am glad to hear it. Because the next time we have one of our heretical masses, I would like you to join in."

"Me? That would be quite improper!"

"Even as a joke? I thought you said you were not too pompous."

"I can share the joke," Photius said. "The idea of you celebrating a Paulician mass, is of course, most amusing. But taking part would be a different matter altogether."

"I don't see why," Michael said. "That theological prank of yours, wasn't it based on the proposition that we each have two souls, one fallible, the other infallible?"

"It was some such nonsense."

"Nonsense? Are you sure? I sometimes feel as though I have two souls. When I act in court ceremonies and preside over the Church, that is the work of my infallible soul. But when I come here and indulge myself, doing the things I really enjoy, then I am guided by my fallible soul. I sometimes feel torn in two, as though a battle is raging inside me."

"With respect, your majesty, the doctrine of the twin souls was a joke."

"And like many jokes, it struck at the truth. We may not truly have two souls, but we have two aspects. We waver, most of us between perfection and imperfection, good and evil. Even you, my patriarch."

"Like all other men, I am a humble sinner."

"Humble? You do yourself an injustice. You are a renowned expert in so many things. Heresy, for instance. Your knowledge would be invaluable in recreating a Paulician ceremony."

"I have studied heresies, your majesty, but . . ."

"I have an idea," Michael said, giving the rest of us a crafty look. "Let us make a wager. If I win it, you will take part in a Paulician mass. If you win it, you will not."

"What would the wager be on?"

"Did you not say something about wine, earlier?"

"I quoted a proverb. One cup for health, a second for pleasure, and a third for a good night's sleep."

"Three cups! I've seen you drink more than that."

"Only when the occasion demands it."

Photius was not being entirely honest when he said that. He was an enthusiastic if undiscriminating drinker. I had tried to improve the quality of the wine he consumed, though I do not think he noticed. But when a man enjoys wine, needs wine, as much as my master did, it seems unfair to deny him. After all, what other pleasures did he have, apart from food? If I have not said so already, I will state here and now that my master was celibate throughout his life. Whatever his enemies accused him of, they never thought of accusing him of any sort of sexual impropriety. Perhaps that is why, despite his supposed dislike of eunuchs, we got on so well. Like an old couple who have been married for decades and long forgotten the ardour of their youth, neither of us was ever troubled by lust.

However, I am interrupting the story.

"Good!" Michael said. "Then let us drink. I will match you cup for cup, and whoever drinks the last cup wins."

Photius groaned, but said nothing.

"Zeno," Michael said. "You know how these things are done. Will you judge the contest, make sure the cups are evenly filled, and keep a count of the score."

"I will, your majesty."

And so the bout began. I was not at all sure which of them would win it, or which of them I wanted to win. Whatever happened, my master risked disgrace, either as a drunkard or as a heretic. Ignoring the desperate glances he gave me, I busied myself setting everything up. I checked the cups and wine, found a stick to keep a tally, arranged the spectators so that they could not interfere in the contest. I set the two guttersnipe thurifers to serve the wine, standing over them to see that they poured evenly and not too much. Then, when I was satisfied that all was ready, I called for the first cups to be drunk.

The two of them, emperor and patriarch, sat side by side on the straw couch, both still dressed in elaborate vestments. Smiling, Michael raised his cup to Photius, then downed its contents. Grimly, Photius copied him. The cups were refilled and the process repeated. The first dozen cups were emptied quickly, and there was little time for the wine to take effect. Another dozen followed, then a third. It was after about three dozen cups, I recalled, that Michael's Ferghanese bodyguard had lost his contest with Inger. I daresay Michael remembered that too. He held his empty cup out. "Are you willing to go on?" he asked.

"Of course," Photius said. The drink had thawed his manner. He looked as though he was enjoying himself.

They drank on, downing cup after cup, until they had finished a fourth dozen. I looked at the emperor expectantly. He held his cup out again, but his hand shook, and he was no longer smiling. Michael drank two more cups, matched by Photius. But after his fiftieth cup the emperor slumped forward suddenly, then vomited, adding a few more splashes of colour to his gaudy vestments. Basiliscianus rushed forward to attend to him, not fearing, as the others did, to lay hands on their ruler. He loosened Michael's collar, mopped his brow and settled him comfortably on the straw couch.

Photius was unconcerned. He held out his cup for a refill. The guttersnipe looked at me anxiously.

"Are you sure?" I asked.

"I am sure," Photius said. "I am going to win this contest outright. I don't want any quibbling afterwards."

My master's cup was filled and emptied ten more times. After drinking his sixtieth measure of wine, he got unsteadily to his feet, took my arm, and asked me to take him home.

"How could you let me down like that?" Photius said, as he lay in bed the next morning. "How could you stand by while I got dragged into something like that?"

I had already sent messages to the patriarchate, warning his staff that he was indisposed. "I am sorry," I said, pouring him another cup of cool water. "But I had no choice, any more than you did. Neither of us can go against the emperor's orders."

"But how did you get mixed up with all his antics?"

"Michael asked for me. He remembered that I took him to the tavern and introduced him to Eudocia. He wanted to go back, to try the same sort of thing again."

"So you have been leading him into temptation?"

"I don't think he needed me for that. He has plenty of ideas of his own."

"So I gather. I daresay you were right not to bother me with tittle-tattle. But you might have told me about these heretical masses."

"I tried to, but you wouldn't let me. You always said he was a good Christian and the guardian of the faith."

"I knew he wasn't perfect. Who is? But I thought of him as thoroughly orthodox. How could I have guessed that he dabbled in heresy? He always took such an interest in the liturgy. And he fought so bravely against the Saracens and Paulicians." Photius thought for a while before continuing. "I suppose, in a sense, Michael is still the guardian of the faith."

"Despite the mock masses?"

"Because of them. He claimed to be worshipping the devil, didn't he? Well, what is that but an inversion of orthodoxy? It is the same with everything. There can be no sin without virtue, no heresy without orthodoxy, no blasphemy without piety. Michael upholds orthodoxy by mocking it, defends the Church by seeming to attack it."

A nightmare
[AD 866]

"Is it true," Bardas said, his face bleak with despair, "that Michael has been worshipping as a Paulician?"

Photius glanced at me before speaking. "I believe so," he said. "If the rumours are to be believed."

Bardas scowled. "Some of the stories are a bit far-fetched. They say that you have taken part in his foul rites, too."

Photius squirmed. "Me? Who could believe that? It's nonsense put about by Ignatius and his followers."

"I knew I was right to depose Ignatius."

"Exactly."

"Maybe I should have dealt with him more finally."

"It is not for me to say."

"I don't know what to believe any more. It seems my nephew is turning into a monster." Bardas tossed down the remains of his wine. "A Paulician, of all things!" He held out his cup and I crept forward to fill it. I was not too proud to act the servant if it enabled me to hear things that might aid my survival. "The Paulicians are worse even than the iconoclasts," Bardas said. "They are, what d'you call them? Manichaeans isn't it?"

Bardas looked to Photius for confirmation, but my master was staring silently at the floor, no doubt wondering how far rumours of his involvement in Michael's antics had spread. "Well," Bardas said. "Whatever you call them, they are liars and hypocrites, I know that much. I've had them interrogated when I've caught them in battle. They always lie to conceal their foul beliefs, even if they are tortured. Their only virtue is that they are fierce fighters. But that makes them little better than brigands. Some of my generals think we ought to leave them on the frontier as a deterrent to the Saracens, much as a farmer might plant a hedge of prickly thorns to keep wolves from his herds. But the farmer who follows that practice is likely to find himself cultivating a field of thorns, having nothing left to feed his flocks on." Bardas paused, pleased with his rustic metaphor, then looked anxiously at Photius. "They are loathsome heretics, aren't they? There's nothing in this idea of leaving them to flourish?"

"I don't know about that," Photius said. "That's a military matter. But the Paulicians are certainly heretics, though not of the sort Michael supposes. They are not devil worshippers at all, but puritan zealots who despise the pleasures of the flesh."

"Puritans?" Bardas shuddered at the thought. "Why would Michael want to worship like them?"

"Assuming that the rumours are true, then I would suggest that Michael chose the Paulicians as his model because they are dangerous, and because their beliefs are supposed to be the antithesis of Christian doctrine. And, as you say, no one can prove him wrong by getting a Paulician to say what he believes in. If there are any Paulicians in Constantinople, they pretend to be good Christians, compounding their heresy with hypocrisy." Photius sighed. "But in that respect they are no worse than some Christians."

"What's got into Michael?" Bardas said. "I tried to make a man of him. I got him interested him in racing. I sent him to taverns for a good time. I provided him with a mistress. But he's taken everything too far. He spends so long running around with those low-life friends of his that he's neglecting his duties. The eunuchs are complaining."

"Do we care about them?"

"No. But the one useful thing they do is make everything run smoothly in the palace, getting everyone in their places, starting ceremonies on time, making sure everyone knows the right words and movements, and so on. What they want is a mechanical emperor, like those golden beasts my brother-in-law had made for the palace. I've never seen the point of them myself. Nothing but a waste of money. But the eunuchs are right about Michael. They say he is turning up late, muddling his words, wandering off to do something else in the middle of an audience. I've seen it for myself. I've had to stand in for him. Nothing wrong with him enjoying a drink, but now he's drunk all the time."

"He always behaves perfectly in the cathedral."

Bardas gave Photius a sour look. "He would. He likes that sort of thing. Don't get me wrong. I know we all have to go to church. But enjoying it's another matter. And it's not as though he's the pious type. I expect your services give Michael ideas for the fun and games he gets up to in the Hippodrome stables. I don't understand it. It's not natural for a young man like him to enjoy dressing up in vestments, and so on."

"I think Basil is behind it," Photius said. "Michael is, if you will forgive me for saying so, odd." Bardas frowned, but my master ignored him. "I think we can all agree on that. Michael is odd. But I cannot believe he is wicked. Basil is another matter. He may be a peasant, but he is Armenian, and we know what Armenians are like. Basil knows exactly what he is doing. If all the stories are true, then Basil is leading Michael into a labyrinth. A place in which he will be confused, and from which there will be no escape."

Bardas took another swig of wine and sank back on his couch. He was puzzled by my master's talk of labyrinths. After a period of silent brooding he came up with an opinion. "Something needs to be done about Basil."

"Yes," Photius said. "We need to get Michael away from him and diminish his influence. Not to mention the rest of his friends. Can't you take him on another expedition against the Saracens?"

"We are due to sail for Crete next month. But Basil is to come with us. Michael has insisted on it."

"I suppose that is understandable," Photius said. "Basil is the High Chamberlain."

"Exactly. Something's got to be done about Basil!"

"True, but what?"

Bardas drained his cup again. "He might have an accident. Battlefields are dangerous places. Who knows what might happen?"

"Or what might not," Photius said. "Basil is very strong, as well as cunning. I suspect he can look after himself perfectly well in battle, just as he does elsewhere. If we are not careful he might end up sharing a Triumph with Michael, and then where will we be?"

"Taking orders from a jumped-up peasant."

"Exactly," Photius said. "But I don't see what we can do."

"I got rid of Theoctistus, didn't I?"

I was surprised to hear Bardas remind us of the murder he had committed in the palace, but Photius gave him a sly look. "That was an unfortunate business," he said. "But you were clearly overcome by anger."

"I was absolved though, wasn't I?"

"Of course! We cannot be held responsible for what is out of our control. And good came from your actions, or seemed to. But anger is a sin, we must remember that."

"In that case," Bardas said. "I'll make sure I don't act in anger again."

"Good. It is best to avoid sin, if possible. But I am sure that whatever proves to be necessary, if it is done for the good of the empire, will be forgiven."

Of course, they were wrong about Basil. Whatever he had done in the past, whatever power he wielded as High Chamberlain, he had been replaced as Michael's favourite by Basiliscianus. I daresay I could have told them that. But I had no objection to something unpleasant happening to Basil, as long as it happened far way, where there was no risk to Eudocia.

A couple of weeks later, just before he was about to depart for Crete, Bardas had a nightmare. He rushed to Photius babbling about the crowds of saints and eunuchs that had plagued his sleep.

"Most distasteful," Photius said. "But I know nothing about dreams and portents. Oneiromancy is a mystery to me. We must send for Leo. He will explain your dream."

The philosopher was nearly eighty by then, and still teaching at the university, though he looked more like a magician than ever, his white beard hanging halfway down his chest, his clothes patched with any colour that had come to hand.

"The eunuchs," Leo asked. "Were they dressed in their court robes?"

"Of course they wore their robes," Bardas said, shuddering. "Do you think I'd dream about naked eunuchs? It was a procession, an endless one. They marched like an army, on and on, round and round the palace, out of one door, in through another, appearing and reappearing. They were like a regiment of women, stinking of perfume, painted and powdered, dressed in silks and jewels. It was horrible! Unnatural! Their shrill voices nagging at me all the time, going on at me for killing Theoctistus, saying I was denying them their privileges, and so on."

"That seems clear enough," Leo said. "What about the saints?"

"I don't rightly know who some of them were. But they were saints, all right. They had golden light round their heads, just like in icons. And they were carrying things. Books, crosses, palm leaves, shrouds. One of them was very stern. He lectured me about my sins. He had a great big key, and was using it to close some doors that shone like the bronze gates of the palace."

"Saint Peter," Leo said. "Shutting the gates of Heaven."

A look of horror spread over Bardas's face. "Does that mean I'm damned?"

"It means you are feeling guilty," Leo said. "Quite apart from what you did to Theoctistus, everyone knows how you hate eunuchs."

"What about the saints? Will I go to Purgatory?"

"There is some doubt," Photius said, "as to whether Purgatory actually exists. It is one of the matters on which the pope and I disagree. In the West . . . "

Bardas and Leo both glared at him.

"Saint Peter," Leo said, "stands for Rome and the papacy. The pope backs Ignatius, whom you deposed."

"I did it for the empire," Bardas said.

"Are you sure of that? Didn't Ignatius condemn you for adultery?"

I was surprised that Leo spoke so frankly to Bardas, but he was a very old man, close to death as it turned out, with little left to hope for, or to fear.

"I deposed Ignatius to give us the patriarch we deserved." Bardas looked pleadingly at Photius. "I did the right thing, didn't I?"

"I really couldn't say. Though Ignatius was clearly far too stupid and ignorant to be patriarch."

Bardas stood silently, his chest heaving, his mouth opening and closing. "What does it all mean? The dream? The portents?"

Leo spoke frankly again. "It means that you fear death, which is natural enough in a soldier about to embark on a campaign. You also fear the consequences of your sins. In that respect, you are no different to anyone else, though perhaps your sins are worse."

"Sins? I did everything for the good of the empire."

"Perhaps you are contemplating some new sin. There must be plenty of opportunities on campaign."

"Yes," Bardas said impatiently. "But what does my dream foretell?"

"Are you sure you want to know?"

"Yes. That's why you are here."

"Very well. In my opinion, having considered the nature and substance of your dream, and the symbols it contained, I would say that you are about to be replaced in the emperor's favour."

"Who by?"

"It is your dream. You know better than I do who you fear."

Bardas, despite being a grizzled veteran of fifty years old, went weak at the knees and collapsed onto a couch. While I went for some wine and summoned servants with wet cloths to revive the trembling Caesar, Leo slipped away.

A month later, I was surprised to see Photius thrown into a fit of violent agitation while reading a letter. "Wine!" he shouted, leaping to his feet and staggering towards the library door. "Bring me wine!"

The parts of his face that were visible between his uncut hair and ever-flowing beard were as white as a sheet of finest parchment. His hand shook so badly that he could hardly hold on to the letter. I led him to his couch and poured out a cup of unresinated Cretan, always the best I think, for quenching an urgent thirst, though not, in view of what had happened, a tactful choice. He downed three or four cups before the colour returned to his cheeks and he felt like speaking.

"The news," he said, holding up the letter. "It is terrible."

"What news," I asked.

"Bardas is dead. My friend and protector, the true ruler of the empire, gone!"

"But how? Did he die in battle?"

"Basil has killed him."

"Basil killed Bardas? I thought Bardas was to . . ."

"So did I." Photius looked around anxiously to make sure no servants were present. I had already made sure of that when I brought the wine. "Whatever we thought," he said, "we were wrong."

"Where did it happen?"

"In Miletus. They stopped there before sailing on to Crete. According to this letter Michael discovered that his uncle was plotting against him, so he ordered Basil to kill him."

It struck me that there was something suspicious about the news, which was the opposite of what we might have expected.

"Were there witnesses?" I asked.

"Witnesses?" Photius waved the letter feebly. "According to the messenger who brought this, it happened in front of everyone. It is incredible! Just before they left, I gave them all the Sacrament, and they all swore on the Eucharist that they would support and protect each other in war."

I knew well enough what Michael thought of the Eucharist, and doubted that Basil or Bardas were any more pious. But I could not quite imagine the scene Photius had described.

Later I found out the truth. There were so many witnesses that it could hardly be kept secret. That in itself was worrying. It showed how bold Basil was, and how little he cared who saw what he did to win power.

Basil and Bardas had argued from the outset, disagreeing about which route to follow, what supplies they needed, how to get the Saracens out of Crete, what to do with the island afterwards, whether to sail on and attack Egypt, and a host of other military matters too recondite to be of general interest. By the time they reached Miletus they were barely speaking to each other. But in public, to reassure the army, and to please Michael, they had to seem harmonious. The three men dined together with local notables, and entertained the generals of the eastern regiments. They reviewed the troops together, and sat side by side on a silk-draped dais, hearing reports, receiving petitions, doing the usual things that emperors and their generals do when they go to the provinces.

But all the time, Basil was planning to murder his rival. He did not intend to act alone, but had with him six conspirators. Two of them were Armenians, keen to help a fellow countryman. The others hated Bardas because their womenfolk had been dishonoured in one or other of his love affairs. These conspirators were to rush Bardas while he was seated on the reviewing stand, all striking at once so that no one man could be held responsible. Basil, knowing when they were to strike, had stepped down from the stand, leaving Bardas and Michael sitting together.

That fact, which all the witnesses agreed on, makes me think that Basil was planning to kill Michael as well, or at least hoped that Michael would be injured in the affray. But the plan, whatever it really was, did not come off. The conspirators rushed from behind the reviewing stand, brandishing their swords and chanting "death to Bardas". But when they saw Michael sitting so close to their intended victim they hesitated. They looked around and saw the huge mass of troops drawn up for inspection, all of them fully armed. Then they panicked and tried to run, throwing their swords away. Some of the soldiers broke ranks and hurled themselves at the conspirators, killing one of them and knocking the others to the ground.

Basil, seeing his scheme fail, might have stayed among the soldiers he was inspecting, and watched the conspirators being executed. But he did not. With a terrible roar, he barged through the melee, leapt onto the reviewing stand and drew his sword, swinging it wildly at Bardas. Michael, utterly terrified, dived to the floor and rolled away, bumping down the steps to the dusty parade ground. When he was helped to his feet he saw his uncle lying dead, with Basil standing over him, a bloody sword in his hand.

"Bardas was a criminal!" Basil shouted. His voice was so commanding that the struggle below him stopped immediately. The surviving conspirators, bruised and dazed, struggled to their feet. Basil pointed at them. "These men are my witnesses. Bardas was going to kill me. He has killed before. He murdered Theoctistus. He would have done it again. And he was an adulterer. These men know that well."

With those words Basil drew a long dagger from his belt and held it high, allowing the sun to glint off its polished blade. Then he bent over the corpse and began to hack at it, tearing off the blood-sodden silk clothes until Bardas was half-naked. He glared at his dead rival for a moment, then plunged the dagger again, slicing quickly and viciously. When he stood and faced the crowd again there was something in his hand. He held it up, dangling it from his bloodstained hand. It was the dead man's genitals.

"Here!" he said, flinging the flaccid penis to the ground. "This is the part that caused offence." He pointed at the severed organ, which dribbled blood into the dust. "That is what led him into sin."

In death, Bardas became what he most despised, a eunuch. But his humiliation did not end there. Basil hacked his body to bits. He swung at it with a great battleaxe borrowed from an Armenian soldier. He wielded the weapon like a butcher, raising the half-moon blade high above his head before smashing it downwards, splitting bone and cutting sinews, reducing the body of Bardas to a heap of mangled flesh and burst guts.

By the time Basil finished, his clothes were drenched with blood, and the silk covering of the dais was splattered with gore. Michael had looked on impassively while his friend butchered Bardas, and made no protest while his uncle's genitals were stuck on a spear and paraded round the camp. The Armenian regiments hailed Basil as a hero, the mercenaries were given extra pay, and any troops who might have been loyal to Bardas kept silent. Perhaps all the soldiers were glad that they would no longer have to go to Crete and fight the dreaded Saracens.

Photius was still gazing at the letter, muttering about the Sacrament, and about the phial of Christ's blood the three men had used to sign their declaration of amity. In the past he had been sceptical about that blood, which was uncongealed, and never ran out, however often it was deployed. But on that occasion, stunned by the bad news, he was astonished that the relic had not saved his friend.

"You don't think the message could be a trick?" I asked.

"A trick? Why?"

"To test you. To find out what you think, what you will do."

"Michael regards me as a friend and guide. He told me so. He would never think of such a thing."

"No, but Basil might. He may have had this news sent to find out what the reaction would be."

"So if I were to condemn the murder . . ."

"That would be a mistake. How can you condemn the execution of a traitor? You did not condemn Bardas when he killed Theoctistus."

Photius shuddered. "Don't remind me. It was a terrible business."

"Yet your friendship for Bardas did not diminish."

"He did what he had to do. For the good of the empire."

"Basil will make exactly the same claim."

Photius drank a little of his wine. "If this is true, it is a disaster. Not only have I lost a friend, but without Bardas there is no one to restrain Michael."

"Except for Basil."

"Whatever happens now," Photius said, "whether this news is true or false, I must retain my influence with Michael.

235

I must write to him before he returns to the city. Will you take a letter?"

Photius dictated a long letter which I later copied out for him to sign. He did not mention Bardas by name, or acknowledge that the dead man had ever been his friend. Instead he expressed at great length his joy that the emperor had escaped the machinations of his enemies, and lamented the wickedness of those enemies, whoever they were. I was amazed at the number of different ways he found to express those sentiments, and all without saying anything of substance. I suppose it was a skill that came from writing sermons and giving pastoral advice to priests who were far more pious than he was.

At one point in the letter, at my insistence, Photius alluded to the possibility that the news might be false, only to dismiss the idea in view of the emperor's great virtue and clemency. He finished by urging Michael to return as soon as possible to Constantinople, which he no doubt intended to do anyway, where he would be greeted joyfully by the entire population.

Photius felt better when the letter was sent, but he soon started to feel anxious again. "If Bardas could be brought down like that," he said, "then anyone can."

I did not want to alarm him, but I agreed.

"I am defenceless without Bardas," he said. "Remember what happened to Methodius when he was patriarch? He died mysteriously, just when they wanted to appoint Ignatius. I always suspected poison. It could happen to me, if I'm not careful. I don't think I will return to the patriarchate. I've never really felt comfortable there. The place will be full of spies, I feel sure of it. There will be plenty of people wanting to replace me. Not just Ignatius, but others. I will be much safer here in my own house. I can get to the cathedral easily, and I can have all my work sent here. You will help me, won't you?"

"Of course I will."

"There's something else."

"Yes?"

"I'd like you to sleep in my room."

"Like the emperor's chamberlain?" I asked, though my example was not perhaps a good one. We were far from sure that Basil had his master's interests at heart.

"Exactly! With you sleeping across the doorway, I will feel much safer."

Years earlier, when I first arrived at his house, Photius had thrown me out of his bedroom. Because of my stupidity, and his embarrassment, it took much longer than it might have done for Photius to learn to trust me. Now he wanted me to guard him while he slept. There could be no greater trust than that.

Questions
[AD 866]

I cannot say that I ever liked Bardas. He had occasionally been
generous to me, giving me money when Photius told him
that I had helped their schemes. He usually ignored me, taking
my presence for granted, as though I really was no more than a
scribe or cup-bearer, and not the confidant of his friend.
Bardas had always made his hatred for eunuchs clear, and I had
no reason to think he liked me any more than the others of
my kind. In fact, I had reason to be glad at his death, as Cyril
could no longer threaten to tell him of my part in Theodore's
false prophecy. But if my master regretted the death of his
friend, then I had cause to regret it too.

By the time Michael and Basil returned to Constantinople
Photius was already settled into his new routine, going to the
cathedral only when he had to, seldom venturing out into the
city, spending little time at the patriarchate, doing most of his
work in the safety of his own house. I could see that he was
happier for it. Relieved not to have been punished or deposed,
he raised no objection when Michael made Basil his co-
emperor. Despite all that had happened, Photius took part in
the coronation without protest. Basil was dressed in purple,
seated beside Michael on a splendid throne, and crowned with
a diadem blessed by my master. Photius knew that doing
exactly as he was told was the price of his office. Under Bardas
he had been able to do that without too many qualms. But
under the combined rule of Basil and Michael, who knew
what a patriarch might be required to do or assent to?

Nine years earlier, before an audience that could never have
guessed what he would later become, Basil had defeated a
Bulgar giant in a wrestling match. Since then, Khan Boris had
sulked, prevaricated, played Rome off against Constantinople,
and eventually accepted baptism and ordered the conversion

of his people. But there were aspects of Christianity that did not please him. He wrote, both to the pope and to Photius, asking for guidance on a variety of topics. I cared nothing for the Bulgars or their beliefs, but I encouraged my master to throw himself into the problem, encouraging him to expand his domain, diverting him with endless details. He, despite the risk of losing the Bulgars to Rome, was inclined to scoff.

"The Khan asks here," I said, reading from his letter, "whether polygamy is permissible."

"Of course not."

"Basil has two wives."

Photius winced, even though my comment was not meant to provoke him. I simply intended to remind him that our new emperor had faults and secrets which might one day be exploited.

"Not officially," Photius said. "If Basil is married to Eudocia, and I can attest that he is, then the other woman is a concubine, and any children she may have produced are bastards, whatever rustic rite she may have gone through. The law is quite clear. Polygamy is forbidden for Christians, and the Khan must be told that firmly."

"Are rulers allowed concubines?"

"No, but we would be foolish to say so."

I made a note for the reply, then studied the Khan's letter again.

"Khan Boris would like to know whether priests are allowed to marry?"

"Lesser orders, yes. Higher orders, no."

"The pope does not allow any of his priests to marry."

"Then I expect my policy will prove very popular with the Bulgars."

"The Bulgars would like to know what beasts they are permitted to eat."

"Then let them read Leviticus."

"Is that strictly relevant?"

"It will do for them."

"The Khan asks whether it is permissible for his people to wear trousers."

"Trousers? Why does he bother me with such trivial matters?"

"It must be important to his people."

"Why should God care whether their legs are covered or not?"

"Someone must have told them that He does."

"A papal missionary, I expect, spreading nonsense to confuse the Bulgars and undermine my good work. Well I say, let them wear trousers if that's what they want. They may be Christians now, but they're still barbarians."

I noted that trousers were permitted.

"Are they allowed to eat cheese during Lent."

"No."

"I understand that cheese is an important element in the Bulgar diet, and that the pope permits it."

"Then the pope is wrong."

"They may find his policy more to their liking than yours."

"I will not compromise the purity of the faith for the sake of the Bulgars' fondness for cheese."

I recorded his views.

"What about praying for their ancestors?"

"That's a tricky one. I will have to think about it. We should revere our ancestors, of course, but not if it involves any sort of pagan magic. And definitely not if they think their ancestors are gods, or anything like that."

"Are they allowed to pray for rain?"

"They may pray for it, but not try to induce it by spells or incantations."

"What about curing illness with miraculous stones?"

"Blatant paganism."

"But I've seen doctors in Constantinople do just the same."

"If so, then they were allowing God's grace to pass through some holy object in order to effect a cure. There is nothing pagan about that."

"Do you think the Bulgars will understand the distinction?"

"Why not? It is perfectly simple."

"They seem very confused about the Procession of the Holy Spirit."

"Only because the pope's minions have been filling their heads with nonsense. Their doctrines are just watered-down Sabellianism. Who could possibly believe that the Holy Spirit proceeds from the Son as well as the Father? That heresy has been condemned by every synod since Nicea!"

Photius composed a long letter of guidance for the Khan, expressed in the most elegant language, modelled on the best of antique literature. It ignored nearly all the practical matters we had discussed, but listed every Ecumenical Synod, giving full details of all their decisions, as though that alone was enough to instruct a wavering convert in the orthodox faith. The rest of his letter described the character, duties and obligations of an ideal ruler, matters that Photius had had the opportunity to ponder, if not to observe. He particularly recommended sobriety.

I tried to modify my master's tone and make him write a shorter, less learned, more useful letter, but it was no use. The result was that the Khan threw out all Photius's missionaries and replaced them with priests from Rome.

For some time I had heard nothing from Eudocia. I longed to see her, to talk to her, just to be with her sometimes. And I feared for her safety. It cannot have been pleasant to have a murderer for a husband, even if he was a husband in name only. For all I knew, Basil might have pushed Michael aside and taken Eudocia for himself. But I knew nothing. She did not summon me, my letters and messages went unanswered, and there was nothing I could do to get in touch with her. She lived in the most inaccessible part of the palace, guarded by servants, eunuchs and ladies-in-waiting. Though my master's business took me to the palace now and again, it was useless even trying to get near the imperial quarters without an official pass. The Ferghanese bodyguards would have killed anyone who tried, and I had no intention of dying at the end of a curved Turkish sword.

Then, about a year after her wedding, Eudocia gave birth to a boy, and I was invited to view the child. Her rooms were grander than I had imagined, glinting with gold, the air heavy with eastern perfumes, the walls draped with purple silk, as befitted the wife of a co-emperor. But nothing in that room could dim Eudocia's beauty. She was like a goddess, like Odin's twofold wife, both Freyja, giver of love, and Frigg the Earth Mother. I wondered where Eudocia kept the idol her father had given her, and whether she had invoked its aid to conceive.

As though in Asgard, Eudocia sat in state, surrounded by wealth, attended by servants, closely watched by a pair of grim-looking matrons who were most reluctant to move away when she dismissed her other attendants. They watched me suspiciously while I knelt and kissed Eudocia's hand. It felt odd to be abasing myself before a woman I had dandled as a child. I suppose many servants must have had the same experience. I did not feel like a servant. I felt like a fellow conspirator. Did anyone else in that magnificent chamber know where Eudocia really came from, exactly what she was? I half expected her to wink at me, to let me know she was in on the joke. But she kept her composure, receiving my homage gracefully, allowing my lips to linger for a moment on her jewelled hand before permitting me to stand.

"Who are they?" I asked, when she eventually persuaded the two matrons to withdraw.

She pulled a wry face. "My aunts."

"You mean . . . " I looked anxiously at the alcove where they lurked. The room was large, but the two matrons might still have been within earshot.

"That's right," Eudocia said. "They were sent by my so-called family, and now I can't get rid of them. They watch everything I do. The only person they are afraid of is Basil."

It was hard to imagine what her life must have been like since she had moved into the palace. There were many questions I might have asked her, but none were politic.

"Motherhood suits you," I said. "You are more beautiful than ever."

"You flatter me," she said. "But everyone does."

There was a touch of sadness in her voice, and I did not

know how to respond. How could I, a eunuch freedman without rank or honour, tell the noble Eudocia how I felt?

"How is the child?" I asked, remembering why I had been summoned.

"Come and see," she said. Instead of summoning a nurse, Eudocia rose from her carved chair and led me to the cradle herself. I gazed down at the boy, trying to recapture something of the affection I had felt for his mother when she was young. Having been almost a brother to Eudocia, the boy would have been a sort of nephew to me, and that is the closest a eunuch can get to fatherhood. Looking at the wrinkled face that peered out from thick layers of swaddling, I tried to think of something appropriate to say.

"What is he called?" I asked.

"Leo."

"Like the philosopher."

"Who?"

"Leo the philosopher, an old friend of my master."

"I don't know him." Eudocia looked down fondly at her son. "His father chose the name."

I could hardly ask her who the father was, even though that was what everyone wanted to know, so I studied the child, searching for clues. A few wisps of dark hair escaped from its hood. But Basil and Michael were both dark, so that was no help. Leo's face was as shapeless as a ball of dough. Only the most doting mother would have been able to see any hint of paternity there. It occurred to me that perhaps all children begin life blank and unformed, only acquiring shape and character when their parentage is acknowledged. In which case, unless Eudocia admitted adultery with the emperor, Leo would come to resemble Basil.

That thought reminded me of Eudocia's plight, and the rest of the visit passed in a slow agony of small talk. I was almost relieved when a smirking eunuch appeared and informed me that it was time to go.

"You have seen the infant?" Theodore said, as though Prince Leo was a great portent or wonder of nature. He had made a point of coming to find me in my master's library as soon he heard that I had visited the imperial quarters.

"I have," I said. "And I can assure you that everything about him is completely normal. He has one head, two arms, and, as far as I could tell, two legs."

"Yes, of course," Theodore said. "But when was he born?"

"A few weeks ago, I suppose."

"A few weeks! It must be less than forty days. She hasn't had the ritual bath yet has she?"

"I don't know."

"And she's still confined to her quarters?"

"She's been confined there since the wedding."

"You must have some idea when the child was born."

"I am no expert on babies."

"How can I cast a horoscope?"

"Have you been asked to?"

"No, and neither has anyone else. It's most odd. Horoscopes are always cast for infants born in the palace. But in this case, no one has been commissioned. And if they had been, I would know."

"You're not interested in knowing the child's future," I said. "You only want to know when it was born so you can work out when it was conceived, and know who its father is."

"You are quite wrong," Theodore said. "I am not in the least interested in tittle-tattle. I am only interested in uncovering the truth." He tried to look haughty, and stepped away from me as though in disgust. But before he reached the door to the courtyard he turned back. "You must admit," he said, "the child's paternity is of interest. Didn't Eudocia tell you anything?"

"No."

"I suppose it's only natural. I wouldn't like to be her, stuck between Michael and Basil. The consequences could be nasty for her, whichever of them is the father. But you know what I think? It's Michael. He's the father. I know what they say, that Michael is always drunk, that he prefers men, that he hasn't fathered a child by the empress. But Basil is worse. They say he went through some mockery of the marriage vows with two other men before he met Michael. He took money for it, too. I can't believe a man of that sort could have fathered a child, even if he is married to the lovely Eudocia."

I did not know what to think. I knew that Eudocia really had been Michael's mistress once. But I also knew that Michael's seed had been used up, wasted in places where it could not ferment and form an embryo. And I had seen how Basil and Eudocia gazed at each other on their wedding night. Despite Theodore's aspersions, Basil's potency was not in doubt. He already had a son by his previous marriage. But I said nothing to Theodore, who could never be trusted with a secret, and somehow turned even common knowledge to his own advantage.

"I'm sure I'm right," Theodore said. "I may not know the moment of conception, but I have consulted the *Chaldean Oracle*."

"Do you expect me to believe in that? Remember, I was there when you cooked up that prophecy about Michael marrying Eudocia."

"Cooked up? You insult me." Theodore tried to look hurt, but he was not very convincing. "The *Chaldean Oracle* knows more than any man. It embodies the wisdom of the ancients. Don't forget, every word of that prophecy came true. Bardas did rule, and Michael did marry a woman called Eudocia."

"The wrong one!"

"Don't blame me. The oracle revealed the truth, and does so again. It confirms what it predicted the first time. The omens and portents are as clear as they can be. Take it from me, Michael is the father, not Basil. The boy is a bastard."

"You had better not say so. Not in public."

"That depends on which of them prevails," Theodore said. "Michael and Basil will be at odds over this. Some say they hate each other already. If Michael comes out the winner, he might be very glad to find he has a son and heir."

"And you intend to take the credit for discovering this fact?"

Theodore said nothing, but smiled at me mysteriously, hoping I would not notice the book he had slid under his ragged coat. I retrieved the book and escorted him from the library.

In retrospect, I wish Theodore had been able to obtain the details he wanted. Had we known Prince Leo's future, we might have taken steps to protect ourselves. Theodore, as things turned out, had more to fear from that child than any of us.

Underground
[AD 866]

"Where are you taking me?" I asked.

The guard strode on silently, swinging his unsheathed sword, lopping off the dead heads of roses, hacking at any branches that hung in our way. I shuddered at each blow, fearing for my own head. He had led me into a forgotten part of the palace grounds, an overgrown terrace, full of unpruned trees and tangled rose bushes. The leaves had already begun to fall. Between bare branches I glimpsed the grey waters of the Sea of Marmora and the misty Asian shore.

At the end of the terrace, rising above the vegetation like eggs in a nest, was a clutch of marble domes. They must once have shone like a beacon, visible to ships rounding the point, but years of neglect had left them streaked with dirt and tufted with moss and weeds. There was a fountain by the arched entrance, its dry basin filled with wind-blown rose petals. The building, whatever it was, looked abandoned, ready for demolition, a fit site for some new imperial extravagance.

The guard sheathed his sword and urged me up the leaf-strewn steps. The doorkeeper was surprised to see us, but offered towels, which the guard declined with a grim shake of his head. The place, I realised, was a bathhouse, though it was clear, as we briskly marched on, that it was not much used.

A trio of young eunuchs preened and chattered in a corner of changing rooms, their high voices echoing like birdsong from the cracked walls. A few pink bodies floated in the warm pool like sweetmeats in syrup. Dense steam rose from the calm surface of the hot pool, but no one swam in it. Nearby, on a worn marble slab, lay Cyril, his naked flesh falling in pale, quivering folds. A masseur was doing his best to knead the old eunuch's body into shape, but he might as well have been a butcher trying to rearrange a heap of wet, slithering tripe.

"Zeno," Cyril said, his jowls wobbling in time to the masseur's strokes. "I am sorry you had to come through the

247

gardens. There is another way, but we can't have you knowing all our secrets." He attempted, unsuccessfully, to turn over. "You will have to excuse me for a moment." Wheezing heavily in the steam, he allowed the masseur to roll his body over and drape him with a towel.

"We've got this place to ourselves," he said, after dismissing the masseur. "The beards don't use public baths very much. They fear nakedness. It must be something to do with their faith. They are afraid that the sight of flesh will excite their passions and lead them into sin. Of course, we eunuchs are incapable of such things. Well, most of us are. We can do as we like, and no one will suspect us of any impropriety." Cyril lay for a while, breathing heavily, then turned his face towards me. "What a long time it is since we last met. I think it was at the wedding of Basil and Eudocia, was it not?"

"It was."

"There was a question I set you to answer. I wanted to know whether it was Basil or Michael who enjoyed her favours that night. You have not supplied me with an answer."

"I don't know the answer."

"In which case, you are not much use to me. After all, you haven't sent me any reports recently.

"I informed you about the drinking contest."

"That was months ago."

"I haven't seen Michael since then."

"Why not?" There was a note of exasperation in Cyril's voice. My damp clothes clung to me. I felt uncomfortably hot and sweaty. "He doesn't need me now," I said. "He has a new favourite."

"Exactly! Why have you not kept me informed about Basiliscianus?"

"I haven't had the chance. Michael has forgotten about me."

"I think not. In fact, I have reason to believe you will be receiving a summons from him very soon."

Cyril, lying supine on the slab, viewed through the steam of the hot room, looked utterly helpless. He was like a spineless sea creature washed up on a rocky shore. A little more buffeting by the waves, and his shapeless body would dissolve into nothing. I did not believe that he had the power to make me do anything. With Bardas dead, what could he threaten me with? I was determined not to betray Photius again.

"No," I said. "I've had enough. I will serve my master, and no one else."

"Your master?" Cyril spoke softly. "I suppose you mean Photius. But what is he without Bardas to protect him? What power does he have now? Haven't you noticed how things have changed? Michael has let everything go. It didn't matter so much when he was just having a bit of fun. So long as we could keep track of him, we could allow that. But he is drunk all the time now. Sometimes he doesn't seem to know whether he is in the palace or at a tavern. He forgets the right words and gestures. And if the emperor cannot perform his ceremonial role, then the social order collapses."

"You mean that the court eunuchs are less important."

"It is not just us. It is the beards too. The nobles, the senators, the generals, the priests, the servants. No one knows how to behave at court, how to present themselves."

"My master the patriarch knows his duties."

"If Michael carries on like this, then Basil will destroy us all, and who will be your master then?" Cyril's voice sank almost to a whisper. "Do you want us all to be thrown out of the palace?"

The old eunuch, I decided, was pathetic as well as powerless. "It makes no difference to me," I said. "I am not one of your kind."

Suddenly, and with surprising ease, Cyril sat up. "You are a fool," he said, in a firm, loud voice. "You have understood nothing." He clapped his hands, then swung his body round so that he sat on the edge of the slab. Alarmed by his newfound vigour, I stepped back. "You can wait there," he said. "The guard won't let you out until I've finished with you."

Two servants appeared, bearing baskets of towels and clothing, accompanied by the guard. They quickly dried Cyril off and dressed him in fresh linen, finishing his costume with a long tunic that disguised his shapelessness. He sat with ill-concealed impatience while another servant dressed his hair into its usual pigeon-wing style, then he stood and gripped my arm. His plump hand was far stronger than I expected.

"Come with me," he said. "Then you might understand where your duty lies."

Cyril led me quickly away from the hot room, the guard following close behind, his sword sheathed but ready. The steam diminished but the darkness increased, so I had little idea where we were going. Stumbling over loose paving stones, following Cyril down steep steps and along narrow, sloping passages, I glimpsed empty chambers, cluttered store-rooms, heaps of firewood, and glowing furnaces stoked by hunched slaves. At Cyril's command, one of the slaves plucked a firebrand from a brazier and went ahead of us, lighting the way as we went deeper beneath the palace.

We halted by a grated archway, rather lower than a man's height. Cyril rattled the bars and called out, demanding to be let in. Wanting no such thing, I held back, but the presence of the guard, and the knowledge that I might never find my way out of that dark labyrinth, prevented me from fleeing. I waited uneasily while an unseen figure heaved the grating open, then allowed myself to be pushed through the archway.

Almost as soon as the grating crashed behind me, something grabbed at my ankles. I lurched forward and fell against the wall, failed to find a grip on the slimy surface, then toppled into a heap of stinking straw. As I lay there, the slave swung his firebrand, and I glimpsed a horrible creature scuttling away from me. It had been a man, perhaps, but had no legs, and used its arms to swing its truncated body along the floor.

"Do get up," Cyril said.

I did as I was told, though I dreaded following the creature that had felled me. But I had no choice, and the guard urged me on until we reached the end of the tunnel, and stood in a domed chamber thick with foul air. It stank worse than the Hippodrome menagerie, but there was no ventilation except a tiny air hole high above our heads, at the apex of the dome. I wondered where the hole came out, picturing it among rose bushes, looking like an innocent wellhead to strollers in the palace gardens. The courtiers going about their business above our heads could never have imagined what I saw when I looked around the chamber. Cut into its wall, lit by a few smoking, guttering torches, were a series of cells and niches, some big enough to hold several men, others no bigger than a sarcophagus. All were inhabited by freaks of nature, caged, fettered, or free to wander, according to their kind. There were dwarfs, hunchbacks, a fat woman, a crouching giant, cripples of all sorts, gibbering idiots, a human skeleton, dome-headed imbeciles, a scrawny Negro with a huge penis, creatures with flippers instead of arms, a hairy ape-man, a pair of twins joined at the head, and others, whose deformities were hard to make out in the feeble, flickering light.

"What are they?" I asked.

"Unfortunates," Cyril said. "They were born like it, for the most part, and are kept here for amusement."

"Who could be amused by them?"

"There are people who like deformity, even lust after it. The beards are a strange lot, and it is sometimes useful to be able to cater for their needs."

"And to blackmail them afterwards."

"You are catching on, Zeno." Cyril led me through a door to another smaller chamber. It too was lined with cells. "Not all the inmates are deformed," he said, gesturing at the nearest prisoner. He lay on the filthy floor, twitching and foaming at the mouth, dressed in rags that had once been purple. "He claims to be Theodora's son," Cyril said. "And Michael's half-brother. That would make him useful, if it wasn't for the fits."

Beyond the epileptic pretender was a group of men who looked quite normal, compared to the other inmates.

"These men are supposed to be dead," Cyril said. "They are the disappeared. We keep them here just in case. It might perhaps be in our interests to release a few of them."

He showed me another cell, where half a dozen men were chained up, all deprived of ears, noses and tongues. "Others," he said, "will never be released."

"Who are they?"

"Men who have defied us, or have let us down, who did not understand where their duty lay." Cyril thrust the firebrand towards the cringing prisoners. Hearing voices, they held out their manacled arms and tried to speak, but all that came out of their flapping, empty mouths was a hideous, wordless croaking. The sound, echoing round the subterranean domes, set off the other prisoners, who answered by shaking chains, rattling bars, calling out obscenities, wailing and shrieking, barking like dogs disturbed in the night.

Cyril did not need to say anything else. He let me gaze at the mutilated prisoners for a while, allowed the chill of the dungeon to seep into my bones, let the horrible noises made by the freaks and imbeciles assault my ears.

"Do you understand?" he said.

"I understand."

"Good." Cyril gripped my arm and led me away, talking as we went back to the light. "When Michael summons you, you will go. You will attend him on whatever jaunt he has planned. And you will make it fail. It is vital that we undermine the influence of this Basiliscianus."

"That may not be necessary."

Cyril stopped and pulled at my arm as though he would lead me back to the dungeon. "I thought you understood. Did I not show you enough?"

"I understand. But I also know that the influence of Basiliscianus will fade soon anyway."

"When?"

"When he is rewarded by Michael."

"What do you mean?"

"Michael is weak, and easily influenced."

"I did not bring you here to learn that."

"Wait, there is more. Michael can be led, but only by nobodies. When his favourites are rewarded with power or status, they lose their influence. Perhaps, having something to lose, they no longer take risks. Or it may be some quirk of Michael's that he only loves the powerless. But I'm right. Think of it! Eudocia was a tavern girl when she met Michael. He was in awe of her beauty, utterly in love, until Bardas

252

installed her in a fine house and made her his official mistress. She lost her power then, and Basil replaced her. He was a peasant, remember, a stable hand, and Michael was in awe of him. But as soon as Basil was made chamberlain, his power over Michael waned. Basil has relied on brute force since then. Now Basiliscianus is following the same path as Basil and Eudocia. He has influence, but only until Michael rewards him."

"At last!" Cyril said. "You have told me something useful. Have there been others who could influence Michael?"

"There was a youth called Gryllus. A fat buffoon. But he lacked ambition and failed to win a reward. He was pushed aside by Basiliscianus."

"Whose influence must be undermined."

"But there is no need. I am trying to explain."

We had emerged into the bathhouse. Cyril stopped and turned to face me. "What you say is interesting, Zeno. But I think you exaggerate. And it makes no difference whether Basiliscianus is about to fall. He is Michael's favourite now, and Michael's madness must be stopped. Otherwise, we are all finished. You must go on this next jaunt, and make sure it fails. And if you do not, you know what awaits you."

The Divine Member
[AD 866]

It was no pleasure to be in that procession, shuffling along behind Michael as he drunkenly wandered the reception halls and colonnades of the palace. I felt a fool dressed in Leo's old vestments. I had never worn them at the palace, and was sure that all the courtiers would know I was not a real bishop. I risked being exposed as one of Michael's cronies, the despicable sycophants that had dragged him down into debauchery.

The emperor lurched and stumbled, gripping the muscular arm of one of his favourite charioteers. Basil walked slightly behind him, as was proper for a junior co-emperor. I could see him glaring at the creatures Michael had introduced into the palace, particularly at Basiliscianus, who walked far closer to the emperor than he had a right to. Basil's haughty look suggested that he had forgotten how he reached the palace, and thought himself just as noble as his patron.

As Michael passed, courtiers and ambassadors bowed and prostrated themselves, flinging themselves to the ground as though that act of abasement could make their ruler admirable. Wherever we went, organs played, and the choirs called out their acclamations, requiring all onlookers to worship and revere the most effulgent of emperors. Michael looked startled by the words, which might have been taken as an ironic comment on his complexion, which varied from puce to crimson. The choir faltered and began again, puzzling the emperor even more. None of us dared look up, for fear of catching the eye of another.

We went on like that for hours, passing from one part of the palace to another, pursued by the smell of incense and rosewater, dazzled by displays of gold and silver ornaments, while Michael was greeted and acclaimed by diverse groups of citizens, priests, guildsmen and nobles. The court eunuchs kept as close to him as they could, gently touching his elbow, whispering in his ear, intoning ritual formulae. I could not

254

decide whether all court ceremonies were as long and point-less, or whether things really had fallen apart because of Michael's drunkenness.

Cyril was there, supervising everything from the sidelines, prompting those who forgot their lines, urging forward the shy and humble, subtly curbing the pretensions of the over-eager, frowning if any of the eunuchs made a mistake. He did not acknowledge me in any way.

Eventually Michael and Basil disappeared into the imperial living quarters and the eunuchs ushered the petitioners and delegations away. Basiliscianus tugged at my sleeve. "Come with me," he said. We passed rapidly through the palace gardens until we reached a small gate that led into the Hippodrome stables. Some of the buildings had been clad with marble, just as Michael said, but their shining walls were already spattered with dung and stained yellow with horse-piss. Basiliscianus led me into a vaulted room that might have been part of a bathhouse, but for the heaps of foul straw and broken tackle that lay every-where. Only a few of the stalls were occupied by horses. A dozen grooms and stable boys were perched on grain sacks or old saddles, swigging wine from skins. Though vested as a bishop, I was obliged to sit with them and share their wine, listening to their dull talk until the emperor came.

"The patriarch's eunuch," Michael said when he saw me. "You used to guide us didn't you?" His vagueness was puz-zling. He was still a young man, and it was less than a year since I had last attended him. Had drink brought him so low? I bowed my head in silent assent. Michael had taken off his ceremonial robes, and was dressed in a simple tunic, like any other nobleman. "Today," he said, "I will guide you. We are going somewhere we have never been before. You will never guess. It is not a tavern. Or a cookshop."

"Or a brothel." Basiliscianus sniggered.

"We are going to church," Michael said. "And when we get there we are going to look for something that will play a very special part in my little ceremonies."

★

255

There was a mist on the Sea of Marmora. I longed for it to thicken, to turn into a fog that would rise up and cloak us. But it remained thin and patchy, hinting at concealment without providing it. The oarsmen were old friends of Basiliscianus, who had once rowed with them, and they teased him for most of the journey, though Michael eventually tired of their banter.

"Do not annoy my friend," he said. "For that annoys me."

They rowed in silence after that, and we all sat anxiously until it was time for us to scramble ashore. We stood in the shadows while Basiliscianus paid the guards to let us through the sea gate. A more conscientious emperor might have been concerned that his officials were so easily bribed, but Michael was always glad to be able to do exactly as he liked. We set off, bearing lanterns, some of the party concealing sacks, swords, staves and axes beneath their cloaks. Michael was well used to the route, even in the dark, as he had often ridden in procession through that part of the city, as all Triumphs began at the Golden Gate. But on those occasions the citizens opened their windows wide and hung their houses with bright weavings and green branches.

We walked through empty streets, past shuttered houses, our passage marked only by the yapping of guard dogs. Soon we neared the church of Saint John the Baptist, with its great monastery where the iconodule zealots were always plotting to undermine Photius. Even at that time of night we could hear the droning of their perpetual chant. It would have been good to silence them, to end their schemes. I hoped for a moment that the monastery might be our destination. Whatever mischief was planned, it would be in my master's interests if it harmed the supporters of Ignatius. But we went on, past other churches, beyond the last of the houses, into the empty land that lies inside the walls.

"What are we looking for?" I whispered to Basiliscianus, as we struggled across the rough ground, tripping over rocks and tussocks in the darkness.

"A little church, in the middle of an orchard. It shouldn't be far off." He raised his lantern, and its faint light showed that there were some trees just ahead of us.

"And when we get there?"

"We will search for a relic," he said. "A very holy one."

The church was closed up, but that was why we had brought the axes. A couple of the grooms took turns to hack at the timbers, and soon had the doors swinging open. We rushed inside, and under Michael's direction, began to search the church. The men with lanterns thrust them into alcoves and held them behind pillars, looking for anything of value. There was not much, but lamps, candlesticks, dishes and thuribles were thrown into sacks. But the noise we made roused the guardian of the church, a grey-bearded old man, who staggered sleepily through the broken doors, feebly waving an antique sword. He looked around in amazement, saw my episcopal vestments, and dropped his rusty blade with a clatter.

"My lord bishop," he said. "You had only to ask, and I would have opened up for you."

Michael laughed at his mistake. The old verger looked at him, then recognised his emperor. Slowly, a look of awe spread across his face. "Your majesty," he said, before flinging himself on the floor.

Michael looked down at him with contempt. "He knows me," he said. "That means we will have to kill him."

No one moved.

"I said we will have to kill him," Michael repeated. "We don't want any witnesses."

I realised with horror that I, like everyone present, was about to witness something worse than Michael's usual follies. There had been no killing before, but neither had there been any ransacking of churches. If the verger was to die, what might happen to me? I knew too much to feel safe. Silently, touching the idol of Thor that hung round my neck, I cursed Cyril for having dragged me back into the emperor's circle.

"Will no one rid me of this foolish old man?" Michael said.

It was Basiliscianus who stepped forward. He reached down for the dropped sword, inspected its edge, then smiled grimly at Michael. The verger was still lying on the floor, whimpering with fear and confusion. Basiliscianus raised the sword and brought it down on the back of verger's neck. The old man screamed, and lunged at Basiliscianus's legs. Though blood flowed from his neck, it was clear that the blunt blade had only nicked him. Basiliscianus kicked the verger away, flung the sword to the floor, then grabbed an axe from one of the grooms. He raised it high above his head, then swung it down, burying its blade in the old man's shoulder. His screams were terrible, and he twitched and writhed in agony. Basiliscianus heaved the weapon out and swung it again, but he was an oarsman not an axe-man. His clumsy blows hit the floor more often than they hit the verger. We all dodged anxiously out of the way, hoping he would get the business over so we could take whatever it was we were looking for and get away. After half-a-dozen swings, Basiliscianus finally buried the blade in the verger's head, splitting his skull, ending his writhing, polluting the floor of the church with the blood of its guardian.

"Well done," Michael said, putting a silk-clad arm round his friend's blood-spattered shoulders. "I knew I could rely on you. Now, the rest of you, get searching! It must be here somewhere."

Basiliscianus was shaking with fear or exhilaration. I wondered whether he had ever killed a man before. It was certainly a long time since I had seen one killed, and the experience reminded me just how dangerous it was to be an emperor's plaything. I joined the grooms, who were searching the back of the church, tearing down screens and curtains, tapping the floor and walls in search of hollow places.

"What are we looking for?" I asked one of them.

"Don't you know?" There was an odd smile on his face, though what it meant, I could not tell.

"No," I said.

"We're looking for the Divine Member." The groom jerked his head in Michael's direction. "That's what he calls it."

"The Divine Member?"

"God's prick," the groom whispered. But the domed

church amplified his voice, and Michael must have heard him clearly. "Christ's penis," the emperor said, removing his arm from his friend's shoulder and walking towards us.

"His penis?" I said. "Did He have one?"

"Of course He did," Michael said. "Did you imagine that He was a eunuch, like you?" I did not think it the right moment to explain to the emperor the exact nature of my mutilation. "Remember the Creed," he said. "You ought to know it, being the patriarch's eunuch. Christ is both perfect God and perfect man. And Man is the image and likeness of God."

"And His member is in this church?"

"So I have been told. But now that I see the place it seems unlikely. I hope I have not been misinformed."

"It's what the priest told me," Basiliscianus said.

"Priests! What do they know?"

"He told me the whole story, how it was brought by Joseph of Arimathea . . ."

"I don't want to know all that. I want to know where it is."

Basiliscianus moved away to join the search. I tried to follow him but was called back by Michael. "Not you, my mock patriarch," he said. "There is something I want to ask you. And you had better be sure to give the right answer."

Whatever Cyril had ordered, I knew it was hopeless to try and thwart Michael. Despite his earlier drunkenness, I had never seen him so determined.

"I will try, your majesty."

"In the liturgy, one thing can stand for another, can it not?"

"It can."

"And the essence of one thing can enter into the other?"

"In a symbolic sense."

"No more than that?"

"A sign, or image, according to Dionysius the Areopagite . . ."

"Spare me the chapter and verse. What I want you to tell me is this: are things transformed . . ."

Michael never finished his question, as just then there was a loud crash followed by a cry of triumph from the back of the church.

"I have found something," Basiliscianus said. He was crouching by the altar, part of which had been smashed by an axe, which lay on the floor amid a pile of marble fragments. "It's in here," he said, reaching into the hollow space his axe-blow had revealed. While we all gathered around, Basiliscianus drew out a glittering object and placed it on the top of the altar. "This must be it," he said. "What else could it be?"

The bulk of the reliquary, even allowing for its thick crust of gold and precious stones, which gleamed in the torchlight, suggested that the Divine Member was of superhuman size, but that was only to be expected. On the other hand, a reliquary the size of a man's head may turn out to contain nothing bigger than a tooth or a knucklebone.

"Open it," Michael said. His voice was powerful. He sounded like the soldier he sometimes was, not like the dissolute pleasure seeker we knew. Even so, Basiliscianus hesitated.

"What are you afraid of?" Michael asked.

"If it is what we think it is," Basiliscianus said, stepping back from the altar. "Then it might be dangerous to open it."

"For you, perhaps," Michael said. "But I am not afraid of punishment. Not in this world, or the next. I *am* the emperor, after all. And the guardian of the faith. Who would punish me?" He reached out for the jewelled reliquary, running his hands over it as though it was made of soft flesh. Finding a clasp, he unclipped it, loosening the lid, which he lifted slowly. Inside, nestling in a hollow of faded red silk, was a greyish wizened object the size and shape of a finger. If Michael was disappointed by the Divine Member's proportions he did not show it. "This is it," he said.

Basiliscianus looked anxiously at the smashed doors, beyond which the blackness of the night was visible. "Shall we take it away," he said. "Back to the stables."

"No," Michael said. "We will use it here."

"Use it? How?"

"You will see, Basiliscianus. And you Zeno. As for the rest of you, go to the doors and guard them make sure no one comes in. You must be ready to depart the moment I give the word."

The others went, leaving the three of us by the altar. Michael turned to me. "We did not finish our theological discussion," he said. "And there is no time now. Before I leave here, which must be very soon, I wish to be entered by the Divine Member."

"Entered?"

"Exactly. Just as the Holy Spirit enters us when we swallow the flesh and blood of the Saviour, I wish it to enter me by means of this Member."

This desire of Michael's was a new departure. All his previous efforts had been devoted to mocking God, or to worshipping the devil. Perhaps his wish to be entered by the Holy Spirit was a promising sign. However, I was fairly sure there was something wrong with his theology, that he may actually have uttered a heresy. Michael did not give me the chance to formulate a more considered opinion. He leaned over the open reliquary, probed the shrivelled member with his finger, then turned back to me. "It is as I suspected," he said. "What I hoped for will be impossible. The Member is far too fragile. That is why I asked you about essence and substitution. You will have to speak the words that will transfer the Divine essence from this relic to a human member."

"I will?"

"That is why I chose you, because you are the patriarch's eunuch, and can act in his place. You know the words of the liturgy, don't you?"

I was not sure that I did. While working in my master's library I had devoted more time to heresy than to orthodoxy, and I had only rarely attended church. Nor could I tell what the emperor had in mind. But I could see that my fate depended on my being able to say something. "In this case," I said, "a new formula will be necessary."

"And you can speak it?"

"I can."

"Good. Now, Basiliscianus, undress!"

Michael had spoken in his voice of command again, and whatever Basiliscianus may have thought, he obeyed, struggling out of his clothes until he stood naked before the altar.

Michael lifted the reliquary from its place and offered it to me. When he was satisfied that I held the jewelled box in a suitably respectful way, he adjusted his clothing. He untied his drawers, hoisted up the long skirts of his tunic so that his lower half was naked, then lay face down on the altar where the Divine Member had been. "Are you ready, Basiliscianus?" he asked. "And you Zeno?"

We both assured our ruler that we were ready to do his bidding, and he told us to begin. But I had no sooner begun to recite, than Michael told me to stop. "That is no good," he said. "That won't work at all. You must touch both members."

"Both?"

"God's, and Basiliscianus's. You must grasp them both as you say the words. Otherwise the substitution will not take place."

With extreme reluctance, I did as I was asked, placing the jewelled box on the edge of the altar, touching the relic with one hand, and grasping Basiliscianus's flaccid member with the other.

"Flesh of God," I began, addressing the shrivelled relic and trying to avert my gaze from the imperial buttocks. "Generative organ of the Creator," I intoned. "Know You that we cannot ascend and participate in what is Yours. I call upon You to come down to us and participate in what is ours. By means of Your most Holy Member, give Yourself to us." I went on like that for some time, mixing half-remembered phrases from my master's theology books with mumbo-jumbo of my own invention, aware that if I finished too quickly or was too easy to understand, Michael would not be impressed. As I spoke, no change came over the shrivelled relic, but the real member, the one I held in my other hand began to swell, growing gradually firmer until my cupped fingers could hardly encompass it. Basiliscianus swayed and fidgeted, rubbing his erect member against my hand with increasing urgency until I realised that I must quickly finish my extemporised rigmarole. "Send down Your Holy Spirit to us," I concluded, giving Basiliscianus's penis an extra tug. "And make this member Yours."

"Now!" Michael said. I let go of my throbbing handful, grabbed the reliquary and stepped back. Basiliscianus rushed forward, ascended the altar and clambered on top of Michael. Considering that he had just endured a meaningless ritual while standing naked in a cold church, watched from the doorway by a gang of stable hands, his enthusiasm was inexplicable. I am sure that, had I been whole, I could not have performed as eagerly as he did. Perhaps he believed that the Holy Spirit really had entered into him, or that his member had been transformed into that of God. Whatever the reason, he was possessed by an inhuman energy that caused him to plunge his erect penis between Michael's buttocks, burying it repeatedly in the imperial flesh. Michael cried out, calling on God to enter him, groaning with pleasure or pain, his voice echoing round the dark church, growing so loud that I feared he might even wake the old man who lay dead on the floor with his skull smashed in.

A dinner party
[AD 867]

"I was right," Photius said, repeating one of his favourite phrases. "Whatever his little eccentricities, Michael really is the defender of our faith. He certainly put those papal legates in their place."

It was the end of the great Church Council that had lasted for several weeks and brought together bishops and ambassadors from all over the Christian world. I had attended my master throughout the council, helping him in every way I could, knowing that Cyril would not dare to harm me while I was surrounded by bishops and nobles. On that last day, I was escorting Photius home, not because the distance was far, but because the people, who had followed every twist and turn of the Council's proceedings, were strangely disturbed by the outcome.

"Michael is a changed man," Photius said. "He seems to have overcome what he called his fallible soul. He is more pious than ever. I think his experiments with heresy must have taught him something. Whatever it was, I feel sure he has put all that behind him now. He defends the Church as though it was his own, which I suppose it is in a way. Any affront to it, he regards almost as an affront to his own person. It is as though something has entered into him, as though he has been inspired by the gift of the Holy Spirit. What an example he sets for Basil!"

"Did Basil contribute to the Council?" I asked, hoping to distract my master from speculating on what might have entered into Michael.

"Basil sat there, looking regal, but as for saying or doing anything, what would you expect? He knows no more about the Church than I do about chariot racing."

Photius wheezed a little as he walked. He had grown quite fat from all the official dinners he had eaten, and sometimes had to stop and get his breath back before he went on. I had considered arranging a litter for him, but that would have made us too conspicuous. I looked around anxiously, hoping the noises I could hear in the side streets were not coming any closer.

"The people are not happy at the results," I said.

"Nonsense! Orthodoxy has triumphed. Heresy has been abolished. We have put paid to all that Latin nonsense about the Dual Procession. No one can now say that the Holy Spirit proceeds from the Son as well as the Father."

"Except for those who still obey the pope."

"I have deposed and excommunicated him."

"The people are concerned about the price you paid."

"What price?"

"Recognising King Lewis as Emperor in the West."

"It was well worth it. Lewis has promised to march on Rome and unseat the pope for me. Then who will be the sole ruler of the Church?" Photius turned and peered at me in the darkness.

"You will," I said, though I was not convinced. Whatever King Lewis had promised, there was no way of making him do it. Like Khan Boris, he might switch his allegiance to Rome if he could get a better deal there.

"As for the title," Photius said. "It is a mere formality. No one could mistake the king of the Franks for the equal of the Roman Emperor."

"The people think the imperial title has been devalued."

"They didn't complain when Michael tried to make Basiliscianus co-emperor."

I was surprised that Photius mentioned Michael's plan. It was the kind of thing he had taken to ignoring since the death of Bardas. "I don't think it was widely known," I said. "Anyway, Basil stopped him. This Frankish business is different. There has been rioting."

"The weather is still hot," Photius said. "Warm nights encourage the people to wander the streets in search of amusement. Sometimes they get rowdy. There is nothing new in that."

"The people are angry with Michael. They say he is no longer worthy to be emperor."

"But he was born to the purple, and has ruled them since he was a child. He has won them a series of victories against the Saracens. And he is still only a young man. What is he now? Twenty something, isn't it?"

"Twenty seven."

"Exactly! He has a glorious future ahead of him. Why should the people turn against him now?"

I took Photius by the arm and drew him closer to me. "They have been talking about you," I said. "They blame you too for devaluing the imperial title."

"That will be Ignatius and his follower stirring up trouble again. No one takes any notice of them. The people in general are grateful to me. I have stood up for orthodoxy, defied the pope, banished heresy, and converted the barbarians. Only last month, some Rus ambassadors agreed to be baptised. Soon the whole of Christendom will look to me for leadership."

I led Photius into the house and helped him out of his vestments, but it was a long time before he went to bed. Instead, he stayed up, drinking wine and talking endlessly about Michael's piety and how his patriarchal rights had been upheld.

That same evening, while Photius sat mulling over his triumph, Michael held a small dinner party for a few of his friends. It marked the end of the Church Council, and, as a contrast to the official receptions he had been obliged to host, it took place at a little pleasure palace on the other side of the Golden Horn. The guests were all nobles or courtiers. Basiliscianus, who might not otherwise have qualified, had been made a patrician. Unusually, despite the fact that they were married to each other, Basil and Eudocia were both invited.

That, probably, was Michael's greatest mistake.

It pains me to think that Eudocia knew what was going to happen, but she surely did, even if she never quite admitted it to me. In her defence, I will say that she had been pressed by Basil, who made her swear that young Leo really was his son, and not Michael's, as court rumour suggested. Eudocia had come to despise Michael for the way he treated her, and for his ceaseless search for more recondite pleasures. And I think she loved Basil, in a way, or was in awe of his strength and beauty, just as Michael had been. I am sure that Basil won Eudocia's support by making certain promises about Prince Leo's future, promises that depended on the outcome of that evening's entertainments.

The guests arrived by boat, gathering on a terrace that overlooked the Bosphorus. They had a fine view of the city, with its lights glinting over the dark water. Basil and Eudocia travelled in the same boat, but were careful to ignore each other once they arrived. Basil flirted with Thecla, Michael's ex-nun sister, which must have taken an effort as she was much older than him, and very fat. Eudocia sat beside Michael. She was still his property, whatever she had agreed with Basil, whatever vows she had sworn. She ate every delicacy put before her, paying Michael the attention he demanded, making sure his goblet was filled frequently, distracting him from the irregular comings and goings that might, for a more attentive host, have marred the meal.

Basil, for instance, left the dining room several times. Once, he took Thecla with him, and returned, red-faced, to the ribald cheers of the other diners. Basiliscianus, never having been present when Michael, Basil and Eudocia were together, did not know who to try and impress. He kept changing places, plonking himself down on the ends of others' couches and annoying the guests with would-be witty prattle. Michael, already drunk, noticed nothing. He was pawing at Eudocia, disarranging her dress, making lewd suggestion, quite oblivious to Basil's jealous glances.

Eventually Michael lurched to his feet.

"It's all over," he said. "You can go to your beds now. Or your boats."

The guests who were carried back across the Golden Horn were lucky. Of those who remained, few survived the night.

★

267

Michael took Eudocia to his bedchamber, and, lacking a suitable eunuch, had Basiliscianus sleep across the doorway. Michael was too drunk to do any of the things he wanted to do, but Eudocia humoured him, slowly removing his clothes, tenderly rubbing him with scented oils, promising him unimaginable pleasures, lulling him gently to sleep.

A few hours later, when the palace was dark and silent, Basil, followed by a gang of Armenians including several of his brothers, burst into the imperial bedchamber. During one of his absences from the dinner he had broken the lock, so he only had to barge at the door with his shoulder to break it open. Basil kicked Basiliscianus aside, hacking at him with his sword as he dashed towards the imperial bed. Eudocia, though she must have known what was going to happen, screamed in terror.

I cannot bear to think of Eudocia in such danger. She might easily have been killed, especially at that moment when her screams threatened Basil's scheme. Michael woke, and tried to get up. But when he saw Basil standing over him with a sword, he slid drunkenly back onto the bed, clutching desperately at Eudocia. A moment later a squad of Ferghanese bodyguards arrived, and Michael cried out to them to save him. Some of Basil's men rushed out to fight them. For a short while there was utter confusion, with Turks and Armenians shouting, running, thrusting swords and shoving at each other through the doorway.

While everyone else was distracted, Basil raised his sword over Michael. "Call yourself a man?" he bellowed. Michael clung even tighter to Eudocia.

"You're a coward!" Basil said. "A drunkard! A heretic!"

Michael whimpered and squirmed.

"Get away from him!" Basil shouted.

Eudocia tried to free herself from Michael's terrified grip. She pushed his face, pummelled his hands, kicked his legs. He begged her to protect him, but she finally succeeded in shoving him away.

"You're not fit to rule!" Basil said, but he held back from striking a blow.

As Michael reached out for Eudocia again, one of the Armenians took his sword and slashed it downwards, hacking off the drunken emperor's hands. Blood gushed over the bedspread, splashing Basil and the Armenian, soaking Eudocia's fine silk nightdress. She leapt from the bed, throwing herself into Basil's arms. Basil pushed her aside. In fact, he hardly noticed her, and Eudocia never forgot that.

"What use is that!" Basil shouted. "You've only hurt him."

"He can't be emperor now," the Armenian said. "He's mutilated."

"That's no good. He can still talk."

"Shall I hack his tongue out?"

"No, you fool! He must be killed. And so must all the witnesses."

The Armenian raised his sword, holding its hilt with both hands. He brought it down on Michael, plunging the blade into his belly, twisting and turning it until the already bloodstained sheets were covered with slithering innards and gobbets of half-digested food.

One of the Armenians burst in, and seeing Michael's butchered remains, dropped to his knees. "My brother," he said, "You have succeeded. You have won the empire."

"Not yet," Basil said. "Not until I control the palace."

Leaving the dead and dying behind them, Basil, Eudocia and the Armenians rushed to the waterside where a boat waited to ferry them across the Golden Horn. Though the sea was rough by then, they took the long route, rounding the point and rowing past Hagia Sophia to the palace. But the sea gates were closed, and in the small hours of the night, not even the co-emperor's name could get them opened. Basil ordered everyone back on board.

"I'm seasick," Eudocia said. "I can't get in the boat again. Let's wait here until morning."

"No. We must get into the palace before they hear the news."

"Why? Michael is dead. Isn't that enough?"

"No. Some of the eunuchs are loyal to Michael. They might put someone up against me, some relative or other."

"Not before dawn. Let's wait here."

Basil grabbed Eudocia and pulled her towards him. "Little Leo's in the palace, isn't he? What if the eunuchs decided he was Michael's bastard?"

"He's your son. I swear it!"

"Maybe. But what if the eunuchs put him on the throne? They'd like that, wouldn't they? A one-year-old emperor would suit them well. It might suit you, too."

"No! No, it wouldn't."

"Are you sure?"

"Yes, I swear it!"

"Good." Basil let her go. "Let's get into the palace before the eunuchs try anything. Now, get into the boat."

"But I'm seasick!"

The Armenians bundled Eudocia into the boat, then rowed for a fisherman's harbour. They rushed through deserted streets to the palace, but did not attempt the main gates, which are made of solid bronze, and could never have been forced. Instead, Basil led them to the university. As far as I know, he had never been there before, but someone must have told him about the iron door Bardas had used when he killed Theoctistus. With the help of a couple of the Armenians, he kicked down the door, then rushed to the imperial quarters. There was a quick purge of palace officials, then the news of Michael's death was announced.

Shortly before dawn, Basil the peasant, with Eudocia the former tavern-girl beside him, sat in the throne room, sole ruler of the Roman Empire.

As you will realise, I did not see Michael's murder myself, though Eudocia later told me much of what happened. Had I witnessed those events I am sure that Basil would have had me killed, and these memoirs would not have been written. Even so; what followed was bad enough.

Downfall
[AD 867–8]

"What happened?" Theodore said. He was dressed in rather shabby vestments, and had obviously come straight from a service, though I had never known him to take part in any of the liturgy.

"Photius has been arrested."

"I know that. Everyone knows that. But how? Why?"

"The guards came for him. The Ferghanese. It was early in the morning. That was the first we heard of Basil's coup. They wanted Photius to go to the palace and administer the Eucharist to the new emperor."

"And he refused?"

"Yes."

"The fool!"

"He said he wouldn't share the sacraments with a murderer."

"I can't think why," Theodore said. "He's done it before. He celebrated the Mass with Basil after he killed Bardas, and with Bardas after he killed Theoctistus. It was a test of loyalty, that's all. Ignatius was stupid enough to fail the test when he refused to share the sacraments with Bardas, but I didn't think Photius would make the same mistake."

"He wanted to preserve his integrity."

"Well, better late than never. But I still think he's a fool. If he'd said those few words, he might still be patriarch."

"He didn't want to serve under a peasant usurper."

"He served quite happily under a drunken madman." Theodore frowned, and tugged at his beard. "Have you heard what people are saying?"

"I came through the marketplace on my way here. People were going about their business as usual. They were saying nothing."

"Exactly! They were sick of Michael. They knew all the rumours. And they didn't like it when he recognised King

271

Lewis as emperor. It debases the title, diminishes the Roman Empire. They know that Basil kept silent throughout the Church Council. He took no part in those decisions. As far as they're concerned, a new emperor can be no worse than the old."

"So you don't think they'll rise up and depose Basil?"

Theodore laughed. "I don't think so. Anyway, you wouldn't want that, would you? If Basil goes, then Eudocia goes too." He thought for a moment. "Have you tried talking to her? She might persuade her husband to release Photius."

"It was the first thing I thought of. As soon as they took Photius away, I ran to the palace and tried to get in. But the bronze gates were shut, and so were all the others. I couldn't get near her."

"Well, there's not much to done, is there? We will just have to wait, to see what our new emperor decides. But there is one thing that occurs to me."

"Yes?"

"Photius's house. You'll be in charge of it, I suppose?"

"I will look after it, as before."

"And you'll take special care of all the books, won't you? There must be hundreds in that library. They'd be worth a fortune if they ever came on the market. Of course, we must hope and pray that Photius is soon released, and is able to enjoy his library again. But if anything were to happen to him, it would be shame to let those rare old volumes go to waste."

Basil did not hesitate. It was as though he had planned his coup for years, and knew exactly what he would do afterwards. How can an illiterate peasant have had so much political skill, so much foresight? After deposing Photius, Basil summoned Ignatius and offered him a second term as patriarch. The zealous puritan, who had been deposed for defying Michael and censuring Bardas, accepted, and became patriarch to a usurper. Photius was exiled to an obscure and uncomfortable monastery. I was not even allowed to say goodbye to him. All the decisions of the Church Council were set aside in order to please the people and appease Rome. My master's work was undone.

After Photius was sentenced I returned to the house, only to find that the gatekeeper would not let me in. He gazed blankly at me as though he did not know who I was, and said that he had instructions to admit no one. I pleaded with him, reminding him that I had lived in the house for years, but it was no good. Behind him, in the courtyard, I could see some of the other servants laughing and smiling at my plight. No doubt they planned to run the house for their own benefit, living on whatever money and stores were left. As I walked away I regretted having annoyed them in the past. I might so easily have let them carry on supplying my master with poor wine, and with their other little swindles. Photius would never have noticed, and the servants might have liked me more. But I had wanted to serve my master well, making up in those small ways for the times I had been forced to betray him, as well as paying the servants back for the time they beat me.

I had nowhere to go. Surely, someone would take me in, would give me a home? But who? Constantine had gone to Rome, to wrangle with the new pope over who was to have the honour of converting the Slavs. He was not likely to be back for some time. Leo was eighty and had lost his wits. The last time I visited him he babbled about dragons and earthquakes. If, as some said, he had sold his soul to the devil in exchange for wisdom, he had made a bad bargain.

I wandered for a while, feeling the cold wind in my face and the slippery cobbles under my feet, wondering what to do. It was dusk when I reached the palace. I knew that Eudocia was inside, married to a murderer, doing her duty as empress, protecting her infant son. Surely she would help me if she could? But the guards at the bronze gates were as implacable as ever. There was no entry for ordinary people like me, whatever pretext I might be able to think of. I skirted the high walls, hoping perhaps that a postern might still be open, that a guard or official might know me and take pity.

But they did not, and I was alone and friendless as I wandered deeper into the twilight.

In a small square beneath the looming bulk of the hippodrome, I was confronted by a strange and pallid figure. Everything about it, matted hair, slack flesh, ragged clothes, was grey. It was as though one of the statues that had often watched over my nocturnal jaunts had descended from its pedestal to confront me. But the figure that stood before me was no emperor or god. Nor was it a senator or charioteer, or any of the other notables the city had thought worthy of commemoration. With its hunched posture, lolling head, the hands clutched desperately to a downward tilted face, it was a perfect representation of abject misery. And it was no statue, but a living being, one that wailed and shook, rocking backwards and forwards, wordlessly proclaiming its suffering to anyone who would listen.

It was a bad place to beg. There were not many passers-by. Two black-clad monks had just scuttled round the far side of the square and left it by an alley. I would have followed their example, and seen no more, had not a linkman hastened past. The torch he held, blazing briefly through the square like a meteor, lit the wailing beggar, revealing more than I had seen before. Its clothes, which I had taken for grey, were filthy bloodstained rags, which barely covered the creature's pale, slack flesh.

At that moment, prompted by the linkman's noisy steps, the beggar raised its arms and cried out. The linkman hesitated, turned his head slightly, then dashed down the alley, leaving nothing but the smell of burning pitch behind him. The square was plunged back into darkness, but the beggar's face stayed with me like a scene lit by lightning. I saw, and can still see, the skin hanging in folds like an empty sack, the white hair falling down over a creased brow, and the hollow, blood-crusted sockets where the eyes had been. For that poor wretch, deprived cruelly of its sight, the darkness of night was perpetual.

Then it called out again, speaking intelligible words for the first time. "Give me alms," it said. "For God's sake, don't let me starve."

The voice was Cyril's. The creature that stood before me had been the chief of the guild of court eunuchs. Bardas had often talked of ridding the palace of all eunuchs. Basil had obviously begun the process, at least with those who had offended him. Cyril had made my life miserable at times, but seeing him like that, I could not hate him. His condition reminded me that there were far worse fates than the one that faced me. Without saying a word, I pressed a few coins into his hand and rushed away.

I paced the city all night, not caring where I went. Broad avenues, narrow alleys, parks, gardens, mean squares and great forums, were all the same to me, though I kept well away from the place where I had seen Cyril. Once or twice I took refuge in church porches, but no one took pity on me or offered me a bed. Why, I wondered, was I so much unluckier than Basil, who had slept in a porch, been rescued by a priest, and set on the path to greatness?

At dawn, finding myself at the Golden Horn, I stood for a while looking down at the grey water. All around me, fishermen were landing their fresh-caught hauls, cookshops were frying fish and onions, and people gathered to eat and chat. I handed over a small coin, received my loaf and fish, and ate them by the quayside. Then I set off again, following the sea walls to Blachernae, remembering the Rus raid and my part in repelling it. Surely the city I had helped save could not be so indifferent to my fate! But no one knew me. I was just another eunuch, a wanderer from the quarter where eunuchs are usually found, but otherwise unremarkable.

The land walls loomed over me, reminding me that I had reached the city's western edge. I went through a gate and out, towards the tavern, thinking it might provide me with a refuge. I had sunk so low that I was prepared to work there, to pour drinks and serve food, to endure the taunts of rough sailors and fishermen. But even that was denied me. It was only a couple of years since I had arranged a pension for the nieces in return for their silence about Eudocia's origins. My mistake, I suppose, had been to reinforce the offer of money with threats, and to reappear when I had no power to offer or threaten anything. The nieces saw me off, accusing me of blackmail, threatening to call the prefect's men.

There was only one person left who could help me, though I was reluctant to ask him. Wearily, I returned to the city, and after pacing the streets until long after night fell, I took refuge with Theodore.

"Have you brought any of the books?" he asked.

"I couldn't bring anything. I have nothing more than the clothes I'm wearing."

Theodore's lodgings were worse than I remembered. The house he shared belonged to a little church not far from the one that had once held the Divine Member. He was attached to the church in some way, though he did not, as far as I could tell, serve as its priest. Nor was his priestly status enough to persuade the housekeeper to keep the place remotely clean, though that did not trouble Theodore.

The time I spent with Theodore was not happy, and I do not intend to describe it in detail. To pay for my keep I had to help him with his work, copying out old texts and cobbling together new ones, though the money my writing earned always went into his purse, not mine. He sent me on errands to booksellers or monasteries, to the houses of anyone who wished to seem learned. I delivered anthologies of poetry, histories, books of anatomy and astrology, ancient dramas, hagiographies, catalogues of heresy, romances, herbals, and accounts of wonderful voyages. I collected books from people who had no further use for them, taking them to Theodore for valuation. I must have seen every book in the city, except for church bibles and the volumes locked safely in my master's library, and Theodore made a profit on all of them. I often took books to the university. Theodore no longer taught there, but he still dealt with the teachers and students. Sometimes, after handing over a manual of philosophy to an eager student, I wandered slowly by the palace walls, remembering the past, longing for my lost love. But the gates were guarded better than ever under Basil's rule, and a glimpse of the gardens was the most I ever saw.

"I can't understand why Eudocia hasn't got in touch with me," I said, after delivering *On the Generation of Animals* to a young Aristotelian. The spring weather had made my memories unusually poignant.

"I can," Theodore said. "I can understand it perfectly."

"You don't know her."

Theodore gave me a condescending look. "I helped create her," he said. "It was me, was it not, who made the prophecy that won her a life of luxury. And it was me who wrote her genealogy and found her a noble family."

"And it was you who called her son a bastard."

"I only speak the truth, as does the oracle. And the truth is that Eudocia no longer needs you."

"Of course she does. You don't know what we were to each other."

"I know exactly what you were to her. A means to an end. She used you to win wealth and power. Now she has what she wants. She won't help you."

"You are wrong. I was like a brother to her."

"A creature like you can be nothing to anybody."

There was a silence, during which I tried to swallow my anger. I could not afford to annoy Theodore. If he threw me out, where would I go? But it was clever of Theodore to make me angry. I forgot for a moment that he said nothing without an ulterior motive, and that he had a scheme ready for every occasion.

"I served Eudocia well," I said. "And she is grateful to me. It is not my fault that she is locked up in the palace."

"You will never see her again while Photius is in exile."

Again, I swallowed my anger. "Then I will never see her. Basil won't bring Photius back."

"Don't be so sure," Theodore said. "Ignatius is a fool. Basil knows that. He only made the old eunuch his patriarch to win over the zealots. There are questions Ignatius cannot answer, difficulties only Photius can resolve."

"Perhaps."

"Think of it! What does Photius know more about than anyone else?"

"Heresy."

"Exactly!"

"Basil is not interested in heresy," I said. "That sort of thing was more to Michael's taste."

"Just at the moment, Basil is most interested in the Paulicians. He wants to stamp out their heresy, but he is finding it very difficult. They are like hornets. Every attack makes them more ferocious, especially now that they are led by that renegade John Chrysocheir. He was an officer and a gentleman, and they are the worst sort when they go bad. Some say he is halfway to joining the Saracens. He's certainly doing their work for them. Do you know his last raid got as far as Ephesus? His men and horses defiled the cathedral. The house of God, polluted by the dung of beasts and the mockery of men! Can you imagine it?"

"No," I said. But I could imagine it all too clearly.

"The army could do nothing to stop him. Now the heretics will pour across the empire like a foul flood, polluting everything they touch. They are the enemies of civilisation, enemies of everything Photius believes in. And if they cannot be defeated, they must be tamed."

"I am sure you are right," I said, puzzled by Theodore's sudden fervour. "But I don't see how this concerns us."

"You don't? I thought you wanted to serve Photius."

"I would, if I had the chance."

"Now you have a chance," he said. "Basil and Ignatius are sending a mission to the Paulicians."

"So?"

"You must join the mission and go east."

"What use would I be on a mission?"

"That is what I am trying to tell you."

"How can I join the mission if it is being sent by Ignatius."

"I can get you attached to it."

"How? With Photius out of favour, how can you achieve anything?"

Theodore gave me a pitying look. "There are many ways

to get things done. Do you think I would rely on one patron?"

"Have you been taking orders from Ignatius?"

Theodore said nothing, but looked at me strangely. I could not tell whether he really had been working with my master's enemy, or whether he merely wanted me to think him crafty enough to have done so.

"I cannot see any sense in what you are saying," I said. "Why should I work on behalf of Ignatius?"

"You wouldn't be working for him. Photius wants to make this mission his own. He has been writing to the Paulician heretics, urging them to return to orthodoxy. In fact, he has been writing to all sorts of people. Some of the letters are quite pious. I don't know what's come over him."

"How do you know that? He is my master, not yours."

"I make it my business to know whatever is useful to me. And so should you."

"You have made sure I can find out nothing."

"I have protected you, given you a home, kept you safe from the hostile world outside. I can see that I am to receive little gratitude. However, if you won't thank me, surely you will help Photius."

"How?"

"There are two possibilities. You could undermine the mission, ensuring that it fails. Or, if it succeeds, you could make sure Photius gets the credit. The first option would be easiest. Ignatius has chosen an abbot called Peter to lead it. That was a great mistake, as the Paulicians hate monks. According to them, the monastic orders originated with the devil. And this Peter, as well as being a monk, and an ignorant zealot like his master, is a feeble coward quite unfitted to his task."

"And what, exactly, is his task?"

"Peter's task is to convert the Paulicians and secure the release of their prisoners of war." Theodore smiled grimly. "I do not think there is much chance of him succeeding. Especially if you do all you can to impede him."

"I haven't agreed to go."

"How can you turn down an opportunity like this? All you have to do is undermine Peter the Abbot, then step in and take his place. Persuade John and his followers away from their heresy. Get the prisoners released as well. If you can do those things, and do them on behalf of Photius, then his return to favour will be a few steps nearer."

"You make it sound so simple."

"It could be, if you remember the doctrine of economy."

"Which is?"

"A trick used by missionaries. They are economical with the truth. They only reveal what they know will be acceptable to the people they are trying to convert. There is no point in making impossible demands. I fear Photius made that mistake with the Bulgars. He ended up driving them to Rome. You must do better with the Paulicians."

"I am no missionary."

"Didn't Constantine train you for just this task?"

"He did, but it was years ago, and Photius decided I would be more use to him in the city."

"Things have changed. You would be more use to him in the East."

"I'm not sure."

"Only you can do it," he said. "Everything depends on you."

I did not believe that everything depended on me. Nor did I relish a journey to the borderlands, or time spent among the heretics. I had already had enough of Paulicianism.

"I have consulted the oracle," Theodore said. "It foretells a great triumph. The heretics will be overthrown. Photius will be restored. You will see Eudocia again!"

Perhaps you will think me foolish for agreeing to do what Theodore asked. Yes, he baited me, flattered me, played on my feelings for Eudocia, even used the *Chaldean Oracle* to justify his scheme. I knew that he was a trickster, and that he had misled me in the past. But he had also helped me, though not always in the way I wanted. And I was not entirely sure that the oracle spoke falsely. The ways of the gods are mysterious, and they may reveal the truth even through charlatans. I was willing to try anything that might bring Photius back from exile. Theodore was right. Only when my master was back in Constantinople and restored to favour could I hope to see Eudocia again.

The Paulicians
[AD 869]

There is not much to say about the journey, except that it was made at the height of summer, and that the heat, dust and privations of travel put us all in a terrible temper. It was no surprise to me that no one in Santabaris, which Theodore claimed was his hometown, would admit to knowing him, or would advance me the money he had promised. At Sebastea there was much talk of John the Heretic, of his strength and power, the audacity of his warriors, the range and suddenness of their raids, the hazards of travel near the frontier. Even the Saracens, they said, were afraid of him. Worst of all, the heretics destroyed holy images wherever they found them, and hated monks.

Peter the Abbot refused to go on. He declared himself ill, installed himself in the guesthouse of an Armenian monastery, and announced that he would conduct the mission from there. That, at least, was just as Theodore had predicted, and I immediately volunteered to go to Tephrike on Peter's behalf. Groaning on his sickbed, Peter could not summon up enough energy to forbid me to go, though he would not trust me with the gifts Basil had sent for John the Heretic. Nor would he let me take a guard or porter. Unencumbered, I set off for the frontier, travelling most of the way with some merchants bound for Melitene.

The head of the valley was watched by some armed heretics, who sat beneath a spreading mulberry tree, their heads wrapped in cloth like Saracens. I reached inside my tunic and touched my idol of Thor. Since my master's downfall I had been careful to keep it with me. It was carved by a cunning man of the North, from the tusk of a fabulous beast. Such things have their significance. And gifts have a power of their own. Something had preserved me. If not Thor, then what?

The guards inspected me carefully. They were ruffians from

the backwoods, and had never seen a eunuch. But they did not rob me, as I feared. Instead, they invited me to sit with them in the shade.

"Partake of the living water," one of them said, offering me a swig from his wineskin.

"Welcome to the Earthly Paradise," another said, offering me a dried fig.

"Is it truly here?" I asked, trying to sound enthusiastic. Travelling on my own, deception was necessary. I had decided to present myself, not as an emissary, but as a seeker of the truth.

"Of course!" The fierce guard smiled at me, his face filling with unexpected joy. "The Scriptures tell us that the Garden of Eden was here in this valley. Now John has led us back, and we have left sin behind."

The valley of Tephrike was delightfully green, especially after the dry uplands I had crossed to reach it. But when I looked more carefully I saw that the land had been abandoned. Overgrown vines tumbled down steep terraces, neglected orchards clothed the lower slopes, and the valley floor, which might have been covered with wheat fields or vegetable plots, was bare and dusty. Adam and Eve did not till the soil, so why should the Paulicians?

At the far end of the valley I could see the town itself, flat-roofed houses rising up the slopes beneath the great citadel that dominated it. I felt like the hero of a fanciful romance. In order to see again the woman I loved, I had to enter an impregnable castle and release the prisoners who were held there. Then I had to win favour for my master by converting the heretics. Such feats are easy for heroes, but I am only a eunuch. Alone, unarmed, and without a plan, I set off for the Paulician stronghold.

Tephrike was filthy. The streets were strewn with rotting food, heaps of dung, dead dogs, and rubbish of all sorts. Scavenging birds hopped and flapped everywhere, despite the curses rained on them by the old men who watched from doorways. All the heretics, and there were not many of them, were old and feeble. How could a handful of greybeards have terrified the East?

Unmolested, I wandered the dirty streets looking for food and shelter. Half the houses were roofless, their rooms choked with crumbling timbers and broken tiles. There were no shops or taverns, but some of the houses were stacked with sacks, barrels, jars and baskets from which a few old men helped themselves, carelessly spilling what they could not use. They avoided my eye, and mumbled to themselves, but would not speak to me. After searching the lower town thoroughly I found an empty house that served as a hostel for travellers, and lay gratefully on a bed of loose straw.

The next morning, having begged bread from a toothless dotard, I began my task. It was clear that things could not be as they seemed. Sitting in my doorway, I watched the Tephrikians carefully, though I did not go so far as to mumble or drool, as they did. They shambled past, wandering from one house to another, picking their way through the filthy streets, without any obvious purpose. There was little life left in any of them, and I could not see what use they would be to me. But I had to talk to someone, or my journey would have been in vain. Eventually, I chose a man of monkish appearance. He was just as old as the others, though sprightlier of step and brighter of eye. He spoke to the other men as he passed, and afterwards they trembled and gibbered a little less.

"Father," I said, falling in with him as he walked one of the winding streets. "I wish to know the truth."

"The truth?" he said, stroking his grizzled beard. "Who can know the truth?"

"I can see wisdom in your eyes," I said, gazing at him raptly. "What is your name, Father?"

"Men call me Zacharias."

"You are an adept, are you not?"

"I am thought wise by some. But why should I share my wisdom with you?"

"So I can ascend to a higher level of existence."

"So you can climb up there, more like." He pointed up to the castle, which loomed over us.

"Is it so bad to wish to reach the castle?"

"No. It is understandable. We all want to reach the castle. It is where John dwells, and he is the most perfect of us all. He can call up demons and bid them do his will. With their aid, he can send storms and pestilence against our enemies, strike deep into their countries."

"Is he there now?"

"He is always there."

"Then I would like to meet him."

"Meet John? That is impossible. Only the perfect can aspire to that."

"Then I wish to become perfect."

"You? But you are a eunuch. You were rendered imperfect on the day you were cut."

"There are those," I said, "who have made themselves eunuchs to enter the Kingdom of the Heaven."

"Not among us. We become perfect by overcoming our base desires, by driving from our minds all thoughts of filthiness and bodily corruption."

"That is simple for my kind," I said. "We never think of such things."

"Never? Do you think I believe that? I can see from your fancy clothes that you come from Constantinople. I'm right, aren't I?"

"Yes."

"We all know what a pit of filth that city is. No one there, whether man, woman or eunuch, thinks of anything but the next occasion for polluting the body with shameful acts. The men there are always spilling their filthy semen, and they care not where they leave it. On the ground, in the nether orifice of a boy or eunuch, in a woman's womb where it may ferment and form a child, it is all the same. Ask yourself this: was there sexual intercourse in Paradise?"

I asked myself, but without coming to any conclusion. Adam and Eve had children, that much I knew. But how they were conceived, and whether it happened before or after the expulsion, were questions I had not previously considered. "I don't know," I said.

"Typical! You false Christians know nothing."

"That is why I came here. I wish to learn."

"Then think of this: all sin comes from lust, and it is by means of lust that sin is passed on. Cain was born of the seed of Satanael. The Evil One took the form of a snake and coupled with the first woman, making her the first adulteress. He spilled his filthy seed inside her and brought forth the first sinner. No good will come of the spilling of seed. The bodies of sinners are no better than rotten carrion. They are corpses shackled to debased souls. How much better off they would be if they were slaughtered, if their carcasses were cut away from the spirits they enslave."

Zacharias grabbed my arm with his bony fingers and stared at me with his small, cold eyes. "That's Constantinople for you," he said. "A city of corpses, shuffling their way to Hell."

He reminded me of Ignatius, who was probably at that moment denouncing the sinners of Constantinople from the pulpit of Hagia Sophia. How similar all zealots are, whether orthodox or heretical! There is little to choose between them. They think of nothing but what they ought not to do. Yet they manage to squabble as though they agreed on nothing.

"I agree," I said. "Constantinople is a sinful place. That is why I came here.

Zacharias gripped my arm tighter. "Can you tell me honestly that you have never indulged in shameful filthiness, even passively?"

"Not me," I said. "I am incapable of such acts."

Dismayed to find that I was thought inadequate even to become a heretic, I let Zacharias walk on. But the next day I approached the old man again, and after a while, when I had convinced him that I was in earnest, he agreed to instruct me.

"The first thing you must understand," Zacharias said, while we sat in the shade of an overgrown vine-arbour, "is that the Creator of the World to Come is not the Creator of this world."

"So there are two gods?"

"In a manner of speaking. The Creator of Heaven made our souls, which He will receive after the Judgement. He sent his Son down to us, but not in material form. You must remember that! Christ was not made of flesh, and was not born of Mary."

"And the other god?"

"The Creator of this world also created sin. He sent his son, Satanael, to spread sinfulness among men."

The Bulgars, I recalled, believed much the same thing. Yet they were savage pagans, and the Paulicians claimed to be the True Church. I had confirmed that they were indeed heretics, and not Christians at all. Photius was wrong in thinking them mere puritans. Had Michael been right in thinking them Satanists?

"Which god do you worship?"

"We revere the Creator of our souls, and fear the Creator of sin."

Zacharias told me that his kind would not take part in any of the sacraments, regarding the bread and wine as ordinary substances, foisted on the simple-minded by false priests in place of true knowledge. It was inconceivable, he claimed, that God would turn Himself into mere matter. Christ could not have fermented in the foulness of a woman's womb, endured infancy and childhood, been ignorant and gained wisdom, or learned a trade at his father's side. Nor could He have eaten, drunk or slept like a mere man. All those things were illusions, like His seeming agony on the cross, designed to instruct and redeem mankind.

The heretics only accepted a small part of the Scriptures. In fact, the heretics rejected most things, including the Trinity, the cross, priesthood, relics, icons and images, candles, incense, the baptism of infants, the intercession of saints, and just about everything that the orthodox hold dear.

I was tempted to ask Zacharias what was left to believe in. But I knew the answer. He would have told me that whatever was left was the truth. There was nothing attractive in the Paulician faith as he revealed it. There were no great myths, no sublime mysteries, no beautiful liturgy, no fellowship of worship, nothing but denial. Yet I kept company with that old man, sharing his meagre rations of bread and water, studying for weeks, learning whatever I could, thinking that dissimulation might get me into the castle, if not into the World to Come.

It was the return of the warriors that changed everything. They arrived suddenly, flooding into the town, pouring along its narrow streets, leading pack-mules, driving bullock-carts, laden with loot and slaves.

"Who are they?" I asked.

"John's men," Zacharias said. "They are back from raiding the Black Sea coast."

The old man tried to continue his lesson on the nature of evil, but I found it hard to pay attention as the streets below us were suddenly filled with activity. The soldiers unloaded mules and carts, threw sacks to the ground, rolled barrels through doorways and drove their women after them. A squad came into the hostel, which they quickly transformed into a tavern, flinging their weapons into a corner, broaching their barrels and drinking toasts to victory.

"Are these members of your faith?" I asked.

"Lesser members."

"Can they become perfect?"

"Not if they carry on like that."

"Why do you tolerate them?"

"They are John's men. Their raids bring wealth to Tephrike, and without them the emperor's men would soon drive us out."

"So they are allowed to sin?"

"There is no help for it."

One of the warriors hauled a woman onto his lap. She was dark-eyed and beautiful, a good catch for an ugly soldier. Seeing that Zacharias was staring at him, he called out. "Old man! What are you looking at?"

"He is concerned for your sinful soul," I said.

Zacharias glared at me, but said nothing.

288

"I'm a sinner all right," the soldier said. "But what can I do about it? Look at her! She's a beauty! Wouldn't you be tempted?" He pretended to offer the woman to Zacharias, who shrank back against the wall. "What I reckon is," the soldier said, "what you can't help isn't a sin. And the more beautiful the woman, the less you can help yourself, so the less sin there is."

Pleased with his feat of logic the soldier took a great swig of looted wine.

"That's nonsense," another soldier said. "Take a look at my woman." He thrust her forward so that we could see her clearly. "She's as ugly as they come."

We could hardly disagree. She was short, red-faced, and had a squint, though a devotee of plumpness might have found something to please him. Her owner leaned forward and addressed Zacharias. "There's no sin in what you don't enjoy, is there?"

Zacharias nodded. I was tempted to query that proposition, but the soldier went on, jerking a thumb at the owner of the beautiful woman. "He's wrong," he said. "He'll enjoy having her, so the sin is worse. I won't get much pleasure out of an ugly woman like mine, so I'll hardly have sinned at all. There's no arguing with that, is there?"

In fact, there was quite a lot of arguing. Another soldier stood up and said the first two were both wrong. "It depends how you do it," he said. "Suppose it's dark, and you can't see her, what then? And what if you think about a beautiful woman when you're having an ugly one?"

"Or the other way round," someone called out.

"Yes, doing it the other way round's a sin."

The soldiers went on, debating the sinfulness or otherwise of every permutation of the sexual act they could think of. The discussion was so heated that I thought they might forget to do anything with the women they had captured.

"I don't know about sin," one of them shouted. "But I'll tell you this: the best way to Heaven's through a woman's cunt."

"The only way to heaven," Zacharias said, "is through self-denial."

289

But none of the soldiers noticed. They had begun to practise what they had preached.

The following day, after sharing my room with several drunken soldiers, I went to Zacharias for my lesson, picking my way through the sleeping bodies, discarded clothing, spilled food and pools of vomit. The Paulician warriors, I decided, were very like the Rus. That might have been expected. I had been told that they were more brigands than heretics. But guards at the head of the valley were pious. And the men in the castle, John and his circle, were pure and enlightened. Zacharias had assured me of that.

"I still do not understand," I said. "How can members of the True Church behave like that?"

The old man sighed. "They are too ignorant to understand. When they are drunk, they think themselves already perfect. And even when they are sober, they imagine that for the perfect there can be no sin."

"Like the Messalians?"

He looked at me oddly. "What do you know about them?"

"The Messalians believed that once sin had been driven out, no action could be sinful."

"Are you sure? You could be confusing them with the Marcionites?"

"No, I don't think so. They . . ." The old man's expression warned me that I had made a mistake.

"How do you know this?" he said.

"I must have heard someone talk about the Messalians."

"Not among us, I hope. I have certainly never mentioned them. And if anyone else has talked of their foul doctrines, you must lead me to him immediately. That vile sect believes that Christ was a man. But you knew that already, didn't you? Just as you knew about the Marcionites. In fact, it seems that you are quite an expert on heresy."

"No, I can assure you . . ."

"You can assure me of nothing. You said you were an innocent, searching for knowledge. But it is clear you are nothing of the kind."

The castle
[AD 870–873]

My arms held firmly by two strong guards, my feet dragging and bumping over uneven stone paving, I was conducted rapidly upwards. Streets, gateways, narrow passages and steep steps, all disappeared behind me as I was hauled deeper into darkness. When my arms had almost been pulled from their sockets, I was shoved backwards through a doorway, then flung roughly onto the floor. I lay with my face on the cool flagstones, fearing to look up in case I found that I was in a dungeon, surrounded by hopeless and starving prisoners.

"You may rise," an imperious voice said.

Cautiously, I lifted my head. I was in a vaulted chamber, a deeply shadowed place, lit only by a few mote-speckled sunbeams that struck down from small windows high above me. In the centre of the room, illuminated by a pool of light, was an apparition, a stiff, white-faced, silk-clad, jewel-encrusted figure, which sat rigidly in a carved throne at the top of a three-stepped dais. It might have been an effigy, had not the Paulicians been bigger image-haters than the iconoclasts.

I stood, half crouching, half bowing, before the figure, which could only be John, leader of the heretics.

"A eunuch!" he said, his voice distant and echoing. "What a long time it is since I saw one of your kind."

John's silk robes were as fine as any I had seen Michael wear. His hat had clearly been a bishop's mitre, and his feet, which rested on a jewelled reliquary, were shod with soft red leather, an emperor's privilege. No doubt his clothes, like his throne, were looted from a cathedral, perhaps from Ephesus, revenge on the faith he had rejected.

Zacharias stood beneath him, on the lower step of the dais, looking pleased with himself for having found a way into the castle. Beside him was an even older man, whose ragged clothes and grey skin were caked with filth. John's other attendants, dressed in an odd assortment of Roman and Saracen clothes, stood silently in the shadows like a waiting congregation.

"So," John said, beckoning me with a jewelled hand. "Zacharias tells me you are a spy."

I stepped towards the dais. "No my lord. I am a humble seeker of truth."

"Don't believe him, my lord," Zacharias said, looking up eagerly at his earthly ruler. "He's come here to learn the truth all right. But only so he can go back to Constantinople and denounce it as lies."

"Is this true?" John said.

"No my lord, I assure you, I came here only to study the true faith at the feet of this venerable teacher."

Zacharias was not moved by my attempt at flattery. "Why do you know so much about heresy, then?"

"I have made a study of lies, in order that I may know the truth."

The filthy old man stood on tiptoe, straining towards his master, and whispered something. To my surprise, John did not shy away or hold his nose in disgust, but listened with respect. Zacharias looked resentful. I sensed that there was rivalry between the two old men.

"I am going to set you a test," John said. "Describe to me the beliefs and practices of the most fallacious heresy you know."

I thought for a moment. Perhaps John expected me to describe orthodoxy. His costume and accoutrements suggested that that might please him. But it might also be too obvious. Seeing the old man who had set my test, and noting John's splendid appearance, I had an idea. I described for John the sect of the Borborites.

"They claimed secret knowledge," I told him. "They believed that the world we see is not real, but an illusory emanation of the outermost of several ethereal layers. Each layer was governed by a spirit, which knew, and could reveal to anyone who led a pure enough life, the secrets that would allow them to ascend. The Borborites hoped, as a result of their devotions, to see beyond, perhaps even to climb through, those illusory layers until they reached the arms of the being they called the Kind Stranger.

"To the Borborites, the world we see was never meant to have been created. To them it was at best an accident, at worst a mistake. Others thought the world was created as a test, and designed to be as unpleasant as possible. Both types agreed that all pleasure was to be avoided. Some went further, mocking and perverting everything that others thought good and necessary. They ate food so filthy that it would have poisoned normal men. The foulness of their food confirmed that this world is debased and despicable. The Borborites never washed, dressed in rags, and slept with unclean beasts. They were, my lord, disgusting."

John smiled as he looked down at his ragged advisor. I always thought of the old man as the Borborite after that.

"Their devotions," John said. "Tell us about those."

I took another step towards him and dropped my voice to a loud whisper. "Unspeakable," I said.

"Go on, tell us more."

I did not know any more. I looked around the room, assuming an anxious expression. "It would not be advisable," I said. "Perhaps another time."

"Perhaps you are right. But it would be interesting to hear more of these, what did you call them? 'Ethereal layers.' Was that it?"

"It was, my lord."

"Most interesting. And there might be something in it." John turned to the Borborite. "Why have you never told me any of this?"

"Because it's all lies."

"You mean there never were such people?"

"There may well have been. But we are concerned with the truth, not with lies some ancient sect may have believed."

"Everything is symbolic, isn't it?"

Zacharias edged his rival aside. "Many things can be interpreted allegorically, my lord. That is why we are able to conform outwardly when we are in enemy territory. If we are obliged to worship in churches, or even mosques, without compromising our true beliefs."

"I thought so," John said. "That's why I want to hear more of what this Zeno has to say. Leave him with me, will you."

When Zacharias and the Borborite had withdrawn, John beckoned me to his dais. I ascended the first step and stood deferentially, waiting for John to formulate some tricky theological question, hoping I could answer it satisfactorily. But when the ruler of Tephrike spoke, it was not about the Borborites, or any other heresy. He asked me about Constantinople, about people and places he had known, and the latest gossip from the court.

I was confined to a cell after my interview with John, but it was a comfortable cell, no worse than the hostel I had come from. I could see that there was little hope of converting the heretics to orthodoxy. But I hoped that, if I flattered John enough, I might be able to win some concession, perhaps even arrange for the release of some prisoners, if they had not been sold into slavery. If done in my master's name, that might be enough to secure his freedom.

But I had seen John in an uncharacteristically cheerful mood. His true nature was revealed soon afterwards, when Peter the Abbot arrived at the castle with some of his followers. I was astonished to see Peter after all those weeks. I thought he must have gone back to Constantinople, or succumbed to illness at Sebastea. Yet there he was, standing meekly before John's throne, presenting Basil's costly gifts. I hung back, hiding among John's attendants, hoping I would not be noticed.

Zacharias surveyed the presents sulkily, prodding the heaps of silk with his foot, stirring the gold with a bony hand. The Borborite stood beside him, staring at the gifts as though they were a heap of dung dumped by a farmer. John hardly even looked at the treasures he had been offered.

"You insult me!" he shouted. "You offer me what I have already." He sat up straighter and extended an arm, displaying the magnificence of his robes. "And as for the rest of it, it is already mine. I can take goods of that sort whenever I like."

Peter hung his head, not knowing how to deal with John's anger.

"Look at his shaven head and black clothes," the Borborite said. "He's a monk. He is here to do the work of the Creator of this world."

"I am indeed," Peter said. "What nobler work can there be?"

"There! You have it from his own mouth. He is true servant of Satanael."

"It is you and your kind who are servants of Satan. I am a servant of the Lord, and of the emperor."

"A peasant usurper who sends me worthless trash," John said. "Has Basil nothing better to offer?"

"I have this," Peter said, pulling a book from under his coat.

The Borborite took the book, looked at it briefly, then handed it up to his master.

"Lies!" John said, flinging the book to the ground. "Again, you insult me. Do you imagine that we do not already know the truth?"

"I imagine no such thing," Peter said, stooping to pick up the book. "I know that you and your followers, like all Manichaeans, are blinded by error, and are doomed to damnation. I have come here to offer you salvation." He held the book up, waving it at John. "But if you reject it, what am I to do?"

Peter took a few steps back, clutching at the cross that hung from his neck. "Look on this and repent!" he said, holding out the cross.

John looked at him with contempt. "We do not worship wood."

Peter turned his back on John, which I did not think wise, and walked away from the throne.

Then he saw me.

"Zeno," he said. "I thought you had run away."

John rose from his throne. "Do you know this eunuch?"

"I knew him," Peter said. "He was one of my party. But he deserted us."

"You sent him as a spy!"

"I would not send a creature like that. He is nothing to do with me. You can keep him."

"Another present," John said, settling back into his throne. "How generous you are! You offer me wealth that is not wealth, a book that is not true, and a man who is not a man. But the eunuch, like so much else, is already mine."

Peter stayed at Tephrike for nearly a month, half prisoner, and half guest. He questioned people in the streets, reproached the soldiers who guarded him, preached to Zacharias, argued with the Borborite, and debated with John, annoying all of them. He called me a traitor and apostate, and I could hardly prove him wrong by revealing my true purpose. By the end of his stay he had achieved nothing, which was what Theodore had hoped for. But I had achieved no more, and without the prospect of returning.

Before Peter left, the Borborite presented him with a book. "It is a history of our faith," the old man said. "It tells how we have been persecuted and hounded out of the empire. It tells of our tribulations in the East, and the battles we have had with those who have sought to deny the truth. You would do well to read it and reflect. In the World to Come, there will be no place for heretics like you."

Peter took the book, but held it away from his body as though it stank. John, addressing his own followers as well as Peter and his party, made a final announcement.

"I have a message for that jumped-up peasant you call your emperor," he said. "You can tell Basil that he can have the West, if he thinks he's man enough to hold it. But the East is mine, and I intend to take it."

John celebrated Peter's departure with a feast, a meal of such luxury that it would have horrified Zacharias and the Borborite, had they been allowed to attend. Secure in his high castle, surrounded by warriors and sycophants, John ate roasted meats doused with rich sauces, drank sweet wines from the East, and listened to the wailings of a band of Saracen minstrels who claimed to have entertained the Caliph of Baghdad, whose recent murder had left them unemployed. After the feast, his head full of flattering words sung by the Saracens, John watched dancers whose movements were every bit as lascivious as those who had entertained Cyril and the court eunuchs.

It was no surprise to me when the feast descended into an orgy. Nor was I surprised to learn that such things happened often, whenever there was a victory over the imperial army, a successful raid, or a new influx of loot and slaves.

Who could wish to read yet another account of gluttony, stupidity, drunkenness, and debauchery? Not me. I have seen enough of the perverse and baffling effects of lust. Men of all kinds and every faith are led astray by their appetites, and seek to justify their weakness in any way that suits them. What purpose is served by further enumeration of their crimes, follies and excuses?

Yet I suppose it is my duty to report the hypocrisy of the Paulicians. The men of Tephrike claimed to revere the Creator of the World to Come. Yet the men in the castle, John and his immediate followers, worshiped the Creator of this world. Even according to their own system, that is much the same as devil-worship, the very thing the orthodox accuse them of, and which Michael sought to imitate. It is true that the Paulicians did not mock the sacraments, as Michael did. That would have meant nothing to men who believe that Christ was a spirit who did not take material form. Nor did they mock the clergy, who by the Paulicians' reckoning were already a mockery.

But John's men indulged in every sort of lust, spilling their seed in every orifice, taking their pleasure with any partner, doing everything that Zacharias and the Borborite condemned, all to glorify the Creator of sin. And that was the secret of the Paulicians, that among them there were worshippers of the devil, as well as zealous puritans, and men too brutal and stupid to understand what they were doing.

★

For the next three years I hardly stepped outside the castle. Despite the heat and sun outside, it was a dark, cold place, its vaulted chambers echoing with eerie cries, its cell-like rooms inhabited by trembling sycophants, all dominated by the moods of a deluded heretic. I was the only eunuch in that place, the only eunuch some of the men had ever seen. They poked and prodded me, stroked my smooth skin, lifted my tunic to see what the cutting had left. They did not prefer me to their women, who submitted and kept silent in a way that I could never have managed. It was always a relief when some-one new came to the castle to divert attention from me. But we had few visitors. One or other of John's commanders might report a raid or skirmish. Saracens came to buy slaves or loot. A few heretics drifted in, members of Eastern sects no longer tolerated, either by Christian or Saracen. They would be questioned by the Borborite, their heterodox beliefs drawn out for John's amusement. Sometimes, if there were enough of them, they were set against each other like theological gladiators. Afterwards, if they were able-bodied they were sent to join John's warriors, a gang united only by hatred of orthodoxy and a love of the freebooting life.

John kept me near him, making me watch the follies of his men, or entertain him with examples of heterodox theology. It became my practice to expound a new heresy every day. I told him of heresies I had learned from Photius's books, and from the texts I had copied, or concocted, for Theodore. When I ran out of ideas, I repeated heresies I had already described, or sneaked in obscure but orthodox doctrine. John did not seem to notice. He was happy to be amazed at man's capacity for error, and to be reassured that the Paulicians' doctrines, whatever they actually were, and whether he believed in them or not, were a fixed point in the middle of a swirling sea of false belief. I suspect that, having rejected orthodoxy, John believed in nothing but his own power.

What a torment that time was, and what a waste! What use is a eunuch away from Constantinople? Only there can my kind thrive. In the provinces we are like bees cut off from the hive. In that castle I became something worse than I had been before. I was a buffoon and a sycophant, but to no purpose.

In the darkness of my cell, I cursed Theodore for sending me on a fool's errand. I dreamed of Photius in exile and Eudocia in her palace. How could I hope to help either of them? I often clutched Inger's gift and begged Thor to protect me. I was still not sure whether I believed in him, but the Thunderer proved in the end to be more powerful than the god, or gods, of the Paulicians.

Escape
[AD 873]

I knew something was wrong when I found that my cell door had been bolted in the night. I waited for hours, hearing the tramp of feet, distant shouts, the clank of iron, and a hundred other sounds that spoke loudly of trouble without revealing what the trouble was. Eventually I was dragged from my cell, marched through the crowd assembled in John's audience chamber, and flung roughly on the floor.

"How did you summon them?" John said, his voice trembling with anger.

I raised my bruised head as much as I dared, but could only see John's red-shod feet. "Who, my lord?"

"Basil's men."

"My lord, I know nothing of Basil's men."

"Then how do you explain the army he has sent, if you did not summon them?"

"I cannot. I didn't . . ."

"It is not that his army can harm us. What can they be but men in Basil's own image, peasants, grooms, stable hands, swineherds and drovers? What can men armed with pitchforks and dung shovels do against an army like mine? No, I do not fear them, but I hate spies and traitors." He leaned down at me from his throne. "How did you get the message to them?"

"I can assure you my lord that this army is nothing to do with me."

"I'll punish you for this! I'd cut your balls off if it hadn't been done already!"

"Sir," I said. "I hate Basil, and would never betray you to him. Let me prove my loyalty. I will do anything you ask."

John called out for wine. I lay as flat as I could, hoping my humility would calm his anger. His servants rushed to his side, competing for his favour. He drank, then cursed Basil in every way he could think of. I lay there for some time, prostrate on the cold floor, while servants came and went, and messengers brought news that John's men had started to desert. Used to the whims of their master, they all ignored me.

Then Zacharias and the Borborite arrived, weeping and wailing, trying to outdo each other with terrible predictions. Still I lay on the floor, my head aching, my limbs cold and numb. The two heresiarchs had been at it for some time when an officer reported that the imperial army was almost at the head of the valley.

"Then go and fight them," John said.

"There are too many of them," the officer said. "We will all be killed." He was unarmed, but dressed for battle, with a long mailcoat and heavy iron greaves.

"Then be killed." John sounded calm, almost reasonable. "What are you afraid of? The World to Come awaits you."

"Most of the men have run away," the officer said.

"From a gang of peasants?"

"From the biggest army the emperor has ever sent against us."

"The emperor? That usurper!"

"My lord, some of the men will fight. But only if you lead them."

John's face turned almost as red as his boots. "Do you think me unfit to rule?" he shouted. "I have royal blood, you know. My family is ancient. They did not just rule valleys like this one. They ruled whole provinces, principalities, nations, empires. I am a better man than Basil. I am a true King of the East. I am inspired by the Creator of the World to Come, and I mean to be the ruler of this world."

John leapt from his throne, drew his sword and swung it at the officer. The officer stepped back, but the blade gashed his throat. He staggered, clutched vainly at the air, then slumped to the floor with a clatter of chainmail. I felt his body roll against mine, and his warm blood seeped into my tunic.

"Traitor!" John said, kicking the body. He paced the room, shouting at his few remaining supporters. I lay as still as I could while John was near me, then rolled over and dived into a corner.

"We cannot stay here," John said, jabbing his sword wildly at the vaulted ceiling. "We will be entombed in darkness. We must go to the light, to the East. There I will be a King!"

"What does it matter whether we flee or fight?" the Borborite said. "The righteous among us need fear nothing. Not the sword, not fire, not even torture. Whatever punishment they subject us to, we will be saved. If they tie us to a stake and pile blazing faggots around us, we will not burn. Angels will snatch us from the pyre and bear us away to the World to Come."

The thought of being burned terrified me. I began to edge towards the door, ready to sneak out and take my chances, to throw myself at the first imperial officer I could find and beg for mercy. No one could mistake me for a soldier, and there might be time to explain myself before I was struck down.

"We go to the light!" John shouted, and dashed after me, his silk robes flapping around him. I ran, scrambling down the stairs, John and the others behind me, trying to get out into the open before they did. In the courtyard, John pushed me aside, shouting at the gatekeepers. They saw the bloody sword in his hand, obeyed him, then ran through the gates they had opened. We all rushed after them, down into the town, along the winding streets, through the crowds of weeping women and wailing heretics. At the edge of the town our path was blocked by a gang of John's warriors. The Borborite leapt into the middle of them and began to urge them on.

"John is a hypocrite," he shouted. "He is a son of Satanael! He has deceived us!"

The warriors formed a circle around us, jeering and jabbing their spears angrily. Some of them picked up stones and looked ready to throw them. John did not hesitate. He reached out and grabbed me, pulling me roughly in front of him. I felt a stone hit my leg, then another. In a panic, desperate to escape, I lashed out at John, hitting him in the face and clawing at his hands. He was so surprised that he failed to resist, and without really meaning to I managed to snatch his sword. But then my anger subsided. I stood with the sword in my hands, my chest heaving with effort, wondering what to do.

Then I heard the Borborite's voice. "Kill him," it said. Others joined in. "Cut him down," they said. "Kill the hypocrite."

The bruise on my head throbbed. I felt dizzy. The shouts deafened me. Without thinking, I obeyed, swinging the sword at John's neck. It was the first time I had attempted such a blow, and I can hardly claim that my aim was true. But I did hit him, and the sting of the blade as it glanced across his chest sent him reeling back. John glared at me. I pointed the sword at him. When the chorus of heretics urged me to strike again, I struck, lunging upwards with the blade. Its point drove deep into John's throat. I let go of the sword and it fell between us. John clutched at his throat, blood trickling from his mouth and seeping through his fingers.

". . . plans," he said, in a faint, gurgling voice. "I had such plans."

He swayed, grimaced, then pitched forward onto the dusty ground.

I staggered back, and the heretics all rushed forward, waving and thrusting whatever weapons they had, trying to land a blow on their former leader before he died. Seeing what was happening, more of the Paulicians arrived, shouldering me aside as they fought for a chance to claim the glory of ridding their sect of a false leader.

I fled, happy to let anyone who wanted it take the credit for John's death. I was in such a tumult that I hardly saw where I ran. I had killed someone! I, a eunuch and scholar, had wielded a weapon! I felt proud and elated. Was that what it felt like to be a man? My chest swelled and my stride lengthened. I felt I could run forever, that I could dash through the abandoned orchards like a deer, or a wolf. Had I become a beast? Shame and fear mixed with my pride. I was as bad as Basil, as Bardas, as Basiliscianus, as the savage Rus who had raided Tmutorokan. My pace slackened. Inger's idol bumped at my neck. Had Thor the warrior guided my hand? Or was that violence always in me? Could I, if the need arose, kill again?

By the time I reached the head of the valley and saw the

first imperial troops, my confusion had turned into an unnatural calm. I was going to escape. I was on my way home. All I had to do was explain myself. The soldiers, seeing a blood-spattered eunuch, treated me kindly. I found that they were commanded by Petronas, whom I had met once or twice at court, and had been a friend of Photius when it was safe to be so. He sent me west, to the shores of the Bosphorus, where my master was still in exile.

At the monastery, the first person I met was Theodore. He was sitting in the shade of a plane tree, going through a box of books he must have found in the abbot's library. The tree dwarfed the monastic buildings, which were low, spread out, and more like a rustic hamlet than a spiritual retreat.

"What are you doing here?" he asked, scowling at me.

"I came to find my master."

"You've left it a long time. Photius has been languishing here for years. As you can see, it's not a luxurious place. Whoever founded this monastery was not planning for an easeful retirement. Luckily I have been able to arrange a few comforts and diversions for Photius. You were his servant. You might have been able to do something for him yourself, had you got here earlier."

"How could I? You sent me to Tephrike."

"Sent you? I think not. I suggested a way in which you might have helped your master. I made some arrangements, helped you with money. That was all."

"There was no money. No one in Santabaris would admit to knowing you. I was stuck in Tephrike for three years. There was no possibility of converting John or releasing the prisoners. The whole project was pointless."

Theodore gave me a reproachful look. "A prophet is often without honour in his own land. However, you are right about one thing. Your mission was pointless. But how were we to know that Basil's men would kill John the Heretic?"

"They didn't!"

"Of course they did. Basil has given thanks for it in the cathedral."

"But I killed John."

"You?" Theodore laughed. "That's a good one! Zeno the eunuch, slayer of heretics." He laughed again, so loudly that some of the monks came out and stared at us, frowning at his unseemly merriment.

"I did kill him," I said, when Theodore's laughter subsided.

"That's travel for you," he said, wiping away a tear with a grubby sleeve. "A couple of years in the East, and you come back full of tall tales."

"It's not a tall tale."

Theodore rocked with silent mirth. I hated him for mocking me, for not taking me seriously, for assuming I was capable of nothing. But I noted the effect my story produced, and resolved not to mention it again.

"Whoever killed John," Theodore said, "we should be glad that the heretics are finished. But it has spoiled my other plan."

"What was that?"

"With my help, Photius has been writing a history of the Paulicians, and an account of their beliefs."

"But you know nothing about them. I spent years in Tephrike . . . "

"You do not seem to have made such good use of your time as Peter the Abbot. He may be one of Ignatius's creatures, but he has compiled a most interesting account of the Paulicians."

"He was only at Tephrike for a month. He knows nothing."

"No, his account makes it clear, he stayed for nearly a year. He debated with the wisest of their initiates, and found out everything there is to know about the heretics' history and beliefs. Of course, his style is rough and uneducated. Photius has added polish, as well as his own theological insights. Alas, the book will not be needed now. We will have to devise another plan to get Photius back in favour."

"Can I see him?"

"I expect so. I will have a word with the abbot. He is a simple fellow, but he listens to me."

★

It was six years since I had last seen my master, but he had aged much more than that. He was in his middle fifties, and his close-cropped hair and spreading beard were almost white. His face was deeply lined and greyish from lack of sun and air. He had, however, lost some of the weight he had acquired during his time as patriarch. There would have been no banquets at that monastery, nothing but prayer, contemplation and scholarship.

Some pages from his history of the Paulicians rested on a small writing desk, and Peter the Abbot's report was propped up behind them. I longed to look at what Photius had written, and see what Peter had made of his brief visit to Tephrike. I could not help feeling that Peter's book, and my master's use of it, betrayed me in some way. But my feelings about that were unimportant. I was back with my master. That was what mattered. He rose from his desk and stepped towards me. He held out his arms. We embraced. His arms closed around me. I felt his beard tickling my ear. He spoke a few soft words of welcome. We were not just master and servant. We were old friends, reunited at last.

"If I am to get back in favour," Photius said. "And away from this place, then I must give Basil something. A valuable gift. But what could he possibly want? He already has the empire, the heretics are defeated, he controls the Church, he has a beautiful wife, and several sons."

"Not all his own," Theodore said.

"What do you mean?"

"Prince Leo is Michael's son, not Basil's. I'm sure of it."

"I hope you will not repeat this rumour," Photius said. "We must offer Basil something he wants, not offend him with idle gossip."

"Basil might be glad to know the truth, if we could prove it. He wouldn't want the empire to go to a bastard. He's got other sons."

"No!" Photius said. "If you are a true friend of mine you will not mention this again. It is far too dangerous."

"So what would you give him? You said he has everything."

I remembered John the Heretic's grandiloquent rants, how he had claimed patrician ancestry and scoffed at Basil's peasant origins. "I know something that Basil does not have," I said. "Ancestry."

"He has it," Theodore said. "But he does not care to have it known."

"Then we must supply him with an ancestry he can be proud of," I said. "We did it for Eudocia. We found her a new family, devised a genealogy that made her look noble. We must do the same for Basil."

"What a good idea," Photius said. "People of his sort are always sensitive about their humble origins. It ought to be possible to prepare a genealogy that makes him seem noble. He would surely be grateful for that."

"He would be more grateful to know the truth about his son," Theodore said.

"No!" Photius said. "Zeno's plan is a good one. It would be better to give Basil good news than bad."

"Basil's family came from Armenia," I said. "That is conveniently far away. We could trace him back to some noble family from those parts, preferably long extinct. Perhaps the Arsacids."

"Persian royalty!" Theodore scoffed. "Why stop there? Basil's mother was Macedonian. Perhaps she was descended from Alexander the Great."

"It would be best not to overdo it," Photius said. "We must flatter the emperor, not mock him."

"I am sure I could devise something suitable," I said. "The Armenians . . ."

"Zeno is no genealogist," Theodore said. "He won't help you get back in Basil's favour. What use was he to you in Tephrike?"

I was angry with Theodore, but I did not want to argue with him in front of Photius. He was too good at turning everything to his own advantage, and I knew that my scheme would not work without his cunning.

"You leave it to me," Theodore said. "I will concoct a history so full of pathos and nobility that it will have the court weeping with sorrow and sympathy. There will be an ancient lineage, heroic bravery, patriotism, honour, defeat and exile, followed by a slow drift into poverty. I will depict Basil's father as a figure from Hesiod, not a peasant, but an honest farmer, content to till the soil with his own hands."

I swallowed my anger and let Theodore talk. He took an idea I had only just thought of, and expounded it as though it had been in his mind for years. I managed to add a few refinements, and toned down some of his flights of fancy, but it was Theodore, not me, who added the plan's masterstroke.

"I will write the finished document in a mixture of cipher, cryptic verse and archaic Persian," he said.

"But no one will understand it," Photius said.

"And I will arrange to have it hidden in the imperial library."

"But no one will ever find it."

"Of course they will," Theodore said. "I will make sure of that. And when they do, I will be on hand to declare that you, Photius, are the only man in the empire wise enough to understand it. Of course, I will have to interpret parts of it myself. I will have to hint that the document is important, that it will bring great credit to the emperor. Then it will be up to you. You will be brought back from exile. Then you can give Basil the noble ancestry he craves, and win back your privileges."

Later, when Theodore was consulting with the abbot, Photius spoke to me. "Zeno," he said, "There is something I must ask of you."

"Anything, master."

"I do not quite know how to put this. Theodore has always been a good friend and supporter. He has helped me in many ways. What would my library be without him? But it seems to me that, in this case, there is a possibility . . ."

"You think he may interpret the genealogy himself, claim all the credit for it, and leave you in exile."

"I wouldn't put it as harshly as that. But things can go wrong. The court is a treacherous place. I would be happier if you went with him and made sure things turn out as he proposes."

Restoration
[AD 874–878]

"It is an insult," Photius said when he returned from the palace. "Basil has asked me to teach his young sons. Has he forgotten I was patriarch of this city? Does he mistake me for a village schoolmaster?"

"I don't suppose," Theodore said, "that Basil ever saw a village schoolmaster when he was a boy. And being tutor to the young princes is hardly the same thing."

"Prince Leo is eight. Alexander and Stephen are even younger. I hate children."

"It could be worse."

"How?"

"Basil hasn't asked you to teach his other son, the one he had by that peasant woman he was married to."

"Prince Constantine? What could I teach an empty-headed youth like him? He is a peasant through and through, despite the honours Basil heaps on him."

"At least you are back in your own house," Theodore said. "That must be a relief after those years in the monastery."

"Look at the state of it!" Photius said, glaring at the half-empty pool in which dead carp floated, the waterless fountain, the moss-crowned statues, and the dry leaves that lay in deep drifts all around the courtyard. "The whole place is filthy, inside and out. They've drunk the cellar dry, and you should see the library. An awful lot of books are missing."

Theodore looked shifty. "Servants can never be trusted," he said. "But if they have sold any of your books, I promise you, I will do everything in my power to track them down for you. I know all the booksellers in the city. They won't dare hide anything from me. If those books are anywhere to be found, I'll get them back."

"I will get the house cleaned up," I said. "Just make it clear to the servants who's in charge, and I'll organise everything."

Photius walked into the house and sadly surveyed the dust

and grime. After wandering the empty, echoing rooms and finding few of his old servants still there, he was happy to hand responsibility to me.

"Do you think you could arrange some food?" he said. "And some wine, perhaps. That Monemvasian you used to get was very good. The abbot was not very generous with his cellar. He seemed to think that the worse the wine, the more virtuous the drinker. I have never shared the view that where there is no pleasure there can be no sin."

Pausing only to issue orders to the bewildered servants, I rushed out of the house to look for a wine merchant. I could have sent someone, but I wanted to go myself, to jostle with the crowds, to smell the fish frying at the quayside, to feel the breeze from the Bosphorus, to see the idlers in the market-place, to taste the wine and haggle over the price. I was back, with my master, in the greatest city the world has ever known.

Constantinople was not quite as I remembered it. Basil, powerful and popular after his victories in the East, had adorned the city with statues, squares and elegant colonnades. Places I had known well were transformed, and not just in the official quarter. There were gangs of shaven and shackled prisoners everywhere, some of them flogged through the streets, others displayed outside churches to discourage wrong-doers. On imperial orders, most of the low taverns, cookshops and brothels had been closed down. Basil, more than anyone, would have known where they were.

None of those changes concerned me. I had no intention of returning to my old life, and with Michael and Cyril dead, no one would make me. The only part of that life I wanted was Eudocia, and I had heard nothing from her. Could it be true, as Theodore claimed, that she had used me, and no longer needed me?

Unable to reach Eudocia, I devoted myself to Photius, making his life agreeable, supplying him with comforts, and with such diversions as his age and nature permitted. His greatest pleasure was to invite a few friends to his house, where they would eat a good meal, drink the fine wines I supplied, and discuss books. On those occasions, Photius became again what he always had been, a wit and scholar with a taste for good company, particularly when that company was content to listen. Gradually, by those means, Photius rebuilt his network of friends.

"I cannot believe that Basil is still taken in by Ignatius," Photius said, after hearing the patriarch preach at the cathedral. "I proved he was a fool years ago, and nothing has changed. The old eunuch is just as foolish as ever. I sometimes think that Basil likes being surrounded by fools."

"Ignatius is wise in one thing," I said. "He has learned to flatter Basil, to praise him for purifying the city."

"Purifying?"

"You heard the sermon? Ignatius praised Basil for 'sweeping away dens of iniquity' and building new churches in their place."

"Churches that are in the hands of ignorant zealots."

"The people like Ignatius, and the priests he appoints. They don't expect their priests to be learned."

"Well they ought to! How can Ignatius be trusted to govern the Church? Even the papal commission thought he was too stupid to be patriarch. Anastasius, the pope's librarian, declared that Ignatius was 'conspicuously lacking in the knowledge expected of a churchman'. Yes, he said that! And he could hardly be counted as one of my friends or supporters."

There was a story I had not dared tell Photius. Some of his missing books never reappeared, and there were rumours that a mysterious priest had sold them to that same Anastasius, a member of the delegation that came to Constantinople to denounce Photius and all his deeds.

"No," my master said, shaking his head sadly. "The fact is, Basil fears learning and values ignorance. That is the peasant way."

"He has not closed the university. You must be glad about that."

"I suppose so. But Basil might have let me teach there,

instead of making me teach his sons. They are stupid and ignorant, just as you might expect from the sons of a peasant."

I did not remind him that Leo, the eldest, was rumoured to be Michael's son. Photius had always rejected that possibility.

"You might think," he said, "that princes would see the need for an elegant oratorical style. But no! They seem unable to grasp even the basics of rhetoric."

"They are very young."

"You don't need to tell me that. I feel more like a nursemaid than a teacher. It's a humiliation. Sometimes I think I might be better off in a monastery. At least I could do my own work, and not be distracted."

"No, your destiny is here in the city. You have great work to do, I am sure of it."

Photius said nothing. Surely, after all my efforts, he was not going to give up and go back into exile? If he did that, I might never see Eudocia again. I considered asking Theodore to make another of his prophecies. Then I thought of a more practical scheme.

"I could help you," I said. "Remember how I taught Eudocia?" My master's expression showed that he did not. "Take me with you for a few sessions," I said. "Tell them I am your assistant. Then, after a while, you can leave most of the lessons to me."

Photius only hesitated for a moment. "That is most generous, Zeno," he said. "And I will take you up on it."

"Look at all these new buildings," Photius said as we strolled through the palace grounds. "All these churches and chapels. Why are they so elaborate? Surely Ignatius would prefer something simpler. And these reception halls." Photius waved vaguely at a domed building surrounded by scaffolding and swarming with labourers. "Do they need to be quite so costly? There's gold, onyx, porphyry and serpentine everywhere you look."

I struggled along behind my master, carrying his books, of which, considering the ages and abilities of his pupils, there were far too many.

"I don't know how he's managed it," Photius said. "Michael was always short of money for public works."

"But not for improving his stables," I said. "He clad those with marble and mosaics."

Photius looked uncomfortable. Perhaps I ought not to have reminded him of the scene of his drinking contest with Michael. "Basil feels insecure," he said. "He was more grateful than you could possibly imagine for that genealogy I gave him. He said it confirmed what he already knew. These new buildings are the same. They confirm his opinion of himself as a great and noble ruler. But I think there is something rather vulgar about it, something of the peasant suddenly come into money."

Photius wisely fell silent as we neared the imperial quarters. All around us workers were sawing, hammering, polishing and sweeping.

I was wary of entering the heart of the palace. I hoped to see Eudocia, but was afraid of meeting Basil, of him remembering me, knowing me for the eunuch who had witnessed his debaucheries. We were greeted by a court eunuch and ushered into the imperial schoolroom, which was small, and had not been embellished with costly materials.

"Eudocia isn't here," I said.

"Why should she be? I am educating her sons, not her."

"So you never see her?"

"Of course not. Why should I? Women know nothing of education."

The three little princes arrived, and Photius, the greatest scholar of the age, taught them a lesson that might have been appropriate for young men preparing to enter the imperial bureaucracy. Knowing better than to interfere, I watched, noting my master's mistakes, remembering how Constantine had taught me, resolving to teach something more suitable when my turn came.

When Photius handed the princes over to me, I abandoned his attempts to teach them high-flown rhetoric and tried to entertain them. We read romances, adventures, and accounts of wonderful voyages. I wanted the princes to enjoy their lessons, not for their sakes, but for mine. I hoped that they would tell their mother what a good teacher I was, and that she would remember me.

I allowed the court eunuch to lead me into Eudocia's presence, glad that I had put on my finest clothes, that my appearance was only a little less elegant than his. Being in charge of my master's finances, I had bought some long linen tunics in various delicate shades, an embroidered silk coat, some soft shoes of dyed leather, and a selection of belts, purses, hats and trinkets, such as are fashionable at court. I even employed an expensive barber to dress my hair stylishly and get rid of the grey that had crept into it. Such things are unimportant, but Eudocia was the empress, and I did not want to let her down.

As instructed, I hung my head as I entered her chamber, but I saw that she sat on a carved and cushioned chair, with a little dog curled up at her feet.

When the eunuch touched my elbow, I knelt, then prostrated myself, lying face down on the cool marble floor.

"Zeno of Tmutorokan," the eunuch announced. "*Assistant* to your majesty's sons' tutor."

"You may rise," she said.

I rose, as gracefully as I could. Eudocia looked almost lost among the grandeur of her new apartments, though she wore a silk gown that shone with almost as many colours as the mosaics on her walls. She was over thirty by then, but her beauty had not faded. Nor had she become fat, as women often do when they are confined to their quarters with little to do. I gazed at her lovely face, wondering what to say to her.

The eunuch nudged my elbow again. "You may deliver your report," he said.

"Tell me about Prince Leo," Eudocia said. "How is he progressing?"

I did as I was asked, then reported on Alexander and Stephen. I made sure that my comments were as dull as possible, so that the court eunuchs, the stern matrons, the

315

maidservants and guards, would all lose interest in anything I said. Eudocia listened, and asked one or two questions. Then she rose from her couch.

"Come with me," she said. The dog woke up and gazed expectantly at its mistress. The court eunuch looked anxious. I hesitated. Eudocia beckoned me with a jewelled finger. "We can talk better outside."

At her silent command a pair of carved wooden doors swung open, and Eudocia led me through them into a large walled garden. It was planted with fruit trees and rose bushes, and here and there among the paths, pools and fountains were tubs of flowers and sweet herbs. A peacock strutted in the sun, spreading its gaudy tail.

"I almost didn't recognise you," she said, when the doors had closed behind us.

I longed to take Eudocia in my arms and hug her. But how could I? She was no longer the child I had cared for, the young woman I had taught, or the neglected mistress I had consoled. She had become something else, but I was not sure what. I did not know how things stood, whether we were truly alone, what Eudocia would permit.

"I've grown older," I said.

"No, it's those clothes. I've never seen you dressed like that."

"I didn't want the court eunuchs to look down on me." I did not like to admit that my new appearance was in part a disguise, that I feared being recognised by Basil.

"I prefer you dressed as a man."

"I will remember that. If you invite me again."

Eudocia did not answer my implied question. "Why didn't you come to see me before?" she said.

"I tried, but the guards wouldn't let me in."

"Why didn't you write to me."

"I did."

"I didn't get any letters from you."

"Nor did I from you."

"I'm not much of a writer," she said. "You know that."

There was fear in Eudocia's eyes. She turned away from me.

I could see that she would say no more about our years apart. With the dog following at her heels, she took me to the far end of the garden, where a roof sloped down from the high wall, shading a collection of cages and hutches. There were birds of all sorts, some chosen for their plumage, others for their song. She had cats, tame squirrels, and several monkeys. Michael, I recalled, had kept a menagerie. Its inhabitants were fierce, savage, grotesque. Michael had teased them, just as he teased his friends and followers. Eudocia's pets were soft, gentle, companionable.

"Let us sit in the shade," she said, leading me to a carved wooden seat beneath a spreading fig tree.

"This is my empire," she said. "And my world."

"Your world?"

"It is all I see, and all I can control."

"But you share the empire with Basil."

"I share nothing with Basil. I hardly ever see him. He spends all his time fighting wars, or building churches, or praying."

"Praying?"

"I would never have believed it, but he is quite pious now. He prayed constantly that those heretics would be defeated. And they were. You should have seen him when he heard that their leader was dead. He was on his knees for hours, giving thanks to God."

Something flashed in the sunlight. A round, glittering object moved across the marble paving. Slowly, it jerked and wobbled, dragging its heavy body on feeble legs. At first I took it for a gilded automaton, such as Leo the philosopher had built. But when it crawled closer I saw that it was a living thing, a tortoise, whose humped carapace had been burnished and set with jewels.

Eudocia reached up into the branches and picked a ripe fig, which she dropped in the creature's path. It burst on the ground, spilling its purple flesh. Extending its wizened head, the tortoise nuzzled the fruit, then opened its toothless jaws and bit into the sweet pulp.

"It reminds me of the patriarch," I said.

"Ignatius?" She giggled. "You are right. I hadn't thought of that. He shall be called Ignatius from now on."

"Have you heard him preach?"

She pulled one of her sour faces, the type that told me better than words could that she remembered what we shared, and what we both knew. "Of course I have. Basil makes me go to the cathedral whenever he does."

"My master envies the patriarch."

"Photius? I can't imagine why."

"He wants his old job back."

"Are you asking me a favour?"

"Perhaps."

"I've told you how things are. Basil doesn't listen to me. Except when I tell him about his sons." She thought for a moment. "I'll tell him about you," she said. "I'll tell him what a good job you are doing, teaching them."

"I'd rather you didn't. Mention my master's name, not mine. Make sure he gets the credit."

Eudocia did not say anything. I had the feeling that our reunion had not been a success, that I had awoken in her unwelcome memories. She stood, and walked out into the sunlight. I followed her, full of remorse, hoping I had not offended her. She paused by the doors to her chamber.

"Do you remember," she said, "how we swore never to desert each other?"

"I remember."

"Well, now that I've found you again, I won't desert you. But please, don't ask me for more than I can give."

The doors opened and we stepped through them. The court eunuch conducted me briskly away.

I felt sorry for Eudocia, confined in that world of women, where silks rustle, and perfumes hang in the still air, and long afternoons pass without incident. She did not spin or weave, as respectable women are taught to do. Nor was she pious, or interested in good works. Despite my attempts to educate her, she did not read. Her only diversion, apart from watching over her children, was her garden and her pets. She must often have sympathised with the caged birds, which fluttered their bright plumage, unable to escape.

A strange thing happened after my reunion with Eudocia. Her jewelled tortoise, which she had just named Ignatius, fell into a pond and drowned. It was found floating in the water, its wizened limbs swollen like dried fruit that has been steeped in wine. And soon after that, weighed down by his gold-embroidered vestments, the real Ignatius collapsed and died. I must make it plain, in view of what I tell elsewhere in these memoirs, that the patriarch's death was entirely natural, and not the result of intrigue. Ignatius was nearly eighty, and had never been robust. When Bardas deposed him he had to be beaten to make him resign, and he was later injured when the Rus attacked his island monastery. I think he only lasted so long to spite my master.

"Is it true?" Photius said. "Can the old fool really be dead?"

"They will announce it in the morning," Theodore said.

"I feared he would go on for ever. He had a shrivelled, mummified look about him, like those corpses the Egyptians prepared. According to Herodotus . . ."

"You will be the next patriarch."

"How do you know? Have you heard something? Have you consulted the oracle."

"No. There is no need. No one is better qualified to succeed Ignatius than you."

"You flatter me."

"I wouldn't dare," Theodore said. "You see through flattery like the clearest Syrian glass. But I hope that when you are appointed, you will remember those who helped you."

I was there when Photius was invested as patriarch for the second time. I stood in the great cathedral of Hagia Sophia with all the nobles and notables. I heard the unearthly voices of the choir, saw the shimmer of lamplight on the mosaics, smelled the incense as it wafted between the marble pillars. And I watched Basil presiding over the ceremony with assurance, correctly pronouncing each of the formulae, making the

319

gestures required of him with the utmost dignity. He made a better job of it than Michael had, at Photius's first investiture, almost twenty years earlier. The silk clothes and jewelled accoutrements of an emperor suited Basil. They did not look vulgar when he wore them, but were a fitting ornament for his tall and muscular body, the outward signs of the power he had taken by brute force but wielded as though born to it. To everyone present, Basil appeared to be what we had made him out to be, a descendant of Alexander, Constantine, and the ancient kings of Parthia.

I could see why Eudocia was afraid of him, why she kept to her quarters and said little. And I understood why she had not let me near her during those difficult years. Between us, we knew too much.

Theodore behaved as though my master's restoration was entirely his doing. He could not boast openly of having concocted Basil's genealogy. Even he could see that that would have undone everything. But he did talk constantly, in a vague and suggestive way, of the work, the influence, the sheer cleverness, that he had deployed to get his friend back into power. Photius was more or less obliged to make Theodore a bishop, giving him the see of Euchaita, an obscure town in the East, to which many Paulicians had fled. It was the least he could do, or so Theodore said.

I do not know whether Theodore ever visited his diocese. If he did, he cannot have stayed for long, as he always seemed to be in Constantinople, usually hanging around Photius, whether at the house or the patriarchal residence. He encouraged Photius to make the most of his reappointment, to gather into his hands whatever powers he could, storing them up against a time when he might be attacked again by popes or emperors. Of course, Theodore did all this subtly, citing precedents, putting forward theological justifications, unearthing obscure points of law, discovering ancient texts, experiencing dreams which he later interpreted at great length.

A necessary act
[AD 879]

I must tell now of the worst thing I have ever done. I would much rather not, but there would be little point to these memoirs if I concealed the truth. In my defence, I will say that it was not done for my own benefit, but for Eudocia's. And in her defence I must point out that she did not, in so many words, ask me to do it. She did not need to use words. Who could resist her sky blue eyes when they brimmed with tears?

"You like little Leo, don't you?" Eudocia asked as we sat in her garden. Despite my fears, she had taken to inviting me there after my lessons with her sons. I was, once again, the patriarch's eunuch, and no one could object to me. "Leo's so good with his books," she said. "He's much better now that you are teaching him. He found Photius difficult. Leo's such a shy boy. He doesn't like being pushed. Basil does bully him, always wanting him to go riding and hunting and watch the racing. That sort of thing doesn't suit him at all."

"I can see that," I said.

The quasi-avuncular sentiments I had felt for Prince Leo when first viewing him had long since faded. I had seen too little of his infancy for such feelings to take hold, and by the time I got to know him better, his nature was already spoiled by the peculiar circumstances of his upbringing. I could not really say that I liked the boy, but I felt sorry for him. Basil's blustering displays of manliness would have made anyone feel inferior.

"Basil is always comparing Leo with Prince Constantine," she said. "And Leo always comes out of it badly. Basil says he wants his children to have the education he didn't have. But Constantine hasn't had it. Constantine had toy swords instead of storybooks. He went to war instead of school. Basil dressed him up in golden armour and sat him on a white horse and told him he was a hero. Basil made Constantine co-emperor.

He hasn't done that for Leo. When Basil dies, Constantine will be emperor."

"But his majesty is barely forty." I looked around anxiously. We were not alone in the garden. In the distance, beyond the strutting peacock, a couple of servants trimmed and tidied the plants. "With God's grace," I said, raising my voice slightly, "it is to hoped his majesty will live for decades to come."

Eudocia pulled a sour face. "Yes. But I am likely to outlive him. I and my little Leo will have to live under Constantine's rule."

I leaned towards her and spoke softly. "Didn't Basil once make you a promise?"

"It was more of a bargain," she said, shuddering slightly. "Leo was supposed to succeed him. But Basil never really believed he was Leo's father. He pretended to, to win me over, to get my help. He made me swear to it." Her pale face flushed with sudden anger. "Did he make that other woman swear that Constantine is really his son? Why does he trust her and not me?"

I could think of nothing to say. I could hardly remind her that she had abetted a murder to win Basil's promise, or tell her that Leo's uncertain paternity was still the subject of palace gossip, thirteen years after the boy was born. She knew those things anyway, if she cared to remember them.

Eudocia drifted off into a reverie, staring blankly into the distance for a while before speaking again. "Do you remember what the nieces at the tavern used to say? They said I had the evil eye."

"I remember."

"It can't be true."

"No. I expect it's just a superstition. Photius says . . ."

"I'll tell you a secret. If it was true, Basil's favourite son would be dead by now."

She gazed at me, giving me an imploring look, letting her words sink in. Then she took my hand and led me back into her chamber. I withdrew solemnly from her presence, and, as I walked back through the palace gardens, I thought deeply about what we had said.

Like Eudocia, I had no love for Prince Constantine, who was a vain and stupid youth, who would make a far worse emperor than his father. Those raised in expectation of power seldom use it wisely. Michael was proof of that. I could see that Constantine's elimination might benefit the empire, as well as pleasing Eudocia. But was Leo any better? Whichever of his putative fathers he took after, he would not make an ideal ruler. Yet he was certainly Eudocia's son, and she was beautiful, unhappy, and in need of help.

I had already killed a man, though largely by accident. But for that I might never have believed myself capable of violence. I tried to imagine how Eudocia might be satisfied. Murder might not be necessary. Princes have often been removed from the succession by castration, or by depriving them of their eyes or tongues. Ignatius was one such. But his life showed how troublesome it might be to leave a mutilated prince alive. Browsing through my master's history books, I found that emperors have been brought down in many ways. Caesar was stabbed by his friends, Caligula was killed while watching a dance, Commodus was strangled by a wrestler, Elagabalus was killed in a privy and dropped down a sewer, Maurice was murdered by mutineers, Phocas was hacked to pieces and thrown in the sea, Justinian II was beheaded, Constantine VI died of a botched blinding, Leo V was cut down while singing a hymn, Constans Pogonatus was clubbed with a soap-dish while lying in his bath. So much blood! So much violence! The thought of it sickened and terrified me.

Even supposing that I could nerve myself to such an act, that the gods permitted me to succeed, what would be the result? I would be caught instantly and punished. I would be shaven and flogged, chained in a deep dungeon, tortured, left to languish in filth, surrounded by freaks and imbeciles. Before I died, I would lose my eyes, ears and tongue. My tongue would be last. They would make me confess, and implicate others.

Would that ensure Eudocia's happiness, or the succession of her sons? I did not think so. To get her what she wanted, I would have to be cleverer than those treacherous friends and servants, those wielders of clubs and daggers, those stranglers and ambushers. I would have to kill Prince Constantine without anyone knowing who had done it or how it was done.

It was Prince Leo who gave me the idea. He would have been pleased, had he known the results of his innocent complaint. But I never told him, or anyone else, not even Eudocia. We were in the schoolroom on a hot August afternoon, going over a passage from the *Iliad*. Not caring much for soldiers, horses, chariots and things of that sort, I have always preferred the *Odyssey*, but Photius had decreed that the siege of Troy was a better example for a youthful prince than the wanderings of a trickster. Young Leo cared little what text was set, as long as he could quibble over the meanings of obscure words, find defects in the narrative, and try to catch out his teacher with unanswerable questions. I am much more forgiving than Photius, who would never allow himself to be caught out. Even so, I despaired of ever reaching the end of the chapter, in which Patroclus applies a healing herb to Eurypylus' wounded leg.

As we struggled towards that improving conclusion, Leo questioned the lineage of several Achaean heroes, thought their battle tactics defective, wondered at the primitive equipment they bore, criticised Homer's extended metaphors, called the Olympians demons, and doubted the morality of robbing dead enemies.

Then he said something that made me forget all about Homer.

"Honey cakes!" Leo said. "Hecamede gives the Achaeans honey cakes. Just like Constantine! He's always getting cakes."

"And you do not?"

"Mother says they are bad for me, and will make me fat. But Constantine can have as many as he likes, and no one can stop him. Mother can't stop him, because she's not his mother. Constantine's mother sends him cakes. I expect she makes them herself. She is a peasant. Did you know that?"

Knowing that servants were likely to be nearby, I avoided the prince's question and urged him back to the text. But I could not think about the *Iliad*. I had remembered another example from my master's books. Claudius was poisoned with a dish of mushrooms. They were his favourite food, and he ate them eagerly, heedless of any danger. There was no need for violence, no need to be nearby when Constantine died.

For the rest of the lesson, my head full of conflicting hopes and fears, I let Leo pick holes in Homer as much as he liked.

I went, cloaked and veiled like a woman, to an old crone in the Armenian quarter, and asked her advice, claiming that I wished to dispose of a sick but much-loved dog. It sounded plausible to me. I dislike dogs, but Eudocia complained that Basil preferred his deerhounds to her.

The crone's shop was reassuringly dark, and full of sacks, pots, flasks, and bundles of drying herbs.

"You'll want something painless then?" she said.

"That's right," I said. "A potion I can put in its food. Something that will kill the old dog in its sleep."

She peered at my veil, trying to make out my face. "Would it be for your husband?" she said. "They're beasts, men are."

Surprised, both by her quickness, and by her willingness to believe me a woman, I muttered something ambiguous.

"Nothing shocks me, dear," The crone said. "It's all right, I won't say anything. I can't can I? I don't know who you are, after all."

It occurred to me that what the crone supposed was as good a story as any I might have made up. If anyone questioned her, her answers would not lead to me.

"What would you recommend?" I asked.

She rummaged through her stock and pulled out a well-stoppered pot. "I'd swear by this," she said. "I made it myself from mountain herbs. It'll kill anything, from a cat to an ox."

"How long does it take?"

"A few hours. Put it in his dinner." She winked at me. "Let

the old dog sleep. And the next morning he'll wake up dead."
She cackled at her joke, which she must have used often. "You
won't regret it," she said, pulling the stopper and pouring out
some of the potion. "It's just what you want. And to a lady in
your position, I'll sell it cheap. One gold piece, that's all I ask."

I walked away with the phial concealed under my cloak,
feeling invulnerable in my new disguise, and almost god-like
with the power to dispense death. I was like Loki, who
assumed the shape of a woman to kill the noble Balder. But
my elation did not last long. Back at my master's house, my
doubts returned.

Photius once said that whatever proves to be necessary, if it is
done for the good of the empire, will be forgiven. I hope he
was right. I pray sometimes, though without conviction, to
God, and to the gods of Asgard. Whichever of them awaits me
in the afterlife, I hope I am judged leniently. The Christian
God requires us to be meek, yet urges us to smite His enemies.
Heaven must be full of righteous smiters. To the Rus, no man
can be a hero unless he has killed. Valhalla is full of murderers,
who spend their days fighting, rising from death each evening
to feast and drink again. When the Norse gods' twilight
comes, Odin will lead those heroes to one last battle.

I felt anything but heroic as I poked at honey cakes, trying
to work out how poison might be inserted into them. I
destroyed many cakes before I perfected the technique. Then
I went to a shop by the Golden Gate and bought a batch of
the finest, sweetest Macedonian honey cakes, which I dosed
with the crone's potion by means of a quill. My hands shook
as I worked, and I feared poisoning myself almost as much as
being detected, but I managed to dose all the cakes and place
them back in their basket as good as new.

I had rehearsed the next part of my plan endlessly in my
mind, but I was terrified when it came to carrying it out.
As the princes' tutor I could get into the palace easily, and
had the run of Eudocia's quarters. But Basil and Constantine
lived slightly apart from her, and I had no right to go to their
rooms. I might wander as though lost, but would be seen and

recognised. The answer was to enter the palace as myself, then to deliver the cakes in disguise.

I went through the bronze gates carrying a heavy bundle of books. The guards did not give me a second look. I strolled through the palace grounds, avoiding the labourers and gardeners, until I reached the old bathhouse that overlooked the Sea of Marmora. The terrace it stood on was still neglected and overgrown. I slipped into a clump of bushes and put down my bundle. I drew from it a cloak and veil, and slipped them on, making myself look like a lady. Then I picked up the little basket of cakes and set off for the imperial quarters.

The palace gardens had never seemed so strange or dangerous. With every step, I remembered the prisoners who languished beneath my feet. Were they still there? I hoped never to find out. I daresay I trembled beneath my cloak. I know I jumped whenever I met a toiling gardener or hastening messenger. But each time I considered turning back I thought of Eudocia, neglected, unhappy, and fearful that Prince Constantine would one day rule the empire. For her sake I had to succeed. I tried to shift my shape like Loki did, to think myself a woman, to walk, to carry myself, to hold my head as a woman would have done. It was no worse, really, than pretending to be a bishop to please Michael. I had carried that off, even in the palace, surrounded by courtiers. That memory reassured me, and by the time I reached the imperial living quarters I felt strangely calm.

I knew which doors were guarded by the Ferghanese, which were used by nobles, and which by servants. I chose one of the latter, waited until some kitchen-hands went through, then slipped in behind them. Gathering my cloak around me, looking straight ahead through my veil, I walked almost as though asleep, passing from room to room, until I reached Basil's chambers. There I found the servants who looked after the emperor and his favourite son. Affecting a Macedonian accent, pretending to be from Constantine's mother, I handed over the cakes, and a few coins for the trouble of delivering them to the young prince. He would be glad of them, I was told, when he got back from his day's hunting.

It was when I got outside that the shaking started again. Anyone watching me walk back to the bathhouse would have thought me a palsied old crone. But I got there safely, took off my disguise, pissed in the bushes with relief, then left the palace by the nearest gate. Back at my master's house I waited. When Photius came home and talked endlessly about his negotiations with the pope, I hardly listened. When the time came for bed, I lay restlessly by my master's doorway, starting at every sound, expecting the Ferghanese guards to burst in at any moment and carry me away. Sleep, when it came, brought terrible dreams of eyeless, tongueless creatures gibbering and twitching, clutching at me with slimy hands, dragging me down into endless twilight.

Dawn came and drove away my dreams. I rose, dressed, attended my master, but could eat nothing. The morning passed in an agony of waiting. How many times did I fling down the book I pretended to read, then rush to the privy only to wonder why I had gone there? Time crept as slowly as Eudocia's jewelled tortoise. Every sound from the street presaged my arrest and downfall. But no one came for me, and at noon the announcement was made: Prince Constantine was dead, the city was in mourning.

How could I have known that Basil would go mad with grief? He was strong and cynical, and had taken power ruthlessly. He had killed and butchered without flinching. He had other sons to succeed him. Yet the loss of Prince Constantine undermined his sanity. There must have been a special bond between Basil and Constantine, who was born when his father was still a stable hand, when neither of them could have hoped to rule the empire. The prince was strong and brave, if not particularly intelligent, and Basil must have seen the boy as his true heir, whatever he had been told about his other sons. Perhaps he only trusted in his own peasant blood, and feared the foreign taint in Eudocia's.

Basil's grief seemed normal at first. Photius was quick to celebrate a mass for the dead prince, and did not object when Basil asked for another. When those first masses turned into a regular series, Photius continued to oblige, and was only alarmed when Basil started to show an interest in the Bible.

"Elijah!" Photius said. "What business has he wanting to know about that? I tried to put him off, said that the Old Testament needn't concern him, but he wouldn't listen. In the Sanctuary itself, almost as soon as the ceremony was over, he insisted on pressing me further, wanting to know about the prophet and his ascent to Heaven, babbling about fiery chariots, glowing angels, burning eyes in the sky, and so on."

"I can understand his enthusiasm for chariots," Theodore said. "Basil was always interested in racing. Wasn't it at the Hippodrome that Michael first saw him? You could say that a chariot bore him to power just as it bore Elijah up to Heaven."

"But it didn't! That is the point. A fiery chariot parted Elijah asunder from Elisha, but it was a whirlwind that bore Elijah up to Heaven. Basil has muddled the story with Ezekiel's vision of God in the form of a fiery chariot."

"It's an easy mistake to make," Theodore said. It was easy to forget that he was a bishop. He often forgot it himself.

"Not for Basil." Photius said. "The *Book of Ezekiel* is extremely obscure. There is a whirlwind in it, and a chariot, or perhaps a throne, it depends how you interpret the text, not to mention the wheels of fire, or the four-faced angels with calves' feet. In the *Book of Kings*, where Elijah's deeds are described, there is much mention of chariots. King Ahab seems never to have dismounted from his chariot, though it is not, as far as I can recall, the one that did the sundering."

"It seems a minor point to me," Theodore insisted. "Anyone might have confused the two prophets and their chariots,"

"It doesn't make sense!" Photius said. "You would need to know the verses quite well, then to have half-forgotten them, to come up with the nonsense Basil has been spouting. Do you think he gave any thought to the Old Testament and its prophets when he was murdering his way to power? Or since, for that matter. Of course not! Basil wouldn't come up with all that symbolism and theophany himself. He can barely read. If he has been studying the Scriptures, he must have had help." Photius sat silently for a moment, sinking deeper into his old couch. "Elijah and a fiery chariot! Who could have filled Basil's head with nonsense of that sort."

"I have no idea." Theodore took a deep draught of my master's Monemvasian, then held his empty cup out to me. I ignored it.

"I suppose it is only natural," Photius said. "Grief can throw a man off balance. Basil seems to teeter between melancholy and mania. When he is not enthused by all this nonsense about Elijah, he sinks into the deepest gloom. It really is most unfortunate that Basil should be so irrational at this particular time."

"What is so special about the present?"

Photius frowned at Theodore. "The negotiations!" he said. "Have you forgotten? I had such hopes of reconciliation with Rome. Pope John seems more reasonable than his predecessor. He is almost ready to rescind the anathema against me. Of course, he hopes for concessions in Bulgaria. And he needs our help against the Saracens in Italy, which might explain why he is so keen to compromise. But I can't bring the business to a conclusion. What we need is a resolute emperor who is ready to send an army. And what we have is Basil ranting and raving and babbling about Elijah. It is almost as though Prince Constantine was killed by agents of the Saracens, or by someone who wants to frustrate me yet again. It was murder, wasn't it? Who could have done it?"

Theodore held his cup out again. I did not fill it, but watched his face carefully for signs of craftiness or deception "The people say it is God's doing," he said. "Punishment for Basil's sins."

"That may be. But I suspect an earthly agency."

"If so," Theodore said, "I have no idea who it might be." For once, I believed him.

"What can I do?" Photius said. "Quite apart from my

difficulty with the pope, it is not healthy for emperors to be interested in the Bible. They start thinking they understand it, and come up with ecclesiastical policies of their own. That was what led to iconoclasm. Yet I can hardly tell Basil that. And his sudden piety may be a sign of remorse, as well as grief. I am not sure I will be able to bear it if he says he is sorry for killing Michael and Bardas and asks for my forgiveness."

I relented and filled Theodore's cup. "I don't think it will come to that," he said. "It's grief. And I think I see how we can take advantage."

"Take advantage?"

"Don't get all pious. We may not know who committed the murder, but let's try to get something out of it. People are at their weakest when grieving. Emperors are no exception. Let's give Basil something he wants. It worked with the false genealogy. That got you out of exile. If we can work the same sort of trick again, then Basil will give us something we want. If we can get him to concentrate for long enough to order a fleet to Italy, you will get your reconciliation with the pope and everything that follows from it."

"Yes," Photius said. "I can see that. But what does Basil want."

"He wants his son back."

Photius almost choked on his wine. "Are you proposing a miracle?"

"I am proposing something that will seem a miracle."

A few days later Theodore, tidied up and vested as Bishop of Euchaita, was presented to the emperor after the service at Hagia Sophia. Basil, distracted by grief, did not remember Theodore's role in discovering the false genealogy, but was most interested in the prophesy he recited.

"Tell me again," Basil said. "What is it you predict?"

"In only a few days," Theodore said, in his most oratorical voice, "his majesty will find what he desires most."

"And this book. The . . ."

"*Chaldean Oracle*, your majesty."

"Yes! Is it a proper Christian book?"

Theodore stood a little taller, though he could not match Basil for height, and glanced down meaningfully at his newly cleaned vestments, silently invoking his episcopal authority. "It is sacred!" he said.

Basil reached out and gripped Theodore's arm with a surprisingly firm hand. "Consult the book again!" he said. "Find out exactly. Where and when will he come back?"

"We have fixed the place," Photius said. "It is out of the way if anything goes wrong."

"It won't go wrong," Theodore said.

"But what are we going to do? You can't really call up the dead. Can you?"

Theodore gave my master one of his inscrutable looks. He never minded how dark his powers were thought to be, providing he was thought to have them. "It is possible to call up the dead," he said. "But they do not always answer. In this case, to be sure of success, the deed must be done with trickery."

"But how?"

"We will get Basil to the grove near the hunting lodge. That is all arranged. And he will come alone, with not even a hound to keep him company. I told him that Constantine's spirit will not appear otherwise."

"But how are we going to make it appear?"

Theodore and Photius began to bicker, each blaming the other for having raised Basil's expectations. As they spoke, it suddenly occurred to me that, having got Basil into the grove, the best plan would be to kill him. There would be no need to produce Constantine's ghost, supernaturally or otherwise. And Basil's death would please Eudocia better than anything. It would make her regent until Prince Leo came of age, and she would be in need of wise counsellors to guide her. Leo, though a difficult pupil, showed no signs of his father's folly, and there would be plenty of time to train up Leo to the task ahead of him. I imagined a new Golden Age, in which the empire would again be guided by Photius, with a little help from me. Perhaps I would achieve high office. Eudocia might make me her Logothete or High Chamberlain. With Basil dead, everyone would benefit, and two murders would be avenged.

I was on the point of proposing this new plan when I realised its disadvantages. Basil was a strong man, and would be hard to kill. It was unlikely that two old scholars and a eunuch could bring him down. If we involved anyone else, they would talk. Theodore would talk anyway. Basil was bound to tell someone where he was going, would certainly have body-guards within earshot. We would all be caught and killed on the spot. The plan was hopeless.

Then I noticed that Photius and Theodore were staring at me.

"He's about the right size," Theodore said.

"You're right," Photius said. "And Constantine was a beardless youth, or nearly so. With the right clothes on, and in the dark, Zeno could pass for him."

"No!" I said. "I am much older than he was."

"You are still slim and fresh-faced," Theodore said. "That is the one advantage of your condition."

"I look nothing like him."

"You will wear a disguise."

"You are forgetting my voice."

"Voice?" Theodore said. "Do spirits speak? And if they do, do they speak with earthly voices? I think not! You will play the part, and play it well. Our good fortune depends on it, if not our lives."

They wore me down, convincing me that they were right, that the fate of the empire, as well as their safety and happiness, depended on me appearing before Basil in the person of his dead son. Neither of them, I am sure, had any idea that I had killed Constantine. And neither of them had any idea how to make me seem a spirit. But I did.

"A ghost must appear suddenly," I said. "And it must disappear equally quickly. There is only one way to achieve that."

"How?" they both said.

"With a beam of light. Did you ever see old Leo's steam-

333

driven sphere?" Their blank looks told me that they had not. "It was powered by light," I said. "Heated by the sun's rays, which were concentrated by a highly polished concave metal disk, not unlike a shield."

"And you have seen this shield?" Theodore said, with a sneer in his voice.

"No. And that is the point. I saw the sphere turning in the middle of a darkened room, and the light that bathed it, but not the reflecting shield. It was hidden."

"So," Photius said, "if we can get hold of this shield, we can light you from hidden lamps and make you seem a ghost?"

"Exactly. The shield can be swung this way or that, bathing me in light, or plunging me in darkness."

My armour was made of pressed papyrus covered with gold leaf, which was light, and made no noise when I moved. The lance I carried looked like Constantine's, though it was a lightweight cane, also gilded. My face and hands were dusted with white powder, such as women use to beautify themselves. In that guise I made my way to a woodland grove near the emperor's favourite hunting lodge.

I had to hoist the stiff skirts of my corselet and piss again before I got there. We eunuchs are weak bladdered, and fear had made my condition worse. I had already emptied my bowels so often that I felt like a dried out wineskin. I walked through the leafless trees as silently as I could, but my knees knocked, my guts grumbled, and my hands shook so much I could hardly hold my lance, which caught in roots and low branches and threatened to trip me up. I had begged for a less military disguise, but Photius and Theodore insisted that Basil would expect to see his son in parade order.

Photius and Theodore were nearby, tending a collection of lamps and lanterns in the shelter of a half-ruined woodman's shack. Erected beside the shack was old Leo's reflector, which we had found, after much enquiry, in a storeroom at the university. It must have been there for years, and was very rusty. The head porter was glad to get rid of it, though we had to swear that its use was philosophical, and not connected with the black arts of which Leo had been suspected. After carting it back to Photius's house and cleaning it up, I experimented, working out how best to illuminate it and send its light wherever it was needed. Theodore soon stopped sneering and claimed the shield as his own. I was glad he was willing to operate it. My own role would be difficult enough.

Basil arrived as promised, breathing heavily, snapping twigs and stirring up freshly fallen leaves as he walked. He had always been big. In middle age he had become fat. Had it not been for the small lantern he carried, I might have taken him for a questing boar. He halted at the centre of the grove, looking up at the hazy crescent moon. He lowered his lantern, then reached to his waist and tugged a hunting horn from beneath his cloak. The richly carved oliphant glimmered in the faint moonlight. Basil raised it to his lips and sounded a signal. The horn's tone was plaintive, full of loss and grief, heavy with dashed hopes. The notes hung dying in the chill air. I shivered, but that melancholy sound was my cue. I threw off my enveloping cloak and stepped forward. Somewhere in the darkness, Theodore and Photius swung the polished shield.

I was bathed in light. My gilded armour, the snowy tunic I wore under it, the lance I held in my pale hand, all glowed with a brilliant yellow radiance. The thin night-mist caught the light, creating a nimbus that hung round me, shrouding my face with a ghostly luminescence.

"My son!" Basil said, letting the oliphant fall. "Oh Heaven, forgive my sins!" He dropped heavily to his knees, then pitched forward onto his face. There was a sharp crack, the shattering of carved ivory. His lantern fell over and went out. Basil began to hammer on the ground with balled fists, flailing his arms, covering his head with dead leaves. "I have won the world," he wailed. "But I would give anything to have my son back. Send him to me, Almighty God, and I will never sin again."

I stood there, wreathed in golden light, enjoying the sight

of a Roman emperor abasing himself before me. Did Basil remember the time when he was a stable hand and I was a servant? Did he ever recall the debauchery he had led Michael into, or the shameful things he had done to win power?

My pleasure only lasted a moment. The light from Leo's reflector picked me out, pointed at me like an accusing finger. I feared that Basil would see me for what I was, would know that I was the cause of his grief. He may have been mad, but he was cunning too. He might well have known all along that I was the murderer, discovered that I was to impersonate his son, and agreed to our ploy just to get his revenge. He always carried a long knife at his belt. He had used it to castrate the corpse of Bardas, and my false armour would not protect me for a moment against a weapon like that.

Basil struggled to his feet, trampling the shards of his broken horn. "My son," he wailed. "Constantine! Come back to me!" He flung his arms wide and rushed towards me.

At that moment, the shield swung away, plunging me into darkness. I leapt back, escaping just in time from the emperor's embrace. My heart pounded as I crashed through the branches and out of the grove, pulling my cloak around me as I went. I feared that Basil would follow me and realise that I was no ghost. But he blundered noisily in the darkness, calling again and again for his son to come back.

"He's ready," I said, when I reached the woodman's shelter.

Photius and Theodore were crouched inside, lit by the lanterns they were busy snuffing out.

"We will go and comfort him," Photius said. "Come, Theodore, we must reach him before the Ferghanese do."

They rushed out into the darkness, leaving me to clear up. I threw off my false armour, put out the remaining lamps and bundled everything into a sack. The shield could not be carried away, so I rolled it into a hollow and kicked leaves over it until it was covered. As I crept away from the shelter I could hear grief-stricken sobs and calming voices, and the tramping of the bodyguards' feet as they escorted Basil and his comforters to the hunting lodge.

The twelve guises of evil
[AD 883–886]

I am sure that Thor protected me in that woodland grove, and that he watched over me afterwards. The Thunderer preserved me from Basil's anger, making sure that no one knew that I had murdered Constantine or impersonated his ghost, just as he got me away from Tephrike after I killed John the Heretic. With his strength and simplicity, Thor has led me safely through many dangers, enabling a mere eunuch to achieve what might have eluded a man. Inger did me a great service when he gave me the god's carved idol, though he cannot have known how I would use it.

God seemed to watch over Photius. When the Church Council met in Constantinople, the pope's legates gave my master almost everything he asked for. He was so grateful for Basil's support that he agreed to canonise Prince Constantine. One more saint made little difference, or so he said. The theological errors of the Latins concerned him more. He began a treatise on the *Mystagogy of the Holy Spirit*. It was to be his great work, the book that would establish his reputation as a theologian and prove definitively that the priests of Rome are wrong, that the Holy Sprit proceeds solely from the Father, and not from the Son.

I was not much interested in the Dual Procession of the Holy Spirit. The very mention of the subject made me feel queasy, reminding me of the time Michael stole the Divine Member and imagined that the Holy Spirit had entered into him by its means. But I was glad Photius was writing the *Mystagogy*. The work kept him at home, where I could help and watch him. It would, I hoped, be like old times, a reminder of the years when I toiled in my master's library and smoothed his path to power. I had neglected Photius while consoling Eudocia, and hoped to make up for that. But I had forgotten about Theodore. He could never resist an opportunity to sell books, or to practice divination, and he had a knack of making our schemes go wrong.

Theodore knew his business, and understood my master's project. He arrived at the house with a bundle of books, among them a commentary on Saint Augustine and other Latin Fathers, which Theodore had had translated into Greek.

"Proof!" Photius said, picking up the book enthusiastically. "Proof that the Latins are deluded, that their so-called theology is nothing more than Platonism."

"That book was very hard to come by," Theodore said. "And I had to promise the translator a considerable sum. There are not many in the city who can understand Latin of that sort. Fewer still who know anything of theology. Knowing that you would not want to be in error, I searched everywhere, and eventually found a Sicilian who could do the work. And there were other expenses."

"A Sicilian! Are you sure he is orthodox, not tainted with Latinism or influenced by the Saracens?"

"He is perfectly orthodox. I made sure of that. Now, about my expenses."

"I will write a note for you to take to the patriarchal treasury."

Theodore looked anxious. "I would prefer cash. The Sicilian was most pressing, and you know what they are like."

"I suppose so. Zeno, will you bring the chest?"

Theodore looked much happier when he had slipped some gold coins into his purse. "I am sure this *Mystagogy* will be a great success," he said.

My master's face brightened. "Do you think so?"

"Of course! Who can resist the truth?"

"Many people, it would seem. Much of the world prefers to wallow in a swamp of error."

"But not for much longer. When they have read your work the Latins will return to the truth. The Slavs and Bulgars will accept the word of God from you, rather than from the pope. And the Church will triumph, with you at its head."

"Really? You are sure?"

"I can see it all, with the help of this." Theodore reached

into his bag and pulled out the book he claimed was the *Chaldean Oracle*. Who knows whether the thin and tattered volume he had carried for so many years really did contain the ancient wisdom of Zoroaster? It could easily have been one of Theodore's forgeries, something he had concocted to serve his own peculiar purposes.

It struck me that Theodore smelled worse than I remembered. It may have been fragments of decaying food lodged in his clothes or beard. Many were visible, along with stains and grease marks, remnants of meals he had cadged, of untended drinks he had finished off. Or it may have been the result of some inner decay, the failure of a crucial organ, the rotting away of his soul, if he still had one. If the rumours are to be believed there can hardly be a scholar in the city who has not signed away his soul to the devil.

Theodore sat at my master's writing desk and opened the *Chaldean Oracle*. He covered his eyes with a hand, and stabbed randomly at the cryptic verses with the other.
"I see everything," he said, rocking backwards and forwards. "I see the future. I see what lies before us, how everything will turn out."

I thought Theodore's performance ill-judged. Photius knew as well as he did what trickery could be achieved with the *Chaldean Oracle*. But on that occasion, as on so many others, my master was willing to be taken in. I suppose it was understandable. There were times when the book, or Theodore, really did seem capable of predicting the future.

"What do you see?" Photius said.

Theodore ran a grubby finger over the verses, as though he could absorb the words without seeing them. Then he uttered his prophecy.

"I see darkness where light once was."

"Are you sure? Shouldn't it be the other way round?"

"I see what I see," Theodore said. "One who is now above ground will soon be below it. I see a dark chamber full of monstrous men. Men and beasts shambling in the darkness. I hear terrible cries of pain and anguish. One who now hears the soft voices of women will be among the beasts and monstrosities. He will hear nothing but the tearing of flesh and the gnashing of teeth and the harsh cries of the mutilated." He paused for a moment, swaying slightly and breathing heavily. "That is not all. One who sees light and beauty now will soon see nothing but darkness. Red hot daggers will plunge into his eyes, depriving him of his sight."

"Who?" Photius said. "Who?"

"Wait, there is more. I see it now. The son who is not a son. He has conspired against the father who is not his father. He will be punished."

"Who?"

Theodore opened his eyes and pushed the book away. "Isn't it obvious?"

"No."

"Leo, of course. He will be imprisoned and blinded for defying Basil."

"Basil would not blind his own son. I cannot believe that."

"But Leo is not Basil's son. He is a bastard."

Photius looked shocked, though he had heard Theodore's aspersions before. "I presided over Basil and Eudocia's wedding," he said. "I baptised Leo. I will not have it said that he is a bastard."

"But it is obvious. Leo is Michael's son. Anyone can see it! He behaves just like Michael did, carrying on with that mistress of his."

"Whatever Prince Leo may have done as a youth, I cannot believe he still does it now that he is married."

"No one believes the marriage is consummated. Leo's got a mistress called Zoë. The whole city knows it, even if you prefer to ignore the truth. Leo is an adulterer, just like his true father, and now he's going to pay the price."

"You must not repeat any of this."

"The emperor might be glad to know what the oracle foretells."

"You must not tell him."

"Basil would be happy to see me again. I am sure he

remembers my last prophecy, and the time we comforted him in that grove. I wonder what he would say if he knew that it was Zeno who appeared before him."

"No! You must not approach him. Not in his present state. There is no knowing what he might do. I am your superior, and I forbid you to speak to him."

"Then I must obey," Theodore said. "But there are ways round that. One can always approach an emperor though his friends and familiars."

"Have you done this before?" Photius frowned. "Have you approached Basil without my permission."

"No, not Basil." Theodore attempted a smile. "Of course not. I was thinking of Michael."

"What do you mean?"

"It was nothing. There were some items I thought he might be interested in. Books, relics, curiosities. You know what Michael was like. Anyway, why shouldn't I talk to the emperor if I want to, if there are things I know that he would be glad to hear?"

Photius was puzzled by Theodore's words, and by his tone. His old friend was defying him, turning against him. I remembered a conversation in a church near the Golden Gate, words spoken hastily between an emperor and his favourite while a corpse lay bleeding on the floor.

"It was you!" I said. "You told Basiliscianus about the Divine Member. You pushed Michael over the brink and into madness. You gave Basil the excuse to kill him!"

"What is all this?" Photius said.

"It is nothing," Theodore said. "Zeno is babbling."

"No I am not. I suspected it before. Now I know. You have been working against my master for years. All your tricks and forgeries, all your schemes, everything you have done has undermined him."

"My dear Photius, the eunuch is talking nonsense. They are unreliable creatures. Haven't I always said so? You should never have trusted him. I apologise for my sharp words just then. You must understand: I am your oldest friend, your staunchest supporter."

"He is not," I said. "When you were in exile, it was Theodore who stole your books and sold them."

"Is this true?"

An honest liar would have denied the charge straightaway. But Theodore could never resist the temptation to seem cunning and mysterious. He faced Photius silently, allowing a half-smile to reveal the truth. For the first time my master saw what sort of man he had trusted and promoted.

"My books!" Photius said. "I can see from your face that Zeno is right. A man who would steal books would do anything. You are no friend of mine. Go from my house and never come here again! I forbid you to visit the palace. Go from this city. Return to your diocese and stay there!"

Theodore left the house, cursing us both as fools, but he did not go to Euchaita. He was seen around the city, consorting with various foreigners and unsavoury types, spreading lies and rumours. Photius was upset by his friend's treachery, but he was good at forgetting what was not convenient, and soon had cause to feel more cheerful.

I would not like it to be thought that my master was prone to gloating. But given his long dispute with the papacy, his reaction to Pope John's death was not surprising.

"It proves what I have always known," he said. "God is on my side, not theirs. The priests of Rome are heretics and schismatics. They tried to get round me by revoking Pope Nicholas's excommunication. But God had already punished him by striking him down at the very moment I was exiled by Basil! They revoked Pope Hadrian's anathema. But God struck Hadrian down as well. It served him right for meddling in Bulgaria and trying to undermine my good work with the barbarians. And now Pope John is dead, murdered by his own family! Poisoned like a dog, then beaten to death when the poison didn't work. The signs cannot be any clearer than that. God will not be mocked or misrepresented. All this nonsense about the Dual Procession must be swept away!"

Photius was so pleased by the way God had revealed His will, that, after delivering a triumphant sermon in the cathedral, he tried to explain the *Mystagogy* to Basil. He did not get very far. As soon as he mentioned that his treatise concerned the respective natures of the Father and Son, Basil flew into a rage, thinking that Photius meant to criticise his attitude to Leo.

"It was terrible," Photius said afterwards. "I thought he would beat me. And I was still dressed in all my vestments. You would think he might have some respect for my office, if not for my person, but no! He went red in the face and raised his fists and shouted. He called me an interfering fool. There were plenty of cathedral staff around. The place was full of deacons and vergers, but none of them came to help me. In fact, they all slunk away. Don't they realise who their master is?"

I could not think of a tactful answer, and let Photius carry on.

"Basil told me that his son is an adulterer. Can it be true?"

"You know it is," I said. "Theodore told you."

"I have learned not to believe in him."

"It's true. Eudocia told me all about it. If you think Basil was rough with you, you should hear how he beat Leo for falling in love with Zoë. There was blood all over the floor, according to Eudocia."

"Leo ought to have learned his lesson. It's not for princes to fall in love. They must do their duty."

"Not everyone can. Michael loved Eudocia, even after he was married."

"How much better it is to be celibate, like us. We are not troubled by such things."

"But we are."

"What do you mean?"

"I mean that we cannot avoid the consequences of Leo's love. Eudocia is afraid that Basil will do something terrible."

"Such as?"

"She fears that Basil will blind Leo, just as the oracle predicted."

"Have you told her what Theodore said?"

"Master, I tell her everything."

"Everything? Why? What have you been up to?"

Seeing how bad things were, and how shaken my master was, knowing that Theodore could no longer come between us, I decided to speak frankly. "Years ago," I said, "when you made me free, you said I was to be your eyes and ears."

"Did I say that? What can I have been thinking of?"

"If I understood you, what you wanted was someone to do your dirty work."

"Dirty work? What an unpleasant phrase. I have always tried to be above such things."

"Exactly. And I have tried to take care of everything you wished to be above. I have got my hands dirty while you have kept yours clean."

"Oh, Zeno! Am I such a bad master?"

"No. You have made me what I am, and I am grateful. I would be nothing without you. And neither would Eudocia. She is your creation."

"Michael fell in love with her, not me!"

"Yes, but you made her, you and Bardas. And you used her."

"No!"

"You did it through me," I said. "To further your career. And you have triumphed. The pope's death proves that. Now you must protect Eudocia, and her sons."

"Basil still has the power to depose me. All my good work would be undone."

"You must risk it."

A few days later I took Photius, cloaked and hooded like a monk, to Eudocia's quarters. I have never seen him look so scared. Even though I chose a time when Basil was away hunting, and took him round the back way, avoiding all the eunuchs and courtiers, he pulled his hood so low that I had to lead him like a blind man.

"What a lovely garden," he said, attempting a smile.

"Is it?" Eudocia said. She was plainly dressed, and her hair hung loose. "It feels like a prison yard to me. I can't go anywhere or do anything. But it's worse for my Leo."

"Why? What has happened?"

"Basil has locked him up."

"I expect he means to keep Prince Leo from temptation."

"No. Basil has accused him of treason. Leo is in prison somewhere. I don't know where."

I hoped Leo was not in that dreadful prison beneath the bathhouse. Theodore's prophecy had hinted at it. Was it revealed to him by the oracle? Or did he know of the place already? Surely he could not have been taken there by Cyril? My mind filled with unpleasant possibilities.

"Treason?" Photius said. "There has been no announcement."

"There won't be. Not for a while. The guards are busy rounding up all Leo's friends and supporters. They'll all be accused of conspiracy. Tortured, I expect. Until they confess."

Photius looked alarmed, and gripped his hood, as though anxious to reassume his disguise.

"Don't worry," Eudocia said. "No one could accuse you of being one of Leo's supporters. You're safe enough."

"I am sorry your majesty . . ."

"Your *majesty*!" She mocked my master's tone. "Do you remember what I am? Have you forgotten what Basil was? We are not *majesties*. We are common people picked up from the gutter and used by people like you."

"I am sure . . ."

"You made us. You used us. But the joke's on you. You can't control us now. You don't dare face Basil and tell him he's wrong!"

"It is very difficult. Only the other day, Basil *thought* that I was rebuking him, and he flew into a rage."

"D'you think I don't know what Basil's anger's like? I've been married to him for twenty years, near enough."

Photius would not meet Eudocia's eye. He gazed vaguely at a rose bush, as though trying to think of another polite comment about the garden. Women and their emotions had always baffled him. Like most scholars, he thought they were imperfect and inferior. I regretted taking him there, and wondered what I could do or say.

Then Eudocia flung herself on the ground at my master's feet.

"You must help me," she said, clutching at his ankles. "I beg of you! Go to Basil. Tell him to free Leo. Tell him not to harm my son."

Photius trampled a clump of aconites in his eagerness to retreat. I helped Eudocia up, and led her indoors where her maidservants could look after her. I did not like leaving her, but she had her servants, and Photius only had me.

"Did you tell her to say those things?" Photius said, as we made our way back to his house. "She said what you said, that I used her."

"She is the empress," I said. "And I am the patriarch's eunuch. I cannot tell her to do anything."

Photius held onto my arm. "I am getting old," he said. "I don't have the strength to do as she asks."

Photius refused to confront Basil in person, or to advise him indirectly, as I suggested, by preaching a sermon in the cathedral. The best I could get out of him was a letter on fatherly forgiveness, drawing on the story of David and Absalom. It was the kind of thing Photius might have sent to a newly-christian ruler; rhetorical, long-winded, abstract, full of vague allusion, lacking any identifiable reference to real people or events. Basil, if he bothered to have it read out to him, would have had little idea what his patriarch was getting at. By then, Theodore had got himself into the palace, and was busy repeating his prophecies to Basil, thus ensuring their fulfilment. He fed the emperor's hatred by asserting Leo's illegitimacy, and made treason plausible by supplying the names of conspirators. No doubt my master's name was on the list, and mine with it.

Have I described the twelve guises of evil? According to the Paulicians, the devil works through men, women, priests, bishops, monks, teachers, serpents, birds, and several other things, which I have forgotten. It is not surprising that the Paulicians fear serpents, but who, if they had not spent years

346

among them, would have guessed that those heretics hate above all things magpies and ravens? A bird that can talk, according to them, does the work of the devil better than any man.

Perhaps the Paulicians are right. Had I not been distracted by a talking magpie, I might not have been captured and castrated by the Rus. However, it might be argued that the bird brought me as much good luck as bad, that I would hardly have a story to tell had I lived my whole life in Tmutorokan. But the parrot I bought for Eudocia was surely a creature of the devil. How else could it have done so much harm?

I saw it in the animal market by the Golden Horn, drawn by the cawing and chirping of the caged birds. Thinking that I was a bird-fancier, the dealers offered me blaspheming magpies by the dozen, as well as crows that could tell riddles, parrots that could repeat anything they heard, and birds from India that could recite Persian poetry.

I listened politely, and was about to walk on, when an idea struck me. It was clear that Photius could not influence Basil. But if the patriarch of Constantinople, unchallenged ruler of the Orthodox Church, could not persuade Basil to release Leo, then who could? The answer was a talking bird. Such a creature, I thought, lacking fear or scruples, repeating the same words endlessly, might be more persuasive than a man.

I engaged the bird sellers in earnest discussion, learned what there was to be learned about talking birds, and left with a grey parrot, brought I was assured, from darkest Africa. I hid it in an empty room, where I knew none of my master's servants would go, and trained it to say two words. When I was sure it had learned its lesson, I took it to Eudocia.

"It is not a pretty bird," she said, looking at its drab plumage. "Not like my peacocks."

"No, but it is clever."

I tapped my finger on the parrot's cage, attracting its attention. It glowered, clicked its tongue, then repeated the phrase I had taught it.

"Free Leo!" it croaked, cocking its head to one side. "Free Leo!" it repeated, the words echoing from the walls of Eudocia's garden. "Free Leo!" it shrieked.

"Stop it!" she said. "Stop it now!"

I threw a cloth over the cage and silenced the parrot. "I thought you would be pleased."

"Pleased? By a bird that mocks me?"

"I've got a plan. You're to give the bird to Basil, or to let it free in his quarters. When he hears it squawking those words he won't be able to stand it."

"Is that the best you can do? I thought you loved me. What about Photius? Why can't you get him to say something?"

"He's afraid. That's why I thought of the bird. It won't be afraid. It will go on until Basil frees your son."

"Basil won't take any notice of a bird. He only thinks about Constantine now. I thought things would get better when Constantine died. But they haven't. I don't know what's worse: hearing Basil threaten to harm Leo, or hearing him go on about Constantine's ghost."

"The ghost," I said. "It was me."

"You? How could it be?"

I told Eudocia how Photius and I had made the ghost appear. I did not mention Theodore's part in the scheme, or that we had done it to advance my master's cause rather than hers. Nor did I confess to her that I had killed Constantine. Even so, she seemed impressed.

"Zeno," she said, "did you really wait for him in the dark like that? You know he always carries a hunting knife. He might have killed you."

"I know. But it was worth it."

"I didn't know you could be so brave." She looked at the covered birdcage. "I'm sorry I was rude about the parrot. I know you were thinking of me. I'll try your idea. I suppose a bird can't do any harm."

I was not the only one to wait anxiously for news of Leo. The young prince's fate had touched the city, the people were turning against Basil and his cruelties, and some of them even rioted, demanding that the emperor release his son. Basil brooded in the palace, leaving the prefect to deal with the rioters. When, after a month or so, it was announced that Leo was to be freed, the citizens were overjoyed. I rushed to Eudocia, struggling through the cheering crowd that besieged the palace.

While her servants looked on, Eudocia greeted me warmly, allowed my kiss to linger on her hand, graciously helped me to my feet. Then she led me to her garden, making sure the door was shut firmly after us, and that we were alone. We sat in the cool shade beneath the fig tree, watched only by the caged birds and beasts. Seeing them, I wondered how I could ask Eudocia whether Basil had obeyed the parrot or the people. But she did not give me the chance.

"I've been thinking about what you told me," she said. "You know where the place is, where Basil saw the ghost."

"I do."

"If Basil was to go there again, would you lead some people to him?"

"What people?"

"Some friends of Leo."

"Are there any who are not in prison?"

"A few. And they will do anything to help him."

"Anything? Such as?"

"Don't ask. Just say you will do it." She gazed at me with those blue eyes, giving me a look that would have unmanned anyone. "For me," she said, softly.

"I will."

She took me in her arms and kissed me on the mouth. She was not an empress then, but my oldest, closest friend. "I knew you would," she whispered.

"How could I not?"

"It will be for the best," she said. "Now, let me tell you what you must do."

Photius was in his library working on the *Mystagogy*, painstakingly turning abstruse thoughts into obscure words.

"Master," I said. "I must ask a favour of you."

He looked up, his brow furrowed by thought, as well as by age. He was almost seventy by then, and his many reversals had left their mark on his once-handsome face.

"What is it?" he asked.

"You must send a message to Basil."

"It would be no use. He takes no notice of me."

"He would, if you wrote clearly and said something he wanted to hear."

"Such as?"

"That the spirit of his son will appear again in that woodland grove."

"Why should Constantine's spirit do that? You are not proposing to put on that costume again, and repeat all that business with the lanterns, are you?"

"No. I will not be impersonating the ghost. I will be guiding some of Leo's friends to the grove."

"And what will they do there?"

"They will wait for Basil."

"What for?"

"It is best if you don't know."

Photius looked horrified. "I am the emperor's patriarch. I could not be involved in anything like that."

"Think how Basil has treated you!

"Don't remind me!"

"He is not fit to rule. Something must be done."

"No, I couldn't do it."

I let my master think for a while.

"I suppose I could ask Theodore," I said.

"You wouldn't? After all he has done! Anyway, he would hardly help you now."

"I think he would, if he thought it was in his interests."

"No."

"Then you must do it. You must write to Basil. Tell him his sainted son will reappear. Tell him the time and place. And there is one other thing. Tell him to go without a bodyguard, otherwise Constantine's spirit will not appear."

It was a long time before Photius replied. "I will do it," he said. "But there is one condition. Whatever Leo's friends do, you must not be there when it happens."

Leo's friends were a villainous-looking lot, but I did as I was asked, and led them to the grove. What they did there I do not know, as I left them as soon as I could, making sure that they did not know my name and that I did not know theirs. I was already back in the city when Basil's body was brought in.

His death was an accident, or so we were told. A gigantic stag, bigger than any seen before, had appeared before the emperor in the forest. Taking the beast for a portent, he rode after it, launching his spear at its flank. Goaded, the beast turned on Basil and lunged at him with its huge antlers, catching him in their spreading tines. The stag was so strong that it lifted the emperor out of his saddle and ran with him for almost a mile before it slowed enough for another party of huntsmen to catch up and kill it. The carcass was never produced for inspection, though its antlers would surely have made a splendid trophy. Basil, with his dying words, confessed all his sins and begged forgiveness from all those he had harmed. At least, that is what we were told by Stylian, the leader of the huntsmen who rescued him. By an extraordinary coincidence, Stylian was the father of Zoë, Leo's mistress. He was rewarded with high office as soon as Leo was crowned.

Postscript
[AD 900]

I sit here, under the rustling plane trees, cooled by breezes from the Golden Horn. Beside me as I write is a cup of wine, and a little figure of Thor carved from narwhal ivory. I am not in the city, but near enough. I can visit Constantinople whenever I want to. Strangely, that is not very often, though it is a comfort to know that the city is there, and that my mistress still dwells in the palace.

The tavern is mine now. I have evicted the nieces. They were, in truth, far too old to be an attraction. The place smells better than it did. I had the building scoured from top to bottom, to get rid of all traces of those slatterns. I have servants now, and they keep the tavern spotless. I have lived like a gentleman and dined at the palace. I will not live in a squalid house, or a disorderly one. I have made sure the food here is as good as any you would find in the city, but are the customers grateful? Of course not! Most of them are barbarians, and would not know good food from filthy offal. Among the barbarians are many Rus. They come to the city to trade, not raid. Sometimes they bring slaves to sell. I smile while their wine is served, bantering with them in what I can remember of their language, trying not to think of how they acquire their merchandise. There is a dim memory among some of the older Rus that a legendary countryman of theirs once drank heroically under this roof. I tell them all about it, if they ask.

I would not have chosen the tavern, but it is better than prison, and preferable to exile. And living here means that I can see Eudocia again. There have been times when I longed for the obscurity I now enjoy. When Photius was deposed, for instance, and I had to take refuge with Theodore. Or when I was obliged to be both fool and pander to Michael. Worst of all was my master's second downfall, when he was forced to abdicate by Leo, then tried for treason. My life was in danger then. Of course, Photius, unlike Theodore, never conspired against Leo. He tried to protect the prince, as I did. It is true that our methods were not very effective, and that some could not be admitted to. But we meant well. Who could have guessed that Leo would be so vengeful and unreasonable, so keen to punish those he thought had thwarted him? Photius was well known to be Theodore's friend and patron, so he was arrested. I was implicated in the charges, and spent some time in the cells, though not in that dreadful dungeon beneath the palace. Even so, it is not a time I care to remember.

Leo's investigators were never able to prove much, despite Theodore's frequent and contradictory confessions. In the end, Leo was merciful. He had Theodore blinded rather than killed, which seems appropriate, considering his attempts to see into the future. Before his eyes were gouged out, Theodore begged to be allowed to retire to a monastery he had founded near his see of Euchaita. The idea was incredible, but turned out to be true. Theodore really had founded a monastery, using all the money he got from selling books, faking, scrounging, swindling and prophesying, not to mention the misappropriation of diocesan funds. He had risked his soul in order to have the means of saving it. Or perhaps he had long since sold his soul, and founding the monastery was the Devil's work. The Paulicians believe that monks and priests are creatures of the Evil One, and it is quite possible that Theodore was not a man at all, but a demon, one the minions of Satanael, a creature with a special mission to lead men astray and frustrate all their plans.

Whatever the truth about Theodore's nature, Leo refused his request and had him imprisoned elsewhere.

Leo was kinder to his old teachers. Photius was merely banished. He was even allowed to take some of his books. I went with him, sharing his exile in remotest Armenia. I devoted myself to attending my master, making his final years as comfortable as they could be. As well as finishing the *Mystagogy*, Photius wrote hundreds of letters during that time, all of them dwelling on his saintliness and suffering. He gave much advice to the faithful, and some of them were quite grateful. I cannot say that he was a hypocrite. His circumstances had changed, so why should his opinions not change? In exile, having little else to support him, he found his faith. I only wish that I had found mine, but I still do not know which of the gods is true, or the most powerful.

When Photius died, his remains were brought back to Constantinople. I came with them, and stood in the great cathedral of Hagia Sophia, listening while my master was praised by the emperor Leo, and by all the dignitaries of the Church. They were dissemblers, the lot of them, but even so I was glad to hear Photius given the recognition he deserved. The only thing to mar that solemn occasion was the praise given equally to Ignatius, my master's zealot enemy. The Church has declared a posthumous truce between them, and anathema on anyone who stirs up their old quarrels.

If there is a Heaven, I hope there is a special place in it for popes, patriarchs and bishops, a Valhalla for heroes of the Church. I imagine those prelates rising each day to do battle, debating the Incarnation, Christ's Will and Energy, the Trinity, the Eucharist, the nature of sin, and all the other controversies that have split the faithful into competing factions. Each night, the presence of God Himself, presiding like Odin over an eternal Last Supper, would confirm or refute their various conjectures. Each Heavenly morning those righteous champions would rise again to renew their theological combat, finding new hairs to split, revealing fresh flaws in their enemies' arguments. Such an afterlife would suit Photius very well.

I am seventy years old, and my health is good. We eunuchs, not having burned up our vitality with unceasing lust, tend to live longer than other men. I hope to be here for a while, though I do not expect the remainder of my life to be eventful. I take no part in public life. Leo is still emperor, and is loved by the people, who mistake his pedantry for wisdom. He has married three times, and still has no heir. His brother is drinking himself to death. The patriarch is a pliable nonentity. No one remembers me, except for a certain lady, who comes here now and again, heavily veiled, and drinks a cup or two of sweet Monemvasian wine while we talk of old times. But we have to be careful. There are things we both know, but never mention.

Historical Note

What we call the Byzantine Empire was known to its inhabitants as the Roman Empire. When Rome fell to the barbarians in the fifth century, the eastern half of the empire, ruled from Constantinople (or Byzantium) survived, and endured until 1453 when it was conquered by the Ottoman Turks. (This event is described in *False Ambassador*.) The Byzantines spoke Greek, called themselves Romans, and considered theirs to be the world's only legitimate empire. It was a Christian state, in which the emperor's control of the Church was as important as his control of the army.

In the seventh century, after invasions by a fresh wave of barbarians, and the loss of its eastern provinces to the Arabs, the empire entered a period of decline. (This period forms the background to *Theodore*.) Though Constantinople was safe behind its impregnable walls, trade was interrupted, schools and universities were closed, and many provincial cities were abandoned. During that time, the empire was split by a series of theological controversies, the most serious of which concerned the worship of icons. Iconoclast theologians attributed the military successes of the Moslems to their abhorrence of idolatry, and sought to win God's favour by suppressing the use of religious images among Christians. They believed, among other things, that an icon could only portray the human aspect of Christ, and therefore denied His divine aspect. For over a century the iconoclasts dominated the empire, though icons were hidden away and worshipped in private.

In the ninth century the Byzantine Empire revived. The iconoclasts were defeated, and orthodox worship was restored. The army began to push back the Moslems in the East, and in Southern Italy. Missionaries, led by Constantine (later known as St Cyril), were sent to convert the Bulgars and Slavs, bringing the Balkans under Byzantine influence. There was also a revival of learning, based at the newly re-founded university.

The leading figures in this Golden Age were Bardas and Photius. Bardas was undoubtedly an adulterer and murderer, as well as a great general. Photius was a more controversial character. Many of his writings survive, including his library catalogue, essays on scientific, philological and philosophic subjects, words of advice to newly-christian rulers, an incomprehensible theological tract, and nearly three hundred letters. Reading those works today, one gets the impression of a learned, curious, pompous, arrogant, but ultimately pious man. His career as a scholar, civil servant and patriarch suggests that he was very able, though not always of the soundest judgement. His contemporaries did not think he was pious. He was accused of scepticism, love of pagan literature, blasphemy, mocking the liturgy, drunkenness, and practising magic. Some of these accusations show how little secular learning was valued or understood at that time. They also show that Photius was a complex, contradictory figure, who would have fitted better into the Renaissance than into ninth century Byzantium. It is at least partly due to him that books and learning survived in Constantinople, and were available when an interest in such things eventually revived in the West. Unfortunately, his quarrels with the papacy split the Church, divided Constantinople from Rome, and may have delayed that revival.

The ninth century was also the great age of the Vikings, or Rus, as they were known in the East. Even though a few Rus had reached the city earlier, the arrival of a huge Viking fleet off Constantinople in 860 was a surprising and terrifying event. While the Rus were exploring the great rivers of Russia, they were also raiding Britain and France, and it seems likely that one part of their fleet sailed round Spain and through the Mediterranean to reach Constantinople. They could not conquer the city, but were soon founding cities of their own, which quickly merged into the Principality of Russia. It was under Photius that the first Rus leaders accepted Christianity, which led later to a huge expansion of the Orthodox Church.

Basil, despite his peasant origins, and the crimes he committed to win power, proved to be a very able emperor. He continued the conquests of Bardas, reformed the laws, and endowed Constantinople with many new buildings. He founded a dynasty, the Macedonian, which lasted for two centuries and included several great emperors, as well as some notably feeble ones. However, it is quite possible that Prince Leo was Michael's son, in which case the new dynasty was a continuation of the old one. Either way, and despite the complications of their private lives, the emperors of the ninth century began a period of growth and prosperity which was only halted by the arrival of the Turks in the eleventh century, and the subsequent disaster of the crusades.

Christopher Harris 2002

Theodore – *Christopher Harris*

Theodore, described as the heretical memoirs of a gay priest, was 7th in the *Guardian*'s Top Ten Paperback Originals.

"it portrays the young Theodore as curious, sensual and very human, anxious to understand what exactly constitutes enlightenment, assailed by religious doubts and constantly at odds with the frequent irrational beliefs of the religious men surrounding him. The greatest strength of Harris' novel is the clear and simple presentation of its often complex moral ideas. Ultimately, this is a novel of curious decency, simply and movingly written by a first-time author of real promise."
Christopher Fowler in the Independent on Sunday

"Theodore of Tarsus – who became Archbishop of Canterbury in 668 – was a significant figure in ecclesiastical history, and his story is told in this well researched first-person novel . . . what follows is an interesting account of the homosexual saint's life during strange and turbulent times."
Andrew Crumey in Scotland on Sunday

"At its heart, however, Theodore is a beautiful and poignant love story, examining the passion between twin souls – a love too intense to remain chaste. The author challenges us to consider that while Christianity owes a lot to such love, it will never acknowledge the debt."
Murrough O'Brien in The Daily Telegraph

"The story is based around the complex subject of sexuality and religious faith at a time when the Byzantine Empire was overrun by pagans, weakened by civil war and divided by religious strife. Fleeing war and persecution, Theodore sought certainty and love in his ceaseless wanderings through a collapsing world. Though born a heretic and troubled by religious doubts, the Greek monk was chosen by the Pope to be Archbishop of Canterbury. Arriving in England, he found a land torn apart by war between petty kingdoms, in which Christianity was half-forgotten. His efforts to reorganise the Church were opposed by Wilfrid, a rival bishop, who ensnared him in intrigue and denounced him to the Pope. Despite such difficulty, Theodore was highly successful and – with the help of his lover Hadrian, an African monk – established the Church in England in a form that has, in many respects, lasted until today."

Ros Dodd in The Birmingham Post

"The headline 'Archbishop of Canterbury in Gay Sex Shock' may be every tabloid editor's dream, but, in the seventh century, it was a reality, at least according to Christopher Harris's first novel. However speculative the premise, Harris's research is impeccable and he displays remarkable organisational abilities in chronicling the life of Theodore, first as a clerk in the service of Emperor Heraclius, then as archbishop at 'the world's misty northern edge'. The theological debates on the nature of the incarnation are somewhat fusty, but the scenes of war and episcopal intrigue are vividly described. Despite the novel's lack of an authentic sounding voice, its very modernity underlines its relevance for the self-deceptions within today's Church."

Michael Arditti in The Times

"These fictional memoirs of Theodore of Tarsus, a homosexual priest with heretical tendencies who became Archbishop of Canterbury in the 7th century, will appeal to admirers of *Memoirs of a Gnostic Dwarf.*"

The Gay Times

"the author is adept at evoking the feeling of the time, from the strange world of the Cappodocian monks and the hollow grandeur of Constantinople, to the decay of Rome and the squalor of England. The author explores Theodore's humanity and faith by depicting him as a homosexual, giving the book a philosophical twist that well matches the uncertainty of his times."

Roger White in Heritage Learning

"While we wait for the historical Theodore to emerge from the labours of professional scholarship, we have the Theodore of Christopher Harris' ambitious and wide-ranging novel to educate and entertain us."

Catherine Holmes in The Anglo-Hellenic Review

"This is Harris' first novel and Dedalus, an innovative and imaginative small publishing house, are to be commended for finding a new author of such talent and storytelling skill. This book was a pleasure to read."

Towse Harrison in The Historical Novel Society Review

"a fascinating window on the period and indicates lengthy and meticulous research."

Sarah Singleton in The Third Alternative Magazine

"The fictional memories are both moving and inspiring in their honesty and the text is a compelling read. Theodore's sexual revelations and religious self scrutiny draw the reader into a world far removed from our own yet develops themes relevant to these times."

Buzz Magazine

£8.99   ISBN 873982 49 6   340p   B.Format

False Ambassador – *Christopher Harris*

"Christopher Harris's first novel, *Theodore*, the heretical memoirs of a gay priest, was published to some acclaim last year. His second novel is no less eclectic. Beginning in 1428, this swashbuckling romp recreates a brutal medieval world on the cusp of civilisation. Despite his scholarly inclination, 15-year-old Thomas Deerham is sent by his father to be a soldier with the English Army. Our hero's adventures take us from savage encounters in France to Rome via Constantinople, with much murder, rape and pillaging along the way. At the slightest provocation, Thomas and friends whip out their swords to prove their manhood. When Thomas unwittingly adds fratricide to his already heavy burden of mortal sins, it is little wonder he seeks salvation. This authentically gory story requires a strong stomach and a sympathetic imagination."
Lisa Allardice in The Independent on Sunday

"Another fine historical tale from the author of *Theodore*. This time he takes us on a journey through the bloody savagery and the no-less-bloody nobility of fifteenth-century Europe in a welter of mishap, mayhem and debauchery. An absorbing read that delights and disturbs in equal measure."
Sebastian Beaumont in Gay Times

"Set in Renaissance Europe, this entertaining novel tells the story of Thomas, a young soldier in the English army. After deciding to desert, he falls in with a gang of ruthless mercenaries, endures hideous privations, is enslaved and escapes the fall of Constantinople before ending up in Rome. Harris, who has an imaginative grasp of the squalor and violence of the time, has thankfully not sugared this latest offering."
Angus Clarke in The Times

"Harris stays with history in this follow-up to *Theodore*. Renaissance Englishman Thomas Deerham deserts from the army in France and is launched on a journey which takes him round Europe and the near East. This voyage brings him into

contact with the philosophy and heresies of his age, causing him to engage in a struggle with his own flawed soul."
Harry Blue in Scotland on Sunday

"well written and readable."
The Historical Novel Society Review

"Harris has thoughtfully crafted a novel with a certain panoramic vision and a definite talent. Ultimately this book is suited for those interested in intelligent historical fiction."
Andrew Hook in The Third Alternative

£8.99   ISBN 1 903517 00 1   303p   B.Format